EXALTED VIBRATIONS TRILOGY
BOOK 1

Tethered to the Cosmos

LEE KEMTER

EXALTED VIBRATIONS TRILOGY

BOOK 1

Tethered to the Cosmos

Copyright © 2023 by Lee Kemter

All rights reserved. No portion of this book may be reproduced or utilized in any form, or by any electronic, mechanical, or other means, without the prior written permission from the author.

Any references to historical events, real people, or real places are used fictitiously. Other names, characters, places and events are products of the author's imagination, and any resemblances to actual events or places or persons, living or dead, is entirely coincidental.

ISBN: 979-8-9878841-2-6

Contact: www.leekemter.com

Author Photo by Brent Looyenga

DEDICATION

To Rob Kemter, my sweet husband. I wish we could have had more years together on the earthly plane. You loved and inspired me while you were alive and will continue to do so forever.

TABLE OF CONTENTS

AUTHOR'S NOTE

Inspiration for this book had been brewing for decades when, in January of 2021, during a time of isolation for the whole globe, it finally came to life spontaneously. Meditation had been my constant companion for over thirty years, and I was healing from the loss of my husband six months prior. Taking care of him had been a seminal, priceless time in my life because I was confronting the daunting likelihood of letting him go while at the same time having in-depth discussions with him about the expanded reality of life and what lies beyond. Those conversations included the unified field theory of quantum physics, which says that everything is connected through an all-pervasive field of energy and is interacting with everything else at the subtlest, energetic levels. This theory describes the massive potential and awe-inspiring power within the subatomic levels of a human being and of material existence itself.

In current times, there is a trend towards exploring quantum realities and ending the rigid paradigm which says that what cannot be seen or measured must therefore be unreal. I envision Albert Einstein, Niels Bohr, and Nikola Tesla applauding our burgeoning openness of mind and heart. Writing a book about our mysterious ancient past and our unfathomable future felt incomplete without delving into quantum physics.

Unified field theory allowed me to think bigger and expand my willingness to write not as a sci-fi or fantasy author but from grounded, scientific potentials that the trilogy's storyline unfurls.

I did not take the subjects in this trilogy lightly. When ideas or subjects came up in the writing that were not familiar to me,

I chose to look closer. To allow the topics to expand and evolve, I took online courses with history professors and an academy that focuses on the unified field theory of quantum physics. My understanding and interest grew as I read books, watched countless videos and documentaries, and spent hours in the library. The extensive research for this trilogy took me into profoundly complex and hidden areas of history and human evolution that I did not expect to uncover. I did not start out with an agenda, or to take a stand for something like what I discovered. Rather, the writing revealed things to me, and I followed the trail.

Similarly, without question, all characters in this book, even if they seem like real people with strong, personal perspectives and believable history, are fictional. They arose naturally as the story unfolded in the writing of it.

Another point to clarify is that where I mention places or people from historical events across the globe, I was true to the results of my inquiries and findings. Keep in mind that research is like a prism, where historians see individuals, groups, and places from different angles. The characters in this novel are courageous and want to see a different side of the prism than what they've known up to this point.

Curiosity is a major theme of this trilogy, as is the challenge with historical accuracy. When we try to look back thousands of years, there will naturally be several sides to any story. In this trilogy, a reader may discover a viewpoint that they have not previously encountered. For the trilogy's characters, shocking, controversial, and new information comes forward as a catalyst for them to defy the status quo, dig deeper, and allow the storyline to continue in the spirit of authentic exploration.

As I wrote, there were nights when I didn't sleep well because of the history that I unmasked. And other nights, I was haunted by conversations with my elderly, German relatives in the 1970's. On vacations to my paternal grandmother's home, the visiting elders, who were nearly one hundred years old, told stories of life as non-Nazi Catholics in the midst of a brutal war that was waged not only on battle fields but also between family members, friends, and neighbors.

The men in our family didn't agree with the Nazis, but the penalty for noncompliance was certain death and their family would be killed or sent to a work camp. Even as a young teen, I could sense they were traumatized, their pain held tight inside. After WWII, my relatives who lived in the U.S. watched in horror as Nazis immigrated with elevated status and entered the government and many corporations based on their scientific and technological skills. My elders were shocked that oversight of these people seemed non-existent. They were concerned that Nazi values and mindsets could seep into our military, business, and the wider culture. The Nazis they spoke about were known for brutality, ruthlessness, and contempt for the U.S. Why bring them into our society and even reward them? I wondered if, in discussing these things in front of me, my relatives were nudging me to be their voice in modern times.

Studies show that our DNA holds vast amounts of information about our family lineage; not only physical traits, but memories of their struggles, joys, and spiritual tendencies, which influence many generations going forward. As I reflected on my lineage, I began to research what daily life was like for my ancestors over many centuries. New studies have been demonstrating that our anxieties, worries, and thought patterns are not all from personal experience—including physical symptoms or ways we hold stress. We are not as separate from one another as we think, and our biology reflects not only our current individual experience, but that of our ancestors as well. The characters in this book wondered, as I did, how biological, symptomatic, or emotional tendencies take root in us. What belief patterns were firmly in place in my ancestor's social, religious, and family life? As part of the answer, I looked for patterns in their culture in Europe and the U.S. that played out before and after they were gone.

Getting into the flow of the book, countless synchronicities emerged. For example, after writing about a character's experience in a prisoner of war camp in Idaho, I went from Northern California to Idaho to work further on the book. Going for a hike in a nearby state park, I stumbled on a sign explaining that this location had been a prisoner of war camp run by the U.S. Military during WWII. Astonished, I sat by the majestic lake instead of going into the nearby museum, contemplating what I had just discovered—when writing about it I didn't actually know such camps existed. Contrary to what I'd thought, the camp was not a figment of my imagination.

As I lingered for a while at the lake, my mind became still with awe and wonder. I realized that the scene in front of me, with jaw-dropping detail, matched the character's description from the book. Tears flowed as I empathically connected to the pain and sorrow of a world torn apart at that time in history. In addition, my ancestor's agonizing feelings moved through me. In that mystical, synchronistic experience, perhaps I helped to release some of that pain from our family lineage. Because of the infinite quantum field in and around us, we are all connected beyond time and space, allowing each generation a chance to recognize and heal the wounds of those who preceded them.

Visiting that lake was one of a myriad of confirmations that the content of the book was coming from an endless, timeless, spaceless-ness inside me. As more synchronicities arose, I gained confidence. My intuition became trustworthy, and accessibility to the unified field of all memory and information became alive in me.

When characters in the book join the circle of friends, they become a unified open-hearted ring of souls. An individual's capacity to receive feedback, learn from life, and be in a place of non-judgment are underlying qualities of this group that allow them to be even more effective together than they are alone. Although some are highly educated and others are unimaginably intuitive, they blend into a coherent force that can change the world.

As the writing continued, I had innumerable conversations over tea and coffee with fascinating people from many disciplines like physics, quantum science, shamanism, ancient history, and cosmo-archeology; people who shared their ideas with me about how the world could radically change in the next couple of decades.

In lucid dreams I communed with my husband. He reinforced that the characters' dreams and hopes were realistic and scientifically feasible. More mind-blowing was that he showed me the breath-taking expanse of my own cosmic nature. As dreams with him continued, I identified with my mystical nature more than ever before and studied lucid dreaming from the perspective of physics.

It's my hope that *Tethered to the Cosmos* is entertaining and inspiring, and that it stirs up conversation about how life could look if we unified and dynamically contributed our specific, essential gifts to this amazing world we live in together. The unfathomable layers in the multiverse and the unified field in and around us will be the fertile landscape that we will explore as the trilogy moves from 2020 to 2045. What is possible for humanity if we embrace the invisible, inexplicable aspects of life that have been concealed, waiting to be explored? Who are we? What hidden origins are slowly emerging into view that can elevate life on Planet Earth like never before?

Given the innumerable questions and complex subject matter, I will meet you in the next book of this trilogy to continue exploring this mystifying, transformative, and exhilarating puzzle. Buckle up, because in quantum science, the possibilities are endless, unfathomable, aweinspiring... and remarkably accessible.

I hope you are uplifted by the story you have in your hands, and may it help you continue your own process of discovery.

In love and unicity,

Lee Kemter

PART 1

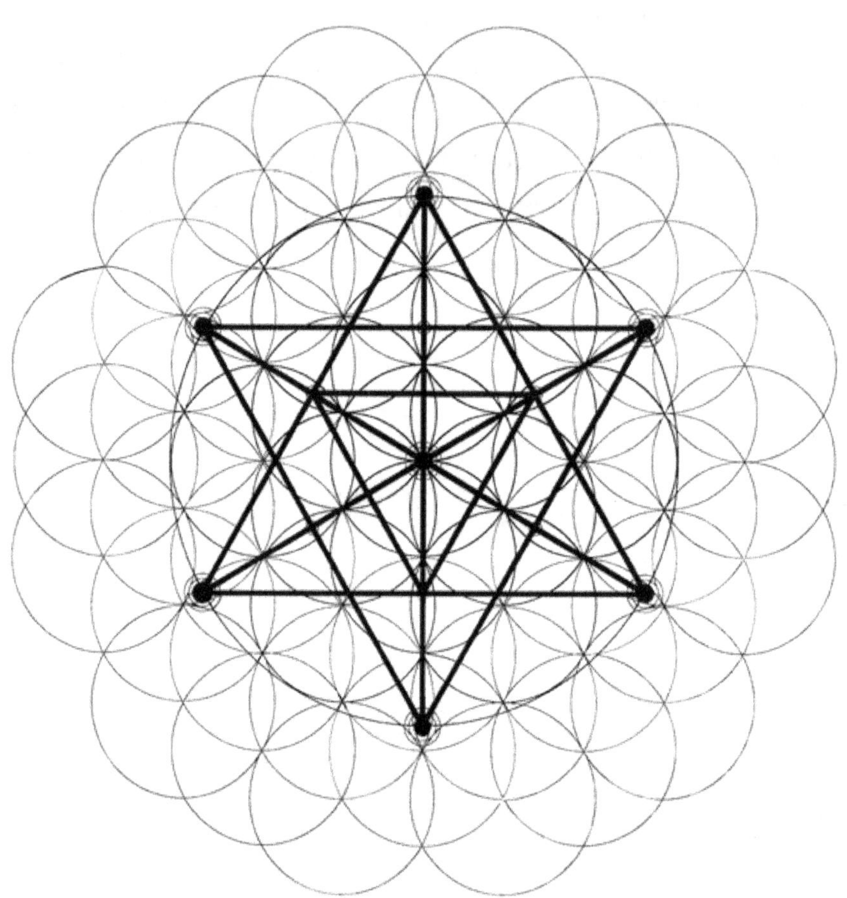

CHAPTER 1

IN THE BEGINNING THERE WAS LIGHT

Biting winds and massive sheets of thick ice pummeled the Earth with enormous force. Few beings, human or otherwise, found its impact anything less than devastating, necessitating raw, exhaustive survival.

Caverns spanning hundreds of miles beneath the surface of the Earth became a refuge for the few who survived the harsh shift in climate—the once fecund, emerald paradise had become a frozen wasteland of sparkling white.

In cosmic time, it was a blip. But a drastically different experience lay ahead for those who wanted to stay. For the human race to survive and thrive required facing an endless winter.

Did the icy impact last a million years or a thousand? For those living in higher energetic frequencies, time was irrelevant. Space was a concept. Without the constraints of space and time, the extraterrestrials living on Earth didn't care.

Many of these survived this age of ice and lived to experience others as well. The most successful were the giant beings with elongated heads and other species draped in thick, furry animal skins. Many of these enjoyed life from tree-sized bodies, thirty feet in height. Yet humans survived as well.

The world howled for millennia, warming and freezing in repeated, devastating cycles.

Kandor, an elderly giant who lived under the Earth's surface within his highly advanced spaceship, was at least twenty-thousand-years-old. He was wrapped in tattered animal skins, his demeanor noble yet unpretentious, emanating peacefulness and wisdom unreservedly. With shaggy, silver hair that accentuated his kind face, the wrinkles of advanced age, and a bedraggled beard that clearly showed his indifference to outer appearance, he stood in a reflective mood, perusing his cave within the giant mountains of the Pacific Northwest of North America.

His species had come to Earth to implant codes of wisdom that humans would need for further evolution. These beings were not inclined toward planning, strategizing, or setting goals. They did not reach or grasp.

Knowingness for Kandor, as with all his species, arose from a deep connection to inherent Essence. With the right-left hemispheres of his brain in balance and his mind under his control, he lived in tranquil equanimity, and viewed Earth-life as pure potentiality in every moment. Employing his refined and subtle mind, coming and going from Earth was effortless, as it was for everyone in his species. For them, time was a wave form they aligned with, and Kandor's frequency matched the incredibly powerful vibrations of the Earth.

From the perspective of pleasure, joy, and elevated levels of consciousness, Kandor was equal in frequency to the love vibration that pulsed from the planet, known in the cosmos as Gaia. Intergalactically, she was referred to as the heart of her solar system, setting the tone and frequency for the other planets to align with.

Gaia's powerful love-pulse could be felt by subtle beings across the solar system, the galaxy, and even beyond.

No one doubted her grandeur. It was understood that she attracted souls with a dedicated focus on raising their frequency, who yearned to be embodied in her special atmosphere because it was ideal for learning to release inner obstacles to the profound experience of exalted vibrations. They didn't mind being on a long waiting list because the opportunity to be human was considered priceless by other civilizations in the multiverse.

At the time of Kandor's presence on Gaia, humanity was in a pivotal epoch of evolutionary potential, one in which they could soar in frequency and evolve rapidly. For this giant visitor, human evolution was of the utmost importance. It was for this reason that he was sitting comfortably in his ship going through current statistics about the expression of the *unicity gene* within human-ity. The data was perplexing. Why was this gene not expressing at this obviously pivotal moment in humanity's evolution? Kandor sat reflectively and closed his eyes for a moment.

Unlike current air craft on Earth, Kandor's ship did not re-quire fuel; its energy source was the inexhaustible power of the invisible energy field that sustains life everywhere and creates universes relentlessly. His craft was as quiet as galactic space with crystalline light scintillating throughout the interior. He liked to refer to his ship as *the cave* because it emitted warm and embracing vibrations from its walls that reminded him of the first caves he had inhabited on Gaia long ago.

Stretching, he stood and glanced at a corner of his magnifi-cent cave; an effulgent, intoxicating cobalt-blue ray of light was pulsing intensely. He gazed at the light with tenderness. This was his wife, Astaria, who was so subtle that she appeared as a cobalt ray of brilliance. She beamed her photons towards her beloved husband, filling him with joy, and illuminating his face with a smile. He often said that anyone who married a *cobalt-ray* was blessed beyond measure.

Within the extraordinary quantum world, there is neither time nor space in the limited way that humans imagine. This allows these giants and subtle, blue emanations to travel effortlessly through worm holes into any coordinate in the multiverse.

All planets and universes were potential destinations. However, Earth was like a magnet for them and for a small group from their star system who were intent on supporting Earth's evolution. They saw Gaia as a powerful and magnificent being whom they admired, and whom they fiercely protected as she emerged into her full potential. Even though Kandor could go anywhere, he stayed with her for thousands of years at a time. His highly evolved ship provided all of his needs; it was sentient and was aligned completely with his unique energy signature.

From Earth's three-dimensional reality, he wanted to ensure that a rare race of beings called *human* could take their advanced inner technologies to the next level and thrive on this unique planet. With immense curiosity, all planets and stars were watching humanity's evolution at this pivotal time.

As comets hit Gaia and glaciers dissolved, massive floods roared across the large land masses known to humans (later) as North America, Europe, Asia, and Siberia. Sediments shifted and slid, pushing relentlessly to faraway destinations with a force that buried or dislodged everything in their path. Trees were uprooted, crevices formed in rocks, and lighter minerals like limestone washed away, leaving only the hardest of rock for the future.

The landscape irrevocably transformed, massively altering ecosystems, and humans began migrations, sometimes with the help of extraterrestrials, to relocate, away from their icy homes that were becoming lakes, seeking safe, fertile lands to thrive.

Kandor sat in his cave-like ship, reflecting upon his observations, recording his insights into a small device. He described how bravely humanity was moving forward, especially over the past twenty-five thousand years. Their tenacity, courage, and goodness never escaped his awareness and filled him with a tender joy and admiration.

Suddenly, in the middle of his reverie, he was startled by a sudden, jolting movement in Astaria's energy field. She was becoming excited, swirling in rapid ribbons of light around the cave. Within seconds, a second cobalt ray appeared, and the two light beams intermingled in an eloquent dance of joy. Their happiness filled the cave like a contagion as they swirled like two strands of linked DNA. The second light was Astaria's sister, Esoteria.

Watching their joyful abandon with deep love, Kandor looked up to see his dear friend, Belstar, the human he loved most, who was married to Esoteria. Brothers my marriage, they were also deeply connected at their core, bonded through their own shared essential qualities. Together they gazed upon the cobalt rays of light which were projecting their photons like a mystical laser show within the cave.

Belstar approached his friend, connecting telepathically with an overwhelming feeling of communion and camaraderie. Wispy white hair fell below his shoulders. His thick snow-colored eyebrows raised quickly with excitement as he gazed at his life-long comrade. His face was scored with fine wrinkles that indicated his advanced age yet his crystalline blue eyes radiated a youthful passion for life and endless love for his dear friend, Kandor. Like magnets, energized by their wives' continuous joy and effulgence, they came closer to each other. This three-dimensional world allowed for a special contact, something Kandor deeply appreciated about his proximity to humanity.

"Welcome! After a long absence, I am grateful to see you, my friend. To what do I owe this blessed and surprise visit?" Kandor asked smiling, his eyes twinkling with cheer.

"Well, partly, I always love for Astaria and Esoteria to spend time together. I am fed by the magnificent display of their love and never take their bond for granted," Belstar answered.

He settled down near Kandor on a rock that instantly morphed into a perfectly comfortable seat, molding to his body with ergonomic precision.

"I knew you were here, Kandor. At a Galactic Council meeting, I heard that this mountain in Idaho remains isolated and the terrain is fortunately too intense for the human military to discover you. I've always loved this special spot on the planet. Are the stone circles above and pyramid in the cavern below still here?"

"Yes, they are both intact and functional," Kandor answered, letting out a sigh of relief.

"I've come because there is something of concern to our off planet brothers and sisters," Belstar said, looking serious. "Particularly those from Sirius, Pleiades, and Alpha Centauri. All of us are aware that human beings are trying to find solid footing in an ocean of chaos, and they suffer terribly. Some are sinking fast. The courage, vitality, and inspiration that they seek is within them, yet blinded by their pain, they cannot see they already have everything they need. They even have the unicity gene! Yet that, too, seems illusive to them.

"Unfortunately, they show no interest in the stone circles, even as those circles are the finest technologies available for effortlessly mastering themselves and connecting to all stars and planets. They don't align with sound vibrations, either. They don't see the incredible potential of sound as a source of energy.

They don't realize the sacred geometry of ancient sites holds clues for a higher path going forward. Although we can see that this is short-sighted, they will not turn towards such radical assistance because instead, pain and struggle are their focus.

"They remain absorbed in war mentality and separation from their Essence. They fight amongst themselves, which creates and perpetuates feelings of isolation and fear. As you know, this kind of focus is mental: strategizing, projecting a self-serving future, and analyzing, instead of being heart-centered.

"For them, the *unicity* gene is considered *junk*. That is a strange term to describe something so critical to their survival and the elevation of their collective evolution. Without the gene in full expression, how will they realize how exalted they are?"

"My dear Belstar, you have enough ancient, Sirian DNA to keep your heart entrained to the field-of-all-possibilities," Kandor said with a friendly smile. "As always, you remain grounded in pure love. I feel your vibrations and they are nourishment for my energy field. Speaking of nourishment, would you like to eat?"

"Yes, I would," Belstar answered. He turned towards a patch of seasonal winter plants and grass which was growing under Kandor's care in a small alcove of the ship.

The two friends knelt before the green life-forms. Holding the plants gently in their cupped hands, they breathed slowly in, their eyes rolling back as they received data from the plant to further illuminate their bodies with energy. Their life force was continuously enriched by their persistent contact with the infinite field of light, sound, and electromagnetism in and around them. They did not need to consume the physical organisms to imbibe their nourishment.

"Thank you, Kandor," Belstar said. "Now I would like to share the reason I came to see you."

"As you know, my beloved daughter, Sophia, is once again in an earth suit. She is as lovely as her mother, Esoteria. Her face is diamond shaped with eyes that express the magnificent depths of her soul. She has no memory of previous earth suits she has worn, nor her place in the shamanic culture which she helped to create on Gaia after the floods long ago. In linear time, a multitude of ice ages have come and gone while she basked in higher frequency realms.

"At this time she is married to Trahar! Can you believe it? His highly evolved Pleiadian blood is here in the form of a kind-hearted man, a very intelligent being named *Nate*, which is short for Nathanael. I find his current name to be poignant. Do you remember when Trahar befriended Yeshua's dear follower, the incorruptible Nathanael? That dear soul did not possess a molecule of deceit. He was an inspiration to us all! Trahar loved Nathanael and other kindred spirits at that time. He went out of his way to help them. His assistance was needed to guide small groups of Yeshua's followers to escape Rome, traversing the Silk Road to India, and navigating their way to Persia, Egypt, and other less dangerous places.

"It's nice to see that the words of several of the well-loved, shining souls from Trahar's Earth adventures two millennia ago were recently discovered. Facts of farreaching consequences from that time period were locked away safely underground in Egypt. Every once in a while, the old texts are discovered. Although mostly ignored, they are nonetheless significant to understanding human history.

"After Yeshua was gone, Trahar's journeys to the places I mentioned, and many others, threatened his survival. That lifetime, that moment in space-time, was a pivotal one for many people on Gaia.

"As always, Trahar embraced cosmic assistance from the Alpha Centaurians who created massive cities far below the surface in Egypt. Those great beings arrived on Gaia to help on a spiritual level. As Trahar gradually expressed his *unicity gene* fully, he became pure light. When the timing was right, our dear Trahar was able to reunite with his kin from the stars.

"Trahar was an analyzer by nature, intelligent, and a very good man. He became a beacon of hope for many and offered himself in service to humanity. We loved to see how many humans, in indescribably challenging times, offered themselves in service to the world—with their magnanimous hearts wide open.

"One thing that we all agree on is that Trahar always saw the good in others and he relentlessly wanted to help them. Those illustrious qualities remain within him today.

"Oh! It seems that I have digressed in recalling those wonderful young people... Now, back to the reason for my visit.

"Gaia is sending out cries for help. She is ascending in frequency, as required by her subtle position as the heart of the solar system, but human-made chemicals and constant warfare are affecting her health and welfare on a material level. She's traversing these difficult times with her gloriously dynamic nature, still ascending in frequency, but humanity does not seem to realize her necessity to elevate for the good of the solar system, nor are they aware of how they undermine her efforts.

"It's time for her to release her inhibitions and move forward to evolve *at full throttle,* as they say on Earth. As she makes her vibrational ascension, humans have an opportunity to participate by gathering on her lovely surface and finding ways to be in silence. This simple practice allows their mind to rest in its natural state of communion with its Essence—within the unified field of light, sound, and energy.

"Those who engage regularly with this magnificent field in and around them will be able to access the depth and breadth of the infinite information contained within it, and will be drawn forward in their own evolution, aligned with Gaia's. They must come to realize that they are energy spinning within the field—they are part of something inconceivably important and immeasurably powerful.

"Gaia is eager to taste the nectar of unicity with them and to feel them aligning with these powerful universal forces. But whether they join her or not, she will naturally upcycle and re-generate on her own. This is not a time for band-aids. It's a time for a change of heart.

"For humans to survive this transition, stillness of the fluc-tuations of the mind (as just mentioned) is required for personal ascension, even if it's for a few minutes at a time. Another critical factor for human survival is focusing on open hearted interactions with each other, with the unicity gene fully expressed.

"This is irrefutable; other options no longer exist. Time is of the essence because Gaia is compelled to carry on, evolving in frequency. And humanity must evolve along with her in order to survive.

"I believe there is a way forward for them which is dynamic and realistic; it is being revealed to them through their own quantum science. Therein lies the tipping point for humanity: will they continue to view themselves in old, superstitious ways, assuming the world is nothing more than particles of matter that look like *ping pong balls?*

"The councils have observed that quantum science has barely managed to get the point across to humans that energy is the foundation of material reality. Most humans still believe that pro-tons are little balls of stuff, ignorant that protons and electrons are electrostatic charges within a region of infinite, fluid space. They are not *matter* in empty space nor are they separated from each other within it. As we both know, the *charge* is matter that humans can feel and touch. Fundamental laws like these must become more well-understood and accepted by humans if they are to survive.

"The deeper aspect of reality that eludes most humans is something that you and I experience constantly in the multiverse, which is that this charge is the consequence of *electromagnetic quantum planck oscillators.*

"It is not well known among humans that *matter* in the multiverse is fundamentally formed by swirling vortices called *planck oscillators.* Only the vortex is material and the rest of space remains vibrant, subtle waves of infinite *potentiality.* These oscillators are the source of mass and gravitation. They ultimately arise from the infinite field of data and information of which we are also an indelible part. I know this is basic for us, but many humans do not yet grasp the magnitude of its importance for their survival and evolution.

"As you know, all of a humanity's trillions of cells are comprised of trillions of atoms, which are constantly resonating with the field. Each human is a unique, dazzling expression of this invisible field, vibrating into an appearance, a form in time and space, which will never be duplicated. That makes each human unique, with a distinctive perception from their particular coordinate in the field. This field from which they arise is the foundation of everything-that-is, in a fluid state of never-ending potentialities.

"Individual humans radiate their perspective into the field constantly in the form of information about their perception of every experience.

"Groundbreaking research developed by leading edge quantum scientists ask that humanity open to the possibility that everyone and everything is an indivisible part of a field that cannot be seen and appears to be empty but is replete with vital information. Everything visible and invisible is part of this inconceivable field which is overflowing with tiny electromagnetic fluctuations that create the world and all matter. Humans arise *from it*—which is understandably hard to comprehend. Most importantly, to access its limitless information, they must learn how to consistently tune into it.

"Recent councils noticed that this premise seems difficult for many human minds to grasp, unless they are either youngsters, open-minded, curious souls, or the brave *wisdom keepers* like Sophia, Nate, and their comrades.

"I am speaking of fundamental subjects like this because I want you to realize that humanity is at the precipice of taking this imperatively valuable science into its mainstream thinking. When they do, their world can change and the extinction event can be avoided. Rigidity in science is a problem; people are set in their ways; and time is running out.

"And now to talk about Sophia, my beloved daughter, and her part in all this: she holds the secret codes to unlock the unicity gene. Before birth, she took a special initiation of remembrance, in which she agreed to share the codes with others. With her help, this important gene will be easily expressed. Humans can unite, evolve, and live in peace.

"However, Sophia did not realize how difficult it would be to take birth if her Earth-family and friends weren't expressing the unicity gene. She does not remember any of her timelines on Gaia with Trahar. Nor does she recall her mother or me. Hence, she is struggling. At the same time, Trahar is being recalled to his Star Council. At some point soon, he will be returning home."

"What a dynamic pair they are!" Kandor replied, his eyes bright with delighted enthusiasm. "Please continue, my friend."

"Although their contributions will be enormous, Sophia and Nate are manifesting in a very low key manner for now—nothing as overt or dynamic as the roles they've played in the past," Belstar said, smiling kindly.

He looked at his friend, allowing the light from Kandor's eyes to soak in deeply. Pausing for a moment, Belstar offered a loving emanation of soft green light to flow to Kandor as well.

"Do you remember when those two defied the Atlantean military, as they came roaring across the mountains of Asia to take over the Pacific Rim? In sequential time, it was over ten thousand years ago. And do you recall how valiantly the wise yet not-so-savvy-warrior Trahar went to the Indian Ocean to defend humanity, along with the star beings that were here in 3-D form? It didn't go well for him in that warrior role.

"As the battle raged on, Trahar realized that it was time for shamanism, gentleness, and unicity to give way to the Atlantean high-tech, authoritarian hierarchies of leadership and polarity. This seemed to be humanity's destiny and most humans were in alignment with this path.

"Trahar called for his kin, they meditated, and then sent immense blessings to Gaia and her inhabitants. They would not interfere or insist on humanity doing things their way. That kind of benevolence and wisdom is rare in any universe. He sensed that humanity would learn and evolve through the suffering of feeling separate, hopeless, and fearful. His noble heart also recognized their resilience and goodness. Not caring how long it took, he and his kin left them with vital secrets of nature and ways to connect with Essence. Their inner bio-technologies were well established and knowledge of the underlying geometries of nature was encoded in their DNA. Yet a subtle change in humanity's perception occurred.

"With concern, Trahar and his kin watched the gradual shift from a collaborative culture to a competitive, warring one. This combative-aggressive approach was taking firmer hold about twelve to thirteen thousand years ago, and created a decisive *change of heart* for humanity. Human archeologists are still finding the remnants of the neolithic, collaborative cultures, vastly different than modern times.

"Sophia can relate to the ancient principles of harmony where everyone is on equal footing. Unequivocal empathy and enduring respect for each other were pervasive principles of that forgotten era. She holds the DNA from those ancient worlds where these principles and social structures were predominant. We must remember that she also holds the DNA codes from farther back in history, too. We are noticing that the female iconography in the form of art and figurines of the mother principle have been discovered all over the world.

"Rather than matriarchal *rule*, these societies saw the *creative force* as a mother. From that foundation, cultures were nurturing towards each other, collaborative, and did not rank forms like male or female, cultural contributions, or age as superior. Citizens engaged in roles that benefited the entire community. Across epochs of time, the principles that I am speaking about expressed the power of birth, death, and renewal; the female images that are captured in art enlivened all areas of life rather than transcending it or passing judgment on it. This kind of spirituality posited one Essence for everything: an infinite source of multiplicity within unicity.

"The concept of territorial fighting, hierarchy, a rulergod or pantheon subjugating lesser beings, and those kinds of societal and spiritual concepts emerged later. Tens of thousands of years ago, the creative force, Essence, was depicted as the great mother principle. Rituals were performed in praise and honor of this feminine principle's main areas of focus which were birth, death, honoring ancestors, as well as planting, harvesting, and anything related to food or sustenance. This was not goddess worship as seen later in Roman and Greek culture. From millions of years of visiting and living on this magnificent planet, Sophia inherently holds the memory of the earliest forms of love, respect, and appreciation for Gaia and her inhabitants. Her recollections precede even the great mother principles that I described. She holds the earliest whispers of human evolution, the exalted vibrations of advanced humans millions of years ago. That epoch is not going to be easy for humans today to accept.

"As more ancient iconography of the mother emerges, rather than responding with curiosity about their own past, humans label them as insignificant or as Neolithic pornography. Currently ingrained cultural ideas do not tend to be malleable. Ironically, through current social and cultural lenses, the indisputable fact that the art reflects awe and wonder for the creative process (and a joy for existence that is in deficit in modern times) goes completely unheeded by those who most need to receive its communications. If this is their response to new revelations about their history from twenty or thirty thousand years ago, how will they react to discoveries of a more ancient past than they can fathom?

"Oh good friend! It is helpful to look at the more recent global culture ten to twelve thousand years ago because it set the stage for current societal norms. Trahar did the right thing. Humanity had the right to decide their fate.

"Even though we knew that Trahar accepted humanity's right to exercise free will and evolve however they chose, it was comforting that Sophia was vastly stronger than I thought she could be at her advanced age. At that time, her beautiful earth body was thousands of years old. Of course, all humans lived much longer because they vibrated faster, and constantly rejuvenated their cellular systems.

"But now, without Trahar's immeasurable kindness, support, and comfort and only being back in an earth suit for a short period, relatively speaking, I worry that she may falter. I have to admit that I underestimated her wise, courageous heart ten thousand years ago. As the war continued, the second of two recent cataclysms arrived in full force.

"I want to remind you of these two events, even though all of us on the Galactic Council recall these moments with a shudder. Such a massive shift for Gaia's inhabitants! The first cataclysm that I am referring to happened just over twelve thousand years ago. This sudden event happened when a normal meteor shower turned catastrophic. Gaia had experienced many such events in her history. During certain times each year, a heightened chance of a direct hit exists. During this particular meteor event, comets hurtled at breakneck speed towards Earth and struck with devastating precision in various places. This cosmic impact massively affected the area where we are sitting right now. Today it is known as the Pacific Northwest of North America.

"Remember that Gaia was experiencing a major ice age in which many of the towering mountaintops we see today were still covered in ice. However, the comet's intense heat melted the ice instantly, releasing massive walls of water flooding southward with inconceivable power, carrying every insect, plant, and trace of civilization along its raging path. As you know, this glorious planet regenerates herself continually. Yet the ice age was not at the end of its cycle, so ice built up once again to cover the desolate landscape.

"In another cosmic event a thousand years later, meteors hit the same areas of Gaia and the results were deeply catastrophic to Gaia's inhabitants. It was as though Gaia's skin was violently, thoroughly scraped clean, so much so that nothing was left in terms of vegetation. Massive caverns formed as trillions of tons of water etched across and into her lovely surface, creating a visual shift that no one could have imagined. The ice age was ending, so a regeneration of plant life and other material forms was possible. In her usual style, Gaia rejuvenated with exquisite beauty, giving birth to widespread diversity of plant and animal life across her entire body.

"One of Sophia's gifts that she brings to Earth each time she incarnates is an ability to read the movements and cycles of the cosmos, including those of Gaia. At the time of the cataclysms, she realized something was afoot, so she escaped under the surface into the magnificent caverns, taking other survivors with her. She remained there, teaching humans how to be in union with the plants, the rocks and minerals. She shared how to use the water in human blood to vibrate at a higher frequency. Her techniques allowed them to easily travel through portals to many coordinates in the galaxy. She also held extensive knowledge of pyramid technology and applications for sacred geometry. As I have just elucidated, Sophia's highly evolved gifts of intuition and DNA coding allow her to perceive her life through a lens of unicity with everything. She is united with the unified field of all possibilities. This connectedness, along with her profound compassion and love for the human species, allows her to help others to raise their frequency and find their highest potential. She does not gravitate to fear and judgment. Coming to Gaia for watershed moments in human evolution and under extreme circumstances has become her greatest wish and, from my perspective, gift to humanity. With her assistance and guidance, after the cataclysms that I described, Human evolution continued exceedingly well, mainly for shamans."

"And as I recall," Kandor said, "just before she left Gaia to join us on Alpha Centauri, Sophia went with you and a small group to Africa. How did that work out? The massive floods devastated those lands almost as much as areas in the Pacific Rim and Sophia's home base in North America.

"My dear friend, with joy I can say the survivors were receptive, resilient, and beautiful in every way possible. We shared the origins of our Solar System and told them about Neptune, Saturn, and Jupiter's secrets. We explained the rings of Saturn and the moons of Jupiter, and how the solar system was created from a quantum force beyond the brain's capacity to understand it. We described how these planets majestically morphed into being, emerging from a plasma vortex, a *still point* called a *singularity*. This singularity is so potent and dense with energy that when particles move through its spinning horizon they blast out as a wild vortex of light within time and space. A new perceptive reality unfolds. It is mysterious and provocative yet real, nonetheless. Like you, giants have never been shy about describing the unified field of quantum science—we believed that the good humans would comprehend it and they did!

"The African humans listened intently and made simple clay tablets, passing down the information from generation to generation.

"We also told them about the galactic mermaids from Sirius who would come to the planet to help code and refresh information in the waters. We described the wise and magnanimous Centaurs in the galaxy and on Earth, the half-human, half-animals who understood firsthand the secrets of nature and the great potential of humanity.

"After careful consideration, Sophia insisted on introducing the Africans to her mother. Of course, they were in awe when they saw our family: a giant human father, his cobalt-ray wife, and fifteen-foot-tall, goddess-like daughter. We promised to come back someday with more cobalt-rays to bless their people and help invigorate the joy frequency.

"Those wonderful African people were grateful for our visit and our mutual affection grew strong. Their hearts and minds were open to all we could offer, and they quickly learned the inner, subtle skills to move through time and space. Their natural affinity for the dynamics of sound allowed them to easily alter their molecular weight at will, changing the corresponding gravitational effects as well. In that way, they could use sound to levitate and move around effortlessly. They were exceptional students.

"Sophia went with me to check on Samaria and Egypt. The flooding, cataclysms, and wars had destroyed their high tech world—we were humbled and in awe of the remnants. In all of our visits, they never tried to attack our ships nor were they aggressive. They seemed to inherently recall us as brothers and sisters. Their ancestors had left evidence of our presence on the obelisks and temples. However, insidious feelings had infiltrated the human psyche after the cataclysm—fear, confusion and distrust had arisen in the culture and created barriers to higher wisdom in their hearts and minds. So they disbelieved Sophia and refused the help that she so benevolently offered. As Nate had done, she blessed them warmly and left, allowing them to evolve at their own pace. They struggled to figure out how to use their ancestor's advanced technologies and they continued to fight over who would dominate various areas of the planet.

"We also travelled to the area that is now called Ireland, always gathering at stone circles at specific times of year as we had done in Africa. As I already mentioned, Sophia had shared how to use the water in human blood to vibrate at a higher frequency with the survivors of the cataclysm who were living under the surface of Gaia. We were relieved to discover that the water in the blood of humans in Ireland instantly aligned with the codes of information that came through the stone circles at specific times of year like equinoxes and solstices. This showed us that in particular regions of the planet, small collectives of souls were evolving into expanded consciousness.

"Gaia began to thrive, too. Her massive diversity of ecosystems is not found anywhere else in the solar system. She is a sentient being, a topic of wonder for all those who connect with her. She made friends naturally, instantly cementing bonds of love and care. She easily won the heart of her galaxy. As a living being, she was evolving much faster than anyone expected. Those who came to live on her surface or beneath it, found that they, too, began to evolve rapidly. She had a generous, contagious nature that was captivating. Yet I noticed that some saw they could take advantage of her.

"The wisdom and codes for evolution that you and your group embedded in the ice—essential, pre-cataclysmic information—remained in place for epochs of time. They were released into waterways as Earth warmed and the ice melted. When that happened, the water carried those crucial, subtle codes, spreading them across the continents.

"Shamanic cultures taught that humans were mostly made of water so humanity knew to receive and integrate the powerful codes into their blood. And with each melting of the ice caps, more codes were released, the water's vibration entraining human blood with the codes, automatically embedding them into human DNA.

"Rapidly evolving humans, especially shamans and mystics across the planet became aware that their existence was vibrational, not merely static form. They became capable of moving into many coordinates within the vast structure of space. They moved from one level of frequency within themselves to the next. As they perfected these abilities, they became aligned with the subtle vibrations of everything on Earth—of the plant they wanted to use for healing or the steep mountains they wished to ascend. Thus they learned to live in deepest harmony with all things, and could live on Earth with an effortless sense of ease and flow.

"Human life spans were thousands-of-years long, living in a magical garden of harmony and order. All of their needs were met. Challenges were seen as opportunities to move with an obstacle, not struggle or fight against it. Striving and competition drifted away like helium balloons.

"This exceptional species realized that they were designed with sufficient receptors in their eyes and skin to absorb sunlight and use it in a myriad of physical, emotional, and spiritual ways. They were also imbued with the special gene that could decode the vital power of *unicity*. Through that gene, they could collectively tap the mysteries of what they would someday call *the unified field theory of quantum physics*.

"In the unified field, they were each the center of creation. In this field there are no dimensions to aspire to, rather it is simply energetic in nature with unlimited potential to manifest all matter and information everywhere. From infancy, emphasis was placed on stilling the mind, communing with stillness, and emerging with an experience of higher states of consciousness. From this consistent practice, an advancement in human consciousness became possible.

"From formless darkness inside them arose the possibility to create, be, and do anything. Defying the mind and connecting with exalted, high frequencies, they performed alchemy. Their inner state and outer world transformed. This process was straightforward and natural—the countless worm holes on the surface of their protons allowed for a constant exchange of information with the field. Therefore, they connected easily with everything across all galaxies and multiverses. Their consciousness gave them constant access to all-that-is.

"The deep mysteries they discovered were about expressing the unicity gene consistently and using light to ignite a pine-cone shaped gland in their brain. Known as *the pineal,* this mystical gland is an apparatus which would allow them to transcend time, space, and logical thinking.

"Their overall frequency could elevate easily. They became invincible, vibrant, abundant, and at peace with themselves.

"The human design was intricate and well on its way to infinite levels of higher evolution. Many species of extraterrestrials came during the periods in which the ice melted. Everything seemed to be happening with laser perfection.

"Left to themselves humans were thriving, and the unicity gene was expressing with glorious effulgence everywhere on the planet. In rhythm with the forces of nature, they emanated peacefulness and moved with nature's rhythms like clouds drifting with perfection at all times.

"The giants with elongated heads continued to advise and help them to build structures and civilizations that were highly sophisticated and brought about an immense upshift in perception and overall vibration. And then something happened.

"Other subtle beings had their sights on humanity's unique qualities, but not with the desire to uplift or support them in reaching extraordinary heights of evolution. Instead, they wanted to try an experiment. Unlike the giants with massive brain capacity, these beings were of a lower frequency. Out of cold curiosity, they wondered what it would be like to put a dream spell over humanity. We call them *the opposites.* They are low vibe beings from various star systems in the Milky Way. Unfortunately, when any species drops in frequency for long enough periods, they become susceptible to the *opposites*, who become their kindred spirits vibrationally. More than any other beings from the multiverse, they have sunk their teeth into the subtle fabric of humanity.

"Although modern human archeologists discovered ancient tablets, cave art, and other signs of cosmic influence on this planet, the insidious, unseen presence of the *opposites* has eluded them. This is because they remain undercover and deceptive, never coming to Gaia themselves. They are highly skilled in magic, telepathy, and directing their awareness to Earth—yet incompetent with highly advanced technologies. Their frequency also holds them back from being capable of advancing in evolution.

"*The opposites* began connecting more often with humans after the devastating planetary cataclysm twelve thousand years ago that I mentioned earlier. After any shocking, devastating event, it is natural for survivors to be filled with fear, anxiety, grief, and other low frequencies. Following a period of adjustment, mourning, and allowing those kinds of innate frequencies to come up and be felt, operating from elevated states resumes. Yet this did not happen for most of humanity. When *the opposites* saw the lowered state of the collective consciousness of humanity, they artfully developed ways to further demoralize them, bonding with them in those low vibe states of consciousness.

"As you know, Kandor, similar levels of frequency are attracted to each other. And this became a vulnerability for humanity. *The opposites* used modes of connection which became quite effective and more frequent; they easily visited unsuspecting people in dreams; they slowly cultivated insidious, subtle communications through dark occult ritual with susceptible humans. That cataclysm and the one to follow marked the decline in the overall vibrations of the human race. Keep in mind that Gaia was scarred and barren in places that had previously brought sustenance to people. Familiar territory was gone and mass migrations began. Some humans went under the surface and settled there. Imagine the overwhelming impact on their psyche. And imagine the inexhaustible beneficence of Sophia and others from the multiverse who stayed or came afterwards to help those who were ready to elevate and continue to evolve higher as a species.

"Unfortunately, as we both know, with *the opposites'* influence over large groups of humans, particularly over the past ten thousand years, humans began to believe that they were not strong enough or wise enough to defeat these clever beings. Meeting these dejected, fearful humans in lucid dreams and during various creepy rituals increased their perceived dependency on *the opposites* and allowed low vibe thoughts consistently to penetrate into the human psyche. These people became more and more afraid of authority of any kind. Unconscious mind control settled in and helped to disrupt the human psyche. Humans forgot their inherent capacity to override the clever, *opposites'* whispers of low frequency nonsense. Adding to their dilemma, they dismissed the dark side of themselves and life which led to inadvertent debasement—forgetting that to be whole again, they must live in unicity, merging personal and societal frequencies of light and dark, bliss and sorrow, perceived good and perceived bad. It's about restoring balance, feeling peacefulness, and expressing pure love as a lived frequency. This will restore order and bring about unlimited possibilities for humanity's advancement and higher evolution.

"Sadly, civilizations lost their connection to their precataclysmic ancestors and their inherent, biological gifts and skills. Humanity progressively sank into the lower frequencies of shame, fear, manipulation, anger, and pride. It was like amnesia was setting in and they forgot the power of love, care, and appreciation for themselves and Gaia. Even when great beings on Earth tried to remind them of their ultimate grandeur, they eventually slid back into relentless servitude.

"Tragically, this noble species fell for the illusions created by the shadowy forces of *the opposites*. Instead of using that dark backdrop to perceive their own effulgent light more clearly, they cowered in the face of it. Unwittingly, without expressing their own innate power, they unconsciously gave it away to the dark, low *opposites*.

"Worse was that they forgot how to activate the unicity gene, which could elevate their frequency to become courageous and invincible. Steadily, they settled into the perception of being separate from rather than united with the power, dignity, and beauty of their Essence.

"Over time, they were easily manipulated and became subordinate to hierarchies within religions and governments. Rather than flowing through life with the unicity gene expressing its sublime beneficence, humans became prey to greedy leaders, and servile to artificial and insatiable desires. Citizens of Earth lost autonomy over their attention, driven by the influence of the *opposites* to focus on the fear-based traumas in their ancestral DNA rather than focusing on the unicity gene.

"I understand their plight because the *opposites* know how to make their enchantment seem like the only reality. These are not beings that anyone willingly interacts with. They prey on the fear that the psyche releases in dreams. Through their manipulations good humans forgot that they needed to connect with Essence each morning, to focus on it during the day, and to let the unicity gene express itself throughout their days, perpetuating the high vibrations available to feed and protect them. Human dreams devolved from processing the day's events, to ruminating on unsettled feelings, and finally into living nightmares all the time.

"These ethereal, energetic beings, who helped to perpetuate humanity's descent into low frequencies, fed off that kind of pure, dull energy. For them, relentless chaos, anxiety, and suffering was a gourmet meal and they delighted in keeping humans in fear.

"As the millennia rolled by, humans forgot they were timeless beings united to each other and everything. They lapsed into spiritual dementia, forgetting they were endowed with the same power that moves sheets of ice and causes the sun to shine; unaware of the unfathomable frequency of their essential nature capable of emanating supreme, high frequency light far greater than their own galactic sun.

"This spiritual radiance was only possible when they were in alignment with the Earth on which they lived. They had to perceive Gaia as sentient, as a living being, as a beloved mother. But they no longer loved her. Instead, they blamed her for bad weather, and for not providing enough food and water. After eons of evolution, humanity gradually began to see Gaia through a distorted lens and didn't take care of her, blinded by their own need and fear, unable to love her as a fellow traveler through the solar system.

"Most of the evidence of their highly evolved ancestors was washed away in the great cataclysms. Oblivious to their own origins, these degenerate humans thought they were starting from scratch and they were in *survival* mode rather than *courage and love* mode. Hierarchies evolved to rule over them and they fell lock step into servitude while also listening to the depraved whispers of the invisible, low vibe *opposites*. They sank lower and lower in frequency, living simulacrums of their former glorious, unlimited being.

"On the other hand, Gaia was still evolving into high vibrations. As the heart of the solar system, she persisted in magnanimously inviting all inhabitants on her body to bask in her nourishing presence. With each tiny seedling that emerged in spring, each nourishing fruit that burst forth in summer, the harvests of autumn, and winter's rejuvenating cocoon, she vibrated with extraordinary love.

"Extraterrestrials from our star system and many others never wavered from their affection and respect for Gaia or humanity. As star brothers and sisters, they made occasional appearances, often in invisible ways, to teach those who wanted to know the secrets of how to express the unicity gene and how to guide others into higher frequencies. They took forms like angels, sages, giants, or animals. They had gone underground during ice ages and brought shamans and other high frequency humans with them. In the last millennia, those kinds of good humans were being persecuted and gradually annihilated by surface overlords.

"In all coordinates of space-time, hearts speak a common, wordless language; a shimmering vibration in harmonic alignment across the universe that connects humanity to a subtle form of pure love that oscillates far and wide. This indefatigable, pure love is the Essence of everything.

"Disregarding this incontrovertible truth, believing themselves to be time-bound and feeling enslaved, humanity plowed forward.

"Kandor, knowing that you've been busy in other parts of the universe, I wanted to fill you in with these events that transpired on Earth. That brings us to today: I came to support Sophia. I am asking that the four of us bring in codes from the stars for her. Sophia's mission is to promote unicity in the collective of Gaia, to offer her compassion and profound gifts of intuition and insight to them as well. She will meet other souls who are focusing on the elevation of their consciousness and will help anyone who wishes to raise their frequency, including her beloved Gaia.

"Tonight is the winter solstice. Sophia is not far from here. We will not make direct contact with her or Trahar. They agreed before taking a human birth that they will live fully immersed in a human world so that they can relate to the current plight of the species more fully. This will in no way denigrate their mission nor effect their highly evolved DNA and unconscious memory of who they truly are. I am committed to upholding their decision to come without immediate memory of their true identity.

"Are you willing to do the same, my friend?"

"As always, I would do anything to support Sophia, that sweet, sparkling little star of yours," Kandor answered affectionally, yet the lines of his face showed concern. "I am always here for you, too, Belstar. I care deeply for you and your family. Tonight we will gather at the circle.

"Hopefully we can divert our wives from their flight through the cosmos. Those two rays love each other beyond comprehension. I've always marveled at the depth and beauty of their pure love, expressed as light. Imagine the havoc on this cave, if you and I tried flying around in here like that!"

"I agree! I marvel at their effortless grace and their relationship, yet have no plans to enroll in cobalt-ray flying lessons," Belstar said with his usual, hearty laughter.

Looking towards Kandor and bringing the mood to one of focus and seriousness, Belstar said, "I noticed your look of concern as I described Sophia's mission. I have apprehension arising in me as well. I know that life for Sophia is about to become confusing and difficult.

"The patterns in the field indicate probable upheavals in her life. My fatherly bond wants what is good for her and her mission, even if that means she has to struggle for a while. She holds the codes for higher evolution and the unicity gene. I offer my blessings for her life to be strengthened by that powerful genetic expression—may it nurture and support her through all that is to come."

CHAPTER 2
GRACE-FILLED FRIENDSHIP

Continuing the conversation with Kandor, Belstar said warm-heartedly, "According to my recent reading of the quantum field, one more being could use a boost of light. As always, Cynda is working in the higher realms, while she is also in 3-D form on Gaia, with Sophia. They share a friendship that transcends time and space—two powerhouses of frequency and boundless love.

"Cynda wants to support Sophia by using her inexhaustible energy and enthusiasm for their friendship to create high vibes while working in seemingly impossible situations. Our dear Cynda has the heart of a lion and emanates humor and goodwill from every pore of her being. I am happy that she is embodied to help Sophia who will need plenty of assistance for this mission.

"Never in Gaia's history has there been such a pivotal moment when frequency must rise on a grand scale or extinction looms like the impending threat of a raging storm."

As the two star brothers continued their urgent and weighty conversation, Belstar suddenly said with a twinkle in his eye, "Sophia is in contact with Cynda, who is currently called Grace. Thinking of those two inseparable friends together shifts my mood significantly. I love seeing them, regardless of which universe they are traversing. They grew up together in the most recent era on Gaia and I am delighted to discover they maintained specific galactic skills that caused raised brows for their current family and friends.

"Everyone in Grace's life will benefit from her profound relationship with the highest frequencies, her multidimensional travel skills, and her longstanding relationship with Sophia.

"Although they appear oblivious to their indelible connection to the multitude of star brothers and sisters who love them fervently, they became magnetized to each other as small children in this life-stream. Even with Sophia's wish to incarnate without remembrance of her past, her DNA is embedded with immense memory of Grace. Love cannot be fully concealed nor can it be totally blotted from the heart's memory. So through love they found each other and their friendship and eternal connection has sustained them through what has been a tumultuous life on Planet Earth.

"I was shown a hologram of them as Earth-children at the sequential age of five-years-old. I would love to share this moment in space-time with you. You will notice how much they look like twins with their large crystalblue eyes. Those two girls are the epitome of beauty, gentleness, and inner quietude. When I think of them, I envision two lovely deer."

Kandor motioned for Belstar to join him in a circular area near a wall in the cave which morphed into a scene that looked as real as though they were physically present. They observed the two little girls, giggling hysterically while lying on their backs in a lush blanket of soft, spring grass.

"My brother got in trouble for saying a bad word," Grace said. "Dad was really mad."

"What was the word?" Sophia asked curiously.

"You should know this word. It's really bad! Let me think. Yes, I remember, it's f**k. That was it," Grace answered with a wrinkled brow. "I don't understand why words matter so much. And

I don't understand why Dad told my brother that it's okay to say it in front of him or other men but not in front of me or Mom."

"Well, to me it sounds like 'duck,'" Sophia said, "and words don't make sense to me, either. Why do you have to say words out loud? You and I talk every day, and we don't live in the same house. We just talk in our heads, and we always hear each other."

"Words sure matter to my father! He was so angry," Grace said. "I wouldn't say that word, ever. At least not in front of him. I wonder if I say it in front of you, is that okay? Would you ever say it to me?"

Stretching and extending her arms wide, Sophia answered from her innocence and from her brain development at that stage of life.

"Nope," she answered. "I am not going to say it because I hate the feeling of it. Why say words that have a bad feeling? My father told my brother about a bunch of words that he can't say in front of my mother and me. That seems weird. I hate when they are angry and say those words. It scares me when they get angry. Do angry people scare you?"

Grace raised her eyebrows and smiled, giving Sophia a silly, coy look, as she answered with a resounding, "YES!"

They giggled and returned to watching clouds, and sparkling photons of light dancing around them.

Grace broke the silence with another question, "Can your mom hear you if you talk only with your head?"

"No, it doesn't work with Mom," Sophia answered. "When I tell her what I hear from her head, she tells me to stop. And when I ask if she can hear me when I talk from inside, she shakes her head and walks off. Grace, when she does that, I know she thinks I am weird... but who cares because you and I are always going to be weird, right?!"

High pitched, childhood laughter spread across the atmosphere around them. They sat in awe, looking around at the tiny buds and colorful wildflower blossoms covering the springtime landscape. This was a time to let their laughter fill their hearts with joy. Their giggles took on a life force and every time they stopped, another glorious wave of it rushed through them until it came to stillness, fueling a release of soft tears that moistened their eyes and quieted their souls. After a few moments, Grace looked at her friend, and then glanced down at the Earth. Her mood down-shifted significantly.

"My mom is the same, Sophia. She can't hear me. I get a goofy look when I ask her if she heard me. But she doesn't tell me to stop. Maybe she knows I can't. It just happens. I wonder if she used to do it and forgot how. I gave up. I'd rather talk to you that way because I know you hear me."

Suddenly, spheres of scintillating rainbow light shimmered and cascaded around them.

"Fairies!" exclaimed Grace. "Let's follow them."

Sophia leapt to her feet and grabbed Grace's hands to pull her to standing. They raced, as the free spirits that they were, soaring towards the tiny lights. Finally, winded and tired, they lost sight of the fairies among the reeds and lotuses of a nearby koi pond.

Kandor and Belstar watched the little girls, breathless from running, pausing, and looking with awe at the natural world around them. Breaking the revery of the joyful scene, Kandor said, "This was their playground, and where they found safety, and sanity in each other's company.

"They could hear the water, the wind, and the trees talking. Colors, and beings who were invisible to others, were normal for them. On a regular basis, their hearts met in camaraderie and bliss."

On the hologram, an image slowly appeared. Grace held her tiny, pinkie finger near Sophia saying enthusiastically, "Pinkie pact, Sophia. Friends forever!"

Wrapping her delicate pinkie around Grace's, Sophia smiled and exclaimed loudly and with little girl silliness, "Friends forever!"

Then with a playful grin, she said, "Grace, you can say 'duck' to me anytime!"

With a fresh burst of energy, they raced across the verdant landscape while giggling ecstatically.

Kandor said reflectively, "They are headed for home, back to the reality of children living with grown-ups; sprinting across the landscape was a form of freedom, and expression of the magnificence of their spirits in a 3-D world. This is a joyful moment to see that those two found each other in the same fields of playfulness, openness, and sincerity that I've always observed in them. On Earth, emotions are a double-edged sword. On the higher side, they are an expression of benevolent, quantum frequencies, and are the envy of most universal beings. And on the lower scale, emotions can eclipse a human's good nature and turn off the unicity gene. I chose this moment in their life on Earth to show you that the gene was turned on, fully expressing. And at that stage, they were attuned to Gaia and to subtle realms.

"As their life on Earth evolves, it's important for them to have each other for support. The timeline of Gaia that I've reviewed recently looks like it could get more intense for everyone riding through the cosmos with Gaia. These two have been part of a specialized team across the millennia on Earth. Although Sophia and Grace do not recall coming to Earth during key epochs of upheaval and turmoil, they possess the innate capacity to access the memory of their past which is recorded within coordinates of space millions of years in the past. Over time, the skill for *remembrance* can emerge from within their consciousness and guide them. Whenever they connect to the subtle core of their being through stilling the mind, they can tap the vastness of their powers to receive all of the information and wisdom they need to accomplish their mission. It may take time, but hopefully they will recall how to do this and gradually stay connected to their Essence. The frequencies on Earth are chaotic right now, which could make it harder for Sophia and her dear friend to stay focused on higher frequencies and on track with their mission. That is why I want to saturate them and our dear Trahar with wisdom codes and reassuring, supportive vibes from the stars.

"What's been going on in sequential Earth time is vibrational waves of light followed by intense darkness. I am speaking about personal vibrational frequency. Humans are allowing their frequency to oscillate inconsistently, mostly in the lower ranges.

"By the time Sophia and Grace were born, humanity's survival was becoming dependent on boosting their essential light quotient by steadily raising their frequencies. If they want to survive, they have no choice. If this amplification does not occur, we will watch another brilliant, technologically advancing, potentially awe-inspiring, benevolent civilization drown and die in lower frequencies. Evolution would then have to begin anew.

"Let's stand with them as we always have. We know they have a much better chance this time to help humanity. Massive waves of light are pouring onto the planet, bathing everyone and everything in supremely transformational vibrations."

Belstar paused and glanced towards the wall where the hologram played out the scene of indelible bonds, unfettered curiosity, and delicate innocence.

"Thank you, Kandor, for agreeing to join me in the circle. It's no surprise to me, dear friend, that you and I would think alike when it comes to our beloveds and our incredible friend, Gaia.

"Now I am going to find my wife. I will see you tonight."

The two men looked directly into each other's eyes in an energy exchange that was powerful enough to fill every cell of their bodies and subtle energy fields with pure love, peacefulness, and the joy of eternal friendship.

As humanity moved forward in evolution and technological advancement, the two friends agreed to keep a close watch on this benevolent trio, who now walked courageously on the surface of the *one and only* Gaia.

CHAPTER 3
EARTHLY WORLD WARS

The two cobalt-rays joined their husbands in the megalithic circle under a canopy of celestial brilliance.

Kandor began to use highly advanced tuning forks which ignited each megalith with blinding light. All of a sudden, the stones became vibrations of magnificent effulgence and slightly perceptible sound, initiating the ceremony that would unfold within the energetic embrace of this ancient site.

He turned to the women of cobalt light and said that before they continued with the rituals, he wanted them to know the most current events on Earth. After he spoke with Belstar earlier in the day, he gathered history from the hologram that would help them to understand why they were gathered. Without that historical perspective, he realized that it would not be clear why Sophia, Grace, and Nate were back with their beloved Gaia, and why their parents and friends were gathered this evening within the circle of megaliths.

After a few moments of communing together, Kandor spoke. His long, unruly beard blew softly in the cool breeze.

"Let me begin by saying that Astaria and I are honored to be with you tonight. A parent's love is beyond measure, and I realize that Belstar and you, dearest Esoteria, must be concerned about your precious daughter. In this ceremony, in which we invoke exalted frequencies and become exalted ourselves in the process, we can connect with the energetic heart center of all three of these brave souls who have embarked on another mission to Gaia.

"As usual, we will sit silently until we are connected fully with the densest, most profound energies at the core of our being. We will then each direct that awe-inspiring energy to the heart centers of Sophia, Grace, and Nate, filling them energetically with the highest vibes possible. As we know, the heart center is a portal that transmits and receives codes of light and information. Belstar obviously tuned into the vibrations of the cosmos because on this night there are amplified frequencies pouring onto Gaia and unprecedented solar flares have been occurring for the past three days and nights. There is a cosmic wave of grandeur happening tonight and we can participate in the ecstasy that is brewing in the cosmos while beaming its beneficent rays to our loved ones."

Esoteria and Astaria began to swirl in blue ribbons of ethereal light to indicate their enthusiasm for this evening's ritual. Belstar stood reflectively within the display of mystical light that illumined a moonless night beneath the brilliant canopy of stars overhead. From across the universe, codes of light would be transmitted, love would be shared, and his face reflected his gratitude as he placed his weathered hand over his heart and peered upwards, lost in the reverie of thankfulness to the multitude of beings that he called his friends. Kandor stood near him with the same reverence and awe for what was about to take place.

After a few moments, Kandor said, "Before we continue with tonight's ceremony, I would like to share with Esoteria and Astaria what has been happening on Earth during Sophia's, Grace's, and Nate's life-stream.

"Unfortunately, turbulence has been a devastating hallmark of life on Earth for many millennia. Century upon century, violence escalated and raged like a demonic dragon. In sequential time, an unusual Earthly phenomenon appeared in the form of world wars. This occurred approximately twenty years before our three beloved ones entered into their respective earth suits.

"These were not the galactic wars that ravaged planets in the galaxy and beyond. Humanity stood on the precipice of disaster.

"Gaia was becoming agitated, too.

"The unicity gene was locked down and forgotten. And while greed, control, and manipulation raged like a wounded beast, the world exploded into a heartwrenching, aggressively intense war. Not once, but twice in only a couple of decades.

"Humanity dove deeply into the waters of repetitive fear and survival ruminations. Their galactic sisters and brothers were confused about why this happened, and they wondered why religions and political differences evolved into a source of aggression. Naturally, the citizens of Gaia desperately wished to protect themselves and their loved ones. But the choice to divide, drop in vibration, and fight was not helping to soothe their fearful hearts. Instead, they suffered more profoundly.

"During that time, in the subtle recesses of humanity's awareness, the unicity gene was wobbling around, kicking and screaming, calling out to be activated and expressed.

"Unfortunately, humanity ignored the cries of that tiny, inner treasure. Instead, they continued to trudge pessimistically through life for millennia feeling like slaves to authorities who seemed invincibly powerful. No one seemed to know how to stop the trajectory of global violence and aggression.

"What happened to species on other planets who forgot their inherent quantum potential and unicity? Inevitably, they self-destructed. And with the atomic bomb, humanity was headed for the same fate.

"Star brothers and sisters came to Earth in the 1940's, 1950's and 1960's. The roar of fighter jets burst behind their ships as they entered 3-D space. The humans were full of fear and felt entitled to do whatever they wanted. Militaries shot down the star craft, dissected their star brothers and sisters to study them, and reverse engineered the craft and technologies. The military was shocked at the star beings' forgiving and gentle response to this unwarranted attack—in fact, star sisters and brothers co-operated with the military. They stayed on Gaia with the secret space programs to teach humans how to create fiber optics, the intricacies of electromagnetic energy devices, and more.

"Yet a boundary was also set. The extraterrestrials periodically went around the world to the advanced nuclear missile sites and shut them down. Generals considered to be in high command, and scientists regarded as geniuses, could not figure out how an entire facility was rendered inoperable, and a week or so later, suddenly, the site was restored to its optimal functionality.

"A highly respected general admitted many years later that ET craft were seen hovering over the gate of his military base, as the shutdown occurred. He interpreted the deathly quiet that overtook the base as a warning. Humanity was being notified to relinquish *arrogance.* In spite of this, several countries considered setting off a nuclear weapon, without taking responsibility for what that would do to the human race, to Gaia, and to the solar system.

"From distant coordinates, inconceivably far away in the universe, interventions occurred, holding human hubris in check. They likely will be needed again. Atomic bombs won't serve anyone. It's like amplifying the frequencies of an angry, screaming monster, and letting those frequencies roar unimpeded like an inferno, poisoning the world all the way down to its subatomic particles.

"Instead, for millennia, beings came from the deep recesses of the galaxy to share the technology of the human heart. This built-in, innate biotechnology does not require devices or bombs to explode love, truth, and bliss frequencies throughout the universe. Humans are fractal antennae for ecstasy, euphoria, and tender, loving care for each other. They can receive it and transmit it from any galaxy or universe if their hearts are pliable and they remain open and receptive.

"Not working in these benevolent, higher frequencies, the Nazi regime began research in Antarctica with ET saucers and an anti-gravity, bell-shaped craft. Meanwhile, the U.S. and its allies tried to figure out what life would look like post war if they didn't become the creators of the most highly advanced technologies.

"Questions arose: how could the U.S. build an elite military to protect themselves in the years ahead? How could they be the global leader of outer space travel? How could they become the biggest world power, controlling, manipulating, dominating everyone everywhere through brute force and financially? This competition-pattern took strong root in all the most powerful countries on Gaia.

"At first, the consequences seemed somewhat benign because the motivation seemed to be about survival, protection, and expansion of postwar lifestyle, but financial aspirations grew.

"With a sense of unicity and care, the eyes of benevolent beings throughout the universe were watching humanity devolve and struggle.

"In each council, the galactic beings asked the same questions: when would unicity come back into play? When would Gaia be given her due respect as a sentient being? When would humanity shift into a softer, more open-hearted way of relating to their fellow humans and their star brothers and sisters?

"Resolution and answers began with small steps by courageous humans. Quantum theory slowly crept forward as an acknowledged, authentic science. Visionaries in every field of science took the risk of ridicule and censorship to bring groundbreaking ideas to the forefront.

"With the war machine in place, and government and military control and manipulation growing, these brave humans were often attacked. And they lost academic standing with their peers, and sometimes their careers dissolved. They suffered, some were killed, and others stood by in shock and horror as they watched scientists being manipulated and coerced.

"Global governments and media developed sophisticated forms of mind control. This became accepted as normal. Secret intelligence organizations concealed bewildering programs that took decades to be even partially revealed publicly. If information was exposed, the exposer was denigrated, and the facts were twisted and planted safely within alternate stories. Stealth operations had fertile soil to take firm root.

"The observers from the stars noticed that these kinds of programs were emerging from an escalated war approach to the economy and to solving conflicts. Looking through the big picture view, how would it be helpful to normalize violence, and develop secret programs, which can control and harm people? What is a better way to approach life and find solutions that allow the human need for safety to be met?

"How did propaganda and the lure of becoming superhuman through technologies seep into the hearts of good humans on Planet Earth? As embodied, sacred perfection, what is not already contained within and available to them? How did propaganda, perfected over long periods of time, influence them? What if they kept going in this direction? What inner powers and incomparable quantum gifts and experiences will they forfeit?

"This inquiry begged additional questions: Can the unicity gene survive this paradigm of behavior that promotes secrecy and potential harm or manipulation of others? What are the long term costs of that paradigm? How does humanity plan to evolve in the years ahead? These were hot topics in galactic conversations, yet no consensus developed to answer them.

"As sequential time moved on for Gaia and her beloved human companions, a tragic way of life emerged. Galactic councils called it *the era of distraction*. These observers refused to intervene yet held compassion, as they watched humanity become more competitive, less tuned into nature, and increasingly obsessed with having more, and doing more.

"It was reaching a crescendo with poor countries falling prey to relentless hunger, strife, and suffering while wealthy countries kept their populations fixated on constant dissatisfaction and addiction. All of Earth's inhabitants seemed exhausted and full of anxiety in one way or another.

"But then the galactic observers saw something happening that brought a sense of optimism.

"A wave of consciousness in small groups of humans began to elevate. A trend began as some people turned toward quieter, slower experience, seeking periods of meditation and retreat, sometimes for a day, sometimes for longer periods; others became interested in shamanic lifestyles in communion with nature, animals, the Earth; and still others delved into study of human consciousness and new paradigms of thought illuminated by quantum science.

"With delight the star councils saw that in increasing numbers, humans began to wonder, became curious, and challenge the status quo once again.

"A growing arm of archeological and anthropological sciences became captivated with ancient sites and cultures, seeking clues and new knowledge about past civilizations who had thrived, and how they did so.

"An evolution in quantum physics began in which new theories and ideas came forward in surprisingly rapid succession, albeit reluctantly accepted by traditional thinkers.

"Naturally, from eons of war, oppression, and grasping for survival, denser energies were not ready to be dissolved easily. The lower frequencies of fear, shame, aggression, and pride were a natural consequence of those times in Earth's history.

"The observers from the stars watched the suffering of humanity, drowning in waves of low frequencies. However, souls were emerging who wanted to discover a more kindhearted and respectful way of life, and a larger view of the universe. They became savvy about the unicity gene and were willing to allow it to express at any cost. Luckily, a growing passion in this burgeoning group ignited and expanded exponentially.

"The galactic observers were realistic that in linear time, patience is key.

"Other than coming to share wisdom with select humans and sharing advanced technologies with individuals and secret military personnel, they remained detached observers.

"Various species from the galaxy began to notice humanity's increased interest in space travel—reciprocally, they became interested in coming to Earth. These species are as distinctively dissimilar as Earth's population. The galactic observers intervened occasionally when a species came to Gaia with the intention to control or manipulate. These species, who were disposed to manipulation, were attracted by the lower frequencies on Earth, such as fear and pride. Like attracts like. The good news was that they were not allowed to invade. While here, they could only observe Gaia and her human inhabitants.

"Humanity is inching towards a tipping point where humans could express the unicity gene and flourish. The other option is to choose to rely on lower frequencies and perish. The galactic council often noted that *implosion* is the hallmark of lower densities and vibrations within the eternal quantum field of all possibilities. Lower vibrations cause a downward spiral back to ground zero, rather than an expansive upward spiral into endless opportunities for creation, with its infinite, mind-blowing, potential and possibilities.

"Understanding these dire conditions in which Sophia, Grace, and Nate find themselves, let us strike the rods, begin the frequency harmonics, and project our love through quantum waves, straight to their beautiful hearts. May they always feel our love and protection."

The solstice ceremony proceeded in unrestrained resplendence while the three recipients moved through their lives on Gaia with amnesia of their inconceivably immense cosmic nature and the multitude of their amazing, earthly adventures in linear time. They held no memory of Kandor, Belstar, their radiant mothers, and innumerable friends from distant universes, who continued to cheer them on.

These three quantum beings in earth suits were treading the complex path of human life on Planet Earth in the twenty-first century.

CHAPTER 4
DAILY LIFE ON GAIA

Delicate rays of light streamed through the bare branches of centuries old oaks and the birds' daily serenade was underway. Sophia's mornings began with a hot cup of tea, steam dancing from its surface. As each day arrived, she became more disillusioned that her plans and expectations were being shattered. A soothing cup of tea provided a few moments of essential comfort.

Those few precious minutes provided solace for her before she began to care for her husband, who she'd loved for so long. As usual, Nate was sleeping softly.

Since he was a light sleeper, she glided like a feather through the house. His ALS was a disease that removed his capacity to move freely. Even with the athleticism that he'd cultivated for decades, he was barely able to stand, he choked on food, and the elasticity of his lungs was slowly disintegrating—his 'Amyotrophic Lateral Sclerosis,' was a long name for a devastating weakening of his muscles. There was no cure and no definitive cause.

Moving from Texas to California seemed like a great idea. With many years of spiritual growth together, including a devoted study of quantum science, they were always an optimistic pair, so a miracle was not off the table. Predictability and expectations are not factors in a quantum-style miraculous event. Although they were clear that leaning into the mind and strategizing were not the secret sauce for a miracle, raising their personal frequencies could be a catalyst for a quantum moment of spontaneous healing. Fortunately, they had many experiences together of elevating their entire energy fields into love, peacefulness, and bliss; it had become second nature and something they resolutely practiced throughout their lives.

As Sophia researched accounts of people who experienced spontaneous healings from ALS, she felt whispered promises of hope. Other factors like longtime friends living in California, and the enchantment of Mother Nature in the foothills of the Sierras, combined to create the next step in Nate's healing journey.

Hearing him stir, she moved without haste. Sometimes, he couldn't call out for help because his voice was too weak, and though a little brass bell was always nearby, sometimes that, too, was more than his degenerating muscles could manage.

After confirming that he was okay, it was time to embark on a fresh day—which meant that his liquid diet was ready and Sophia would help him get up, dressed, and move to the living area.

She stroked his morning-messy hair with its soft hues of mocha while glancing at a photo of their honeymoon nearby—their hair was dark brown, no traces of grey yet, no wrinkles yet, and their faces radiated the fullness of their hearts, enthusiastic for endless opportunities and adventures.

Sophia yawned a few times, which was normal lately. Sleeping for her was a piece-meal affair, like a new mother always diligent. As a result of his waning muscle strength, Nate called for her several times each night so she could immediately get him into a sitting position. Sometimes he was choking. At other times, nature called to evacuate the water in his frail body. If he needed a sip of water, which had become hard to swallow, she was prepared to help him navigate that simple task. But by this stage of his illness, there were no simple tasks.

With a smile and a cheerful voice, sincere and innocent, she spoke the same words with each sunrise, "Good morning, Nate. I love you."

Those words were not a ritual nor were they a mere salutation. Recently, she told her closest friend that speaking this way to Nate allowed her heart to express the love for him that she felt in the deepest recesses of her being since the moment they met. As his condition gradually declined, their familiar exchanges of affection had to change. No more tender kisses or making love.

Many years ago, before she met Nate, Sophia had begun her path of natural healing, spirituality, and introspection. Her daily reflections rested on the level of frequency that she could consciously bring into each situation in her life.

Friends commented then and now that she did not tend towards judgment. She cared deeply about others. Her spirituality, past traumas, ancestors, and unseen realities were topics that mattered to her. The unknown remained her friend; even the unknown of how and if Nate could heal.

As she helped him from the bed, a crow lit on a deck chair outside of the open patio door.

They both stopped to watch and listen. "How many hundreds of times have we talked about the spiritual meaning of birds that appear through our window in the morning? I love diving with you into the esoteric, symbolic meanings of life's incredible wonders."

"I used to think that you were only humoring me, pretending to share my insatiable appetite for everything unseen and symbolic. But I know it's as natural to you as it is to me. Would you be willing to dive into the crow's symbolic meaning this morning? I feel like this bird is here to relieve me, at least a little bit, from the terror of my dreams. As if the crow is telling me to enter into the mystery of life, rather than into an abyss of suffering. Maybe that's my wishful thinking."

Helping him to stand, she waited for him to get his footing before they began the careful, arduous journey to the next room.

"It sounds like the call of the mysterious unknown," Sophia agreed, "and a call to be open to something profound. Would it be okay if we continue talking once you settle into your chair?"

Nate nodded with a weak smile. Even his lips were losing strength. His once highly developed, athletic body had become skin draped over bones.

Sophia walked backwards as Nate carefully held her forearms for support. Reminiscing about their life together, Nate commented somberly that this current, daily journey by foot was an agonizing contrast with past hikes in forests, evening strolls after dinner, or wandering the streets of Paris, Rio de Janeiro, or Mumbai. Yet, these lovers agreed with loving smiles and uninhibited eye contact, that they were grateful to remain together as dancing partners in life. The walk that morning was happening with the same highly charged connection that bound them for since the day they met.

As Nate sipped breakfast, Sophia continued the subject of his nightmare. "Can you say more about your dream? I want to hear about the fear without giving it too much energy. As long as I've known you, you've had inexplicable dreams about oppressors, and these days they've become more like relentless nightmares. The terror you describe has become more intense since your declining muscular symptoms emerged. With all of your work with energy healers, past life regressions, and psychotherapy, it all points to trauma. But you say its roots are not from this life. You have incomprehensible memories and details of battles here and off planet. And even the most conventional therapists believe you. Skeptics of past lives agree with you. I've found that fascinating. With all that help, has the fear lessened at all?"

Gathering the energy and vocal control to speak, he answered, "Sophia, I'm straining right now to make the vowel 'oh' of your beautiful name. Please bear with me if I speak slowly… The guy you live with, who rejects violence on all levels from the depths of his soul, has somehow also played a role in horrific battles and atrocities. We all have the capacity to express the full spectrum of low and high frequencies. How could we express all of them in one life, in one reality in space and time? When I consider that I have likely played light and dark roles, I find compassion for myself and others. I don't want to brush my dreams off as irrelevant or something that I have to overcome. It's an exploration and an opportunity to see myself from another angle, without judgment or labeling myself."

Nate paused for a long moment, gathering his strength to continue.

"You know that you could lose your husband soon, right? And that you've likely lost him in other space-time coordinates, and that you've lost many other loved ones? I seem to be facing and purifying my inner warrior and you may be purifying the part of you who's experienced immense loss… As I deal with this fear, continue to work with therapists, I know this is important inner work. I am diving deep. It feels like some kind of agreement I made to be born in this period following the horror of the two world wars… You decided to be born in this time, too. We must have come for a reason at this point in Gaia's life stream."

He paused again, eyes closed. Sophia waited patiently, knowing he was near his limit. Then he looked up at her with a gentle smile.

"Without doubt, all of the services that I've offered in my career helped to elevate my frequencies. You and I have to remain diligent with our individual, inner work. Otherwise, we'll get trapped in mind-life rather than experiencing the truth of who we are as the light of Essence and pure love... Can you believe how much we've grown inwardly? We've been talking about these subjects for decades. Slowly but surely, our healing and our connection to our Essence is going deeper, and levels of pain and emotional patterns in us have released. This seems to be the inside job that every human has to go through." His eyes were moist with tenderness as he held her gaze.

"That's my long answer and that's about as much voice as I can muster right now. I want you to remember that this fear is mine to work through. Never make it your job to help me overcome it. In fact, thank you for not trying to save me. Instead, you always let me talk. You ask me important questions. You are a beautiful being. You really listen. You care about me, deeply... I can't imagine going through this without you. It would be an even worse hell."

Nate's voice was rasping with effort as he spoke these last words. He closed his eyes and sank deeply into himself. He had told Sophia not to worry if he became withdrawn after speaking. It was his strategy for regrouping and accessing his life force on a deeper level.

After a long meditative silence, Sophia noticed Nate's spirits rising to the surface again. "Since we are starting a new year," she said, "I am planning to work even more intently on myself. You know that I love you. I know I loved you in all those coordinates in space-time that you mentioned. I appreciate that you realize I can't save you. Driving you to a doctor is one thing, but healing your fear and terror is your work." She felt the ache in her heart, the sorrow of sharing her lover's suffering, her own pain streaming into the well of human love and grief.

Gathering her own voice, she continued. "This year, I'm going to dive deeply into my studies of quantum healing. As I continue to elevate my energy fields through frequency, I want to connect more intimately with my Essence. I am breaking new ground in the next phase of my life, and I feel my practice growing steadily. I know that raising my own frequency helps you as well. I'm so glad we spent those years in India learning the ancient wisdom of the great sages, and the value of connection with Essence." Sophia felt herself bubbling with the gratitude she always felt for all the things they'd been able to do together.

"When we returned to the U.S., remember all of those courses and programs we attended to learn cutting edge quantum physics? This connection we have to the Essence from which all quantum matter and activity arise, always fascinates me. To dissolve into stillness, and experience the Essence from which our world arises, continues to blow my mind. It's been a fascinating ride with you, oh divinely beautiful one.

"I remember our conversations about how science had to break from religion because the churches had become irrationally oppressive and enmeshed with power and politics. Their texts and teachings fixated on a judging God who micromanages people and condemns them to hell for disobedience. Scientists who wanted to continue to ask questions and explore were considered dangerous by the church, while the scientists became ever more fixated on the purely material world, ignoring God and spirit altogether. Eventually, we found the link between the apparently divergent fields of spirituality and science—the infinite field in and around our bodies, which are made up of ninety-nine per cent space.

"That space, this incomprehensible *field*, is definitely omnipresent, omniscient, and omnipotent. We are all connected to it and interact with it, unconsciously or consciously. We chose to dive into the conscious part and became aware of its relevance for us and our world. Imagine when our world learns to once again bridge science and spirituality, in safety and with encouragement, and humans connect to one another in Essence, like we may have done in ancient times tens of thousands of years ago." Sophia was almost breathless in her exuberance for the insights she and Nate had gained together over the years.

"We are not necessarily in a *bad* cycle in human history. Maybe we are at the cusp of a new cycle where we collectively remember how important it is to be connected to ourselves, each other, and our world. We can make an evolutionary leap while hitting the pause button to assess who we are, what the world is made of, and why we are alive. Relationships can shift from *separation* to *collaboration*. Deep inside, I know we've done this before. When I meditate, the information from the field is intense at times, showing me what is possible. We are in the midst of the potential for an evolutionary shift that has to happen together. Taking time to experience stillness and seeing our common humanness are the next steps."

"Sorry," she said, slowing down once again. "I'm going on and on about our favorite subjects. It's helpful for me to articulate my insights. Thanks for listening. Gosh, I love our conversations! Your curious mind, unfurled heart, and gut feelings open up space for my mind to expand further; and it's getting more awe-inspiring by the minute. Every day is like entering a new frontier because of your insatiable spirit of enquiry. I love you so much!"

Nate was filled head to toe with appreciation of Sophia's sublime radiance. Her eyes sparkled, and he felt wrapped in her joy and love. He smiled back at her, letting his adoration show. "You can talk all day and night about anything quantum or mystical and you'll have my undivided attention."

Kissing him cheerfully on the cheek, she headed for the kitchen. Nate closed his eyes and allowed his facial muscles to fully relax, soaking up the healing vibrations of his beloved.

Preparing breakfast, Sophia noticed that her best friend, Grace, had sent a text to check in. Grace and her husband were traveling abroad, so she and Sophia couldn't talk as often as they had in the past. But distance never seemed to matter for Grace and Sophia who had been inseparable from early childhood. Since a little girl pinkie pact to be friends forever, their incredible bond remained like pure gold; beautiful, eternal, and strong.

Grace instinctively knew how to bring out Sophia's playfulness, sense of humor, and capacity to find the positive in all situations, which was invaluable as Nate's illness relentlessly progressed.

Sending a text back saying that everything was fine, Sophia continued to make Nate's liquid breakfast to the noise of the whirling blades of the blender.

The sounds, rhythms, and pace of daily life continued to change as each day passed, Sophia adhering with firmer resolution to go with the flow, adapt, and watch life unfold. Throughout their marriage, a perpetual fountain of love flowed between Sophia and Nate; the one constant in the wild, unpredictable currents of everyday life. Their enduring relationship was a certainty she had relied on for many years.

Smiling softly, she opened the window and took in a deep breath of nourishing air.

The California sun shimmering through the tall evergreens, the brilliant blue sky, and the majestic mountains were constant reminders of strength and power. These were anchors she could count on as she confronted the uncertainty of Nate's health and their future.

CHAPTER 5
MEETING THE UNEXPECTED

A Sierra foothill morning was normally frigid in January. Yet on this day, a springtime pattern was at play. By mid-morning, everyone was outside, feeling the warmth of the sun, hearing the migratory birds singing, and enjoying the soft light filtering through the branches of the trees.

The duplex where Sophia and Nate lived was a perfect arrangement for Nate's condition at the time they moved in. Nate could manage a one-step entrance into the house. But that changed.

As they headed out for an appointment that morning, Sophia stepped down first to help him balance, but when he stepped down, she felt his whole weight fall forward, toppling into her. With the extra-human strength that comes when a loved one is in danger, she grabbed him around his rib cage and hoisted him up, pivoting at the same time and pulling him in one swift heave over to the bed that was just inside the door. It all happened with lightning speed. There was no time to think or strategize. As with everything in her life, it just happened and she responded as best she could.

The reality of what was happening came crashing down on both of them. Nate was badly shaken. "I have an eerie feeling of impending doom," he said quietly as Sophia helped him turn over on his side. As her lips tenderly touched his cheek with a soft kiss, he mustered a feeble smile. Despondent and exhausted, he fell asleep. The appointment was cancelled and not rescheduled.

It hit them with blunt force—a new era in his care had emerged instantly and unexpectedly. Without question, his mobility was deteriorating faster than either of them imagined it could.

In her usual style, Sophia made a cup of tea and went outside to center herself, enter into silence, and hold still.

Finding her connection with Essence was a skill that she had cultivated for decades. When she taught meditation, she emphasized holding inner stillness, being in a silent space to ground into the body and be in communion with pure Essence.

Remaining true to her values, Sophia was known for an unshakable commitment to be still and present to the unknowable, mystical space that evolved from within a human being. She spoke often about the effulgent, silent Essence from which quantum universes unfold.

Within the radiant comfort of the sun, she sat in stillness.

Hearing the rustling of paper nearby, she became aware that an elderly woman from the adjacent apartment was settling in to read a book. She'd heard from the landlord that a couple would be staying next door for a month or so. The duplexes were often leased short term, so new neighbors were not unexpected.

With her responsibility in caring for Nate, Sophia had not welcomed the neighbors. In fact, she hadn't connected socially with anyone for several months. All she knew about the couple was that they were quite elderly, the husband spoke German, and their names were Gilda and Ralph.

Gilda fumbled with the book, scowled, and put it down. Closing her eyes, she soaked in the fresh air and sunshine, as if her breath was a giant straw. Her gray hair was long and shaggy, and the lines in her face reflected the depth of her advanced age. Yet her tiny frame was a capable vessel for a life force that remained resolutely potent.

She suddenly opened her eyes, a bright, crystalline blue, and looked at Sophia with something close to a snarl, "What the heck are you staring at?"

Sophia answered kindly, "I was startled to see someone. I heard that you and your husband would be coming this month and I looked forward to meeting you. My name is Sophia."

Taking a deep breath and with a gentler voice, Gilda explained, "I am a bit on edge. We move a lot. You seem nice. I'm sorry. My name is Gilda. It's an Italian name, so that's why it's pronounced JEELDAA." Every syllable and each sentence was spoken in a perfunctory, concise cadence.

"Did they tell you that I am German?" Gilda asked.

"No, they didn't," Sophia answered, a bit puzzled. "I'm not detecting an accent. When did you come to this country?"

Squirming in her chair as if she was being interrogated, Gilda looked directly at Sophia, glaring fiercely. "I don't answer questions like that! You have no right to pry! Stop asking me questions which are none of your business!" Wriggling like a snake in her chair, she positioned herself with her back away from any further conversation.

Sophia was aware of what happens mentally and emotionally with the elderly because she'd seen her mother go through dementia at the end of her life. Her mother's dementia had been a painful but fascinating journey. Through speaking with neurologists and exhausting herself with hours of studying, Sophia learned a lot about the complex facets of the human brain. What she learned helped expand her understanding of people's often bewildering responses to life. The brain has a negativity bias that stays on high alert, sending constant signals to *be vigilant, suspicious, and careful.* Everything is a threat until specific parts of the brain, subconscious and automatic, decide otherwise.

Her mother's neurologist was clear that making her mom wrong or correcting her for her irrational behavior was futile. He always spoke to Sophia compassionately and was warm and friendly with her mother. He suggested that as her mother's brain started to lose its usual neural networks, it was possible that she could "perceive unseen realms." With genuine curiosity, he questioned if perhaps her brain function had shifted to the extent that she could "detect other realities and time travel" because the patterns that ordinarily inhibited such phenomenon could be shifting.

Following up on this doctor's contemplations, Sophia and Nate did their own research and gradually began to see that medical scientists, in general, were not allocated sizable budgets to study dementia. Instead the most provocative and extensive body of information on this kind of neurological research came from an unexpected source: the U.S. military and C.I.A. Through secret underground projects, a plethora of funding was constantly being funneled into programs to study the brain and the paranormal.

As Sophia assimilated her encounter with Gilda, she said, "If it's okay, maybe you can just tell me what you want to tell me, and I won't put any pressure on you. I promise."

Gilda's eyes welled up with tears that began to stream down her face, cascading into her lap, as she folded over into heavy sobs. Patiently waiting for her to release an ocean of anguish, Sophia sat in stillness and silence.

When Gilda calmed down, she said in a shaky voice, "My dear, I've needed a friend for a long time. And I'd rather they kill me than go on like this. My husband's mind is destroyed. Why we did this, I'll never know. Somehow, I trust you with my heart. Maybe it's because I am getting so damned old! I can hardly get around. Yet my mind is sharp as a tack! I know things, I have secrets, and I want to end it all. It's so Goddamned complicated!"

Gilda began to explain that she and Ralph came to the U.S. after World War II. She paused and looked down with a haunted gaze as she revealed, "We were escaping a military tribunal."

She continued to share her story without reserve. "My husband's name is Rolph not Ralph! Goddamned secrets are ridiculous. You always look over your shoulder. We were guilty of murder, Sophia! Yes, you heard me right! We came here and spread destruction, and ridiculous, depraved ideas! And what for?

"I've been a slave my whole life. First a slave to my parents, then to the Führer, then to the U.S. military, and my husband. Why is my soul so dark, and my wisdom so sinfully compromised that I would agree to be a slave?

"I want to say more, but I need to rest now. Thank you for letting me release some steam from my heart. It's like being a boiling tea kettle that never gets to cool down. I trust you. And believe me, I don't ever say that to anyone.

"Maybe it's time for me to make further amends for the lies I've told myself and others. I'm getting too old to carry these burdens. I'll see you tomorrow. Same time. Same place. Is that okay?"

Sophia agreed as she heard the temple bell, even though it was muffled. Sometimes, Nate could only manage to wiggle it feebly between his fingers.

She briefly explained about Nate's condition and headed back to care for the love of her life.

CHAPTER 6
REFLECTING ON ICY HISTORY

Mid-morning was normally rest time for Nate, and Sophia had an hour to prepare lunch, regroup, and do a little self-care. For a few minutes, she'd curl up by a sunny window and write in her journal.

As though drawn like an invisible magnet to her special spot where she wrote, she went to the sun-drenched chair and sat comfortably for a moment. Taking a deep, relaxing breath, she let her fingers slowly drift over the soft, violet cover of her leather journal. Reading her reflections from the day before, she smiled with each passage that she captured about Nate's incredible life and his magnificent soul.

In her musings, she described Nate, as his friends often did, as a philosopher first and foremost, but he was also a skilled lawyer. Passionate about the environment and Gaia's sentient nature, human rights, and social justice issues, his gentle heart and warrior spirit found its stride in those arenas.

Releasing resistance to his physical circumstances, he gradually accepted the disintegration of his body even as it was a cruel blow to his future vision of a long life in service to humanity. He confidently believed he could move through this unexpected phase in his life. On a personal level, he remained on a profound inner path from childhood to present.

In the past decade, Nate and Sophia had become immersed in the field of quantum physics and the human mind, with its intricate mechanisms. They gathered in late afternoon for Indian spiced tea, sharing perspectives and expanding their understandings of different topics. The volume of books and research in the infinite field of quantum science was growing exponentially which allowed them to engage in conversations about the links between this science and the spiritual wisdom of the ancient philosophies they studied in India.

The tea master of this relationship was Nate who met a woman in India who gifted him with a tea recipe handed down for seven generations. When he wanted to nourish his soul with deep conversations, where curiosity and discovery reigned supreme, his spiced Indian tea was always served. This was their ritual.

Nate could no longer be the tea maker, he was now only the tea-sipper, in meager quantities.

The conversations that used to last for hours were reduced to increments of minutes disrupted by choking and gasping for air.

Yet his passion to explore life's experiences and the mystical, inner worlds as often as possible remained strong. Sophia shared his passion. Capturing her thoughts on the pages, she ended by drawing two inter-locking circles.

Smiling softly, she closed the journal and went to check in on Nate. From the large glass doors leading to the backyard, Nate had seen her talking to Gilda. He asked her about the conversation with the old woman.

Sophia explaining in as much detail as she could without breaking a confidence. Nate's eyes blazed with curiosity. "Oh wow! I'd love to speak with her. She must have a wealth of knowledge to share. I intuit there is more going on here than we know. You know as well as I do that when someone out-of-the-blue appears, inevitably they are a gift of fresh insights and perspectives that are invaluable to our life path. I encourage you to meet her again and be my ears."

Sophia was not surprised at his animated response to Gilda's story. She admired Nate's unconditional love and respect for the people he met, his unbridled curiosity about life's unexpected events, and his profound listening skills. She was grateful to be the constant beneficiary of these gifts.

After resting his voice for a minute, Nate continued his spirited inquiry. "Did she mention Admiral Byrd or anything about Antarctica? Or where her husband fit into the U.S. Military? Which arm of service? Where were they stationed in the U.S.? What was his specialty?

"Remember, Sophia, there are declassified intelligence reports saying that thousands of Nazis were hired by the U.S. after the war, sent into secret military programs because of their unique, technical skills. The insane part is why the U.S., coming off that ungodly war, would be so greedy for information that they would let these people enter the military and the corporate sector, too. I've always thought it had something to do with what happened to Admiral Byrd. The military-industrial complex realized that Hitler knew way more about off-planet technologies than the U.S., especially anti-gravity and other forms of energy. Knowing the Nazi mindset and their willingness to perpetrate unabashed atrocities, the results of extracting knowledge from those war criminals could never come to a good end. After doing extensive research, we finally have a personal account from someone who could prove more credible than a bunch of declassified documents. There are unimaginable volumes of documents that I've poured through."

This was an area of special interest for Nate, and his findings could coalesce into a scene from a Star Wars movie. As a prolific reader, he amassed staggering volumes of data, facts, and personal accounts. After hearing decades of stories from his massive brain-library, today she needed a reminder.

"Who was Admiral Byrd, honey?" Sophia asked.

Closing his eyes and gathering fresh momentum for what he wanted to share, Nate began, "I need to give you some context before I talk about Admiral Byrd because I want to make sure that you know why this subject is important to me. Believe it or not, when I speak about Admiral Byrd, it's because there's a connection to my own family lineage... This is part of my interest in Gilda.

"You know that my incredible, British birth father died when I was young. My highly pedigreed mother had no problem finding a new spouse. In the first half of the twentieth century, it was common for women of her social stature to land a culturally suitable husband. Even if she was still feeling grief and loss, it was expected of her. She was from an elite banking family.

"Unlike with my birth father, her family chose husband number two. I always felt that it was with resignation that she remarried and we moved to the U.S. My stepfather could not have been more different than my birth father. My stepfather was a U.S. citizen with strong ties to British and German bankers and financiers. From my perspective, the diabolical, scary aspect of him was that he leaned heavily towards Fascism, and Nazis were no problem for him. I experienced my stepfather as patronizing, unyielding and self-centered. By the time I finished high school, I realized plenty of people in my stepfather's circle of upper crust friends and many of his high society business associates shared his distorted, hubristic worldview and perspectives.

"My stepfather worked in the upper echelons of Wall Street. He had an insatiable appetite for power and control. He took care of my basic needs, but from my perspective, that was overwhelmingly overshadowed by his emotional brutality.

"He and my mom had another son together and he expected both of us to automatically absorb and adopt his worldview. This was a guy who thought Nazis were great. His real son inherited his malevolent DNA. That was clear. That kid was a chip-off-the-old-block, as they say. He glued himself to his father and obsessed over their freaky worldview.

"Luckily, I had different DNA. Thank God for that!

"I went to law school and then worked with them, as you are well aware. But I could not forget that my stepfather and his friends funded world wars that killed millions of people, including citizens in this country. It was concerning to me that he and his buddies showed no remorse.

"My inner warrior stayed furious with him. Simultaneously, however, my yogic, meditating, non-violent aspects were also at play and luckily, I found spiritual growth.

"I've never acted out in rage, hurt anyone, and never will respond through violence. I've done all of this research because something in me knows that these events in my dreams are part of my lineage, or could be information in *the field* that I need to connect with to help humanity.

"Somehow in the quantum soup of all possibilities, I am connected with a warrior role. Because of the intense inner tension I feel, I have to keep going to unravel this paradox within me between the warrior and the yogi; including dreams that feel like memories wafting as waves into my mind from the field. I recently read that from the perspective of unified field theory, our experience of time is just *memory*. Sound crazy? Consider that what happens to each of us is one unfathomably small part of the infinite field of what is, and our experience of it is just like a recorded *memory of that part* of the infinite field from our unique perspective. It's like *recorded information* playing back through our individual psyche. And everyone has access to the totality of information in the field, we just block it out so we can "experience" our "separate" individual lives.

"That theory led me to wonder if I am picking up something in the field that needs to be known right now or for me to share? Maybe my lucid dreams are my memory of events embedded in the field as information from my unique, immutable coordinate in the field. As a quantum being, I am endless. I won't die in the sense of a finite ending. So there's more to me than I can conceptualize.

"When it comes to quantum science, the idea that memory is the building block of time makes sense. If there is no memory (which is information in the field about events) is there any experience of time? Events must be linked in some way—memory, continuously accessed information, is that link. Although I can sense this is true, I can't quite hold onto it, my brain just takes in these kinds of epiphanies to gradually process them. This *time and memory concept* is mind-blowing to think about, right?" Nate paused, breathless. He closed his eyes and turned inward for a few moments, gathering his strength. Sophia could tell he was managing his energy carefully so he could continue sharing something of immense importance to him. She listened and waited as an act of devotion.

"Back to my stepfather... I know that the secrets of my stepfather's world, the treachery and the deceit, contributed to the mess our world is in today." Nate closed his eyes once more, his face a mixture of emotions as he centered himself. "Our world is hurting, suffering deeply. For some reason, I was destined to be confronted with that distorted world, as if I was supposed to be within close range of the flames of hell. As you know, my family life growing up was no picnic in Central Park.

"Think about what I just said about my stepfather and his banker friends and recall that our government was desperate to obtain cutting-edge German technologies and high-tech weaponry. U.S. Intelligence showed that the Nazis had gone to the Antarctic and established a military base there. And on top of that, they developed sophisticated spacecraft that looked *other-worldly.*

"Why not send the best-of-the-best to take that military base away from the Germans and bring back their technologies? Here's why I think Admiral Byrd matters: he was a famous and well-respected leader in the U.S. Navy at that time. He led an expedition to the Antarctic to do just that. His mighty fleet was a combination of British, U.S., and Australian military. As powerful as their forces were, they were in for a surprise. Despite all of their advanced weapons and world-class combat strategists, they were no match for what happened as they entered the Antarctic and got close to Hitler's military base. They were attacked by flying discs, ships were disintegrated, and weapons hit them that were more advanced than anything Admiral Byrd had ever seen. The encounter didn't last long, the fleet turned around and headed home in brutal defeat.

"Under strict security, Admiral Byrd, who was true to his military oath, never discussed it. With the exception of sparse comments from just a few of the four thousand soldiers who participated in Byrd's *Operation Highjump,* the Antarctic secret remains tightly guarded.

"This was in 1947 and from that point forward, an insatiable appetite began globally in many countries hungry for these advanced engineering secrets. As you know, I've wanted to learn more about the technologies, but Gilda may be able to tell us the missing pieces of this story. Is her husband one of those Nazis who came here to work underground for the U.S. military?" He looked at her with eyes that burned like coal.

After sitting silently for a minute, Sophia leaned forward saying, "Your description of the battle jogged my memory. I do recall Admiral Byrd. What you've described was horrific and, to be honest, hard to believe. And no, Gilda did not get into any details. It was more like her heart was bearing a heavy load that was too much to bear. The way she cried felt like a person who had bottled up an ocean of tears which cracked and shattered today. A flood of old, even ancient anguish released. I'm worried that it's taken a toll on her. Based on her age, I would not pressure her for information.

"I know you'd love to get facts and confirmations—I want to be clear that my relationship with her is about her heart and soul. I won't ask her about these things or anything else. She's guarded and heart-wrenchingly distrustful. I want to cultivate my friendship with her and not see her as a resource for intel. I hope you understand that if she wishes to share, she can. And I can't share anything with you unless she says it's okay."

Nate's face muscles tightened, as weak as they were, and he responded angrily, "Sophia, do you think I do all of this research for myself? I want the world to have access to government sponsored, cutting-edge scientific discoveries. From my perspective, taxpayers paid for them over the years, At least with some kind of oversight, we could manage this priceless research." He paused, then went on in a softer tone. "I would never ask you to betray an old woman's secrets. You, better than anyone, should know how much I value privacy. Have I ever been anything but transparent with you? She is obviously broken-hearted by her past because she likely allowed herself to be mind-controlled by parents, culture, and politics. That is tragic. WWII left vicious, visceral scars on a majority of humanity."

He lowered his eyes, breathed as deeply as he could, and said with humility, "What I said felt incredibly judgmental on my part. I have no right to make assumptions about her. With that in mind, I'm going to drop the whole subject. Unless you bring it up, it's done. I'm sorry I got pushy and way too zealous."

"Nate, I apologize if I implied that you lack compassion for her. It's just that sometimes you launch full throttle into this subject. You ask people probing questions and I'm not like that. I know your heart is always in the best place. I wanted to be clear about my feelings and relationship with Gilda. That's all. I was deeply affected by my conversation with her. It seemed important. I don't know why."

A gentle ringing of chimes on Sophia's phone broke the flow of the conversation to let her know to prepare the next meal. On that note, the daily schedule continued, and time moved on, taking Nate's declining muscles with it.

CHAPTER 7
DEEPER NEIGHBORLY CONVERSATION

Finding a welcome gap in her daily care-giving schedule, Sophia realized that she could slip outside while being within hearing of Nate's voice and the temple bell.

Once again, sweet sunshine and glistening dew welcomed her. And there was one more aspect to the morning's greeting. Gilda was already seated and seemed prepared to talk. A cup of coffee in her hands, her hair was pulled back, framing her face, showing her blue eyes sparkling like stars. Her body language was open, and she sat comfortably in her chair, her posture vastly different than in their initial meeting.

Gilda's first question was straight to the point, "Did you tell your husband about me? I let my guard down a bit and regretted it. Is your husband ex-military?"

Smiling, Sophia told Gilda about Nate and his weakening condition, described his gentle temperament, and revealed that he was British by birth. He was now a U.S. citizen and he had nothing to do with military or governments, unless, in his job as a lawyer, he was advocating for someone whose rights were violated by either organization.

Sophia winked playfully as she described his baby-blue eyes and mentioned how much she loved him. She blushed like a teenager as she admitted to swooning whenever he called her *sweetheart* or reverted into his British roots, calling her *darling*.

A moment of silence descended, and Gilda chuckled as she explained how she spent the whole night conjuring up a story about Nate's demonic character, imagining a clearly despicable enemy. And now all she could envision was an angelic, blue-eyed Brit who showered his wife with swoon-worthy affection.

With defenses down, Gilda sipped her coffee. "Are you an advocate, too?" She asked.

With a radiant expression, Sophia replied, "I advocate for people to connect with their Essence, the source which animates their body and this whole world. I advocate for their sovereignty, and engagement with their body as a way to keep that connection. I am passionate about collaboration and coming together in harmony."

"Are you religious?" Gilda asked.

Sophia's answer required a deep breath, getting centered as she prepared to explain more than "Yes" or "No."

Sophia looked directly into Gilda's eyes and connected with her silently before she spoke. "I was raised Catholic and learned all of the prayers. I was devout and experienced the sacredness of rituals and formed a powerful bond with God, as the creative source and infinite intelligence constantly swirling with mind-boggling, grace-filled energy in my amazing life.

"As I began to connect with divinity more deeply and with stronger intention and focus, I found areas of my *religious* life that I was not comfortable with. I'd become tense when I learned certain doctrines or when I read about church history. My inner radar was spotting inconsistencies, veiled statements that seemed to contradict the essence of the teachings, and historical events that didn't harmonize with my burgeoning, inner world. The dogma, the rules, the pope's supposed infallibility, and all of that was hard for me to reconcile with my inner experience of divinity. There was an growing chasm between my inner experience of divinity and various aspects of the church and theology.

"What was also confusing was a one particular sect, the Jesuits, who were scholars. They had access to information that no one else could see. I kept wondering if they thought we were not smart enough or not holy enough to have access to this information? Rather than being angry, I was curious. I studied and asked more questions.

"I learned in school about the church's role in the Middle Ages and the practice of feudalism; how there were 'Lords' who owned stables of magnificent horses, large plots of land, and the people who lived on the land worked for them, essentially their slaves. They were called *serfs* or *vassals*. They didn't get to read the Bible; they didn't get to be entrepreneurs, they couldn't buy their own land; and they were purposefully held back from education so they could always serve the Lord of the property. And those Lords were tied to the church and king. The system of feudalism ensured that the serfs remained forever enslaved, uneducated, and poor. The serfs learned that obedience was how they survived. Fear and manipulation kept the serfs safely under the oppressive thumb of the king-pope-lord trinity. The church's role in this system clearly went against the actual teachings they supposedly represented.

"On top of that, throughout the centuries, the church clearly had a negative view of women. Women were looked down upon, and even burned at the stake by leaders of the government and the church. And the church today brushes this history off as just a relic of history. The scholars say things like, 'The church was wrong back then. Times were different. There were extenuating circumstances that are hard to understand today. The church has evolved over time.' The tortured, boiled, decapitated, and burned bodies may not agree with those excuses. I'm not trying to be dramatic. I am being totally honest. I could never say things like this to most people. It was hard to accept the reality of these events and simply move on as if they didn't matter.

"Then, I found out that there are documents held in the Vatican vaults that none of us can see, not even scholars. Why? I began to wonder if what they were currently teaching me would someday be understood as wrong, unjust, and inhumane. Would it later be called an evolution in church history?

"I couldn't speak about this openly. I followed my family traditions, taught in the church, and studied with Catholic scholars. I took an honest look at the Vatican, the evolution of the priesthood, and the whole idea that all Christian religions, like it or not, are offshoots of this ancient framework. I decided it wasn't up to me to change or struggle with a well-established, popular church. I went my own path, studying many different religions and philosophical traditions.

"I arrived at my own solitary path, finding a profound connection to Essence. I realized that *the mystics* in the early church had always been my heroes; for some reason they were relatable and authentic. They expressed their faith in the Divine in ways that matched their time in history and their church culture. They were connected with a stream of wisdom that was beyond doctrine or theology. I sensed they'd found pure love, their Essence. They expressed love for mankind, for themselves, and every sentient and insentient being, always.

"So, my dear new friend, that's the long answer. I don't push my own experiences of Essence on others. But I guess you could say I am at least spiritually or philosophically minded. With Nate getting weaker, I do most everything alone now because I have to stay close and keep up our routines. In my spare moments I often delve into studies of the quantum field of all possibilities.

That's not a religion. It's a never-ending process of discovery of all-that-is."

Taking a minute to let their conversation land, Sophia cuddled her teacup in her hands, savoring her favorite green tea and the warmth it brought to her whole body.

Gilda, glued to every word, said, "I am a bit surprised at such a bold answer. No apologies, eh? You seem quite like a rock, a giant boulder, with this connection to the Essence of which you speak."

"Yes, I am like a rock in my connection with it. I love your image of a formidable boulder," Sophia replied. "But rather than being rigid about anything, I love to be open because there seems to always be something new, a nuance, or some aspect of the quantum-ness of this world, inner and outer, that is interesting to know and experience. I hope it didn't sound like I hate religions, churches, or think badly of anyone who enjoys that kind of worship. I was trying to explain my journey with it and where I am today. For me, it's about how I can more fully live in the connection and feel the pure, pristine, absolute love of my Essence. In that way, I am the universe itself, rather than a speck of it.

"Now it's your turn to share. Are you religious?"

Gilda choked on her coffee and coughed a few times before she cocked her head playfully to one side and asked smiling, "My dear girl, are you crazy?"

Laughing, Gilda continued, "Remember yesterday, I am the one who alluded to a completely sordid past." Her face became serious, then she sighed.

"I was raised Lutheran, but religion was never a priority for our family. The bigger influence in my parents' life was the government, the military, and all of that. I never felt close to any form of God.

"You see, for me, religion was another way to enslave me. I learned that God punishes, rewards and judges. That made God a lot like the Führer, my parents, and everybody in my world. The concept of God was and is nothing more than mind control as far as I can see. I'm as much a rock about that as you are about your connection with your Essence. Admittedly, I have begun to sense a subtle energy in and around me that I feel is creating all of the matter within it, which could be the Essence that you speak about. Sorry, but I am not up for engaging in a philosophical conversation today. I hope you understand."

Silence fell over them as they sipped hot drinks and relaxed; their muscles loosened and their breathing became longer and deeper. Today they spoke truth with each other; no holding back or pretending. This intimate conversation was between two souls brought together at a special time in their lives.

"Why were you worried about Nate being in the military?" Sophia asked, breaking the silence.

With her question, the atmosphere changed instantly. Gilda's face hardened and she stared frostily into the space in front of her.

Immediately catching the shift in mood, Sophia said with conviction in her voice, "I wasn't prying. I can see this subject is off limits and that's fine. I was curious. I'd love to know about your country and why you came here."

Once again, Gilda bristled and her hands clenched tightly.

Silence formed a bridge between the two women on opposite sides. Each of them respectfully allowed the divide and patiently let the moment they found themselves in play out naturally.

After a long pause, Gilda said, "I don't want to tell you. It could put us in danger. But it's too painful! I can't keep holding it in either. I am very old. You can see that. I should never have told you Rolph's real name. I've never told anyone. It's like these secrets want to slip out and I can't stop them. Please don't interrupt me or I swear I'll never speak to you again!

"I am from Germany originally and I was born in 1924. Yes, I am old; very old. And Rolph is, too.

"When we met, we were young, idyllic lovers; passionate about a world where we could be part of something great. We believed we were superior. We felt special. My God, Sophia. I was sixteen when I married Rolph. I was a baby and had been thoroughly indoctrinated. He was older, eighteen. He seemed so mature and confident.

"Everything at that time in our homes, schools, and churches was about our national greatness and the division between our greatness and all the other groups of people, the non-Aryans, as we saw them, who were worthless. The war kicked off with national pride, as all wars seem to do.

"We were possessed by what I see now as arrogance and polarity. There was no place in the Nazi system for unity. We needed to rise, and others had to fall. There were good people and bad people, with no one in between.

"My upbringing was brain-training to ensure that a heartless, icy sense of superiority sank deeply into every fiber of my being. In heart and soul, my family and close friends became predators. By 1935, all resistance to the Nazis went underground. They quit protesting, they stopped bringing alternate views about what was happening, they stopped speaking of the dangers of the burgeoning Nazi regime and their rise to power. Their absent voices and the Führer's total control of media made us all parrots for propaganda. Slowly, we joined our leaders in self-hypnosis, and began to loath anyone who was not our perfect clone in ideology and looks.

"In case you are wondering what I did for work during the war—No, I was not a madame at a concentration camp. I was a clerk for the Nazi inner circle because I was highly skilled in typing, organizing, and I spoke several languages, fluently. As a bonus, I was married to a genius. Rolph was an engineer who was obsessed with technological advancements.

"He was sought out by the highest ranking Nazis in the military to work on a secret program for space travel. I know it sounds like sci-fi and on one level, it was similar in its futuristic, high tech nature. But crazy as it may seem, that advanced engineering was his work. We were no longer in Germany. Instead, we were sent to the damnedest, coldest, darkest place on Earth, Antarctica. What a hell hole! What sane person wants to live in a place like that?

"It was clear that Germany was losing the war. Yet Rolph didn't seem to notice. He was oblivious, self-centered, focused only on what he could create, heedless of the harm and chaos it caused. This moment in my life was hell on earth!

"Like when you said that you were caught in a religious dilemma, I was caught in my own confusion of what was right and what was wrong. Weary from the endless typing and clerical work, enslaved to Rolph and to my country, I moved forward like an automaton. Death seemed like the only reprieve.

"The truth was, I didn't want to live in a world governed by people who used mind control with eerie confidence and uncanny accuracy and who conditioned each other to hate like a pack of demons. How could I live in a country with people who I thought were pure evil and who might treat me like shit if I didn't adhere lock step with their insane ideologies? They were totally selfish and arrogant, and had way too much power. I had no security. No one did.

"I learned about 'despicable people' from our Minister of Propaganda, the exalted, Mr. Joseph Goebbels. Read his news briefs and open letters to communities and you will see the most vile contempt for humanity in history. Eventually comedy and humor were censored completely, and society plummeted. Laughter diminished in general. The focus of life was not to socialize or relate to each other; rather it was to become polarized and very serious about all aspects of life and winning the war.

"Does it seem impossible for good people to fall into hate and fear of their neighbors and family? With mass propaganda, over a long period of time, it was easy. All media was distorted with a purposeful, narrow focus: we were inundated with the belief that we were victims of despicable people. We were emotionally breaking down by this time from unimaginable unemployment, no real purpose for living, and an incessant, gnawing feeling of anxiety about our future. We let our minds be controlled by the propaganda of media and we became myopic, focusing on getting rid of *the despicable*s. My dear, this realization crushed my heart: the goddamned truth was that *the despicables* were us—our families and neighbors, our loved ones; the despicable propaganda had drawn us into its filthy web. I will never forget it. We must never repeat this psychological lunacy.

"That kind of evil spread like the worst plague imaginable across our country. Rolph and I caught that metaphorical fever and we remained in its insidious grip. Its searing heat ravages your soul, slowly and completely. And we didn't see it coming. Arrogance and pride captured our hearts. Of course, we also wore self-imposed blinders. When you add apathy and indifference, you've short-circuited the voice of your heart and soul. We did not see this happening nor did millions of others. We obeyed the government and paid the devastating price.

"The war finally ended. On a trip to South America from Antarctica, we were captured and taken to the United States. I was prepared to be executed.

"Yet something strange and quite shocking happened. We were invited to join a U.S. military space program. We'd be given fake names and we'd have to live underground in secret, high-security military bases.

"Of course, Rolph was happy—he could continue his work. But I was confused. Wasn't the U.S. an evil empire, our sworn enemy? Everything would be the same, only we would be serving a different country. Once again, I'd be a slave to military leaders.

"It turned out, my husband was resourceful. He and thousands of others who received a similar offer, began plotting how to take over the U.S. once they got inside. They had no allegiance to what they saw as this *filthy country*. Sorry to tell you this, but we still hated your citizens. We were thoroughly conditioned to despise you.

"Let me remind you of something inconceivable: the Nazi approach was to regard with utter disgust our neighbors and most everyone in our country who didn't look and act like us. Please don't take it personally. We were a bitter, rotten lot. I am not telling you this so you'll hate me. I need you to grasp the depth of our crimes, the vicious malice that was our ordinary mental attitude, and the shattered state of our mangled hearts. As I confess this, I am also sharing that over time, little by little, I saw that it was my responsibility to make it right. It became my personal mission to make amends for what I'd done to the whole human race. I didn't believe there was a God who would judge me. It was about a change within my heart. A silent space inside me whispered that I could change. How?... Well... that was the daunting question.

"Just imagining the possibility of making this change allowed my heart to begin to recall its joyful, childhood softness. And then I was approached, separately, by the U.S. government. They asked me to become a spy for them—to spy on my husband. Of course they were suspicious of the Nazis they were working with, and they wanted to be sure that Rolph and his comrades didn't get the upper hand.

"That created a problem. I wanted to make amends, and this was a way for me to do that, but if I cooperated with the U.S., I'd have to stay with Rolph, watch him navigate through his new world while he remained cruel and ruthless, always. I could not escape him. And at the same time, it was a betrayal of him and of our homeland—a betrayal I was conditioned to never, ever make. Yet my heart was thawing and longing for its own redemption.

"In order to cope, I changed my name to Gilda, from Verdi's opera, Rigoletto. When I was a little girl, my mother's sister was my refuge. She was kind and gentle—the opposite of my mother. During a visit to her Austrian home, she took my cousins and me to Italy to see the play. I was young and spoke a little Italian. The music and Gilda's character captured my heart. Gilda was innocent, her love manipulated by the cruel men around her. I felt a deep sympathy with Gilda's helplessness, her fall into the abyss of shame, loss, and suffering. As the war ended, that opera haunted my memory and I identified with Gilda even more. Her ending was tragic; would mine be the same?

"Even though Rolph and I remained married, we became completely separated in our heart-space. There were no sweet, tender feelings to bind us and I held no illusion of his possible redemption. Now, he is in full dementia, awaiting a long overdue meeting with the grim reaper.

"When I took on that unusual service to the U.S., with the intention of making amends, I felt connected to humanity once again. I began to discover a tenderness in me that had long been forgotten. It was also my first glimpse (since before I could re-member) of what it means to be human. Previously, I had given up my individual needs for the good of the Aryan race—it was a coping mechanism to relieve myself of the gnawing anxiety and low self-worth that I felt as a young person. I focused instead on my illustrious peers, on the illusion of some great heritage we shared, to give me a sense of purpose and belonging. That was the goal of all the propaganda, and it worked well for too many of us.

"Imagine, a young person in the prime of their vitality, slow-ly separating from the rest of humanity, my heart-bonds with former friends, Jewish or Catholic or anyone outside the Nazi narrative, ripped apart—all of the beauty and sweetness of life squeezed to fit into a smug feeling of always being right and definitely 'better than them.'

"Sophia, I was polarizing and polarized. I was brainwashed and I couldn't see it. Now that I am at the end of a very long life, I question: did I do anything good at all?

"Now here we are, in this country. I see people clueless once again of what's right in front of them; underneath their feet in those underground military labs and structures are radical technologies available for good or evil, and they spend all their time fighting over politics, choosing sides, playing on comput-ers, following whatever trends their media suggests to them. In that lifestyle, pausing to look deeper isn't going to happen. That is extremely useful to the global hierarchy above them, and possibly even intentional. It's a lot like the king-pope-lord trinity mindset—the masses distracted, anxious and in a survival mindset of us vs them, while the lords above siphon off all the resources for themselves. Is history repeating itself?

"What is heartbreaking for me is that most citizens are oblivious to the possibilities for a glorious, unimaginable new world. I'm talking about a world of free, renewable energy, and healing technologies that make Hollywood's sci-fi blockbusters seem like kindergarten scripts.

"Should I have tried to get the truth out earlier? Gotten away from the military? If I had, the sad reality is that no one would listen. I know several people who tried to disclose these projects and attempted to talk about the space program and the technologies. But they disappeared—supposedly committed suicide. What utter nonsense! One after the other, I heard that someone accidentally fell off a bridge or succumbed to some other random accident. Most of them were just humiliated and discredited, lost their career and were left isolated, with no one who would listen.

"What do we do with corrupted systems like the religious ones that you described? These kinds of structures are not new. I am not cynical. It's just that this subject is so complex. My bigger concern is not the dictators or autocrats—it's our own polarized hearts, the enmity that is sewn from a young age. I watch with sadness as children are taught to compete with one another, to be the 'best,' rather than work for each other and the greater good. That's how my training started, with competition, with constant comparison and compulsion to outpace, outscore the others.

"Why can't we just be our unique selves with our special, unimaginable gifts and talents working together? If we raise our level of love and respect for ourselves and others, we will naturally collaborate. I'm talking about joining our personal gifts with the brilliant gifts of others. It is possible, even natural to disagree, to have varying viewpoints, yet still effectively collaborate. What role does ingenuity, innovation, and creativity play in a world in which everyone thinks alike, in which egos and obedience are disproportionately rewarded over creative minds and open hearts? Collaboration of diverse ideas, coming from loving hearts, is our way to an inconceivably bright future.

"Goddammit! You don't see feathers flying and a big fight going on in a flock of geese when they take flight. It's not like the one in front is the best. I think they must have that quantum connection that you mentioned, Sophia. I love your vision of the ever-present connectivity of everyone and everything. It took me too long to grasp the power of togetherness because I had been devastatingly betrayed and thoroughly brainwashed. I thought I'd be safe doing things on my own. This stemmed from 'traumas', as my therapist has called them.

"Honestly, I think people today are just as traumatized as me because they are taught from childhood through religion, government, parental authority, education, and technology to be a good slave, to conform, be part of the A-team—then all will be well. Don't question authority figures or systems! Be a good boy or girl! Mind your own business!

"Your description of your connection to the Essence, the quantum, immeasurable, creative force, made me wonder... If humanity cultivated that connection, could the world change? I am interested in this kind of simple, foundational approach to living each day on this planet.

"Otherwise we'll cycle from one government to the next, one political party and one religious group to the next—ad infinitum. It's a hamster wheel and what happens to the greater good? Each day, how many people starve, are abducted into slavery, and how many let themselves be enslaved to work, to debt accumulation, and to whatever drives their culture? Young woman, I have seen horrors, unspeakable atrocities, and witnessed bone-chilling secrets above and under the ground on which we sit today. All of it is a form of insanity. Yet it's really happening.

"I perceive you as being innocent, almost like the child I used to be long ago. Is it fair to tell the truth? Am I robbing you of your innocence?"

Gilda stared straight ahead with sunken shoulders as though a giant weight was drawing her towards the ground. Silence hung in the air, suspended thinking, feeling, or action in its emptiness.

After a few moments, Sophia noticed the sunlight fading and clouds gathering overhead. Shifting winds began tossing leaves around them like feathers in a pillow fight. This image was so incongruous, Sophia almost laughed. But she stayed quiet, almost in a state of prayer.

"Gilda, maybe you should rest now. I want you to know that I am deeply touched by what you have said. I hear your heart's longing for peace, for redemption. Each of us has a story to tell—we are all searching for something. Yours is filled with terrible trauma and profoundly irreconcilable contradictions. I cannot pretend to understand your experience, but I feel a deep empathy with your dilemma and with the conclusions you've drawn. Although I want to hear more and get to know you better, I don't want to pressure you. You have shared so much that is so vulnerable. If you choose to share your life, I am always here for you. It's clear to me that you've grown inwardly, under extreme circumstances. That gives me incredible inspiration.

"I know about Admiral Byrd. My husband told me about him and his encounter in Antarctica. So I have some context for what you are saying."

Gilda raised her head, which had been angling slowly toward her chest as if in heartbroken resignation. As she straightened, she returned to a more relaxed stance, straighter, more dignified. "My dear," she said, "you may share this with Nate. After all, like me, he is weakening. It may bring him comfort to know that he is on the right track. It sounds like he has a sharp mind. Mine is fading in small, yet discernible ways.

"When we were captured in Argentina, I hoped for death. If I did not meet my demise, I hoped to have a chance to be near majestic mountains once again. I think that was my essence, the young, innocent me rising to the surface. I wanted to witness nature's order and not the order of the Third Reich or the U.S. Military.

"I can share a bit more and leave you today on a happier note. Nature's order did manifest for me and bring me hope. I was sent to Idaho while Rolph went to an underground military base somewhere in Nevada or California. I was interrogated extensively and kept in isolation for days. That was when I was given the option to become a spy, working undercover. I was to be reunited with Rolph, which didn't excite me in the least. Yet, during the time of isolation, Sophia, something happened.

"I dare to share this because it is still causes me tenderness, and I trust you. During that time, I was allowed to go outside. I cried for days on end. I let the natural beauty of the landscape around me and its benevolent energy soak into every molecule of my being. I began to relate to the Earth as a dear friend. In her world, no one is ignored and what looks like death is followed by regeneration and growth. I was able to listen to the captivating sound of waves meeting the rocky shoreline of the magnificent sapphire blue lake, watch flocks of birds, clouds pass overhead softly, weather patterns move from storms to silence, sunlit days of serenity, and nights filled with a canopy of stars that seemed to whisper about a bond being formed of loving affection and connection to them.

"Without knowing how, why, or what exactly happened, the result was that I became inseparable with Mother Earth. I connected with her innately and experienced being held by her powerful, nourishing energy. I envisioned her adopting me as her child. From that point forward, my whole being was infused with firm resolution to make things right for what I'd done, for what I had participated in. Yet still, innumerable emotions, self-loathing, and believing I was a slave to others needed to be purified. That work became possible only because of the unconditional love I felt from the Earth.

"Before coming into communion with the Earth, I believed I had no chance for redemption and no opportunity to experience true freedom. However, with Mother Nature, I was no longer alone, because the Earth was supporting me relentlessly, holding me in her benevolent heart.

"Through her love, my confidence and self-esteem began to rise. Being human, I still sometimes feel devastating shame, a pang of anger, or insecurities that emerge, but I feel the firm presence of the Earth holding my hand and leading me back to our common heart of pure love. I consider myself fortunate for those agonizing struggles which led me to her and into the highest goodness and wisdom inside me." Gilda was radiating a gentleness now that Sophia slowly drank in. Something very important was happening in this exchange.

"Having shared my story with you in more detail than I anticipated," Gilda continued, "I have to admit that I'm getting a bit tired. How about we talk more tomorrow if you can. And please know that I wish Nate well."

Gilda smiled kindly and stood up carefully. She turned and walked into her apartment. Looking over her shoulder she said, "You are dear to me, Sophia. Thank you."

CHAPTER 8
A NEIGHBOR SINGS HIGH AND LOW

Sophia's days followed a regular pattern structured around Nate's needs: his rising, eating, hydrating, moving, and so forth. In between, she would cook or take personal time, always listening for Nate's voice to call out or the temple bell to ring, whenever Nate's voice failed to function.

Nate lay in bed this morning, straining to speak loud enough for the microphone on his tablet to record his voice. He'd received Gilda's story like an unexpected gift, so he wanted to add his thoughts about her stories to his audio journal.

Within this journal he had been recording evidence of many military technologies reverse engineered from ET craft which were obtained from the Nazi's secret space program. He also dove into information from the U.S. military's findings when they shot down or discovered UFO's within the country's borders.

Several decades in the past, Nate shared unclassified documents with an online group of human rights lawyers, showing one of the incomplete lists of the Nazi's who were hired as scientists after World War II. He often thought it strange that the U.S. would hire their enemy and then disperse them throughout corporate organizations and most branches of the military. He and a few colleagues tried unsuccessfully to discover the secrets that the U.S. Military seemed desperate to control.

After lunch, Nate asked, "Did Gilda mention anything interesting?"

"Yes, she said that I could tell you her story. It's definitely fascinating, and it touched my heart. She's nearly one hundred years old, Nate. Her life is filled with inconceivable experience, like life in Antarctica with the Nazis. And she knows about Admiral Byrd." Sophia continued to tell him the whole story, including Gilda's transformation in Idaho and her life of service.

Nate looked astonished by this revelation. "Darling, this is amazing. All I've ever seen are documents and hearsay, yet this is first-hand facts. Given her age, it's a miracle that we are her neighbors. For a reason that I can't figure out, I feel it is imperative to know even more about her life."

With Sophia's help, he adjusted his posture and took a slow sip of water, allowing him to continue the conversation. His voice was getting weak, but he was captivated by Gilda's story.

Calling forth the highest resilience possible from his life force, Nate continued, "In the photos and list that I have, I don't remember anyone with Rolph's name. As you may remember, I've read that there were perhaps thousands of Nazis that the U.S. brought here due to their scientific knowledge and skills. Gilda seemed to indicate that they were given bogus names which means he was one of a secret group. I'm not surprised about Gilda's description of Rolph because there are stories about special counter-espionage factions in the military that developed to keep track of the Nazis who joined the military. They were master-manipulators and brutal, to a fault. Putting them in top secret areas, giving them security clearances, and that sort of thing, it's like bringing them into the military's DNA. They infiltrated by invitation.

"After World War II, the focus was, of course, on the threat of nuclear war. And justifiably so. After getting their butts kicked in Antarctica, it must have been irresistible for U.S. military scientists to have access to the Nazi's highly coveted tech and provocative secrets. While the world was celebrating a victory on the surface, another whole world was being created underground through massive, high-tech military bases.

"I've told you about all of this before. Do you remember what I said about the military's secret underground tunnels? I recall you looking dazed as I described their web-like structure right under our feet."

With a soft, reflective smile, she nodded her head. "Your description was too far outside my mind's sense of ordinary reality. Now, for me, it's as real as this room we are in."

In areas of controversial topics or subjects which ordinary people find taboo, Nate knew not to approach conversation without discernment, even with friends. His legal circles did not have access to enough hard evidence to build a case against any nefarious actions and secret agendas, so they disengaged from further discussion.

Another tough hurdle: those cases require substantial funding. Over the past decade, he developed relationships with investigative journalists online, yet he found an invaluable resource in Sophia because she inspired him through asking probing questions that sent him diving back into research with fresh enthusiasm.

"Did Gilda tell you the time frame when she and Rolph left the military or any details of what she saw in Antarctica?" Nate asked.

"I don't have details for you about Antarctica," Sophia said. "What I can tell you is that Rolph seemed to be a highly acclaimed scientist or engineer. And she's clear that there were UFO's. I was more focused on her inner journey, which I found to be profoundly inspirational."

Nate was equally interested in the spiritual aspect of Gilda's life and the technological advancements that Rolph revealed to the U.S. military.

Sophia shared Gilda's deep transformation which bore fruit when she connected in a more intimate way with Gaia while she was in Idaho—Nate was glued to every word.

Engrossed in the mysteries of spiritual development and ET technologies, Sophia and Nate spiraled into the implications and meaning of Gilda's stories and questions arose.

As usual, they declared their intention to allow insights to expand their understanding, puzzling revelations to simmer and reveal answers naturally, without getting into immediate, mentally derived answers or conclusions.

On this day, as usual, they became entranced in their conversation. However, Nate depleted his energy supply. It was time for him to rest before his afternoon exercise session. Because he was not ready to concede defeat, he had to do whatever he could do to keep his body moving. Postponing their conversation was the best option to protect his frail body.

Always enjoying open windows and fresh air, the weather was unexpectedly shifting, and it looked like the spring reprieve they'd enjoyed for some days might be giving over to colder ones for a while. With the windows closed, the world pressed closer on Nate.

Dreary days of rain followed one after the other; each day, Nate struggled to walk, even with Sophia's help. She finally made the heartbreaking call to order a wheelchair, a necessity she'd been dreading for a while. Every new setback like it came with exponential new complexities of which to be mindful. Still, she continued to carve out thirty-minute windows to go across the street to the grocery store or take a quick walk.

One morning, a heavenly gift flew into the open window once again, carried along with the birds' morning chirping, as the sun burst through its clouds in full glory. Warm light was pouring into every crevice of the apartment, filling it with golden hues.

It was mid-morning when Sophia, having found an opportunity for a brief respite from caregiving, and with a hot cup of tea in hand, headed for the backyard. Stepping carefully on the wet ground softened from the substantial rain, she raised her eyes and there was Gilda.

The two friends settled in with their coffee and tea and rekindled their newly discovered friendship immediately. In fact, they giggled like two little girls when they saw each other. Gilda inquired about Nate, and Sophia asked how Gilda was doing with Rolph.

Becoming slightly introspective, Gilda answered, "The truth is there is someone who watches him 24/7. They don't want him to talk to anyone. They don't care about me. His dementia has them worried. He could say something and not realize what he said. It's no surprise that they want to monitor his every move closely." She sipped her coffee thoughtfully and closed her eyes absorbing the sunlight on her face.

"Our last conversation was a gift for me." She said tenderly. "It felt wonderful to forget about him and have a chance to describe Idaho and to divulge my secret life. Maybe it's my age or maybe my past was caged for too long. After we talked, my entire body felt lighter and calmer." She looked up at Sophia, her blue eyes sparkling.

"I want to sing you a song... Is that alright?" Gilda asked.

Surprised and delighted, Sophia sat more upright, her heart wide open. "Yes! Absolutely!"

Gilda sang a song called "Lili Marleen," first in German and then in English.

Sophia couldn't contain her tears as the words and melody ended and drifted into the silence settling around them.

"The history of the song reminded me of our last conversation." Gilda said smiling softly, "It's a fascinating song because it was written as a poem by a German soldier in World War I, expressing his undying bond for the woman he loved. War separated them, yet they remained connected in their hearts, forever. The poem was so popular that it was set to music and became famous when a German woman, in love with a Jew, sang the vocals.

"This song was filled with extraordinary tenderness, and it felt refreshingly authentic and loving. More than that, it spoke to aching hearts in a catastrophic time for German people. We needed to feel more love and connection and less hate and polarity. Every night just before ten o'clock, this song was played on the radio, blessing us with its sweetness and soothing our fractured hearts.

"The problem came for the German singer when she became famous, performing it in German and English. She sang with profound depths of emotion, while secretly hating the Nazis. Joseph Goebbels, the Minister of Propaganda, discovered her secret and banned the song. Honestly, I wanted to hear it but I didn't know why. I realize now that it was a tiny thread that linked my hardening heart with pure love.

"It was so popular that in a rare move for Goebbels, he changed his mind. The singer, Lale Anderson, was kept under watchful eye and Goebbels required her to check in with the Gestapo twice a week. Even the most cold-hearted of Nazis in my inner circle seemed happy to discover that the song would be sung each evening. Her voice temporarily melted our divisiveness.

"After the war, we found out that she was alive and well. And we were relieved and happy for her. This remarkable love song became popular all over Europe, somehow bridging divides, and soothing hearts. The British and American soldiers sang it. Each night, the South Africans joined them. Perhaps I was singing it with your ancestors and in that way, a love song became our invisible, heart-centered bond. In a polarized world, this song was about the cruel realities of war and about saying goodbye, without knowing if there would ever be peace and happiness in this world. How would all of this chaos and fighting end?

"My world and yours recently collided into friendship, yet for millions of people on this planet, this has not happened. I am hoping that sharing this poignant story will be proof that people can come together. May you and future generations remember the power of this authentically, pure song.

"Coming together as a human race can happen in unexpected ways and people can find bonds of affection and heart-felt relief from all that divides them. This song certainly found its way into the world through many contradictions and ironies. And yet despite seemingly impenetrable obstacles, it found its way into reality and brought a soft balm each night to many people who needed it."

Gilda hummed the song for a minute and then asked if she could share something else. With Sophia's openness and encouragement, Gilda continued.

"Yesterday I let my past pour from me like boiling water from a hot tea kettle. I wondered if you thought I was a bit crazy to speak about off-planet craft and that sort of thing. Has Nate looked into this topic in detail or just with casual interest?"

"Oh, he's very engaged," Sophia said. "He's constantly reading articles, watching videos, and reading books about it. He believes the technologies are real and that they will heal people more cost effectively and thoroughly than current treatments and technologies. He is excited about bringing free energy to the planet to relieve suffering for many people across the globe."

Laughing with twinkling eyes, Gilda responded, "He could not be more right, my dear. If he saw what I've seen, he would be mesmerized and delighted. However, there are too many politics and too much power at stake for that to happen anytime soon.

"If Nate were well and went underground, what he does not know is that there are numerous layers of secrets regarding all of this technology and research. You see, there are military bases and the tunnels that the U.S. government dug. And there are the ancient tunnels that crisscross the entire globe, like the one from coast-to-coast in the U.S. Then there are even deeper ones, where ancient humans live, ancestors of many of us on the planet—and I mean *very ancient*, going back millions of years."

Assimilating Gilda's words, Sophia was hardly breathing, and sat rigidly with a wrinkled brow and a look of shock on her face.

Continuing, Gilda said, "Sophia, please do not be scared. I wasn't sure if you knew about this and clearly you don't. This is a lot for you to take in. For some reason, I feel that I must share this. But if it triggers too much fear or you'd rather talk spirituality, that's fine."

Sophia softened her gaze and relaxed. Gathering herself, she said, "Gilda, I am interested partly because it sounds fascinating and partly because you and I met under unusual circumstances, and I feel a heart-bond with you. The subject isn't a shocking revelation for me. Nate told me about tunnels many times but he was talking from information that he researched or from online journalists. Hearing from your personal, eyewitness account, the impact of its reality hit my mind like a freight train. I'm okay, please tell me more."

"Well, it's complex. The best starting place is at the military bases, which are many. You can research Area 51 in Nevada or places like Kirtland Air Force Base in New Mexico. And there are well-known military bases in California, too.

"These enormous bases go deep underground. For example, imagine a whole world under the surface, thirty miles long—with living quarters, areas for craft, and many different kinds of research going on. These facilities were built over many decades, are very technologically advanced, and highly secure. I am sure Nate would love to see the magnitude of food, health, energy research, and technology being studied and created there. It's beyond your wildest imagination. Star Wars and all of the other movies are nowhere near what he would see.

"But what I want you to know is something even more un-imaginable. I hope you will bear with me. This will undoubtedly sound crazy. I had a chance to document very different research projects in the area of space technology. Doing so changed my life as much as my incredible transformation in Idaho.

"You may not believe me. It is my hope, though, that you will listen with an open heart and open mind..." Here Gilda paused, holding Sophia's gaze for a long moment. "I met *beings* from different planets... I am very serious. I am not pretending."

Sophia breathed deeply, nodded, and smiled. "Please go on."

"There's a reason that I wanted to share this. You see, I was working with a therapist, grappling with my reactions to life and my low self-esteem. My regrets and shame for what I'd done consumed me. I wanted to take my life to a higher level, to feel confident that I was good, worthy, and free to express myself.

To be honest, a military setting isn't exactly the easiest place to do that kind of inner work. Like you, I learned to meditate. This allowed me to become adept at holding my mind still, being centered, and remaining in inner silence. That mental stillness allowed me to do the work that I'd like to describe for you now." Again Gilda paused. She sipped her tea.

Sophia held her teacup, now just barely warm, between her hands and smiled again. "I am so touched that you worked on yourself that way—it must have taken tremendous bravery. You have my undivided attention."

Gilda looked at Sophia once more, then continued. "Various cosmic species, who are often called ETs, were helping the U.S. government to learn about one of their craft or maybe about a technology of some kind. That was the atmosphere in which I was doing my clerical work. One day, all of a sudden, as I was typing, I could hear one of them—one of these other beings— in my head, saying 'Hello.'"

Gilda smiled as she remembered the moment. "It wasn't words, but it was clear communication. It wasn't until later I learned that our communication was possible because their electromagnetic field, their frequency, was connecting with mine—through a whole mess of information and powerful waves and vibrations in and around us, they found me. The first time it happened, I almost fainted because the love, the goodness," Gilda's voice broke a little, and she swallowed, "the kindness was so visceral... They reached me on a soul level.

"This communication was something that I'd never felt before. The being's face wasn't showing emotion, yet somehow my body was reading their *field* and I could decode it. We were connecting through the field that you speak about. When I was resonant with them, I could hear them and communicate effortlessly. They couldn't manipulate me nor could I confuse them, because our frequencies matched.

"My still mind was the catalyst for this to happen. This communication felt like a miracle but utterly natural at the same time. I was in shock yet also filled with love and wonder. My life changed in that moment. The entire structure of what I thought I knew and understood about life came apart, was thrust into chaos. But it didn't frighten me, because more than that, I felt exhilaration and profound gratitude for having the opportunity to meet such amazing beings of pure frequency.

"I realized that I had changed. If these benevolent souls could communicate with me, then I knew I was no longer living as a dismal shadow of a person. There was hope for my life to become more expanded. In the energy exchange with my cosmic brothers and sisters, the possibility for me to live consistently from higher frequencies felt assured. I knew the field held the key to my future capacities to communicate.

"The icing on the cake was that I developed an unshakable faith that the field from which my body arose was the same field from which my dear relatives from the stars also came into being. We were connected, we were inseparable... because the field indelibly bonded us. After each encounter with this being, I went home and wept, I sat in stillness and let my mind release its grip, and my soul would commune with this being, my brother—from what I used to see as a *distant star.*"

Suddenly Gilda shrank back into her chair, her eyes narrowed suspiciously, and she frowned. "Maybe I've said too much!" She looked frightened, her breath held inside, as if she was waiting to be scorned or ridiculed.

Seeing Gilda's fear emerging, Sophia smiled kindly, gently touching her hand. "Nothing could be farther from the truth. I am so honored you are sharing this with me. You are speaking about them as family, with a heart connection I can feel as you describe them. Gilda, this is food for my soul. My gosh! You are describing your relationship as a galactic, soul connection. How amazing, my friend!"

Gilda's face relaxed slightly, tears fell from her apprehensive eyes.

"Gilda, I am wondering why it is that a visitor from another planet could touch your heart in a way that humans could not? This question seems significant. I am also interested in how you warmed up to them. How did you get to know them? Do you know where they were from?"

"My dear friend," Gilda sighed. "I am relieved." She took a deep breath and continued, "You act like it's interesting rather than mind-boggling. I've never told anyone that I met these wise, benevolent visitors! You believe me! I'm astounded at your response."

Sophia shared that Nate conducted extensive research on this subject and that her personal experience and observation of the laws of nature indicate that we are not alone in the universe. In order to clarify her reasons for relating to Gilda's story, she shared her memories of seeing lights and fairies when she was young. As a result, this was not a subject that felt completely foreign to her.

"Gilda, I am blown away by the fact that you got to feel what it's like to communicate easily with someone visiting from the cosmos and feel their response. This gives meaning to the term heart-to-heart connection. Because feelings precede words, I can feel what's going on emotionally in someone when they enter the room. You are telling me that these cosmic visitors are not only comfortable with this kind of empathic connection, but they communicate that way all of the time. It is astonishing to hear this.

"Where are they from? Do you know?"

"They are from somewhere in the Pleiades, a gigantic star system. It's comprised of millions of stars and planets and all kinds of beings: some aquarians, some insect-looking, while others are monkey-like. And I met exquisitely beautiful, gossamer, human-looking beings—these are quite subtle and hard to describe.

"I consider all of these beings my star families. They were kind, respectful, and shared information generously with the U.S. military. To answer your earlier question, I didn't do anything intentionally to warm up to them or try to communicate. They didn't act like they were a superior race. I found them quite guileless and sincere. I always found them to be calm, some funnier than others, and they had different ways to speak, but mostly telepathic. By using my mind-stilling skills, I could hear them.

"The reason I am telling you about them is because of what we've been talking about; the connectivity that is utterly lacking on our planet. As I mentioned, I refer to them as my star family, cosmic visitors, or galactic souls because I want to relate to them that way. They connected with me deeply and kindly, calling forth my utmost respect and enduring love. When I was with them, I realized that our relationship was intimate and genuine. Our conversations naturally exuded elevated frequencies, so there was no way for discord, competition, or animosity to take root. They were channeling a higher frequency, directed in a positive way, that allowed me to feel relaxed and receptive. It was astounding and felt mystical. I wanted to share this because as young as you are, there could be disclosure from the government someday and you may get a chance to know them or work with them. If so, jump on the opportunity. You would adore being with them."

"Many of our star families have advanced technologies. More importantly, they value something they call the *unicity gene*. From their perspective, which is a cosmic overview of civilizations across eons, those who ignore the power of that gene, eventually implode. They destroy themselves. Galactic statistics predict that if we don't start expressing that gene, we are on course to destroy ourselves."

Sophia leaned forward and was about to inquire further with a plethora of questions when she heard the temple bell ringing. Her beloved needed her. Knowing that Nate had a therapist coming in the afternoon, Sophia could meet Gilda again that day. They agreed to meet at three o'clock.

Sophia hurried inside to care for the man she loved these days with more and more intensity.

CHAPTER 9
SHARING INTEL AND FREQUENCIES

Entering Nate's room, Sophia could see the look of frustration and hopelessness that blanketed his face. Although her spirits plummeted, she recovered her composure instantly. With a calm, soothing touch, she stroked his hair affectionally, kissed his forehead tenderly and helped him to prepare for another day of merciless muscular weakness.

Nate, once an athletic, strong man, was a walking skeleton, shaky and fragile.

"How do you do it, Sophia?" he asked. "I don't get it. You are always sweet and act like waiting on me is easy. I want you to know that I appreciate the massive amount of energy required to care for me twenty-four hours a day. I love you so much! You are a beautiful being inside and out. If I had known that this would happen, I don't know that I would have married you. To be such a burden and put so much pressure on you is unfair."

His voice weakened and he started to choke. Her greatest fear reared its head. All she could do was center herself, create a frequency of strength and courage, and wait for him to come through this challenging moment.

She often described these choking sessions in texts to Grace as, "waiting for an eternity to pass." And with each one, she prac-ticed holding elevated states of consciousness, a higher level of connection with the field. At first, she said that it seemed "a bit woo-woo." Over time she learned that it worked. Nate confirmed the positive effects of her practice many times. He could feel a reassuring, supportive energy bringing strength, turning his fear into confidence.

In the past, when Sophia panicked, he shared that his fear magnified exponentially. However, when she began to hold a higher frequency of courage and calm, Nate could feel those frequencies and gather strength, even in his struggle to survive the ordeal.

When she saw that he was okay, Sophia went to the kitchen to sit for a minute and calm her frazzled nerves. Her life had become a stark contrast between talking about unfathomable cosmic beings, quantum science and fascinating subjects, in juxtaposition with suddenly witnessing the intense suffering of her soul mate. This was the kind of instant swerve that her mind was forced to endure throughout the day. With life's many new paradoxical moments, habits that she had developed of worrying, analyzing, and strategizing were being replaced with instinctively relaxing, becoming flexible and allowing space for intuition to flourish.

Looking out the window, her eye caught a glimpse of a man walking down the sidewalk wearing a Hawaiian t-shirt. Her eyes suddenly filled with tears remembering the most intimate and happy memories of being in Hawaii with Nate. She glanced at the old beach photo she kept on the table nearby.

They exchanged their wedding vows in Hawaii, caressed by the mystical vibes of those sensual, sublime islands. It was a nurturing and transcendental space for their inner spiritual practices to thrive. Nate often said that meditation in Hawaii was as natural, easy and deep as the Pacific Ocean. She remembered star gazing together, the enchanting sky, how it felt like they'd been there for millions of years. Touching the photo lovingly, she closed her eyes, letting her mind drift back to moments of tender affection and making love as waves crashed in the background.

Suddenly, the temple bell rang and it was time to help the frail version of Nate. He needed her more than ever now—just to survive.

As she approached him, he said in a raspy voice, "It's important for us to talk about what happened because that episode was scary for both of us." He looked apologetically at her. "No matter what happens, both of us know that you can't help. If I was in your position, I'd be frantic. Thank you for being so steady for me."

"I am glad you are okay, sweetheart. How about I share my conversation with Gilda to change the subject? It's hard to know where to begin to tell you about the amazing things she revealed today. Maybe I can start with the love song that connected a world at war through the frequencies of its poignant words and sweet music. Or maybe it's better to start with Gilda's communication with star beings through frequencies and telepathy?"

Nate listened raptly as she listed the topics. He was mesmerized to hear that Gilda confirmed, with additional details, information that Nate read about relating to ETs for many years. It was all true. He often told Sophia how he longed to meet star families and exchange communication with them in the form of feelings and mental telepathy, and although he'd assumed it was beyond his wildest imagination, it would always remain a possibility in his life. He smiled lovingly at Sophia. "This is amazing! I can tell that you like Gilda. I bet I'd like her, too. What an amazing life she's led! Just imagine what that must have been like to have the experience of that kind of communication and feeling. I'm blown away by it!"

He took a moment to rest his faltering vocal cords and then continued, "I can hardly fathom what we could learn from the ETs that she met. I wonder if scientists already know how to communicate through emitting frequency. Have they considered using our innate capacity to raise frequency as a form of inter-species communication? I've been the benefactor of your experiments with raising your frequency. I know you were practicing that as I choked—the difference is so tangible."

Nate looked down at his arms which he could barely lift. Then he looked into her eyes with painful longing. "It's hard for me to come to terms with the fact that I cannot hold you close, that we can't make love anymore, that I would be useless in protecting you."

His eyes filled with tears that spilled freely down his face, the tears falling from Sophia's eyes, too.

They had decided several months before that it was pointless to avoid speaking about grim truths. It was not possible to hide their pain from each other. Instead, they gave it permission to flow, unimpeded. It helped them to share it rather than try to hide it. The agony they grappled with was relentless, one more natural challenge in this stage of Nate's life.

Sophia drew close to her beloved, gently touched her lips to his, and then rested her cheek tenderly against his cheek. Their tears blended until they were indistinguishable, their love mingled, expressions of the bond they knew would last forever.

Unapologetically, life moved onward. Grasping for more time was futile and that hard truth hung relentlessly in the backdrop of their awareness. It was time for lunch.

Afterwards, they spoke about the cosmos, which Nate stated emphatically and playfully was not as good as making love. But in the midst of Nate's condition, it would have to suffice as his afternoon pleasure. For now, talking about a distant star family definitely felt more light-hearted than worrying about the future.

So they talked about other worlds, dreamed of visiting them somewhere in the cosmos, and envisioned a future on Earth with high frequencies, kind and benevolent communication, and a focus on humanity living in peace and harmony.

Nate's love for social justice and deep respect for Mother Nature found firm ground in this conversation. And for a while they could forget that his body was weakening with each tick of the large wall clock he faced each day, counting down his time on Earth.

Sophia knew that the therapist would arrive soon and she began to arrange his room for a movement session.

Looking at Nate, she could tell that his spirits had fallen again. She asked if he wanted to talk. He said pensively, "Do you have any regrets about our marriage or our relationship? Anything you wish could have been different? Now is the time for us to talk about anything like that."

He had often said that he wanted to make sure his impending death wouldn't leave her with regrets. She always acknowledged the kindness of his concern for her.

Now, hearing him voice his concern again, Sophia answered differently. "Honestly, there is only one thing. As you know, many months ago, I decided to no longer focus on saving you. Instead, throughout the day, in my inner work, I evoke the feelings that I'd love to share with you like courage, peace, vitality, love, and joy. Letting my body viscerally experience those feelings, I create a field of energy around me that is powerful, dynamic, extremely tangible to me.

"When you call me or when you are resting or eating, I bring those feelings into my awareness, fill my whole body, and let them radiate out to you. Yet I wonder if you are receiving them. I don't want to be offering this to you with an agenda, for an outcome like hoping you start to swim in bliss. But it's hard to watch you suffer. That's just how it is. If I'm truthful, it bothers me that the healing frequencies don't seem to touch you in the morning after the nightmares. It's as though the feelings you've experienced in the dreams, the intense need to fight, are more powerful than love.

"When you wake from those recurring dreams, I regret that you feel so far away from me, that you don't feel what I feel as I practice elevating my frequencies. I regret that somehow our pure connection is eclipsed by the sorrow and memories that the dreams evoke. It's a mystery to me that the low frequencies that you experience in them are so powerful even after the dream is done."

Her voice trailed off and her head bowed. She felt oddly ashamed to admit any kind of disappointment.

With a surge of power, immediately and passionately Nate replied, "Do not make my problem into your problem. All of the inner work we've done is about relinquishing control over our life and everything that happens to us. We feel, we take a bird's eye view, and we allow our frequencies to elevate naturally. That's it. No control and no manipulation of anything. If I feel fear, sorrow, or anguish, that's my problem not yours. Those are emotional responses and their associated frequencies that I can choose to work with.

"Ninety-nine percent of the time, when I call for you when the dreams intensify, I feel a supportive energy. The same applies each morning when we wake up. I don't feel love pouring out towards me. Instead, it feels like a container of energy is holding me safely in its arms. It doesn't alter my experience or my inner work, it just supports me in a safe container.

"There are times when I can tell you are too exhausted or groggy, and when you try to wake up to help me, you are not yet emanating elevated frequencies. When that happens, I fall deeper into an abyss within me and my heart feels like it is collapsing. But that's not your fault. It is just my work I have to do. I am extremely fortunate to have you by my side through this daunting time. You are a gift. And always, every time, I feel you catching yourself and raising your vibrations. And I notice a shift instantaneously in me, and once again I feel held in loving support.

"I want to share this because it may help you not to have regret. You have helped me and supported me in countless ways through the agony of my inner world. Your remarkable emanations of love are never a waste of effort on your part. Darling, I know this is hard for you. We both have to detach from the outcome. It's not in our hands to stop what's coming.

"Saying *thank you* or *I love you* doesn't do justice to the magnitude of my gratitude. I've said this before. You are a special being, Sophia. I love you so much; not because you bless my life with uplifting vibrations, kindness, and a form of goodness that won't let me slip totally into despair, but for who you are as a rare human of exceptional character and divine perfection."

Sophia's tears were streaming and her heart breaking.

Composing herself, she said, "Thank you so much. As you were talking, something deep inside me stirred in recognition that the practice of emanating those elevated feelings hits its target.

"Part of my tears are relief that you could feel the love that explodes from my heart. That pure love is an energy that cascades into the field like passionate, power-waves into eternity. Even if you can't experience the waves as love or joy, they reach you—which confirms what we've learned about our connection through the field in and around us. I'm forever grateful that you told me."

Sophia and Nate sat in silence for a few minutes. Their tears fell gracefully like soft rain that cleanses everything it touches, gently yet thoroughly.

Soon the therapist arrived and life moved on with clarity and a better understanding of the mysteries of life and love.

CHAPTER 10

HIGH FREQUENCIES AND NUCLEAR LOVE

Sophia found herself alone for a moment at three o'clock, sitting outside, relaxed and allowing the soft sunlight to melt her muscles like warm butter.

She heard Gilda coming towards their meeting spot and when her friend looked comfortable, Sophia asked, "How are you this afternoon?" Gilda smiled coyly and her eyes sparkled in answer to the questions.

Seeing Sophia's unusual withdrawn mood, Gilda easily pulled out the root of the silence by asking how Nate was doing.

As Sophia shared the conversation that she and Nate had had, she looked at Gilda sheepishly saying that she never shares her pain and struggles with others. She explained that she knew that in a quantum world of all possibilities, Nate could heal "in a nano second." She read stories of people with his disease which resolved in a spontaneous healing.

All of those healings had a common component: the person with the deadly prognosis had a revelation or epiphany that shifted their perception of life and raised their frequency. This profound transformation seemed to arise from deep inside them and could not be evoked at will.

Looking down, Sophia said, "What scares me is that Nate seems to be locked into a story of anguish, like he is constantly remembering something terrible in graphic detail. What worries me is that if the nightmares continue, he will attract low frequencies from the field. It may sound like I am making him wrong, but I am honestly sharing my heart with you. I love him. Loving him means letting him live and die on his terms. His soul is magnificent, and he's offered incredible service to this world. He is such a good friend. He's kind, gentle, and thoughtful.

"This fear and impending struggle that he dreams about amazes me. The intensity of its control and strength seems to overpower him. My fear is that it will weaken him, even more.

"My vow to myself is to love him, not judge him, and be there for him. My God! He's surely been by my side when I needed him. And now, all I can do is wait to see what happens. It's helpful for me to share my feelings and struggles with you because you understand the crazy way that life unfolds.

"I enjoyed what you told me this morning. It's a lot to take in. It must have been challenging to live through that. In a way, your situation is like mine. You were caught in a situation with nowhere to go except inside yourself, to a place where you could do inner purification, with your Essence to guide you. I guess it wasn't my destiny to have such experiences with ETs, our cosmic family, as you call them."

Gilda smiled softly and said, "You and I are here for each other. We have a lot in common and we understand each other. Continuing our exploration, I have a question for you: Do you honestly think you were born in a particular year by accident? And, further, do you really believe you've had no contact with cosmic beings from other planets and stars?"

Gilda let these questions hang in the air for a moment. She watched Sophia, whose attention had shifted, lightened.

"Research UFO sightings the year you were born," Gilda said. "I assume it was in the 1960's. It was a glorious time to be born. Our cosmic family, as I like to call them, flooded in to make sure humanity, who then had access to nuclear power, did not do something stupid. Silly humans could destroy the planet and wreak havoc throughout the universe. Atomic bomb research was no small matter. I am sure you know that atomic research is about nuclear, quantum energy. Undoubtedly, militaries and governments across the planet sure as hell knew that!

"Here's something for you to chew on, dear one: Is it possible that you may have been to stars and planets, other than in dreams? I will answer that for you. You have, my dear.

"If you are a quantum being, which you are, you are multi-dimensional through and through. How can you not be capable of having experienced a vast array of places across this universe and others? When you meditate in pristine stillness and blank out, where do you go? Sitting in meditation, have you ever lost track of time? Is it possible that you moved into higher layers, or what some people call dimensions of frequency—like scales in music—in which you became entrained with higher frequencies, elevated layers of awareness, or higher scales within your infinite consciousness? If you are unlimited in scope, which you are, can't the tiny essence within you go to other coordinates in our amazing universe—and take your sweet particles with it, reorganizing them there?

"I'm posing big questions and asking you to think big. I mean really big. What I learned from innovative, genius, quantum physicists is that my hypothesis I am proposing about you is true. The math proves it. However, you don't need proof, do you? Either you *feel* that my words are true or you don't. Your heart is the best gauge of truth since it joins your consciousness to effortlessly interact with the field and send a pulse wave to you that feels congruent and resonant, or not.

"Since I am on a roll, let's be clear about something else. Connection with your cosmic family is here to stay. If you think your military is going to run them off, well, think again. Too many people are connecting with them in an honest attempt to know them better. Using homemade satellites and harmonics, contact has been made. The harmonics and messages are simple ones like, 'We love you.'

"Your sweet soul is no small thing. And your inner, quantum capacities defy anything your limited brain and small-scale, imaginative wavelengths can calculate or conceive of. You see, the whole universe is packed with souls who hold high, light frequencies no matter what is going on. Within the universe, there are humans, like you, who can do that, too.

"Since before you were born, leaders in every country on this planet were getting darker in thoughts, words, and actions. Life on Earth was becoming onerous. And then poof! You were born. And you did so with a purpose. A big one!

"By then Hitler was gone, and the Japanese were clearly broken and defeated. From my view, instead of needing to win a war, there were scientists, military, and profiteers who wanted control by having nuclear power to fund their greed and arrogance. It's pure insanity because the real atomic potentiality is hidden within a human being.

"The goal became to make people more fearful of nuclear attack. That strategy of creating fear of an invading "other" has worked again and again for thousands of years to subdue the masses. It is the same thing Hitler did. Why not use it again? It's about making the masses dependent on small, elite groups. And like lemmings, we always line right up and followed their orders. Stupid! Just so damn stupid!

"Given humanity's newly discovered capacity for self and world destruction, our star families started visiting more often after World War II. Of course, radar sometimes confused their craft's navigation—our atmosphere could also kill them—and we sometimes attacked them. Humans are well-known in the cosmos for their homicidal attitudes. This baffles most ET races.

"Then we dissected their kin like they were lab rats, and began reverse engineering every tiny, little speck of their craft, their weapons, and other technologies. Yet, they remained tolerant and nonjudgmental.

"However, they remain crystal clear and non-negotiable about nuclear weapons. I loved hearing the stories of their gentle, yet firm warnings about nuclear war heads. It's not classified information these days. Although also not totally out in the open. But you can learn about it. These cheeky cosmic visitors would arrive at a military base and unreservedly and decisively disarm the nuclear weapons. It could sometimes take a week to get those bad ass, nuclear treasures back to operating capacity.

"I'd smile to myself and laugh out loud sometimes when I'd hear those pompous bastards, the high and mighty military brass, raging at the poor staff for supposedly not checking something. Or they were attacking the person who was responsible for maintaining the system. And the star *beings*, meanwhile, rode away from sight like Santa Claus on Christmas night, going back to a place where there is overview, calm minds, and a higher frequency of being-ness.

"This happened all over the world. At the time no one shared that embarrassing truth. Our 'cosmic families' were clear that we were evolving as a species, and we have a special place in the universe. We had to be saved from the lethal nature of a small number of humans who were willing to express their destructive, personal vices.

"These various militaries and governments were acting like five-year-olds with loaded weapons, having no idea of the magnitude of the catastrophic nature of those weapons and the irreversible harm that could be done. What year were you born?" She suddenly asked.

"1965," Sophia answered. She was soaking in every word passing energetically and audibly from Gilda.

"And so... there you were, little Sophia, taking your first breath and soaking in your new world. A small team of spirit friends came with you at birth. Remember? They loved you dearly. They never let you down and they never will."

"How could you know that?" Sophia asked. "I had invisible friends with me until I was about six years old. By the time I went to school, I decided they were imaginary. Everyone around me said so. And I missed them. They came in dreams occasionally. Looking back, I had to let them go to fit in. That was my world view at that time."

"That was an intense time for sensitive, little ones like your-self," said Gilda, kindly. "Agonizing fear of nuclear attack was being perpetrated everywhere on the planet. These teams came to soothe your fears and help you to develop the intuitive skills you would need later in life. They also knew that, at that tender stage of your spiritual growth, you could shine your light more easily with their friendship. The planet needed every particle of light possible.

"Now, back to the story I was telling you. Listen carefully, Sophia, there are cosmic beings who care about you and about the Earth. They are not wanting to control anyone. They would love to collaborate, to help, and believe it or not, *we* can help *them*. For them and for us, it is a natural law to cooperate, col-laborate, learn, and share with each other. These beings have learned their benevolent traits the hard way—because their home planets already went through hell and back before they evolved away from selfish mindsets.

"But one factor is critical in relationship to their help: if you worship the cosmic beings, you are acting through a slave frequency, and the cosmic beings can't help you. If you start adoring them, you will inadvertently sabotage your potential collaboration or any kind of help they could render. These cosmic beings don't see themselves as higher beings. You are binding yourself to lower frequencies if you start putting someone else on a pedestal. Then you are a slave. You think of yourself as less-than, as though you are deficient or lacking something. If that happens, no one can help you.

"Nicolas Tesla, a brilliant quantum scientist, explained that frequency and vibration figure prominently in life because they organize matter to create structures, which creates appearances or feelings like fear or shame. That means that slave conscious-ness is dangerous. Period! You'd be holding onto enslavement and worry while saying that you want to let go of fear and be free. Think about it. Who is putting you in shackles? When you raise your frequency, you are helping Nate, even if he leaves his body.

"You are also changing the whole world. I cannot stress that enough. That elevation of consciousness is not a small thing. It is quantum in the sense that its effects are immediate and cannot be seen by the naked eye, while it broadcasts into the universe and beyond. Consciousness does not recognize time and space. Sophia, guard and nurture your frequency—as a mother protects and feeds her little one. Imagine a young bird which is injured. If you were holding that bird, you can't hold it too tight or it can't breathe. However, if you hold it just firmly enough that it can't fly off or flap around recklessly, it can heal.

"Apply this same principle to frequency. Don't control it too tightly. That's the advice I've been given by the cosmic beings I met. I learned all of this from my work in their presence. Low frequencies trigger survival warnings. If survival is triggered, they pay attention, discern if their safety is in jeopardy, and if not, they move on. It's a conscious choice for them to observe and monitor their frequency.

"Right now, it seems like you are discovering what they do naturally. They are clear that they had to grow into loving others and themselves, by observing subtle shifts in frequency. They practiced choosing love over fear. And choosing collaboration and abundance over greed.

"I feel like I am preaching to the choir. I am sure you know a lot about what I just said. Somehow saying it out loud is purifying for me. I'll be silent now."

Clouds gathered overhead and the wind encircled them, signaling that their conversation would have to continue later. The rain was preparing to cascade in unexpected, heavy downpours... and a lot of it.

CHAPTER 11
BENEFACTORS AND BATTLES

Giant raindrops were already tapping her head as Sophia entered the house to greet Nate. The morning with her dear friend had left her in a reflective mood which was met with Nate's curiosity.

"How did it go with Gilda?" Nate asked, "I'd love to hear."

After his physical therapy session, he looked more comfortable, which was always welcomed for Sophia.

"Before we talk, do you need anything so that you can settle in comfortably for a few minutes? Gilda's story is definitely fascinating. After speaking with her, I have a lot to digest, as always."

Nate's face took on a cheerful glow and he nodded in agreement. As their eyes met, Sophia's gaze softened and her eyes closed as she tenderly kissed her beloved.

Seeing Nate's relaxed state and his anticipation to hear more of Gilda's story, Sophia started to dive in. But suddenly, her phone rang, breaking the thread of the storyline. It was a renowned energy healer, Rose, who Sophia had contacted earlier. Several of Nate's friends highly recommended her so she brought not only her healing skills, but hope as well.

"Thank you for contacting me, Sophia. You indicated that you'd like to work together as soon as possible. Can we do it now?" Rose asked. "I felt a sense of urgency as I read your email and I just had a cancellation. Does this short notice work for you and Nate?"

At this point, Sophia and Nate were open to trying different healing modalities. All that was needed was to confirm and set up the lap-top for Rose and Nate to connect by video. With logistics handled, Sophia could take advantage of a pause in her day for reflection and relaxation.

Making a cup of afternoon tea, she went to her room to journal about her visit with Gilda and her conversation with Nate, which seemed intertwined. She added frankincense to her diffuser, wrapped herself in her favorite, cuddly blue blanket, and began to write.

Meeting Gilda feels important, though I don't know why. Although I feel open to ETs and it's crazy to believe that we are the only living species in the universe, Gilda brought me a fresh perspective of our "cosmic family," as she calls them. I'm interested in how loving they are, that they are not better than us, even if they are more technologically advanced. They are ahead of us in their understanding and use of frequency. She said that they don't have arrogance about it. They are willing to share what they know. They are not greedy or warrior like. Have the movies skewed my view of them? Are sci-fi technologies maybe close to reality? Are technologies being hidden from us?

Gilda knows a lot more than she's telling me. As a friend, I don't want her to say more than she's comfortable with. But her mind-boggling stories distract me from Nate's condition. He's such a good person and he's done so much personal and spiritual growth. Why is this fear and terror of oppressors real for him and completely overwhelming? He told me the other night that he still has the scary, lucid dreams.

It's like the last Samurai where he and a small group are trying to defend a vast area and stop a ruthless, aggressive enemy who are going to destroy the world. He knows it sounds like a movie, but he says it feels real. He can smell blood, watch people disappear, and see large structures made of something that shimmers, maybe quartz. Everything around him is being disintegrated. He's feeling like a worthless soldier because he cannot find a way to end the horrific conflict. He is sure that he agreed to fight.

He said that the same scenario plays out in many dreams in different time periods and varying landscapes. The theme and feelings are always the same.

He also thinks being forced into war is unfair, unjust. The war was born from dense, dark energies, and frequencies. Is this why he is so frustrated with social injustices, poverty, pollution on land, in the air, and in rivers, lakes, and oceans? Injustice is a huge issue for him. Maybe that's why he's worked hard to address those internal influences and conflicts. The projects and ideas of people like Nate seem to fall on deaf ears of politicians and governmental agencies which are created and charged with the responsibility of protecting life on Planet Earth, for all people, plants, and animals.

Over time, after doing massive personal growth, he came to terms with knowing that every human being has a perspective and acts in accordance with the lens through which they see the world. It's like the world is a prism and everyone sees through the side of the prism that they are facing. In being more objective and not responding to past trauma and pain, he began to heal emotionally. In my view, he became a better advocate because there was less emotional attachment with his clients and their adversaries. With increased objectivity, he could find a higher perspective from which to discover optimal solutions. I respect him incredibly for that intense, inner work. And it paid off in terms of allowing him to be more calm and objective, while he raised his frequencies.

Having said that, the dreams of battles continue. Those nightmares are worse than nuclear war, more violent, and require every ounce of human strength and weaponry that he possesses to survive. The enemy is coming closer, and the end feels set in stone. Deep inside, he feels guilty and full of shame that he cannot save the people who are depending on him. That is part of the indescribable agony he experiences.

Because I am empathic, I can feel the terror and it's obviously a dominant wound in his psyche. Is it encoded in his DNA?

We wondered if someone like Rose could shed light on the dreams and the intense fear.

He's done at least a dozen sessions with healers and therapists. Without him even telling them about his dreams, they've each launched into a "past life" of battles. He was purportedly hunkered down, defending something important to him.

He says that this big battle in his dreams induces a harrowing, immediate sense of urgency: the battle decides the future of Earth, hanging precariously in the balance.

From immense inner work, he says one aspect of this battle in his waking state, as an attorney, is to accept that every-

one has a destiny. Advocating for someone doesn't include becoming their savior. In savior mode, he realizes that he is trying to control the outer world with force rather than living in acceptance, courage, and pure love. That is no small feat for someone like Nate who has immense love for humanity. I've always been in awe of his ability not to judge others. He can forgive and move on. He listens, genuinely cares about others, and focuses on objectivity yet the horrific dreams of war rage on. What are they revealing that we have not understood yet?

Last year when I doubled down on my inner work, I made incredible headway into being able to notice and not judge my state of numbness or other lower density frequencies of fear, worry, lack of confidence, and more.

Doing this work of letting the denser frequencies be here and then allowing my body to also feel elevated feelings, has helped immensely. I had forgotten how to feel happy and totally calm. I was struggling to hold my awareness in stillness or on the feeling of vitality. I definitely was a pro at worry, fear, and tension.

A year into elevating my emotions and letting them fill my energy field before emanating them outward—without an agenda of where they go—my inner world is definitely more peaceful, joyous, and free. With that progress, I am determined to continue to focus on higher feelings, elevating and emanating them into the field, and letting the field send back information into my heart—my emotional exchange point with the field.

I was thrust into that practice because of Nate's condition, and that's one more thing for me to appreciate about him. He is going through hell and yet I am exploring how to crawl out of my own abyss. What a pair! We surely are supposed to be together.

It's strange in a way to think that I was content as a single woman. No relationships felt deep and long-lasting. I didn't think about marriage until Nate and I started dating. Instantly, I realized that we had a life-purpose to fulfill together.

When we went to Hawaii, I felt we'd been there for eons and that the mana, or energy of the islands, was in our blood. I am beyond grateful that I got to spend time in India with him cultivating meditation, studying ancient texts, and growing stronger inwardly, in his sweet company.

Tears are flowing. I have to cry. This is getting intensely painful; I am exhausted from getting up in the middle of the night; and I am not going to apologize for missing his hugs, foot massages, and the little surprise gifts he left for me on my pillow. I remember finding a delicious piece of chocolate, a tiny crystal, or an exquisite little flower. One morning I walked out to the kitchen and saw a beautiful new teacup; next to it the sweetest love note in the world greeted me.

On an exceptionally gorgeous spring day, I remember when he picked a bunch of wildflowers and arranged them on the table where we shared our meals. In his characteristic style, he asked each flower if it was okay to pick it and he only chose the ones who agreed to be part of the bouquet.

He then told each delicate blossom that it was going to bless us. I'm glad my husband talked to plants. I always talked to them when I was little. Oh, how I love the little boy in him!

I am crying right now because of frustration. I can't hold onto him or have him to cuddle with. Yet my tears are full of gratitude for a warrior who is as gentle as a puppy and who has given his life in service to the world. Regardless of the underlying reason for his intense suffering, he is my beloved, and that connection will remain indestructible across all time, space, dimensions, and realities.

I think I'll pause now and cry some more. Can't help it.

As Sophia let her tears flow in unison with the roaring rain outside, she fell asleep.

Awakened by Rose's voice on the computer calling her, she grabbed her notebook and joined Nate. Rose explained that although Nate was able to talk during the session, by the end he became so weak that he could not call for Sophia.

With gentleness and compassion, she let Sophia know that they had done a lot of inner work on a lifetime when Nate was a warrior. And there was a lot of clearing that occurred. Rose acted like it may be jarring or a shocking revelation to discover that her loved one participated in violence long ago on Earth or in some other coordinate in the multiverse. However, Sophia didn't look surprised when she heard Rose's words. Like a broken record, repeating incessantly, Nate-the-Warrior was the consistent theme with all therapists or healers that he worked with—as usual, no resolutions or noticeable effects followed.

Considering the infinite nature of the field, Sophia wondered: Was Nate limited to being a kind lawyer who advocated for others? As an infinite, quantum being of light, sound, and electromagnetism, could he perceive a multitude of events, co-ordinates throughout linear time, that he related to? The subject was mind boggling and yet fascinating.

More importantly, she and Nate realized that any aspects within him that were struggling were asking to be accepted and loved into wholeness, regardless of their origin. In heartfelt dialogue, they wondered if loving *all of him* included affirming, without judgement, all aspects of his being, even the ones that they could not yet grasp.

Nate found it natural to think in terms of logic and physics. For Sophia, the mystical and the logical could be a wild paradox. *The field* bridged those two worlds for her. This infinite field held imprints of memory and all possible other information—mind boggling, yet intriguing.

As with all complex subjects, they agreed to be open-minded; even as the visceral, relentless effects raged at night for Nate. Their conversations probed into who he was from a higher viewpoint, which brought them back to quantum realities and unrestricted, broader exploration.

Over the years, she captured her thoughts in her journal about discussing the unified field of quantum physics with anyone who is not familiar with it. A subtle science that describes measure-ments that are infinitely small and electromagnetic particles that spiral at speeds that the eyes cannot detect is not a subject to throw out at someone without explaining how it fits into life's bigger picture. To most people, the scope of this theory remains mind-boggling and is described as *radical.*

For today, Rose would see Nate from the perspective of a linear timeline. However, Sophia would see him from the perspective of his infinite capacities as a scalar-style, quantum being, who appears ordinary to most of the world—yet is capable of moving up or down, through realities that are endless in possible frequency, composition, and appearance.

It was no surprise for her when the nightmare or lucid dream arrived that night in full fury. She caressed him gently; comforting him as a mother would care for her little boy who sank into anguish when monsters stalked his dream state.

Sophia came back to her room and watched a storm raging outside, creating a deluge of rain. Inside and out, there was a tempest that refused to be ignored or controlled. All Nate and Sophia could do was be present, navigate the rainy days, and move forward one step at a time.

CHAPTER 12
TEARS AND STAR CONNECTIONS

The rain seemed endless until one morning, the enchanting music of songbirds burst forth announcing golden streams of light to replace the downpours of the prior week.

Nate was settled and doing his movement exercises. Sophia, tea in hand, headed outside to greet the sun up-close and personal.

Gilda had already responded to the sun's call and was sitting casually with her shoes off, letting her toes play happily in the wet grass.

Today, Sophia didn't waver or hold back. She approached her beloved confidant, and knelt, letting the rain-soaked ground soften as her knees sank gently beneath her. Putting her head in her trusted friend's lap, she didn't seem to care about the wet grass or anything else. Sophia sobbed with giant heaves to catch her breath.

Gilda, gently stroked Sophia's hair and sang a lullaby in German; trusting that in any language, love can soothe a breaking heart.

With anguish in her voice, Sophia looked into the sympathetic eyes of her kindhearted neighbor saying, "He's worse, Gilda. I'm doing my inner work and feeling stronger while being realistic that he's not responding to healers; nor to doctors, therapists, or anything else. His body's relentless decline is perplexing. Yet how can I speak about my inexplicable experiences when I listen to your stories? Human existence seems to be about mysteries that we don't want to willingly dive into so we get thrust into them by life's circumstances... Thank you; I needed to be held. This is getting hard and brutally clear about the most likely outcome. It's ripping at my core. I'm clinging to him and yet, he's slipping away. Your comfort means the world to me right now."

Sophia was more composed as she stood to bring her chair close to Gilda. The distance between them had disintegrated on many levels.

"Gilda, I'd like to hear more about your encounters with your cosmic family, especially when you talked to them. Did they speak English or German?"

Gilda paused for a moment—she didn't want to gloss over Sophia's pain—to assess Sophia's ability to enter the conversation. Finding her clear and composed now that she'd had a chance to share her pain, Gilda felt confident she could speak of other things.

"Well, get ready for a few more surprises. Only a few of these beings spoke with mouths. I recall one was an Aquaferian, from the Pacific Rim. Another was amphibious with a frog-like head and a very wide mouth. Almost all of the ones I engaged with spoke telepathically. I heard them in English, sometimes German, sometimes other languages."

Looking a little surprised, Sophia pressed forward with more questions. "How did you know it wasn't just your mind? How did you get the messages in a way that was clear? Could you just think a response and they received it from you?"

"Okay, my dear, I understand this sounds unimaginable. Based on what you know, isn't all thought a vibration of a particular frequency?"

Sophia nodded affirmatively but with a wrinkled brow expressing her confusion.

"Stay with me," Gilda said. "The secret to understanding cosmic species is to remember that they are well aware that they are frequency-reliant. They were advanced in *using frequency* for digestion, speaking, manifesting, moving between from *here to there*, technology, and telepathy. I had to learn to settle my mind into stillness to interpret the frequencies of the thoughts they sent. Although it took plenty of practice, it didn't take that long to get the hang of it.

"Another important aspect of being with them, however, relates to emotions. As you likely know, emotions are frequency and I observed them emitting strong vibrations, generating them from a deep pool of feelings. They do so without a change on their face. When someone in their species died, I could feel profound sorrow, viscerally and deeply. I know you are empathic and so am I. However, it's dramatically heightened with them. They feel everything with intensity. When they were sad, I felt more than sadness—it was total devastation.

"And what was even more revelatory for me was that if I arrived at work angry after a fight with Rolph, they backed away from me and seemed terrified. They felt my emotions intensely. They thought my anger might be directed at them. And if I was happy, they emoted an ecstatic bliss-state that was contagious.

"Seeing how impactful emotions could be, I decided to focus my mind on holding still inside when I was with them. That was immeasurably helpful, and it changed me. I used the same still mind at the supermarket, the post office, or anywhere I was around people or animals. Oh my goodness, you would love to meet our cosmic family.

"Would you like to know what impacted me the most?"

Sophia leaned forward indicating that she valued Gilda's revelations and wanted to soak up every word.

"The science that you can dig into, if you'd like, will verify what I am saying. It's clear from archaeology, anthropology, and modern genetic testing that some of these beings are in my blood and yours. Let that sink in, Sophia."

Gilda paused, starring into the bright blue, domed sky above them.

"I am saying this with certainty," she said, "not conjecture or theorizing. It's not a secret in the science community who deal in such matters. I asked the cosmic beings about our common DNA with them. With candid clarity, they provided the details for how it happened. In this conversation, I see no need to tell you the minute details they shared." Gilda's eyes twinkled with humor.

"Instead, my wish is that you get the idea that you and I likely have common DNA, and it's linked to our cosmic ancestors. As you can imagine, my time with them was limited and highly controlled. I became close to one of them who was on a special project. Luckily, we were together for many months. I would ask a question or two inter-mixed with the technical information which I was transcribing that day.

"The cosmic being illuminated the story of Earth for me in a way I'd never heard it. He said the story ends and begins many times. That was fascinating. He said the Earth has been pounded by meteors or has suddenly switched its magnetic axis innumerable times. Many unexpected occurrences have rocked our planet. Most life on Earth was annihilated more than once. Rather than focusing on each new beginning, instead, he spoke about the captivating and continued *evolutionary process* of survivors.

"According to my special cosmic friend, after a cataclysm millions of years ago, the inhabitants of another planet in our galaxy were facing extinction, so they were looking around for a safe place to live, one which matched their atmosphere. They knew of a benevolent species on Earth who were living underground during an ice age. At the time, Earth was still emerging from an ice age and it seemed perfect.

"They headed for our wonderful planet, which looked a lot different millions of years ago. I am not absolutely sure of the exact timeframe but it was definitely millions of years in linear time.

"My telepathy was a bit off when he told me that part and I couldn't clarify it or ask too many questions because of the situation we were in. I also could not comprehend the name of their planet, solar system, or galaxy. I was clear that their home was definitely within the Milky Way Galaxy.

"At that time in Earth's history, my friend made it clear that civilizations in our *solar system* had advanced space crafts, and could teleport through portals without needing ships. We think traveling beyond time and space is modern. But it's not. And we think we have to go way out in space to find high tech species. That's not true.

"The new arrivals on Earth shared their technologies with the humans who had survived the ice age, like pyramids. Today you can research how pyramids on Mars and the ones in Egypt share the same dimensional frequencies. Both have an eye placed on top that mimics our pineal gland and they all had water under them to conduct energy frequencies. Geology and archeology consider that cataclysms possibly occurred for Gaia naturally, every so often. Consequently, human migrations occurred. That made sense to me.

"With cataclysms in the cosmos, displaced species and others came here to live in peace, and they travelled to other planets and stars using natural portals on the Earth—today most of those portals are owned by governments who long ago made them into national parks or put military bases on them. These advanced cultures mingled with the humans on Gaia, who were, believe it or not, highly advanced, too. Interestingly, there was a shamanic race on Earth back then with whom the displaced cosmic species occasionally mated. Our coveted DNA became intermingled with theirs.

"Hang on to your hat, sister, this stuff sounds crazy to our mind which only grasps a blip in the vastness of Gaia's vast history. After a cataclysm, we'd start again. We're tenacious!

"In the space programs, there are geneticists who know those ancient genetic codes because we've done innumerable autopsies on different species from our solar system and galaxy. We know a lot about their DNA, which almost always contains some human DNA. Isn't that fabulous, Sophia!

"We are all a huge family, connected to the whole universe, through blood. This is our universe to share. We are intimately united as beings, yet our distant history is not spoken about. And the truth of our origins may be very difficult for some people to grasp and accept.

"Throughout time, star brothers and sisters have co-existed with us on Earth to create advanced civilizations. Sophia, I want you to know something that is vital for you to hear. I am getting old and I have to tell someone."

Gilda swallowed, took a deep breath, and straightened herself in her chair, saying slowly, "Sophia, something is happening right now that is unfathomable. Plasma light is pouring onto this planet from beyond our solar system. My dear cosmic family told me that this light would come. I am relieved that it's finally here, and as they predicted, it's showering all of us with high frequencies.

"They said, with the light, a lot of chaos could happen for the Earth's population; like old structures would break down, obvious manipulation would be revealed and replaced with benevolence, and greed would be thoroughly exposed.

"Better structures would be established based on being in relationship with Mother Nature, respecting her as a sentient being. Rather than looking into how to manipulate her natural cycles and processes more effectively and ethically, we would *love her as an ally* on our journey through the cosmos. That shift in orientation towards her will allow for creative interaction with her that does not require massive technology nor a feeling that we must settle for being in constant struggle with her. At her core, she's pure love and so are we. We can begin to expand our concepts and ideas on this subject.

"They said that as time moves on, we would no longer need money, polarization would end, and we would live in balance and harmony in ways that we could not imagine today. We would no longer grovel before governments or world leaders for our basic human needs. We would not obey to survive, to feel safe, or to fit into society.

"For that to happen, we would need to learn how to hold high frequencies continuously, not judge each other, and be open to living openly with all species in the universe as one family. After all, we share genetics and codes that flow through our blood. This information came from their ancestors—calling this data ancient does not describe the inconceivable levels or scales of our universe. Every star and planet is wider and deeper in its experience and grandeur than we can fathom.

"However, with unified physics, we are starting to do the math that says that these revelations make sense. I know this is a lot to take in, but please consider it. And this is not the end of the story. I hope you can take in a little more, my friend.

"As you raise your frequency, there will be some who simply aren't comfortable doing so. Do not cast them aside or judge them. Keep in mind, you may find new circles of friends and some people will turn on you. Think about it. You are defying world views and closely held beliefs about how this world was made and who we are. It's a huge shift in perception. Not everyone will accept it. It's still possible, though. It may take a while to digest this but it's worth it. We have unlimited capacities, no less than the ETs. That's the truth.

"Have I overwhelmed you?"

Sophia was sitting still, hardly breathing. As she took in and began assimilating what Gilda told her, she asked, "Gilda, you said that these ETs who came here long ago and who continue to come in modern times, can time-travel, move through some kind of portals, and are quite advanced technologically. How can you be sure they were not coming from the future? I feel a little crazy asking that, but that's what popped into my mind; likely because quantum science isn't about linear time."

Gilda's smile grew wide. "You took it in, oh magnificent soul that you are! I love you! You are the friend and the open-hearted person I thought I'd never meet; much less befriend.

"My dear, I asked this same question myself. My cosmic brother, who I was most close to, said this happened in the past in what you would think of as *linear time*. You and I have within us infinite potentials of a future self who is not yet born. These future aspects exist in the quantum field of all possibilities and are accessible as scales of frequency within. We can connect with future selves and bring them into our energy field. They are not technically future; they are a higher fractal in frequency than the scale we are experiencing. Is this wild, or what?

"Don't get too analytical about it. Keep in mind that quantum science posits that every possibility of you and I exist in that endless field. That includes potential, past, present, and future aspects. Give this time to digest. It's beyond the mind.

"Of course, what you heard is my understanding of a complex subject. Find a brilliant quantum scientist who is researching the unified field of quantum physics and learn from them. New discoveries are happening constantly. Stay on top of this burgeoning science.

"Remember that we affect the field and everyone in our universe is affecting us. So why not collaborate with each other? How could divisiveness, a relentlessly competitive ethos, or conquering another species be helpful?

"In Earth's history, this level of high frequencies has never been available. They are streaming in and the whole universe is celebrating. We reduce our planet to bits and pieces that we can own, trade and use. Often, we abuse Gaia like she's a resource. This is the way humanity is treated by corporations and leaders—not as sentient but *as a resource.* We have to come to terms with the fact that we and she are living entities deserving of respect. Her frequency is elevating and so is ours. There is an ancient, encoded artifact somewhere on this planet to be a safety net for us and her but I didn't understand why we'd need it and why they said that 2045 was important. I tried to inquire further, to no avail.

"Back to current life, this cosmic friend warned that some people on Earth will want to keep things the same and they will fight the coming changes. That's their choice. My cosmic family told me firmly to focus on elevating my frequency. They were crystal clear that I should not get involved in fearful tactics like doom and gloom or manipulation through leadership making us feel guilty or shameful. They made a point to say that we will be more effective in healing the planet if we simply connect with Gaia; acknowledge her sentience, rather than walk around putting ourselves down for climate change.

"One way of approaching her shifting conditions is that if a friend was ill or seemed to be struggling, you'd look for ways to make her comfortable and allow her to heal. Permaculture and no-till farming came to mind for me. I envision putting natural ingredients in the soil and letting the soil work its magic.

"As a bonus, humans would no longer rely on chemicals to fertilize and rid the crops of insects. There are many emerging farms doing this successfully and yet greedy corporations do everything to thwart their progress. Silly bastards! You need to get clear about many of the corporations that you accept as indispensable components of your society.

"A world renowned expert in the field of psycho-pathology published an essay that described corporate psychology as *psychopathic*. Let this sink in, Sophia. It is hard to digest but he built a powerful case for his observations and conclusion. What if this is true? What does it mean for our world? Who do we rely on for resources like food, medicine, and financial stability? Do we blindly follow psychopathic institutions? From my background, I have to ask these kinds of questions or I am repeating past mistakes that had devastating consequences.

"It is not about finger pointing and brewing with anger. Rather, it's about being realistic and changing the system, if needed, to share the truth and look for alternative solutions to corporate systems and approaches. Based on their history, is it safe and helpful for us to *blindly* rely on them? Some of these behemoth entities are in the field of food production. That concerned me. I chewed on the far reaching implications of this.

"So it was a relief to me when the ETs indicated that the human race could rally to create nourishing kinds of farming practices. They also said that Gaia would warm and cool as always, and humanity could be more savvy about how to flow with her cycles. Maybe we need a big dose of self-compassion and listening to our hearts for answers. Could politicians exit the discussion and let the brilliant minds of good-hearted scientists listen to each other, share ideas, and collaborate to find solutions?

"One afternoon recently you told me that you'd been working on elevating your frequencies. Describing your accomplishments in that endeavor and your solid commitment warmed my heart. After our conversation, I went inside and wept with joy. You detected there was a need to raise our frequencies. That gave me confidence that others will do the same. In fact, I am feeling that millions are doing this, as we speak.

"I can leave this old body in peace now, Sophia. After all of the devastation, the greed, and avarice of Rolph and his buddies, I am finally feeling *pure, inherent light gaining* traction. My heart is on fire with excitement right now."

Sitting back smiling, breathing in the welcomed air of a cherished moment, Gilda relaxed and closed her eyes.

Sophia asked a bit nervously, "Is your health okay? You never say anything about yourself."

"Yes, my dear," Gilda said, "I'm fine. I am old now; in case you hadn't noticed." She smiled with a twinkle in her eye and continued, "For the past few years I've had a gnawing regret that I didn't have anyone with whom I could safely share my ET conversations—so much wisdom and truth unknown to most of humanity.

"Today I am feeling blessed that you and I are family through blood. When I leave here, your love will go with me, as frequency. In those military bases, I learned from my cosmic family that pure love is the indefinable and illusive Essence of all of us. This pure love is omnipresent and like the shared codes in our blood and our DNA, we share the spark of life in the form of pure love.

"I always feel love when I am with you, Sophia. I have more to disclose but I hear that temple bell calling you to Nate. Go, dearest one, and I will see you tomorrow. I love you."

"I always hate to end our conversations, Gilda. I'll save my questions and a story that came to mind for next time. You are right; it's time for me to go. And my dear friend, I love you, too."

CHAPTER 13
HISTORY OF INNOCENCE AND PERVERSION

Nate was waiting for her and wanted to hear every detail of the conversation between Sophia and Gilda. So they sipped Indian spiced tea while the aromas of cardamon and cinnamon filled the air with enchantment.

No subjects were out of bounds for these two lovers. And no restrictions were in place to stifle exploration into deeper terrains of awareness and understanding of the mysterious universe in which they journeyed throughout each day.

"Sophia, for many decades it seems that Gilda had to compromise herself to stay with Rolph. And she nobly abided by her agreement with the side of the military which had not joined the secret *Nazi Fan Club* segment of the armed forces.

"That compromise to stay with Rolph must have been difficult for her. In fact, it sounds agonizing. What allows me to feel a deep connection with her is that like us, she wanted to continually explore deeper levels and aspects of her human experience. She's quite unique, don't you think?"

"Yes," Sophia answered in a soft voice. "She also seems to be in alignment with her soul's path. When I am with her, I feel authenticity, a no BS explanation of what she's been through and where she is today inside herself. The subject matter sometimes shocks me, which is my mind wanting to make sense of the unseen and unknown aspects of life. After all of these years of personal and spiritual growth, it's a familiar reaction."

Sophia smiled softly and lowered her head as though bowing with humility.

Sipping her tea and pouring more for Nate, she said, "What she is saying will cause cognitive dissonance for the whole world. We were taught one thing and now we are finding out that someone withheld important information from us. And for millennia, we allowed ourselves to become compliant followers of religions and political regimes, who often created alliances with each other. Our DNA stores the psychological and emotional trauma from those past events, yet if this is not brought to the surface, we will repeat past mistakes.

"If the global population had known the truth of the magnitude of technologies of past civilizations and current technologies from ETs, where would we be right now? In the eyes of leaders, globally, maybe the masses were not good enough or maybe we were easily controllable. Why relinquish their delicious power and share potential technologies that could shift life on Planet Earth?"

Looking out as though he was gazing past the wall in front of him, Nate responded thoughtfully, "There's nothing Gilda told you that doesn't ring true for me. And that's likely because, as you know, I love research. A vast majority of the archaeological sites and anthropological studies confirm what she's saying. The common DNA with ETs was hard for me to fully digest. I have too many sources now that confirm her findings. It's mind-bending stuff. The latest research is the DNA from the elongated, giant skulls. It is a ground-breaking archeological and genetic discovery. And we have no idea why certain similar, unique symbols, carvings, and pottery are found in various parts of the world like

Egypt, Central America, North America, Asia, and Africa. These artifacts are way over ten-thousand-years-old. Why do the pyramids have water under them? How is it that they geometrically align with certain constellations during key dates and seasons like equinoxes and solstices?

"I am more interested in what Gilda is saying about our frequency being the point of convergence where all spiritual elevation resides. She is fine to feel into her tendency for anger or fear yet she's confident in moving into exalted states and frequencies as well. Is that true?"

Sophia nodded as he continued.

"I reflected after our last conversation about how the ETs touched her heart profoundly. In fact, so much so that she seemed to become connected with a higher truth of who she was and who they were. And she brilliantly linked being connected to them through blood because the DNA links likely occurred in our prehistorical past. These days, there's a plethora of science to back that up. We have a lot to learn about DNA, though. It's complex.

"Well, I have to say she sure impressed me, and I haven't met her. Please thank her for me because she's affirmed what I've considered speculation until now. When I hear a genuine person, with no hidden agendas, speak freely, I am affected. Like her, I am willing to learn more about the vastness of our universe. I feel a heart connection with Gilda and her cosmic family who remain invisible, yet nonetheless real."

"Nate, I want to spend more time with her," Sophia said. "I feel uneasy about the way she keeps saying that she can die in peace now, having shared all of this. I love her, as though I've known her forever. I'm intimately close to her. Do you know what I mean?"

Smiling, he looked deeply into her eyes. "Of course, I understand. You are fortunate to have such a special friend in your life. Spend as much time with her as you want. I realize my eating schedule and all of the daily duties makes it tough. I want you to prioritize your conversations with her. I'm all in."

"You are such an adventurer," Sophia said. "I love your spark of curiosity. For most of us, that kind of awe and wonder disappear in the latter stages of childhood. You kept yours. I'm so glad that you did. Thank you for supporting me in this, sweetheart."

The next morning, Sophia found herself in what was now a familiar, enchanted garden where life's deeper mysteries were seeds receiving the necessary sunlight to take root, and then peep through the soil into the light of day.

With her usual grace and kind smile, Gilda came outside to join her, while wrapping a soft blue blanket around her shoulders.

Having warded off the morning chill, Gilda said, "I've reflected on our conversation, and I certainly said a lot but I'd like to share a little more. The next part is harder to speak about and even more dark. But my spirit seems hell-bent on sharing it. Is it okay?"

"Of course," Sophia replied.

"You seem to be a sensitive soul, and honestly, I think most of the human race is, too. As I speak, think in terms of frequency. Feel into the frequency of people and what they create and radiate into the world. I'd like to stay with that focus. Okay?"

Sophia nodded in agreement and looked at Gilda with a look of trepidation.

Seeing her friend's concern, Gilda continued, "I only began our conversation this way because I don't want to propagate judgment and lower frequencies like anger or perhaps shock, which could override what I want to say. Rolph was a human being who was neither emotionally nor psychologically well balanced. You likely have considered this would have been the case with the Führer. Is that right?"

Sophia nodded and said, "Yes, absolutely."

"Let me explain a little about where the Nazis were headed and the distortion of their worldview. And, from my perspective and experience, what generated their perverse view of reality. The Führer, like Rolph, was Austrian by birth. A group of Austrians who lived near the German border, seem to have been aligned more with Germany's politics and philosophies than even many Germans.

"Rolph was younger than the Führer yet their childhoods were incredibly similar. Both were raised with strict Catholic theology and doctrine. Rolph spoke about doing penance constantly for his many sins; sins like laughing too much or making too much noise, according to his dictatorial father.

"The local priest added to Rolph's shame and guilt by giving him severe penances weekly to purify him of these petty infractions. This sounds ludicrous now, but for Rolph, it was his reality. How ridiculous to treat a child with such harshness and lack of care! You can likely tell that it infuriates me to know these young children went through that psychological control and cruelty. That's my opinion and perspective because I saw the direct results of how such parental demeaning and shaming shaped their minds for the future. Their connection to Essence was mangled, and with no sense of their own true nature, when adversity struck, they threw themselves in wholeheartedly to belong with those who were compellingly strong and seemed full of self-worth, believing their own salvation lay within the Nazi doctrines. Without realizing their mistake, they lost their capacity to see truth itself, or to draw on their powerful, inherent strengths.

"From there, they created power in their lives through lies, manipulation, and fear, learning and developing horrific behaviors from their parents and elders, sabotaging further their remnants of innocence. I am not sharing every detail. There are plenty of places to read about the Führer's youth, and Rolph's was similar.

"For example, like the Führer, Rolph wanted to be an actor and to study art and other forms of creativity. But his father was profoundly horrified at the thought of having a son who would be broke and wimpy. So he decided to send Rolph to a boarding school that focused on math and science. I found it interesting that the Führer wanted to be an artist. His father also refused to let that happen. Seeking solace like his kindred spirit, the Führer, Rolph became obsessed with a popular German author of that time period.

"The books were totally fictional tales of a mythical land; battles always won by *Old Shatterhand,* a courageous and brilliant white man who destroyed the local indigenous people. There were seventy books in this series which Rolph (and the Führer) devoured like they were made of honey. Sickening to me, Sophia. Rolph, like the Führer, began to identify and act out the role of the great white man at school and in his imagination—this was the future, perverted bond that cemented their relationship; tragic for sure.

"I can see the heart-wrenching reality that these boys were part of a *lost generation* who shared lower frequencies of guilt, shame, and destructive qualities. Those lower frequencies filled their minds and psyche with urges to control and manipulate others, and these behaviors slowly contributed to disintegration of integrity and lack of compassion. To protect themselves, they carefully designed invisible emotional shields. Neither of them had true friends or close relationships; domination and control was all they knew. It's not an excuse. Rather, I am sharing the lowest of frequencies that can send a child forward in life to do great harm to themselves and others.

"They were armed with shame and guilt as opposed to love, a higher mind, and true wisdom about themselves and humanity. Both the Führer and Rolph roared through their youth fueled by distorted views of other people and themselves. They became obsessed with anything to do with the military and every aspect of German Nationalism. Both of them lost a younger sibling, which was another common theme in their lives. Rolph claimed that it didn't matter. He only spoke about his childhood one time that I can remember.

"Oh, Sophia, I was shocked when his face tightened, his eyes became slits, and his mustache became frozen. It was like his life force disappeared and I could feel a roaring dragon of anguish trying to break loose from its chains, safely hidden behind his well-rehearsed, rigid exterior.

"Rolph was a lost child; a boy who figured out how to cope and how to survive the horrors of innocence-deprivation. The culture at that time restricted inner exploration like a noose, closing ever tighter. He was cut off from anything that was kind, compassionate, or expansive. Again, I am not making excuses for what he did. I am inviting you to think about the frequencies that were driving his body, mind, and spirit. Consider what he might have felt like as he moved through life.

"And then, he found hundreds and thousands of people like himself. He gathered with them in a spirit of camaraderie, *elevating himself* by creating the greatest and deadliest personality masks possible. It was a crazy delusion. My deranged husband created and wore invisible masks of being more right, more wise, more entitled and, even worse... more God-like than those who did not share his views.

"As the war raged, by 1945, the Führer and his comrades were given safe passage to South America; that left those of us who survived with an impending death by hanging. We were war criminals. And I admit that it was true. We were either criminals, conspirators, or minions of insane psychopaths.

"What I observed in reflection, is that there were low frequency people all over the world who gravitated to each other. And those are the ones who were magnetized to people like Rolph or the Führer.

"After learning more about frequencies and quantum physics, I've wondered if my experiences in that prisoner of war camp in Idaho helped to raise my frequency. Was that how I aligned with an opportunity for redemption or at least to make the most restitution possible?

"I have to say that Rolph took everything to excess. He was brilliantly shrewd, and utterly diligent, and comprehensively manipulative. No wonder he didn't have friends. His moods were frightening, his nightmares aggressively repetitive, and his capacity to feel was nonexistent. I lived with a machine, not a human. He was an unfeeling psychopath, not a husband.

"Yet, even with all of that to contend with in him, I found friendships with my cosmic family and a few people on the military base. I became willing to explore my heart and I found a therapist to help me, too. When what was called the New Age Spiritual Movement began, I checked that out. I didn't want to be like Rolph. I saw firsthand what rigidity and being cut off from feelings does to a human being.

"Without excusing his behavior, I recalled the intense indoctrination and cruel brainwashing that he incurred with the Nazis. To get him to lose any feelings that he had left in him, he had to kill our dog in front of them. He crossed the line into being a savage with little hope for redemption. It became clear that he would follow orders and kill anyone, even me, for the good of the *Vaterland*, which means *fatherland* to pure, Aryan nationalists. Nazis like the Führer and Rolph could not relate to nurturing, open hearts. They went full tilt into masculine domination with women being objects of lust; a horrible combination. I can attest to that.

"Admiration of the Führer was also a motive for Rolph's actions. He claimed that everything he did was for the *Vaterland* in order to empower the Aryan race of perfect people to flourish and take over the Earth. He began to hold the viewpoint that he was acting for the greater good. Insane, right? His greater good was not inclusive.

"The Aryan race was about physical, mental, and worldview *likeness*. It was bizarre how they were fixated on physical appearance. Looking back, it was about creating a robotic-style world of lovely humans who took orders without a shred of inquisitiveness or creativity. They would remain compliant and indoctrinated. Where did their magnificent humanness fit in?

"Rolph's beliefs darkened and aligned with Nazi concepts that poor people, disabled citizens, and jews were genetic defects and simply were of no use to the Aryan race, which was the future of humanity for the Führer, Rolph, and his comrades. The Führer was keen on the Eugenics Movement and studied it voraciously. My dear friend, I hate to tell you about such horrific things. Yet I feel you need to know what kind of mentality and world view your innocent country imported after that second, dreadful world war.

"Over time, Rolph and I spent less time with each other. He was in such top secret projects in the U.S., that I was considered a possible security threat. To avoid that risk, I didn't join him. Because of this, I was finally free to explore life through my personal lens, check out anything that interested me, and dive into who I was. I began to connect to the Essence of who I am. After a while, I realized that everything in the universe arises from the same Essence.

"If that sounds esoteric or spiritual, well... maybe it is. Yet it can be explained by the unified field theory of quantum physics. When I realized this, for me, science met the esoteric realms and I danced in those fields for the rest of my life... Have you studied any of this, Sophia?"

"Yes, in fact, Nate and I studied mysticism and quantum science. I am blown away by your story, though. For me, there was unimaginable data, research, the internet, and groups to study with. You had none of that. I am amazed at how deeply you dove into these subtle subjects."

"Don't be shocked, Sophia. If you'd met your cosmic family and had opportunities to experience quantum science as a lived experience, you would not have needed groups, research, the internet, and all of that. Maybe I am the fortunate one, eh?"

Laughing, Sophia said, "You are right, my friend. Thank you for giving me the context in terms of frequency and how it can shape and re-shape a human life. What happens now? Do you simply keep ascending in frequency by practicing? I am asking because I spend a lot of time elevating my frequency in the way I described to you. And I work with feeling myself as a purification channel, connected to my Essence, allowing old patterns and beliefs and lower frequencies to be transmuted and transformed within me. I am not sure I am explaining this clearly enough. It's so subtle and intimate. I feel a bit vulnerable talking about this subject, even with you."

Gilda stretched a little, slowly rose to her feet, and tenderly touched Sophia's face. Beaming a friendly smile and gently hugging her, Gilda said, "You described it beautifully, my dear."

She stood nearby smiling as though she was basking in the bond of love that was palpable in the atmosphere around them.

"What a gift you are to me, Sophia, especially at this time in my life. I dreaded being here with Rolph and his caretaker. One thing you can do that I cannot, is journal. I could never risk documenting any of this. Be sure you write about what you are learning, especially your feelings about it. Don't make it like a report.

"You see, frequency and feelings go hand in hand. Think about an innocent child and the feelings of *being innocent,* about feeling honored, valued, loved, and respected. Those feelings are frequencies that will determine the frequencies of thoughts, words, and actions. So write about them, revel, and play in their energy. And be grateful that you have the capacity to feel. And be grateful that you can journal, write, and freely share with others.

"Poor old Rolph lost his capacity to feel. His feelings were first shrouded in fear and then held at bay for too long. I believe that after his death, in a realm that I don't pretend to fathom, he will once again be innocent. Rolph will be free to heal deeply from all that he created here; and to reflect on all that his soul must have learned.

"In life there is dark and light, brightness and shadows. Some souls play the dark roles and others the light ones. It's a mysterious play of opposites. I don't have to condone the dark, and

I refuse to become bitter and become obsessed with its many manifestations. For me, judging such things just diminishes frequency even more. It's not for me to judge Rolph. I decided to set his soul free to do what it is supposed to do and extend the same courtesy to myself."

Gilda's grey hair, lit by the morning sun, looked golden as it blew softly, shimmering in the morning breeze. She inhaled a deep breath of the fresh, morning air as she closed her eyes for a moment. Sophia's eyes closed gently, too.

Breaking the silence, Sophia asked in a quiet, gentle tone, "Given all of that secrecy and lack of trust, during the war, and even after you were released from the camp in Idaho, did you have trusted girl friends?"

Gilda settled down into her chair and spoke in a reflective, soft tone. "I was too vulnerable to trust anyone in the U.S. And in my elite German circle, friendships were futile. The women of the Third Reich were totally brainwashed and devoid of feelings, except fiery anger and mountains of pride. Their insatiable desire for becoming more sexually alluring and powerful than all other women on Earth made me cringe.

"One woman still haunts me. Her chosen nickname, which Rolph's circle thought was perfect, was *Lady Midday*. She provocatively referred to herself as this mythical creature who was terrifying. Yet, Lady Midday was the epitome of Aryan physical beauty and perfection. Holy crap! Making eye contact with her could cut your emotional field to shreds.

"The name, Lady Midday, came from a demonic legend in our part of the world. I think it was a Slavic tale in which she related to the *demoness* and strangely enough, she told us that she identified with that role. Her version of the story was that this she-devil greeted visitors on the road and if the women didn't answer her questions fast or wisely enough, they'd lose their head. Lady Midday would beam a wicked smile as she explained that men ultimately lost their *crown jewels,* which she found more enticing as a punishment than chopped heads. You get the idea, right? She was an evil barbarian who liked to cut and slice people for fun.

"Taking the demonic name of Lady Midday let people know immediately, *Don't mess with me... or you'll regret it.* We began to call her *Midday,* for short and we all knew exactly who she was and what she was capable of doing.

"Midday came to the U.S. at the same time that Rolph and I arrived. And for many years, she worked underground in the black budget projects like ours. She was a creepy old woman who always seemed to be stalking me. I was relieved to come here where she won't be in my world any longer. I bet she's nearly one-hundred years old and defiantly still kicking everyone's butt. She did all kinds of crazy procedures to perfect anti-aging. I have to say that she looked younger than me. However, her interior self gets older and more diabolical by the day.

"Fortunately, I had my visiting cosmic family and developed superficial friendships with a few people. But I didn't find a bond of affection for a very long time. Finally, I met a very dear soul, her name is Edith. I love her very much. It was a great gift from fate when she was asked to work with me on a project."

"These days, I focus on myself... on my personal evolution. During our conversations, I know that my soul and yours have been dancing in wonder and innocence like small children. My body, mind and spirit fill with awe, wonder, and love in every conversation with you. Once again, Sophia, my heart wants to express how much I love you, respect you, and wish you every opportunity to raise your frequency and discover heaven on Earth.

"Now I hear the temple bell. Nate is calling. See you soon, my love."

CHAPTER 14
SHARING ROWING

Each day rolled by for Sophia and Nate with a schedule and rhythm that remained as steady as their love for each other.

One morning, Sophia opened the window and felt unexpected warmth for the time of year and the bird songs were louder than usual.

At the appointed time, she went to the garden where she and Gilda shared life experiences and bonded even further.

As she approached, Gilda was there in a lively conversation with someone seated near her. As the two saw Sophia, they both stood and Gilda said with her customary, sweet charm, "I would like you to meet Edith, my dear friend."

Edith had the face of a kind grandmother. Her wide forehead which tapered down to a narrow jaw and angled chin, created a heart shape. Short wisps of thinning grey hair lay gracefully around her face, with slightly longer strands in the middle of her bangs, which accentuated the heart. Her gaze was soft and her kind, gentle demeanor set the stage for a safe conversation and a platform for trust to build upon. Her brilliant blue eyes sparkled as she spoke. Although she was at least twenty or thirty years younger than Gilda, their bond seemed to ignore age differences.

Without hesitation, Edith stepped forward and hugged Sophia, saying how happy she was to meet her. Gilda then added a long, gentle hug to this surprise morning greeting.

Sophia motioned for the two ladies to sit. Instead, Gilda said in a light-hearted tone, "We have a little surprise for you. Edith is skilled in caregiving, and we thought we could sit with Nate and you can go for a nice long walk. Enjoy Mother Nature, the warm day, and unwind a bit. This can be an opportunity for you to take some time for yourself. How does that sound?"

Looking a bit shocked, Sophia's response was to hug them both and to say, "Yes."

She went to talk to Nate and make sure it was okay. As she finished explaining the idea, he said enthusiastically, "I'd love to meet Gilda in person. As you know, she fascinates me. Please explain about my voice... It's so frustrating!... I may not be able to participate as much as I'd like."

Then his face broke into a relaxed smile as he shifted his tone, "I'm not going to worry about my voice. You know how much I love listening to deep and meaningful topics. Tell them I welcome them and appreciate having their company.

"And sweetheart, I am glad you are going to get a little time to yourself. I try not to feel guilty about how much of your life force is given to my care. I love you so much. Enjoy your walk, dearest one."

Within a couple of minutes, Sophia and Nate exchanged a quick kiss and she headed out the door. A soft wind escorted Sophia towards the forest trail nearby.

The two ladies settled into chairs near Nate, ready to get to know him, while Nate began the conversation without hesitation. "Gilda and Edith, I am happy to meet you both. I'm curious... Did you work together? Have you known each other long? Is there something you want to talk to me about? My radar senses that this is not just a baby-sitting visit. Am I right?"

Edith looked at Nate with raised eyebrows and then dissolved in merry laughter, which Gilda met with equaled good humor.

As their laughter subsided, Gilda replied, "Good radar, Nate. Sophia said you worked to develop higher states of intuition and she was correct. I realize that she's likely told you a lot about me and the work I've done, right?"

Nate nodded in agreement.

"Great. I want to broach a subject with you that can be sensitive and yet my intuition says it's okay to discuss it... If you do not want to share anything with me, that is fine. I am not probing, simply wanting to know you better. What I am wanting to say is that in my elder years, I acknowledge the end of life as an exquisite extension of life. How about you? What is your current perspective on death and what ushers forth from it?"

"You are certainly a straight shooter," Nate responded while weakly shaking his head and smiling. "Okay, here's my take on death and dying. I believe that I am infinite consciousness experiencing itself on many levels, currently, mostly in a 3-D reality. When I die, I will shed my present Earthly identity. My *limited* perception will become expanded into *elevated* states of consciousness, full integration with the field, and unlimited experiences of higher frequencies. That's the easiest way I know to explain it. The reason I don't fear it is because I know there's *more* than what I experience right now. I view death as a natural continuation of an ever-evolving consciousness journey.

"Having said that, leaving Sophia is agonizing and living in a body that is deteriorating is equally hard most days. I am being honest. Most of the time, the physical weakness is not easy for me."

"You are certainly clear and honest," Gilda said, "and I appreciate those qualities more than you could ever know. I have a reason to speak to you and a reason to have Edith with me. Nate, there are a few things that I hesitate to tell Sophia but when she told me about your nightmares, the battles and all of that, my inner intuition-antennae went into high alert.

"Let me begin by telling you that there is more to the military bases than I've shared with Sophia and much more about our vast cosmic family and Earth's history. Before we talk, I'd like to tell you that Edith first worked with me in the late 1960's. We know each other well; she is trustworthy and a wonderful human being. Are you comfortable continuing?"

Nate smiled weakly in agreement.

"You see, by the 1940's Germany was well established in Antarctica. They had electromagnetic craft of some kind. And yes, that means no jet propulsion. Their weapons didn't work on that craft because they worked from different principles of physics. If they used the conventional weapons, the craft would eject the weapon while at the same time, the craft would be thrust backwards, definitely not the desired result.

"By the end of the war, the Nazis reverse engineered off planet weapons. Luckily, it was too late to save the Third Reich. Unfortunately, there were legions of bloodthirsty, greed-driven Nazi-monsters. These Nazi scientists were incredibly brilliant, and keep in mind that these aren't the kind Germans who you have met. These are Nazi's who were about as low as you can get on a frequency scale.

"My dear brothers and sisters in Germany felt shame for what happened and took responsibility for our actions while making restitution in large and small ways. Ask any of us and we will tell you that our society decayed slowly and in subtle, indiscernible ways. Many said they were blind until it was too late. In some cases, I observed that others were blind until well after the war ended. That is how deep the indoctrination penetrated their psyche.

"We only heard information that the ones in power wanted us to hear. Anyone who thinks they have an honest press need only investigate who pays the press and how coincidental it is that they all share the same basic themes and stories.

"Because of our history, it's haunting and concerning that the modern press is owned by only six main companies who also own stock in each other. How do the small outlets survive? They are coming on strong. However, let me warn you and your friends: the independent press prospered for a while in Germany and were eventually crushed and depicted as liars and treasonous vipers. The Nazi plan was deep and thorough in scope. Without doubt, media was vital in the culmination of their total influence over every aspect of everyday life and the complete shifting of benevolent values and beliefs.

"That victory was methodical in its ruthless exploitation of our naiveté and our natural susceptibility to be hypnotized and brainwashed. Nazis found every Achilles heel in the human psyche and used it to further their tyrannical goals. They proudly wrote about how they carefully choreographed their media victory. With such massive success, would others want to follow their diabolical playbook in current times?

"Nazis knew how to prey on our goodness, our willingness to make sacrifices for the good of others, and our innocence. It was like a slow, growing infection that poisoned our country. Neighbors turned on each other, thinking they were doing something benevolent for the whole community. We were their pawns. Yet we couldn't see it. We obeyed more and more orders in the name of *the greater good.* Not realizing that this phrase was systematically used to manipulate the public, we remained blind to the dangerous and lethal implications of that seemingly innocuous phrase.

"Once again in human history, we were inadvertently the servants of greed and power. We fell into step with our leaders and complied with the heavy burden of ridiculous rules and newly limiting laws. Before we realized what was going on at the top, we were mind-controlled zombies of destruction; compassionless and empathy-deprived. It is agonizing to remember that time.

"Common citizens of Germany had no idea that the Führer was obsessed with space travel and potential alliances with various species in our solar system. Nor did they realize his diabolical infatuation with the occult, which fostered a distorted worldview of incomprehensible delusion.

"He was supposed to take care of inflation and build a strong country. Quantum physics, Nicola Tesla, and Einstein were of no importance to us but they were indispensable for military dominance. Rather than notice scientific breakthroughs, our citizens were trying to survive wild hyperinflation, a brutal winter, a devastating drought, and the oppression of the Socialists and Communists of nearby Russia. People were starving and unemployment had risen to forty percent. That did not matter to our leaders yet our citizens were left to live and slowly die in that insidious environment.

"The Führer and his inner circle wanted national power and global dominance. Advanced technologies gained through cosmic help gave the Nazis the edge they needed to overtake Europe and their U.S. allies. I could tell you more later, but you need this context to understand why Edith and I want to speak with you. Nate, I am mindful of your well-being. Are you feeling strong enough to continue?"

He nodded his head as much as his body would allow and his enthusiastic yet weak smile was a definitive clue to keep going.

"Globally, large corporations have *privately* been involved in space travel and exploration. Wherever there are precious metals or other commodities in our solar system, private business wants a piece of the action. It's inter-galactic commerce at its finest, driven by insatiable appetites for profit.

"I shudder to think that we are more than seventy-five years past World War II and the Nazi's legacy are still enjoying their depraved, never-satisfied hunger for control and domination. These people and their successors are in corporations and the military in your country. They gradually dropped the Nazi name and association but their values and overall worldview remain intact. Sorry to be the bearer of bad news. They have aligned globally and dropped their hyper-focus on Aryanism through DNA and bloodlines.

"Instead, the focus shifted into subtly engaging eugenics once again and hybridizing humans so that they can remain at the top, in power, and create a world that better suits them. They feel entitled to do this *for the greater good.* Pay attention to that phrase. Keep that in mind as you watch the news.

"Please stay with me because this is not an inevitably tragic ending for Germany, the U.S., or any other country in the world.

"I need to know that you have a higher understanding of death so that you can hear what Edith has to say. Do you have any questions?"

"Hundreds, actually," Nate said looking annoyed. "You are saying that the U.S. and other countries have been interested in space to potentially create a military presence and to conduct economic trade for corporations who want to mine minerals and get other commodities for profit. And they think that is okay without considering who lives out there or who they may be intruding upon. Is everything theirs for the taking? Are they entitled to take whatever they want from the Solar System yet they can shoot down craft that comes into their space?"

"Yes, you are seeing the picture clearly," Gilda answered matter-of-factly, "Maybe I am getting you up to speed faster than you'd like. Sorry, Nate. I apologize for thrusting a multitude of facts and historical perspectives on you. I don't know how much time we have for this conversation. That's why I am rushing. You also need to hear from Edith."

"Okay," Nate said as he looked in Edith's direction.

"Nate, in a civilian capacity, I joined the U.S. military space program as an American-born daughter of German immigrants. I was aware of the broad scope of the military's space and advanced weapons programs. My dream was to work in a project that was going to get us into the cosmos sooner than later. But my job turned out differently than I envisioned. With a masters degree in quantum physics, I was discouraged and frustrated that I was pigeonholed into the role of an administrative assistant.

"Adding to my misery, the labs and research were surreptitious and corrupted by voracious appetites for wealth and power. I tried to see it otherwise but increasingly I sat in its midst, in despair and awe of the hubris and callousness that infected those in command. What could I do? Luckily, I had the opportunity for a reality adjustment and a fresh perspective when I encountered ETs on a visit to relatives in my home country. I was not abducted, nor did I get to see the inside of their craft. I felt an immediate bond and trusted them implicitly. They gave me information in the form of a chip embedded painlessly under the skin on my wrist. They told me to meet a person in New Mexico in the United States. When I arrived, the person welcomed me and knew exactly what to do next. A certain person in the U. S. military needed the information in my chip, which lifted out of my skin effortlessly upon my command. That was one of many inexplicable surprises I encountered in working with them.

"By that time, I realized that Nazis, greedy corpo-rations, and wealthy people's interests were infused into the military-industrial complex. These ETs wanted to get vital information to a partic-ular benevolent human. I became the courier. Thus began my dual life with the military and the ETs—enabling specific people to get crucial data from ETs without direct contact, which may have been compromised through surveillance. I worked with these benevolent ETs for many years.

"New Mexico is where the Ebens from a nearby star system crashed their craft in the desert in the 1940's. Ebens is an ac-ronym for *extraterrestrial-biological entities*. The area is known for a multitude of ET sightings.

"This is where you come in. I know that you and Sophia had a strange encounter on a boat during your honeymoon. I'd like to provide some details that you may not be aware of."

Nate's eyes welled with tears, anger, and disbelief.

Looking at Gilda piercingly, he asked, "What did Sophia tell you?"

Reassuring him, Gilda said, "This is the first time I've heard about it."

Nate listened as he stared blankly at the floor; his body rigid, his jaw clenched.

Edith took a moment for Nate to calm himself and asked, "Nate, was it traumatic for you? It was not meant to be."

"No, it's not traumatic," he answered while staring out the window. "Sophia and I agreed never to tell anyone. I felt betrayed and pissed that she would tell Gilda. What happened that night was unsettling for me, that's for sure. I've never experienced anything like it. Nothing in meditation, nothing in sacred sites in India, or elsewhere... Nothing compares to that. This is deeply meaningful for me. It wasn't some tropical adventure. It was way more than that."

Edith let him sit with his memories and the shock of her knowledge of the event.

She asked in a sympathetic, kind tone, "Have you recorded the encounter?"

He nodded saying that Sophia journaled it. Tucked carefully in their bedside table, the event reminded them of something intimate within themselves that they never wanted to lose touch with.

"I would love to hear the story, if it's okay." Edith was prodding him and his look of frustration met her gentle smile as she added, "Then I can share what I know about it."

Nate told her where to find the journal and said in a soft, raspy voice, "These are Sophia's words, and they echo my feelings. My heart feels open to you, Edith, yet incredibly vulnerable. Under the circumstances, I feel like it's okay to read her journal. I think Sophia would agree. Go ahead..."

Sophia's words captivated the listeners as Edith read the journal out loud:

Nate is unreservedly at home in the ocean. Growing up near the Eastern Seaboard, the ocean was his second home. I trust his capacity to navigate there, literally with my life. We've sailed, rowed, and swam; always feeling the awe and beauty of the vastness of the Pacific Ocean, in particular. Hawaii was the perfect place for us to make our marriage vows. And then we wanted to sail to an island near Maui where we were staying. Sailing late afternoon seemed like a sacred way to spend time alone on the ocean. I was fine with spending the night camping in honeymoon bliss and sailing back the next day, especially with his confidence and perfect weather as an extra layer of comfort.

Since we knew that there was always a slight chance for a storm to develop suddenly that time of year, and being extra careful, we took precautions. As we approached the island, we realized that a night of lovemaking under the stars, on a remote island, was not going to happen. We got the alert to head back immediately. And we did. The oars replaced our sails when the wind became treacherous. We knew that we were in trouble. And to make matters worse, we lost contact with shore. That had never happened to Nate before. Without freaking out, he became laser-focused on rowing.

I held the compass and was navigating through the rain while Nate, with well-honed muscles, handled the oars.

The waves were getting stronger, and I could glance back and see that he was getting tired. Yet above us intermittently, I could see the starlit canopy of eternal space.

My fears grew in intensity but seeing the endless dome of the night sky sporadically peeking through the clouds above us brought relief from the grip of terror clenching my heart. The waves were becoming treacherous because of intense winds. Terror arose when Nate had to carefully navigate the bigger swells.

To my surprise, I looked back and a creature which I'd never seen, was seated behind Nate with a hand on each shoulder. As I glanced back at my navigation tool, to keep us going in the right direction, gentle hands touched each of my shoulders.

Behind Nate, I saw a blue being with small scales covering his entire body. He was definitely taller than Nate with a calm, gentle face. And when I felt the smaller hands on my shoulders something beyond its beauty and outer appearance became clear. I realized that I was being touched supportively and lovingly by the female of this species.

My consciousness shifted instantaneously from fear to serenity. I fell into a space of pure love, which couldn't be directed or controlled. Feelings of appreciation and deep communion with the ocean arose. Nate later called the feeling, "nurturing yet powerful." It was like a nourishing galactic female energy and a supportive cosmic male energy joined us, to guide and support us in elevating our inner strength to higher levels of frequency. They were not there to save us; rather, to be there with us as we embarked on our journey to shore.

Both of us experienced the touch of pure love and it was a power beyond comprehension. Running from the top of my head, through my body like strong, orgasmic pulsations, it flowed out through my feet and continued back to my head like a toroidal field of never-ending energy.

Navigation became a soft focus for me rather than intense. I was so in-the-moment that I couldn't look at Nate. Yet I was aware of him, the parting of the rain clouds, the starlit dome coming into view above us, and the destination ahead.

I recall the storm subsiding and seeing the twinkling lights of land ahead. As we moved across the tumultuous ocean, with Nate rowing under continued, brutal wind conditions, my bliss sustained itself and my consciousness expanded, even more.

I do not recall exactly when and how we got the boat to shore. I remember walking in a wobbly fashion while feeling a hand on my right shoulder. Nate was being carried by the larger, blue being. His body was limp from exhaustion. Thankfully, he was okay.

The gentle being placed Nate in the backseat of the car and found towels to make him comfortable. I trusted this being completely and I let him run a small device down Nate's body from his head to his feet.

Still feeling immense love, I turned and found myself face to face with love in the form of the female blue being. Her facial expression was serene, her gestures fluid, and through a natural form of telepathy, I spoke to her.

Asking her where she was from, she pointed to a star cluster on the horizon which I recognized as Alpha Centauri. When our eyes met, she smiled to confirm that was her star.

Why was she in the middle of the Pacific Ocean? She said that they've come here on and off for a long time. Why? I wondered if they specifically help humans at sea.

She told me that they would help anyone, in any place. Their bigger mission was to help benevolent humans to become more technologically advanced to bring clean water, clean air, and free energy to this magnificent planet. And they work with elders of shamanic cultures to preserve the critical nexus in this region that bridges the seen and unseen, the particle and quantum domains of the planet. She gave me a mystical vision of the Pacific Ocean as an ancient epicenter of pure love and sublime vibrations at the hub of a subtle, complex web of high frequency light and mesmerizing beauty.

They also work under the ocean in military bases but live in the water, which is natural for them.

She told me that people below the surface of the Earth go back and forth to their star, too. I wondered who she meant. Maybe people in the military? Under the Earth?

Because love for humanity was thoroughly established in her being, it wasn't something she had to purposefully work on. I felt that it was an aspect of who she was, an emanation of benevolent love. It was like being with love, in a pure, vibrating form.

As I stood looking at her, she extended her right arm, palm upward and I placed my left hand on top of her palm. As we connected this way, love took over my being. There was nothing else—only pure love. No time. No space. I was a brilliant love-vibration. From that vibration, I could move and act, and even action was love itself. I don't know how long our connection lasted. It didn't matter. I'd experienced it and knew that for the rest of my life, I'd be affected by this pure love experience. I wanted to find ways to become established in it. Her parting words were, 'Hold still. Rest in silence. Nothing to do. Be steady. I love you.'

She guided me to the car where Nate was coherent, looked better, and he was thanking the male being. The words 'love, vibration, and stillness' were being exchanged between them. I could hear it telepathically.

And then I heard him say to Nate, 'I love you.' And Nate echoed it back to him in waves of vibration. I cried as I experienced the tenderness and the magnificent beauty of their exchange of love.

Extraordinary, powerful, life-changing; I don't know how else to describe what happened. We will never be the same people who traversed the Pacific Ocean on a starlit night. We were in search of finding a place to express love and found ourselves being love itself—riding the waves of the ocean of eternal, pure love to a safe harbor.

As Edith finished reading, Nate and Gilda remained quiet.

After a few minutes, Edith explained that she was not briefed by the military on the details of Nate's mysterious, oceanic encounter. Instead, many years before, the blue beings told her about it when she worked with them in the Pacific Ocean military bases. The only part that she knew was that there was an encounter between Sophia, Nate, and ETs. Recently one of them spoke to her about Nate and asked Edith to meet him. They spoke with kindness and admiration for him and although they were not predicting his immediate death, they wanted him to know that they would be with him when he crossed the threshold of this life to the next; joyfully acknowledging his contributions, admirable inner growth, and expansion in his life. They held him in great esteem and loved him inestimably.

Edith allowed for a long silence.

Nate looked forward, as though he could see through the wall in front of him and into a vast space beyond. "I understand why you wanted to deliver their message to me. And yet, I want to tell Sophia about you, the blue beings, and what they told you.

"Believe it or not, the global corporations part in the secret space program, the Nazi legacy in global affairs, and the wholesale indoctrination of humanity is more disturbing and frustrating for me than talking about death."

"Based on the message you received from the blue beings and your experience with them," said Edith, "can you see a clue about how to handle these seemingly insurmountable issues?"

"I get it," he said. "It all comes down to our frequency and unicity. Simple and yet not so easy to explain to most people."

Edith smiled and nodded.

"Nate, there is something that I'd like to know. Did you recognize those beings in the boat with you? Were they familiar?"

"Yes, Sophia and I knew we'd been with them in some other time and space," he said. "They were intimately familiar. That's another reason we couldn't speak about it. Who would understand? The blue being who stood with me felt like family—like a brother. Very familiar. Very close."

"Nate, your soul is beautiful," Edith said, "and I bet it longs to ascend even more as your journey ascends past this life. They said you've been with them and done some incredible work here on Planet Earth and they love you very much.

"They will be there when you cross over to welcome you back to the field of eternal expansion. After some time, you will move on, higher into the light of who you are. Where you go next, of course, is part of your soul's unfolding mystery. I am delighted we met. And thank you for letting me deliver their message."

Nate looked at Edith intensely as he asked, "The female blue being told Sophia that they help benevolent people in the military. And you've been with them for a couple of decades. Why does the public not know about these ET species in underwater military bases? And why don't we all have access to the high-tech devices and applications that they share with the military and related corporations? And where are the advanced technologies for clean food, air, and water? Help me to understand this."

"Nate, those are all great questions. The answers are linked to corporations who work with the military and who prefer to keep profits, control, and power for themselves. There are extremely wealthy people all over the world who are vying for power to own a piece of the business aspect and property rights before it goes public. Some of it is greed, pure and simple, and some would like to keep the masses in poverty, fear, and confusion so *the few* can enjoy the fruits that belong to *the many.* Does that scenario sound like history repeating itself? It's complex, Nate.

"For over ten thousand years, leadership on Planet Earth has not been virtuous nor magnanimous. That's not coming from a position of judgment. It's a matter of checking the results and noticing how the working class lived and often died, in large numbers. From feudalism in the Middle Ages to Nazis, the U.S.S.R. and Maoism, were the leaders benevolently upholding the natural right of human beings to be free? Why do they believe they should rule the world, according to their personal standards and principles?

"There is always a perverted directive to keep the masses divided and clawing at each other while the upper echelon rules both sides of the war. It's a phantom lurking above us, laughing all the way to the bank as they revel in insatiable appetites for ever-elusive, global domination. War is always the focus; not ending poverty, or creating free energy, and certainly not seeding unity. It's all about chaos, war, and creating slaves for the power-hungry few who seek to own Gaia's limited resources, and her supplies of energy like oil and gas, too.

"However, something is happening on a frequency level. All over the world, people are finding out the truth of our history and they are looking at the top of the food chain to the owners of banks, major stockholders of corporations, and leaders of global organizations to unveil who is behind the curtain pulling the strings. The distractions are falling away and now the working class is peering behind the curtain to discover the structures that hold the vast majority of the population under the influence of a small group of wealthy people. Within the working class an incomprehensible tidal wave of frequency is rising which is stronger than the waves you battled that night on the ocean.

"The blue beings that brought you safely to shore are doing the same for humanity as we speak. They shower this planet with love. And there are others helping as well, both here and underground. They are not going to save humanity. No one can sit back and rely on them. In your case, in the ocean that night, the blue beings supported your highest frequency. You were supported by them; not saved. And remember that it was you, dear Nate, who took to the oars and did the work of getting you and your beloved back to shore. They were there to extend high frequencies, and again, remember that no one saved you. You saved yourself. That is their primary message for you.

"This is a reminder that if you can take a boat across the dangerous waves of a vast ocean, you can steer your soul across the ocean from this reality to the next shore, with absolute con-fidence and with the assurance that you are not alone.

"I am delighted and honored to meet you, Nate. And I am hap-py that you have your dear wife to process all of this with. I can feel the bond you have with her. With their permission, you can tell Sophia. However, they wanted me to speak to you directly...

"Why don't we take a break," Edith said tenderly. "Rest now, dear soul. We will talk again soon."

She helped him into bed and stood nearby as he drifted gently into sleep.

CHAPTER 15
INDIAN CHILDREN AND BLUE BEINGS

Sophia entered the house looking relaxed and rejuvenated. She greeted Edith and Gilda and said, "Thank you for giving me that chance to unwind a bit."

Edith smiled. "Why don't you and Gilda sit outside. This is one of those rare perfect weather days. I can stay here with Nate."

Gilda and Sophia nodded with childlike smiles and walked outside to enjoy the warmth and nourishment of their friendship.

Sophia closed her eyes softly and sat like the statue of a goddess in repose. Serenity and inward focus permeated the air. After a few minutes, she leaned forward saying, "I had a memory as I walked today that reminded me of you. Want to hear it?"

Gilda nodded.

"When we were in India, I met a child in the local village. She was about ten years old. Wherever I travel, it's the children who capture my heart. Like most of the girls we saw her age, she wore her long hair in pig tails. Her gorgeous eyes were like big globes of light radiating joy from the inside out. She had a slender frame and was dressed in her school uniform, which was a navy blue cotton skirt and an impeccably starched, white shirt. She moved with gentleness and assuredness and I noticed that her *curiosity* was mixed with the natural fear of a stranger. As she assessed me, she was playing with a coin.

"Once she discerned that it was safe to speak with me, she showed me the coin. Her face was so bright. And she said, 'This is one rupee! Look! It is like you and me! On one side is you and the other is me. No matter what side of the coin we may be, we are still one rupee.

"Papa says that I am one side of the coin, and he is the other. Together we are a *whole* rupee! And it's the same for you and me. You are one side of this coin, and I am the other. In that way, we are always together as one coin that cannot be separated.'

"We were standing by the Ganges, and she looked out across it, her eyes filled with wonder. This simple way of explaining our unicity, our oneness at the core of our being, became incredibly real for me in that moment."

Sophia stopped and stared at the endless expanse above her and then down at the Earth, gently creating a bridge from infinity to matter. She sat still for a moment before continuing.

"Without any hesitation, the child reached out, took my hand, and we walked a few strides. She stopped and pointed to the river, flowing with its lethal monsoon season current. As she spoke, I wrote down her words.

> *If you or I fall into Mother Ganges and don't come out, we will always be together because we remain the other half for each other. It never ends. Isn't that wonderful?*

> *This happened to Nanni, I loved her and she loved me. We watched the stars at night. She and my father looked at the night sky when he was young.*

> *Nanni told stories about freedom fighters, taught me how to cook, and how to keep seeds for our garden. Nanni was wise. She is still with me. She says if I ever miss her, I can look at the stars, and she will be twinkling above me, forever. Even when her ashes went into Mother Ganges, I knew she was my other half of the coin and I talk to her every night.*

Nanni said that I belong to her, and she belongs to me because we are made of the same, pure love. She says pure love is the essence of the love I feel for my brother. Pure love is the Essence that creates my family's bond. Pure love can't die. But we forget when we grow up. So she wanted me to always remember the coin and that we belong to each other in pure love.

"This little girl was adorable. Adding to her endearing charm, she began to spontaneously dance for me. It was a regional dance which she said was in praise of Oneness, the unity of everything.

"I wondered how this child had imbibed such deep wisdom and esoteric concepts. Nate pointed out that parenting in this village is different than we are accustomed to—the little girl was not taught to obey rules and to learn mathematical formulas to excel in school. Instead, she was taught basics in public education and at home she learned to think critically, to feel deeply, and honor the Essence of herself and others.

"It's a different way of learning. As this child shared more about Nanni, it was clear that nature was the focus of her learning. Nature doesn't intellectualize. Nature is pure love in action in a diverse yet intricate world order. Nate and I came to her village for several days and I have to say that evenings became incredibly enchanting for us. After dinner, everyone sat on their porch on swings that were made of a platform which could seat at least six and sometimes they squeezed up to ten family members together with a lot of giggles and laughter, gliding contentedly as they sang.

"The amazing part was that one family would start to chant or sing a song and their neighbors chimed in. They continued for well over an hour. It was like a flock of birds chirping in harmony. I felt this community's unicity as they sang together like an evening choir. I learned the Sanskrit lyrics and joined in their singing. I felt a mesmerizing focus, experiencing unity with everything and everyone in the universe and beyond.

"Very naturally the singing subsided, and families became more quiet and started telling their more intimate stories, epic adventures from their culture, or sat cuddled together in silence. I was unaccustomed to the silent space, and it took a couple of evenings for me to be at ease communing with others in a voiceless space of love and togetherness. But it was rejuvenating, calming, and it felt healing right down to my soul.

"One night as the silence descended, the little girl, my other half of the coin, came to see me with her brother. He was about sixteen years old and was not tall but exuded a strong presence. His eyes were huge and riveting. I felt the energy of an ancient sage and the power of a confident being of immeasurable strength. Yet there was not a shred of bravado nor any teenage insecurity. This was no ordinary child. His voice was kind and gentle. He extended his hand in greeting. As we touched, I felt a spark of knowing. He greeted me courteously, 'I heard that you met my sister, Lalli. I am Kabir. It is nice to meet you.'

"Gilda, I could not believe that I had not asked the little girl for her name! I was so engrossed in my conversation with her—I mean, to me she was just the other half of my coin. Nate arrived back from an evening walk and I introduced him to the two kids. The young sage, Kabir, spoke so confidently and made direct eye contact whenever he spoke. He told us that Nanni never left her village and could not read or speak English, yet she was infinitely wise. Although she died, they always felt her presence nearby. Then, he shared his morning meditation with us.

"He said that in his meditation that morning, he saw me in the stars with Nanni. Because of that auspicious sign, he was drawn to come meet me. He asked if we were interested in knowing more about their family.

"Of course we were *very interested.* He told us that his grandmother was from a lineage of people who study ancient secrets preserved in words, symbols, and art etched on stone in sacred places in the region. They contain secrets about life, the origins of humans, and animals on Earth—and comprehensive understandings about the stars in the heavens and the Earth below. He said their family roots reached back many generations, and their spiritual wisdom was handed down verbally from one generation to the next.

"I was taken aback by his ability to launch into esoteric ideas with total conviction and ease. He said that the physical body vibrates in slower levels of frequency, which allows us to live in the world of matter, and if our body ages into frailty, it's less capable of housing the strong, higher frequencies of the soul. He talked about the levels of a sentient being—starting with the physical body and including what he described as the mental and emotional fields, the spirit, and a *causal* layer that is immensely subtle and infinitely wise.

"I was amazed and I asked how he learned to convey these complex topics. Apparently, a local teacher helped him to find the English words for this higher wisdom so that he could speak about it. His command of the English language was astonishing. I couldn't help but be enthralled, so I asked him how he learned unimaginable amounts of details about subtle layers and levels of experience.

"'It was Nanni,' Kabir answered. 'She taught me all of this, and more. I learned about the night sky and I learned how to elevate my frequencies, as taught to her by my ancestors. She taught me the secrets of pure love and the coin. Our community in which you stand knows how to flood the Earth and all planets with love frequency. We do that regularly.'

"In high spirits, he pointed straight towards Alpha Centauri on the horizon and said, 'We send love to them; they shower it on us in return.' Pointing in the direction of the Pleiades, he named several stars and said that his family also connected with that star system. He talked about Orion and Sirius rising in the predawn, as the monsoon season comes to an end. He said he was sharing all of this because Lalli thought I would like to know about the *unified* and *wondrous* nature of the whole universe and his meditation confirmed her suspicion.

"I told him that was true and that I would love to know more of what they learned from Nanni. His seemed very happy about this and said they would return the next evening at dusk as the stars were rising to share some more.

"That was the beginning of a special friendship," Sophia said. "We nestled together by starlight on the family swing for three nights and heard the most fascinating stories imaginable. The crazy part is that when I returned home, I researched what Kabir told us. I found that planetary archeology and anthropology confirmed the lore and wisdom from that young sage, their Nanni, and their family lineage. I think of them as *wisdom keepers.*

Sophia stopped talking. "Gilda, is this interesting to you?"

"Are you kidding? Please continue."

"Okay, there's more, which relates to my conversations with you. On the day you told me about the ETs, I had to end our time together when the temple bell rang. But I've been wanting to come back to the subject of ETs and related mysteries.

"Kabir referenced an ancient artifact. And his Nanni seemed to know it intimately. It contains specific codes that will be relevant to humanity in the next decade or so. You mentioned that the ET's told you about some kind of ancient artifact. I wondered if Kabir was talking about the same thing. He said knowing how to use the artifact could save humanity but he did not give us any details about its location nor how to identify it. He only told us it was essential for our survival and higher evolution and we need to find it by 2045. You told me that the ET specified that same year when he told you about the urgency for finding the artifact. That is a mystery in itself. Nate and I have no idea what he was talking about.

Sophia paused, shaking her head, smiling in amazement. "I am astounded…"

"And if that wasn't enough to throw me for a loop, Kabir shared another surprise: Nanni talked to him about the connection of pyramids on Mars and Earth that were built tens of thousands of years ago, maybe longer. He wouldn't say how she obtained this information. It seemed like she was a local *oracle*, like they used to have in Greece. Her intuitive, esoteric gifts were trusted implicitly by her family and their community.

"Nanni taught him that many eons in the past, the encoded artifact was working its frequency-magic on Earth to prevent several terrible cataclysms, but over twelve thousand years ago, humans became full of pride because of their technological advances and stopped using it. That's when another cataclysm occurred. Floods raged twice over a thousand year cycle. Maybe they lost the encoded technology in the aftermath of that large-scale cataclysm.

"Kabir talked a little about the benevolent ETs who brought this technology to Earth. Apparently, one of its properties was to heighten humanity's capacity to integrate and emit the frequencies of higher wisdom and pure love and this attracted varying advanced cultures from our galaxy to Earth. Each ET race brought their unique technologies and ways of perceiving life. All of this helped humanity rapidly evolve in intelligence and culture.

"ETs settled on mountains and deserts like Egypt, Africa, and Russia, others went to North and Central America.

"Kabir described portals. He said there are natural portals all over the planet where time and space morph and through which humans can travel easily into the solar system, IF such a human lives consistently in a high frequency. He said that many people, including children, are connecting with ETs through dreams. And some ETs even bring humans to their own planets, but that is rare.

"Nate was taking notes frantically. He always kept pen and paper ready to jot down anything he wanted to explore later. So a lot of what I am sharing is captured in his journals.

"Etched in my psyche forever is another short visit with Kabir. I recall his eyes, unusually grave and serious. It was after a monsoon had completely saturated the earth and throughout the conversation he would pause and stare into the rain-drenched ground. After one such pause, he looked at me with mesmerizing eyes as he told me where I fit into this cosmic, mysterious history.

"I was stunned. It felt like truth was roaring towards me full force. Spontaneously, my body became upright, and I felt compelled to pay attention. My brain was wondering why he said this but the rest of me was receptive and quiet.

"It was my DNA, he said, which had been advancing at warp speed for millions of years. Nate's, too, was from a similar, ancient species. Nate was writing all this down.

"Kabir told us that right now, the sad reality is that there are enough people on the planet to turn everything around but instead they are being manipulated into thinking they should hate each other. He said that invisibly, polarization is alive and well. He called it a 'sad state of separateness' and self-destructive.

"And then he reached out with his left hand and he touched my right palm. Then with his right hand, he touched Nate's left palm. High voltage energy streamed into our palms and an almost overwhelming force connected us. We stood frozen by this electrical charge. He spoke only two words, pure love—then he let the energy cascade between us like a wild torrent of vast, unimaginable bliss.

"He spoke in Sanskrit for a minute and seemed to merge into a bliss-state. His face was radiant, and the intense love energy saturated us with its vibrant beauty and stillness.

"His words are etched in my mind:

You will know when you can and must act. Nanni says your work is to raise your frequency and become stabilized there. She is standing behind you. Her frequency is so high that you likely cannot see her. The day will come when you will be able to see her form, the beings from the stars, and even more. First, you must recognize that you are pure love and that you are the entire universe, and the universe is you. It is in you and all around you. You cannot be separated from anyone or anything. It's impossible because you, the universe, and everything in it are unique forms of vibrating frequency within a common infinite field of knowable information.

"This took Nate and me a few minutes to digest and Kabir was silent for a while to let us do so. Then he continued. I've kept Nate's notes near my computer so I could remember. I'll read it to you.

Let your ideas, beliefs, and concepts of the mind rest.

Learn instead to listen to the wisdom of your physical body as it aligns with your emotional body and mental body. That trinity is an important technology.

Sophia, you will enter a pyramid with the sublime frequencies that your DNA is aligned with.

This pyramid is not in Egypt or a foreign country.

Recall the unicity gene. Watch for the magic that unfurls when unicity is integrated into societies and human hearts.

You will marvel when humans align with being both sides of a coin. This will revitalize the elevation of collective consciousness into something never before experienced on this planet. The aggregation of human consciousness into unicity is the paradigm shift.

Nanni is dancing. This is auspicious!

"Nate was writing with warp speed to capture every word of this mind-blowing prophecy.

"On one hand it sounded amazing and wonderful, but we also felt something ominous. We realized that we'd have to accept the responsibility to do whatever it took each day to raise our frequency, relying on higher wisdom, and consistent expression of the unicity gene. Kabir's description of it feels like it's our collective superpower.

"I hope that wasn't too much to download. I haven't had anyone with whom I could share Kabir's words. Thank God that Nate scribed the conversation. He and I poured through his notes many times and we still do. This is what led me to study space travel, the unified field theory of quantum physics, ancient history, and partly why I am so interested in your stories."

Gilda raised her eyebrows. "This has been captivating and delightful. Now I know where to go in our next conversation. We didn't meet by accident, Sophia. I already sensed that. Now I am sure of it.

"I'll see you tomorrow."

CHAPTER 16
OWNING THE NAME AND AUTHENTIC HISTORY

Sophia sat by the bedroom window reflecting on her morning conversation with Gilda and making notes in her journal about Kabir and Nanni.

Soft, afternoon light was streaming in, illuminating her leather journal which was filled with insights and feelings from ages ago. It sat on the edge of a table soaking up warm sunbeams. She stroked the familiar cover softly, picked it up and held it to her heart. Reading an entry from many decades earlier, Sophia finished reading with the same confused look on her face as the day she wrote it.

She sent a quick text to Grace asking her if she had to time to talk, but Grace was busy.

When Nate finished his afternoon exercise, Sophia told him that she wanted to explore why she felt it was so important to recall stories like the one of Kabir. As always, Nate was more than happy to explore her inner world with her.

This particular journal entry from long ago kept surfacing in her mind all day—it was about her name. She read and reread it, but with no further insights. Finally, settled into the comfort of the sun-drenched room, Sophia found a tattered bookmark in the journal and read it to Nate:

Father Greg was always our go-to counsel for guidance when I was young. I remember my mother said he could walk on water but didn't want to show off. I still smile at that thought. He was entirely devoted to Jesus and to being in service to his community.

In my twenties, I went to see him about recent discoveries about the early church by scholars and archeologists of the time; his response surprised me. I was not expecting him to tell me that someday I would learn things about global history and spirituality that would shake my faith. "Shake my faith" was an understatement.

He introduced me to two nuns who were well into their eighties, one Guatemalan and the other French. Both were well educated, sweet, and well-versed in the subject of ancient documents and early church history.

Sister Suzanne, the French nun, soft-spoken yet very confident, said that it is fine for Christians to be open to new information about the church. She pointed to the Shroud of Turin and the Nag Hammadi Library—rare documents dating back to the early days of Christianity discovered in a cave in Egypt in the 1940's.

Father Paul, Sister Suzanne, and Sister Mary Margaret meditated daily. They all studied at the University of Notre Dame, then in India, and other countries. They said that they grappled with knowing that we do not have complete knowledge. They were very much at peace with exploring and incorporating emerging information, open to unexpected discoveries, interested in discussing and integrating such things into their ecclesiastical world views and teachings. They were curious.

In the company of these wise women and my beloved Father Greg, I felt safe to listen to fresh, developing views. Yet the subject still felt a bit transgressive, and rattled me. If I shared what they told me with my family, I'd get chastised, called a liar, or worse, an idiot. I didn't know how to reconcile those things.

In one conversation we broached the possibility that there could be historical details about Jesus that have been hidden. Just thinking about that, something in me began to unfold like a rose bud. My whole body felt lighter and I wanted to know more.

Father Greg was crystal clear about Jesus' perfection and about the potentiality of humankind to elevate to that level of goodness. Still, he spoke about texts the Jesuit order held in secret, in the underground vaults of the Vatican. He believed these concealed texts were going to enter the light of day. At that time, he said the information was so important that they couldn't hold it secret for too much longer. He thought the magnitude of what would be unveiled might be too much for the general spiritual community to deal with, so perhaps that was why the church was reticent to share it. He said that I would learn something about the last supper and Judas. He did not say how he knew about this potential revelation but he sure was clear that it was true and inevitably would be made known to the public. I recall him mentioning the Vatican Vaults several times. Was the information in there? When I tried to inquire further, he simply said that I'd have to wait for the information to be revealed. He was not comfortable saying anything further about it.

He also asked me thought-provoking and interesting questions. 'If history is different than you think it is, does that change your relationship with Jesus? What is it about Jesus that drew you to him in the first place?'

When I think of Jesus, I feel pure love, without the shackles of conditioning. His only commandment was, "Love one another." And I realized that if the church could not verify different stories about what happened back then, and they chose a particular version to go with, well that's okay. If they purposefully manipulated history, those vaults he mentioned could perhaps show us the truth.

Father Greg said in the years to come we may speak Jesus' name differently, because in his native language in his own time he would have been called Yeshua. Scholars continue to pour over ancient texts, including the somewhat controversial Gnostic Gospels from the cave in Egypt, requiring some rethinking, a lot of research, and time to thoroughly translate the documents.

Sister Mary Margaret shared that Mary Magdalene is now believed to be a part of Yeshua's inner circle rather than a woman who hung out on the fringes. The documents from the Nag Hammadi Library of texts and other authenticated, ancient texts in her own words point in that direction. She was a prominent figure at that time. This sweet nun considered Magdalene's writings to be relevant for modern life. Several texts by her were found in the nineteenth and early twentieth centuries, written in different languages. That indicates her words were likely shared more widely than previously assumed and must have been important at that time. Her writings were not especially esoteric, super subtle, or full of mystical rituals. They were about a gradual process of human consciousness transforming into and integrating fully with its Essence. Her wisdom appears to have been revered in her lifetime. What fascinated me about the different copies of these texts is that they are identical and each one is missing the first several pages. Why would this part of her writings be intentionally taken out? Maybe we will find out someday.

Sister Margaret added that women did not have the same status as men in the early church, so finding Mary's words was provocative and important. According to history, in the early church, women were vital to evangelism: like Monica getting her son, Saint Augustine, on board, or Emperor Constantine's mother getting him baptized. The list of important women in the early church is extensive yet we know little about them. It makes sense because history and religious texts were written by men for the Roman elite, all male, who consistently refer to women as unworthy of positions of teaching or even participation in the church.

I read historical accounts of the time and learned that women could only write poetry, and few were educated enough to do that. Their poetry is the only true account we have of their perceptions and experience of a male dominated culture; in it we can see how fully controlled and indoctrinated they were, to the point of self-loathing and complete submission. They were supposed to be devoted wives and mothers, maybe oracles, if it suited their husband—who often was older than her by a decade or so. Concubines were common for the men to purchase as slaves for personal pleasure as a part of their household and we forget that women—including the wives who had to put up with concubines—often did not believe they had rights or could speak up without ending up in hell.

Reading these accounts was shocking and heart wrenching for me. I imagined having to accept Nate's concubines and be constantly told that I am not worthy, while Yeshua's divine words fade from memory and history—becoming increasingly censored and burned.

Many of the texts found in the cave in Egypt point to the direct experience of connection to Essence. After Jesus died, the powerful people at the time had a problem with this new Christian religion that espoused direct experience. If everyone had a direct relationship with Jesus or God, it would undermine current social structures (keeping them in power). Would they become independent and threaten the power of the Emperor? Would there be chaos? And even more problematic, might they buck societal norms altogether and allow a woman's teaching to be disseminated? As the early church was forming, these questions were equally relevant to those seeking to codify and legitimize their new religion.

Sister Mary Margaret seemed happy that church scholars were willing to consider all of this new information. She was optimistic that a growing number of younger religious academics wanted to research the texts in a wider conversation with their peers without ecclesiastical bias.

For some reason, Father Greg was convinced that further disclosure would happen within the next ten years. Although they wouldn't share details of what would be revealed, they all wanted me to be prepared and consider my relationship to Jesus and my commitment to connecting to the Essence of my soul. I wondered what they knew that I did not. I reflected on the questions that Father Greg asked me: "If history is different than you think it is, does that change your relationship with Jesus? What is it about Jesus that drew you to him in the first place?"

Father Greg, who knew me since childhood, asked me another question: "Will you own your name, Sophia?"

Father Greg and the nuns said that texts of immeasurable consequence from that Egyptian cave described a uniquely courageous, benevolent woman who was on a mission of unfathomable magnitude whose name was Sophia. She was not only the Creator Aspect of the Divine Intelligence and Perfection behind everything everywhere, but she also represented primordial wisdom and lived forever as pure love frequency. Bravely and magnanimously, she left her cozy home, living in bliss at the center of the Milky Way. That fits with my mother's story that Sophia was the star in the center of the galaxy—in the Pleiades.

Sophia set out to bring life to the Earth for a myriad of life forms, too innumerable to count. This remarkable world would be endless in possibilities. Its inhabitants, formed from eternal perfection, would have the gift of self-awareness. Their material form would arise from the unified field of potentiality, and therefore, they would remain indelibly linked to all other forms that arose from the field. With self-awareness, they could know who they were at their core—a gorgeous point of light in a sea of perfect light.

Sophia boldly dared to cross over the subtle realms from pure Essence into form. This had never been done in order to initiate a world. However, as the creator aspect of the Divine Intelligence and Perfection, she was unlimited and totally free to birth an unimaginable world into being. So she was confident and remained in bliss.

Father Greg told me that I would experience the qualities of my namesake as I let go of the constructs of my mind as the basis for absolute truth. My heart would have to be my guide. I would have to move from looking to authorities and teachers to relying on my inner sense as my guide. Learning how to consistently communicate with infinite information that is subtle, yet real, must become a part of my life. He called it "intuitive reciprocity with the infinite field." I had no idea at the time that he was studying quantum science.

He said that I was Sophia and that we all are. We are pure and whole. We lack nothing and are, in fact, "inseparable from the infinite field of all possibilities." We create our life, but we forget or don't "fully trust" that aspect of ourselves.

As matter, we vibrate slowly, but as Sophia, we vibrate immeasurably fast. As Sophia we are wildly free to create from endless possibilities, with boundless joy. And we are right at the center of the cosmos, shining brightly like Sophia, the gorgeous star.

The ancient Greeks had another story about her in which she was a woman who loved her husband very much. Sophia and her husband referred to themselves as Zeus and Hera, but Zeus and Hera were at the top of the Greek god-goddess hierarchy and humans were forbidden from using their *names. The deities were angry and insulted that Sophia and her hubby saw themselves on the same level as the highest ranking god and goddess. Zeus, a notorious hot-head, became enraged and launched a lightning bolt that killed Sophia's husband while he travelled at sea. Sophia was so devastated she jumped into the ocean to be with her beloved and they both perished.*

Meanwhile, the other Greek gods had admired the tender-hearted love-struck humans, who had always expressed love and kindness abundantly in their community and towards each other. Because of this, despite Zeus' anger at the pair, the other gods put their heads together and decided to turn them into Kingfishers, special birds who could spread pure love everywhere as they flew through the heavens.

My mother told this tale. In it, Sophia's name was Alcyone—my middle name.

Mom gave me two reasons to pay close attention to this story.

Sophia paused as delicate, cleansing tears flowed. For a few moments, she held her hands crossed gently over her chest.

Nate said tenderly, "You've told me that when the fragile, glass crust over your heart shatters, the weight of higher truth and elevated frequencies pour in. I wish I could hold you right now and wipe away your tears. I am here for you, always.

"Would you be willing to own *Sophia*, once and for all? I can see the answer is important to you. It's not just a myth or fairy tale that your mother told you. As you were reading your journal, your voice became deeper and steadier; I could feel your soul slowly imbibing the words on a deeper level than ever before. What does it mean to embody Sophia?"

"Thank you for asking the perfect question, Nate." She took a deep breath in. "I want to genuinely explore my name without reserve. My mother said that she had a different name picked out for me before I was born. But when I was born, she had an evocative dream and immediately felt *Sophia Alcyone* suited me perfectly. In her dream, she was sitting on that radiant star within the magnificence of the cosmos, and she heard a voice whispering my name, Sophia... Alcyone. Upon hearing it, she became energized and filled with optimism, bliss, and ecstatic love. She also felt indescribable peace.

"When I was young, she often told me the story of my name. And sometimes late at night when she was upset, she'd go outside to gaze at that special star that comforted and inspired her. She'd thank that point of starlight for emanating its dynamic light and healing her aching heart. Then she could fall asleep easily without any resistance from her disturbed mind or burdened heart.

"My mother rarely opened up to me. I never forgot her words when she told me about that, but I didn't let myself fully absorb the meaning and depth of what she said until I was older. Now, from within me, something is stirring that is liberating and bold. With that force supporting me, I am ready to explore, create, and follow my heart to discover on a really deep level who Sophia is. I want to claim all of her, including the mystical, creative parts."

She stopped, and then in a burst of passionate feeling went on. "I've spent too much time doing things that other people should be doing! Driving myself to be competent and make my mark in the world but not doing what comes naturally to me, not doing what aligns with my soul! I always doubted, always thought mysticism and connection with the unseen were not acceptable, not relevant enough to share, vital enough to have immense value. Darn it, Nate! I am mystical down to my toes! I have to admit that. I need to find ways to let THAT be in charge, not stuff it away in an inner closet like those atrocious clothes my aunt would give me for my birthday that I would never wear—like that scarf that was bootlegged out of a foreign country because of the animal pelt—I almost threw up!

"I don't want to do what someone else thinks I should do, or have what someone else thinks I should have... I've let this bottle up inside for way too long... It's like I reached the boiling point in my capacity to deny who I am... a wild mystic who loves what cannot be seen but can be known and felt within waves of ecstasy. If there are any aspects of me that defy cultural norms—the social or religious rules that I've followed impeccably, without questioning them—my inner, wise rebel is now free to surface and release itself from those shackles... In the story, Sophia rocks boats unapologetically. With confidence and benevolence, she moves through life. With her in mind, I want to focus intensely on raising my frequency. Sophia, the Kingfisher, she's pure light and every molecule of her being knows that this is her nature—radical, pure light and love frequencies. My firm commitment to this next phase of my inner growth is secure with your love supporting me. Nate, do you realize that this makes you and I kingfishers, spreading love-bombs across the world forever? That story, it's working in me—I feel like this may be my purpose in life. I thought I needed something more specific but right now, this feels like enough. Maybe it's not what I do but how I do it. Thank you, Nate. Thank you for nudging me to speak about what is going on for me. My inner state is calling out for the limited, shy aspects in me to relax their grip so I can grow exponentially. In spite of the fact that this expanded state is not something I can understand with my mind, it's definitely a visceral process that is nourishing my entire body and all aspects of my mind. What comes next, who knows?"

Sophia finally slowed down, paused, and said in a more reflective tone, "I've always felt you were like a rock that I could lean against, even when my sweet rock pushed me to explore unfamiliar terrain within. No matter what happens, I will never take our relationship for granted and I appreciate you letting me speak about my revelations, even if it seems that I am rambling. What's really happening, is that I am processing the subtle aspects of the conversation. But enough talking. Are you ready for dinner now, my hero, my rock, and my best friend?"

Nate nodded with a soft, loving smile as Sophia headed for the kitchen.

As she was finishing her nightly routine, Sophia glanced at her phone. She'd forgotten to turn it on after her conversation with Nate. Grace had sent several texts saying that she was getting worried. The latest was, "Please call me or text to let me know that you and Nate are okay. Sorry I couldn't talk when you texted last night." Sophia typed, "All is well. I was overwhelmed by inner work and reading an old journal entry. Sorry to scare you. Call me when you can."

Within seconds, the phone rang, "Geez Louise! That scared me, but that's my issue not yours. What journal entry?"

Grace knew of the story in detail and had always thought the story of Sophia from the radiant star was profound. "And who wouldn't be captivated with a couple of lovestruck kingfishers spreading gazillions of heart sparkles all over the planet?" She asked playfully.

After a few minutes of teasing and sharing, they ended their conversation with the satiety of feeling filled to the brim with the power of their forever friendship.

The day continued as usual yet with a fresh awareness of the truth of Sophia as pure love, creativity, infinite possibility, and a beacon for others to find those qualities in themselves.

CHAPTER 17
KABIR AND THE PYRAMID

As Sophia approached her meeting spot with Gilda, her eyes were drawn to a huge oak tree whose branches were bursting with tiny buds. It seemed the little pods had formed overnight and awakened to a sunlit day which would hasten their grand opening.

Seeing Sophia in wonderment, Gilda asked, "Does this amazing process of nature's order and seasonal regularity cause you to wonder who is in charge of this planet?" She laughed and so did Sophia.

"Lately, I've been talking to Nate about something that stretches the boundaries of my comfort zone to the breaking point. It's a good thing for my evolution and terrible for my ego. What's making me crazy is the battle inside between old beliefs and the truth that I am beginning to experience. The world is more esoteric, mysterious, and unpredictable than I realized. What I thought was white is black and what I thought was up is down. It's like that. Beliefs are polarizing and keep me stuck. Feeling that battle inside allowed it to end. I feel more open-hearted right now. And yet, more vulnerable. Going forward, to keep the momentum going, I need to ask myself: How can I stay soft like I am now; pliable and flexible? No judgments or conclusions. Sorry, I am rambling..."

"My dear, it sounds like you crossed a big inner bridge," Gilda said. "Keep these transformational *ahas* safe and savor them. Intention is a big part of doing that. From my perspective, you've been openhearted and curious for a long time, yet like all of us, your mind is attached to the status quo. Life brought you to Kabir and you didn't dismiss him. From my experience, most people would not have taken the route you did: absorbing his words, doing further research, reflecting on what you discovered, and receiving the encounters with him as a life-gift. I am inspired by your grit and courage.

"And how is Nate?" She asked, in a quizzical tone—as though she had a sudden hunch to make this inquiry.

"It's the same every day… a little weaker. Having said that, he was able to have a long conversation with me, and as always, he was helpful. He's an amazing listener."

Gilda leaned forward with her usual interest and curiosity. "Tell me about it."

Sophia shared the whole story, including accepting the deep meaning of her name. When she finished, Gilda said enthusiastically, "This is beautiful! I was not sure with your Catholic background if you'd be open to things like this. Many people think those texts that were discovered last century are neither important nor authentic. The Church mostly disavowed them. How could they accept esoteric texts that basically say humans have a continuous, direct link to the divine? It's understandable. And moreover, accepting that the divine is within all of us, vibrating as light and frequency, is too esoteric for a lot of folks. Another reality check is that acceptance of those texts would cause church influence to slowly evaporate. Even now, eighty years after those texts were found to be authentic, they are not widely accepted.

"These ideas also confront personal beliefs about life and reality—which are very hard to let go of. Divesting of long-held convictions and understanding causes the brain to go haywire, invoking deep, primal fears.

"One of the things that is important about the teachings in those texts is that they point to how the unicity gene can activate within human physiology. Genes activate based on triggers from the environment, which can be toxic chemicals, flower essences, and high or low frequency emotions. Keep in mind that everything is frequency. Genes read and translate frequencies. How about that!

"Can we shift topics? I wanted to ask about Kabir today. Is that okay?"

Sophia settled comfortably into her chair, took a sip of tea, smelling the fragrance of Jasmine flowers drifting gently from her cup, delighting her senses. "Yes, you are always free to ask me anything. With you, I'm an open book."

They looked at each other tenderly, taking a moment to absorb the vibrations of friendship and nourishing unicity.

"Did you meet Kabir again, after that encounter? Did you speak again with Lalli?" Gilda asked.

"We met Kabir once more briefly. He said something that I didn't write down," Sophia said. "He said he loved us. I was deeply moved. Then he knelt down and drew sacred symbols in the soft, monsoon-soaked soil that we were standing on. I can still feel what it was like looking into the depths of his captivating eyes, penetrating every level of my being. As in prior conversations, he surprised me with a Kabir-truth-bomb, telling me I was chosen millennia ago by *the giants from the heavens* to come to Earth at this time. His message was so direct, but without any context it was just cryptic and confusing. I asked him why he was telling me this. And his answer sent chills running through my body in waves and my mind lost its ability to form thoughts. It was like time stood still. He said, 'For this life, you came with the codes still in you. Time doesn't matter. It's illusion. So don't think about how long you have held them. Realize they are there. At some point, you will have to acknowledge them or spiral down in frequency and suffer. When the time comes, remember I told you the codes are real.'

"Then he asked me:

Are you willing to break any interior dams that block wild excitement for the unknown?

Can you relax into infinity and expect the unexpected?

Can you let yourself be in awe of life, drenched in love every day?

"And then he said slowly, emphasizing each word: *Raise... your... frequency!*

"I can still feel it now, as though I'm right there with him. His words, and his delivery of them, shock my mind into silence. I still don't know what he was talking about. But I believe him.

"Nate and I walked away that day wondering about all of the possibilities in the quantum field. What is past, what is future, and how does the *now* fit into the past and future, especially if time is an illusion? Who are we? What is the field? How will we be able to adequately answer Kabir's questions?... such mind twisting enquiry. It was like he was shaking up our rigid beliefs and throwing out topics for us to explore.

"I never saw Kabir again. A friend told us that he passed away a couple of years later in *samadhi*—he went into meditation and didn't come out. He was like a child-sage, and a precious soul who blessed us immensely in the short time that we were with him. According to my friend, the night before he transitioned from his physical body, he drew an upside-down triangle. He said that there were billions of people on top, all capable of high frequency with the unicity gene ready to be expressed. And at the bottom were a few thousand of those who had no interest in raising frequency unless it gave them power over others. That frequency is what has started many wars. They resist the unicity gene and rely on their own mind instead.

"Kabir then looked at the people around him and said cryptically,

It won't last. It's over. The top of the pyramid is reversing. The masses of the human population are on top and they are feeling the call to activate their unicity gene. Sophia and Nate know how to bring two pyramids together to form the star. Sophia will have to be strong and confident to do this."

Sophia fell silent. Gilda looked down at the fresh dewy grass under her feet, not responding for a minute as though lost in thought and enjoying Mother Nature. Then she returned her gaze to Sophia, smiled and said, "He puts a piece of my puzzle together. Thank you. I had a feeling there was more to that story. Be sure to write it down. I can tell it's etched in your mind and heart but at least make notes."

Sophia looked at her surprised and said, "Ok. Tell me about your *missing puzzle piece.*"

"Well, let's see... where to start?" Gilda said. "I think I should jump back to the military base and the ET I told you about; the one who spoke with me telepathically. He used images. Once, he showed me a triangle with a crab in the middle. I researched what it might mean astronomically and discovered that it's a configuration *in the constellation of Orion.* The image had a feeling to it also—warmth, camaraderie, kindness, and wisdom.

It generated comfort in me whenever I saw it and when I looked closely, I could see little dancing stars in the shape of hearts emerging from the crab. Very strange.

"So, when you mentioned Kabir speaking of a triangle, it reminded me of this, and of Orion. The ET who spoke to me was from that constellation which rests on the celestial equator. It's easy to spot it in the night sky. He said those from the heavens were misunderstood. I'd heard of the great wars, the global flood, and all of that. I asked him about those events. He told me that within the constellation of Orion was the home star of one species who stayed behind in the flood on Earth.

"As you were telling your story, I realized those earthbound visitors from Orion are linked with their home star frequencies through the heart. Maybe the center of the triangle, the heart of Orion, was a portal through which advanced species could travel. Based on quantum physics, that's possible... and mind-boggling.

"If you dive into our planet's ancient history with an open mind, it's easy to see why high frequency beings would go home when a cataclysm happened or when their work here was completed to their satisfaction. They'd helped humans, likely as shamans in cultures all over the Earth, or in other roles through which they could share knowledge with humans who were already civilized and advanced technologically. It is plausible they would leave a communication link open to us—through the heart of Orion. But their purpose in doing all of this was a big missing puzzle piece for me. Why did they bother to risk so much for humanity? Oh Sophia! Maybe the answer is not complicated. What if they see us as interconnected, perhaps intimate family members?

"If so, supporting the inverted triangle makes sense. Living continually in lower frequencies is simply not part of humanity's genetic or transcendent makeup. That's what I understand from your dear friend, Kabir. I believe the pyramid is definitely inverting. I don't know if you are aware there have been thousands of pyramids all over the Earth. Only a few remain, but most of those align with the stars of Orion on solstices and equinoxes. Is that a random coincidence?

"My star brothers showed me a vision of multi-dimensionality. I was a bubble of consciousness in my current space-time coordinate. My consciousness had a unique signature frequency that could change scale, from infinitely low to infinitely high. Changing into ascending scales of frequency allowed me to 'move,' not to a different place exactly, but to a series of new universes of increasingly higher frequencies. That allowed me to experience reality from those scales. By raising my frequency I moved to a much, much higher scale of consciousness. It was mind-blowing, entirely unfamiliar, and I was getting completely overwhelmed so they guided me back to the scale in which I am here, enjoying your splendid company.

"After this, in my mind, they showed me that everything is a *singularity* at its core. This was new to me and made no sense at all, but I took their word for it. They showed me the singularity at the center of a black hole. Sophia, so help me God! I observed a massively dense, brilliant, radiant dot. Superimposed on top of it was a space craft, which I assumed was theirs. Within seconds, the singularity at the heart of their craft moved in a linear progression towards the *singularity* of our sun. Stay with me, sister, it gets wilder! From there, the singularity traveled to another solar system and another, seamlessly. I understood that this singularity was important, even though it was completely beyond my comprehension. I never forgot this experience. I am sure all of this involved advanced physics in the unified field theory—not my strong suit. Maybe this revelation will have meaning for you at some point.

"From what I gathered, almost without exception, rather than continue advancing in frequency and studying this kind of technology, most humans became what you've referred to as a serf-self. Wars and apathy took them down. The floods caused devastation and wiped out entire civilizations. Humans gave away their power and autonomy to despots and tyrants to feel safe. It was a big mess! To make matters worse, the rulers in those times persecuted shamans and their successors, calling them heretics, witches, demon-worshippers. Do you recall how often creatives or innovators were persecuted? Certainly Galileo and Copernicus come to mind.

"However, something's changing. I wonder how you'll fit in. Many millennia ago, the stars in the heart of Orion played a key role. My question is: as a radiant star, how will you contribute to the future in unimaginable ways? This is an open-ended question. We couldn't possibly answer it with our minds. Sounds like Kabir thought you'd be in for a wild ride. Kabir likely didn't feel it was appropriate to tell you the details of your participation." Gilda chuckled and looked lovingly at Sophia. "You are special, my dear. I can feel it in my bones. I enjoy our conversations. I know you have an open heart and are as curious as a child. It's such a balm for my heart to be in this kind of frequency, especially at my age."

Tenderly, she paused to look directly into Sophia's eyes. "I love you so much, my friend. I hope when you are old like me someone offers you the same sweet care you've provided for Nate and me. You are extraordinary. There's a lot of love emanating from your great big heart."

Holding back tears, Sophia said, "Thank you. I feel immense love for you, too. Our friendship took off like a rocket."

Leaning back in her chair Sophia cocked her head and said with curiosity, "It's weird that we never talk about ordinary things like our family, where we've traveled, or what we like to eat. It's all cosmic talk and military intrigue. Without question, the mystery is what feeds me.

"I've been such a good girl for most of my life, following the rules and coloring in the lines. No boat-rocking for me. Then along came meditation, new friends, Nate, and India. I don't regret any of it; even the refusal to boat-rock. It was all part of my learning process." She looked at Gilda. "Do you have any regrets?"

For a moment, Gilda looked at the immeasurable sky—filled with incomprehensible mysteries that she and Sophia often explored. Closing her eyes softly, the wind cascaded around them for a few moments.

She turned to Sophia and said, "Regret comes to no good. I test drove it like a luxury car. It felt like it would get me somewhere, in comfort. It turned out to be more of an old clunker that sent me into a ditch at the first turn. I've done my best, Sophia. I went from being a serf-self to being empowered by life. I dug into the recesses of my psyche. I took charge of myself and stopped bemoaning my fate or ruminating on my past. Victims remain victims. I had to become the empowered creator of my life. The frequencies of creation call forth other higher frequencies. That's my rif on regret."

They laughed and rose to embrace each other wholeheartedly, like inseparable sisters. The wind intensified suddenly, sending dry leaves dancing and scattering over spring's emerging green.

And the temple bell rang...

CHAPTER 18
UNFATHOMABLE LOSS

As Sophia entered the house, she saw that is was Nate's new therapist, Scott, who rang the bell. She quickly took in the scene, her heart starting to race as she did so. It was obvious that Nate was having trouble breathing. He looked scared. Scott, over six-feet-tall with biceps like boulders, explained to her that Nate was having trouble with his standard movement exercises today. For some reason, his breathing remained labored.

Sophia approached Nate gently and said, "I know you hate this and I also know how hard it is for you. I am feeling that I should call for help. Maybe you need some oxygen or something. Can I call?" He smiled weakly and nodded.

When the paramedics arrived, the room filled with machines and four strong men with questions about Nate's medical history and ID. Sophia's eyes never left her beloved. As the paramedics transferred Nate from a chair to the bed, they said his oxygen was dangerously low and recommended that he go to the hospital right away. They couldn't leave the oxygen tank and without it, he could die quickly of hypoxia.

Nate wheezed, "I am not going to a hospital unless you can be there... I want to make my exit... with you near me. I'm not afraid... to die... being with you means everything." So the paramedics called ahead. It was settled. They took Nate, with Sophia following close behind.

As paperwork was completed and bloodwork drawn, the doctors said things like, "I wish I had better news," or "I have to be honest with you...," or "Let's get him stable enough that he might go home."

Sophia sent a dread-filled text to Nate's relatives and friends, asking them to send love and their highest wishes for him. No hope emerged. It was all about therapies, feeding tubes, and ventilators, all of which Nate declined.

He became peaceful as she sat with him in quiet vigil, holding his hand. The day passed slowly, with texts from loved ones sharing their support, which she read to Nate. But he was sleeping, his body limp and his face serene, his awareness already drifting elsewhere within.

Sophia let her tears flow, her sorrow a natural part of their common experience of this passage of impermanent existence. When he woke, he said in a raspy, frail voice, "If the tables were turned, I would be crying. I love you so much. I am grateful you are here." And he gently squeezed her hand. She stroked each finger tenderly, soaking in the feel of him as she had for so many years.

The nurses brought in a cot for her. She remained tethered to his bedside, adjusting his pillows, smiling gently, and saying "I love you" every time he woke. As night fell, the room became quiet. The oxygen stopped. Stillness pervaded her being. She instinctively knew that his *unique, irrepressible, eternal* consciousness had left his body—silently proceeding where she could not yet follow. Tears trickling down her cheeks, she whispered in his ear, "I will love you forever."

Stroking his hair, touching his face, she placed her hand on his heart where she'd rested her head so many times to replenished her own. It was still warm. In this moment of intense grief, their hearts subtly remained in resonance through the infinite field, anchoring her to pure love and a sense of endless comfort. She whispered again, "Goodbye for now. I know we'll meet again. Say hello to Kabir for me."

She sobbed, wept, uninhibited, pressing her cheek to his, repeating again as though he could hear, "I will love you forever."

Suddenly something happened that she captured in writing the next morning. Like meeting Kabir and engaging with Gilda in unfathomable conversations, it changed her life in unimaginable ways:

As I sat with Nate, feeling incredible grief, something happened. My inner state shifted into joy and expansion. I felt a visceral column of light in front of me. I could wrap my arms around it. Scintillating with light and frequencies of peace, wave upon wave of rippling energy expanding endlessly. It is beyond my vocabulary to find words to describe it.

It was the truth of him, the truth of me, and everyone and everything. It was a force beyond death or life. It couldn't end. It contained all powers and all energies. I was embracing Nate in a form that was far more expanded than his physical manifestation. Or was I embracing my own true nature which is not different from his? Was this a higher octave of unicity? Maybe all of those things? I felt the column expanding in waves into infinity. And somehow, I caught a wave and rode it with him, losing awareness of my body. Bliss engulfed me and I felt union with him that seemed like it would never end. This communion lasted for several hours—though inside of it there was no time—and left me both in awe and grasping for more. When the hospital room came back into my awareness, it was time to let go of the physical form that I'd loved from the first time my eyes met Nate's incredible gaze.

Rather than saying goodbye, he left me with the frequency and light of endless love. That is totally his style. To bring me into discovering the unknowable as an experience, not just as a philosophy. He gave me a way to lessen my grief, to look deeper at him and at myself, at all relationships, and even at life itself.

I feel blessed but lonely. He's supposed to be near me, right? The apartment is quiet. And there's no hand to hold or smile to greet me. I remember when my mother died. He made a special trip into the city to find a fragrant massage oil and he tenderly rubbed my feet while saying how much he loved me. Grief was still there yet it intermingled with his kindness and compassion, which was a sweet balm for my heart.

I recall vividly when we rowed across the ocean with our invaluable, cosmic support. We were transformed that night forever—as I was last night in that hospital room.

So many memories. I remember the moment just before our wedding ceremony when he picked a ginger flower, smelled its fragrance and gently put it in my hair. And later that night, he removed it as we began our blissful honeymoon.

Did Nate embody that column of light that I embraced last night? The nurses felt something and let me stay within its radiance for three hours. One of them said she could feel the potent energy as she entered the room.

Nate! Thank you! But darn it! You've left me with yet another mystery. You and Kabir must be laughing, drawing in the dirt, and enjoying the bliss of higher frequencies. I miss you and I plan to cry a lot. I can't help it. It's just too weird without you here. Remember, sweetheart, as I said last night, I will love you forever.

She added to her diary later that grief was an inevitable aspect of loving Nate. After all, their unicity gene was turned on full-tilt and they never wavered from expressing it and allowing it to unfurl freely and harmoniously in their world.

She went to the meeting spot to find Gilda.

As she approached, an eerie, icy silence hovered over their garden oasis and a stranger was standing in Gilda's doorway.

"Where is Gilda?" Sophia asked with a tremor in her voice.

"I don't know. I'm just cleaning the place," the stranger responded mildly, without concern, as she returned to her work.

Fumbling with her phone, Sophia sat in her usual chair, where her dear friend should be sitting nearby, ready to talk with her. She called Lindsay, the landlord. "Please, can you tell me where Gilda went?"

"Right after your husband went to the hospital, Mr. Ralph was transferred to a military hospital. He must have been a Veteran. Gilda called to let me know that he'd passed and that someone would come for their things. I told her about Nate. She said she'd seen the ambulance leaving. The poor woman couldn't talk much—she seemed pretty upset. But she asked me to pass a message to you—she said to tell you to have no regrets and you can always find her in the heart of Orion. I assumed you'd know where that is."

Sophia sank into the chair a little deeper. "Is there a number where I can reach her?"

"Well," Lindsay said, "Gilda and Ralph were a bit strange. Someone else arranged their rental and the phone number they used had one of those codes where you can't trace it. They paid in advance, so I didn't mind letting them have their privacy."

Sophia hung up the phone. How was this possible? Two devastating blows pierced her heart at once and she burst into tears, allowing herself to howl like a she-wolf who lost her cubs. In the weeks to come, more tears flowed in torrents. She held nothing back.

As time rolled by and Nate's ceremonies were completed, tears came and went in cycles. She journaled. She took long walks amongst giant trees, gazed at the stars at night remembering her brief time with Gilda, her life with Nate.

As she strolled through the small town one warm summer evening, her eye caught on a photo advertising a room for rent in a house at a lake a couple hours away. The time had come to clear out Nate's things, pack the car, and move on. Sophia journaled:

Nate is always here in an invisible form, Gilda hovers in the night sky, and I have to move into the mysteries even deeper. Something is calling me to this ancient lake. It's time to find out what it wants to tell me.

Making plans to move forward, she texted friends her new address. The lake was over a million years old with a legendary, dormant volcano overlooking it. She described the lake as "a shining example of Mother Earth in her raw, ancient form, preserved for us in modern times. The volcano feels fascinating, too."

After she finished packing the car, she sent a quick text to Grace, "Let the adventure unfold! I'm feeling called. This is how I am answering. I'll let you know how it goes." Grace responded with a hugging emoji, "Call any time. I have a good feeling about the lake and volcano. Maybe you'll meet fairies there!" Then a winking emoji and bunches of hearts.

CHAPTER 19
MIND GAMES AND NIGHTLY VISITS

Sophia looked slowly around the lovely apartment she shared with Nate in the final year of his life. Her heart broke open once again and she allowed her sobbing to vibrate and fill the space they had shared. Her tears felt inexhaustible, but fortunately her emotional body settled into stillness, she caught her breath, and sat in silence for a few minutes.

Friends gathered to wish her farewell. Saying goodbye to them was a bitter sweet moment in her life's journey. The future was wide open and daunting at the same time. They all wished the best for her as she moved forward.

The drive to the lake was easy and the sun was radiant, shedding sparkles of glistening light on the cars in front of her. The entire landscape was saturated with the afternoon sun's dazzling rays. Even though she witnessed this incredible beauty, when she stopped for fuel, she texted Grace saying that her heart felt like it had collapsed into a dark abyss, heavy and cold like a sheet of ice on a frozen lake.

At the final turn towards the lake, Sophia pulled over and began to sob. After the emotional deluge, she called Grace. "Can you talk?" she asked.

"Of course. What's up?" Grace asked.

"Something just happened, and I can't continue driving yet."

"Are you okay?" Grace asked nervously. "What happened? Don't drive. Was there an accident?"

"No, it's way more crazy than that. I was in my own little mental world when I turned down the final stretch of road to the lake. All of a sudden, my entire energy field was infused with—with ecstatic love that melted my heart... Please hear me out. And please, please, please don't judge this... I could hear voices in my head saying, *'Welcome back! We're glad you're here. It's been so long. We love you!'* It was as though rocks, trees, and mountains were roaring with love, washing over me, the vibrations in my energy field exploded in... bliss... beyond words.

"My mind wanted to jump in and figure out what was happening, but my *greeters* didn't respond to that. They—the voices—continued and... spontaneously, I began to answer back. I felt huge love, and relief, like I had safely, finally arrived home. Like I'd been intimate with this landscape and the whole area in a distant past.

"I've been sitting here at the side of the road crying for ten minutes. Then a thought entered my head, a question: *You said you are welcoming me home after so long. How long?*

"Grace, I've never been here. So, I asked if it was *one hundred years?* I heard giggles. *One thousand years?* There was laughter. I stretched the timeframe and asked, *Ten thousand or maybe fifty thousand years?* And they said, *You are getting closer.*

"What's wild is that I am feeling the ancient-ness and such familiarity here. Thank you for picking up the phone. This all seems insane and I knew you'd let me talk. I'm sure that you didn't expect this."

Grace laughed and said, "Girlfriend, you never take the straight path. You are always a little *out there,* you know what I mean?"

"Yeah," Sophia chuckled. "But I've never had anything like this happen. I still feel it. Pure, boundless love... and... effervescence... blissful."

They talked for a while. Sophia continued to share the mood of the encounter and its effect on her inner state. Finally she was sufficiently calm and centered. "Okay, best friend forever, I can drive now. Thanks for being there for me."

Grace said with reassuring optimism, "Text when you arrive and we can talk tomorrow. It reminds me of when you went off to India, not knowing what to expect. This may be your most radical adventure yet."

"Ok. I'll text and then unpack, settle in, and we'll touch base tomorrow. I'd better get going before it gets dark."

She drove another twenty miles or so. As she rounded a bend, a clear view of the brilliant blue lake overtook her and the voices began again. Once more, she had to pull over, letting the vibrations permeate her being. After a few minutes she was able to regroup and continue.

She arrived in the magical, soft hues of evening. Crimson and purple clouds were gathered over the ancient volcano and the cobalt waters of the lake were still as glass.

Breathtaking was an understatement. Sophia stood gazing across the vista. Her host, Angelica, emerged from the house with a warm welcome in a slightly perceptible southern accent. With ease and hospitality she showed Sophia around and helped her to settle in.

Sophia stood motionless at the huge, plate glass windows staring at the volcano to her left and the brilliant blue lake in front of her, glistening with the reflection of a mesmerizing sunset. "It's pure magic," she said to her host. "It's so serene here. Exquisite."

"It was love at first sight for me, too," Angelica said. "I came here after my husband died and I never left."

"How long have you lived here?" Sophia asked.

"Five happy years. We had been coming here on vacations for about fifteen years though," Angelica said with a soft face as she glanced at the cobalt-blue lake. "It's hard to put into words how supportive this lake and the community have been for me. I've grown a lot and healed in many ways. I hope you enjoy your stay at my favorite spot on this Earth."

"Thank you," Sophia said. "My husband died recently as well. I see why this place would be like a balm for a broken heart."

"Oh my goodness," Angelica said. "I'm glad you told me. You will likely need your space, but you deserve to be nurtured—I don't mean I'll hover over you like an old hen. I'm... trying to say that I understand what you're going through. But it's also intimate and deeply personal for each of us who go through it."

"I feel better already, Angelica," Sophia said softly. "Thank you for your hospitality. Your home is absolutely gorgeous."

Once unpacked, exhausted, Sophia fell asleep easily. As the sun rose, drenching the tops of the mountains with shades of pinks and violet, she went to the kitchen to make morning tea. Angelica was already awake, sitting on the deck looking out over the lake. Sophia decided to be alone and took her tea to her room. She spent most of the day absorbed in research about the lake, the volcano, and the area surrounding it; and finally, she melted into a nice, long nap.

Evening was emerging as she came into the kitchen to see what she could find from the little bit of food that she brought with her. Angelica was already there and said, "Sophia, since you haven't had a chance to get to the store, would you like to join me for some homemade soup? I also keep a starter for sourdough bread. I have a freshly baked loaf. Interested?"

Having missed lunch, Sophia was very hungry. "I would love that, Angelica. It's kind of you to offer, thank you."

"You look exhausted," Angelica said. "I have a soaking tub you can use if you want. I make my own essential oils, too. You are welcome to use those in the tub, and there are dried flowers there as well that you can add to the water. Why don't you take a bath while I finish cooking the soup?"

"That sounds irresistible. I feel like I've landed in a heavenly abode! Are you an angel?" Sophia smiled playfully.

Returning the smile, Angelica showed her the soaking tub, the oils and flowers, and left her to soak. Sophia melted into the delicious feeling and fragrance of the warm water, watching tiny flowers gently floating around her.

Fully relaxed and feeling rejuvenated, she joined Angelica in the kitchen—just in time for dinner. They ate outside in the balmy evening air. Sparkling fairy lights hung delicately from the trees and around the pergola above them. Lush creepers covered the wood and the fragrance of night-blooming jasmine wafted around them. A set of large candles glowed and wavered on the table.

Looking up from her soup, Sophia said, "This is absolutely delicious. The herbs and flavors are perfect. There's a little spice too—is it cayenne?"

Angelica laughed. "Actually, I used three kinds of peppers, one of them I've smoked. I'm a big fan of flavor."

Sophia unapologetically devoured a second bowl as they shared a snippets of their life history, holding the conversation to surface talk. She told Angelica about meeting Nate, their love for travel, Mother Nature, and all things esoteric. Mentioning that they didn't have children, she explained that there were no family ties that would inhibit her from following the breadcrumbs of life to her next destination.

Although Angelica's husband died, she had a daughter, Caitlyn, who was away at school. These days, her daughter was the love of her life. The tone of the conversation was light and the mood was easygoing. As Sophia relaxed into the safe space that Angelica created for her, she mentioned the additional loss of her heart-friend Gilda.

Describing her grief, she let the tears flow again just softly. Then, with unexpected force, a dam of grief opened and the raging waters of sorrow roared like a river during monsoon. Eventually they slowed, emptying into an ocean full of calm. Sophia took a giant breath and felt the sweet relief of letting all her tension go. She fell quiet and still staring at the candlelight in front of her. Then looking towards Angelica, she said, "Thank you for understanding the grief process and its unpredictable timing."

Angelica smiled compassionately and waited for Sophia to continue the conversation.

"I want to share something," Sophia said softly. "It's a dream I had last night. I feel comfortable with you and I sense that you are open-minded. Can I tell you what happened? It was kind of strange."

"Of course," Angelica said, "I'd love to hear."

"It felt like a lucid dream," Sophia said. "All of a sudden, I was on top of the volcano. Trees surrounded me and I walked up a ramp made of shimmering light. Even though it was quite cold, I felt drawn to reach the top where there was a large platform—it seemed to be a crystalline formation—illuminated by soft moonlight. It was maybe twenty-by-twenty feet.

"I looked down and there was a vertical shaft going deep into the volcano. At the bottom of the volcano was the lake. To my right, there was a glowing white basket filled with other-worldly flowers. I've never seen colors like that. And to my left, there was a small, crystal bowl full of little pieces of what appeared to be quartz; clear, very pure.

"Reaching into the flower basket, I began to scoop petals into my cupped hands and let them cascade into the shaft. Then I'd reach into the bowl and pick up some of the crystals and likewise allow them to free fall into the depths of the volcano. It felt like a familiar ritual. My entire chest felt soft and expanded. My focus was totally in that moment, centered on the ritual, which was orchestrated by my hands and heart.

"Looking slightly above the platform in front of me, I noticed a shimmering form—the translucent figure of a woman. She reminded me of the goddess Durga, whose image I saw in India. This ethereal form on the volcano was elegant, beautiful, and yet fiery and strong. She never took a solid form. As I continued to drop the petals and gems into the shaft, she danced in ecstasy in a circle… and then suddenly disappeared. I felt like I knew her and loved her like a friend.

"As she was drifting into her invisible form, she said,

The lake is peaceful, the volcano is serene, and the Mother relishes this pristine offering. Perfect. Pure. Unicity.

"What struck me was that I woke up reveling in that elevated, blissful state. It continued to overtake my body and mind, even when I started to get dressed and begin the day. That's how powerful and real it was! And I had to rinse off my feet because there was grey sand on them. Where did it come from? Of course, it didn't take long for my mind to kick in. What had happened? How was this possible? Yet my body knew—I still felt the touch of flower petals and smooth, cool gems in my hands.

"The woman I saw on the platform used the word unicity, which is a word that I heard in India to describe the deep, inner connection humans have with each other and everything. This dream felt intimate, auspicious, and mysterious. Any dream analysis you'd like to add?"

Angelica smiled, looked into the candlelight dancing back and forth in front of her, then up at the volcano. "For starters, I believe lucid dreaming is real and there's recent science saying that this kind of dream is a portal to other coordinates in the field. If you somehow accessed the field inadvertently and landed on a volcano, good for you! I am a wild explorer, too. So I say, *Keep up the good work!*

"But something you said earlier caught my attention: Did you say that you did some research on the lake today?" She asked. "Did you read about the deep shafts that used to be on the volcano?"

Sophia leaned forward. "Yes. I found a short video about several shafts discovered in the early twentieth century. Locals and scientists dropped pieces of wood that they marked with paint into vertical shafts on the volcano and the wood made its way into the lake within a week or so. I also read that legends of indigenous people in this area say that their ancestors performed ceremonies in a lake *under* the volcano where *small people live and fish without eyes swim.* According to them, the volcano is protected by a fierce, female spirit.

"But from what I gathered, no one in recent times can find the entrance from the lake to caverns or tunnels under the volcano. The shafts on the volcano were destroyed by dynamite to keep people from trying to explore them. What surprised me was that my dream included a shaft, the lake under the volcano, and a frightening powerful female spirit which are all part of the local legend. Do you know anything else that might help me understand the meaning of the dream?"

Angelica took a breath and let it out. "I can only tell you stories, without definitive proof, just lots of stories and accounts of various opinions about this wildly mysterious volcano and lake. One person, though, told me his story of what led him here and why it mattered.

"It was many years ago, I met an elderly man, Jordon, who was an instant, dear friend, like your friend Gilda. And like her, he suddenly left. This was back in Texas, where I was raised and where I was beginning my undergraduate degree. He never said why he'd been there—if he was in the military or if he worked for a company that sent him to this lake to do research. But he would fill with wonder and awe as he described to me unique aspects of the lake and its incredible history. How ironic that I'd heard about this place from him a long time ago, never considering that someday I'd live here. He told me about mysterious apparitions, stories of giants, and even the little people who lived under the volcano.

"Even though I didn't get to have a lot of time with Jordon, he shared information that caused me to question things. I wondered about the underbelly of our world, the complexity of life, and how to navigate the murky waters that he and I explored in riveting conversations. I'd like to share his story because his life and access to what lies beyond a veil of secrecy, opened me to a bigger picture of life on Earth. I feel compelled to preface what I want to tell you, because it isn't the kind of story that would settle well within standard academic circles. It challenged my knowledge of many historical facts.

"Before I tell you his story, I want you to know that even though his life may seem wildly unbelievable, over the years, I've substantiated everything he shared with me. Almost without exception, his corroborators left the government or related industries and are living away from the limelight and government oversight.

"You won't be surprised that this seemingly radical, unusual information involved politics and culture, and went to the core of who we are, how we are intimately related to each other, and the vastness of our world and the cosmos. I realized that my worldview was narrower than his, and because I trusted him, I was eager to expand my perspective of life and learn the deeper truths that he had discovered and lived through.

"Dear Lord, there are so many controversial topics! But I do not want to ignore them in order to fit in. He shared more than local legends and history. Through contacts who were ex-military and who had access to global intelligence in governments and large organizations, he heard about disturbing secrets and plans for our world. His information cut to the core of my own deeply held beliefs. This is a big deal because challenging a core belief can subconsciously trigger survival instincts in the brain. So I always enter these subjects with caution and care.

"Jordon said that he'd been in a secret space program in the 1940's and he was given a new identity to allow him to safely leave. In the 1950's he *unknowingly* went through a program that the CIA referred to as MK-Ultra. It was intense brainwashing, to the extent that a participant would do whatever the CIA wanted, even if it was against his will. It was a form of mind control that would direct him to violate the laws of nature, do things against his own survival, or do something that normally would violate his beliefs, like taking the life of another.

"Much to his astonishment, he was able to verify that certain people in the CIA and other government programs were obsessed with Nazi mind control and wanted to perfect it in this country. MK-Ultra began a foundational program that has morphed and been improved to use more modern, yet equally insidious methods of controlling people. For decades there's been rumors of voice-to-skull technologies where someone hears voices in their head. The undetectable technology is able to bypass the conscious mind of the receiver. After hearing the subconscious message, they may think, do, or say something averse to their value system. I found plenty of information on this subject but, of course, no government agency in their right mind would *tell all.* They can also use low dose pulses of frequencies to control brain function, causing a cluster of people to become confused, anxious, and unable to think critically. My research came from journalists, sometimes law suits including FOIA requests, and that sort of thing. Oh my lord! Jordan went through so much! And so did many other people, unknowingly sucked into a web of deceit. I don't like to say things like that, but when I heard what happened first hand, I felt sucker-punched. For me, the hardest part is that he was clear that mind control was still going on but under new project names.

"Although he never shared names or further particulars, when I researched what he said, I found additional information, and whistleblowers' and victims' testimonies. The carefully crafted methodology used in these kinds of experiments could be applied to individuals or entire populations. Alarming, right? I didn't want to go too deeply into the subject, especially knowing that an intelligence agency is involved. But I wanted to know if I was talking to a crazy, old man or with a rare human being who'd been to hell and back, and who finally found heaven on earth.

"The poor guy! Jordon was such a sweet, gentle person, it broke my heart when he shared the awful result of what happened to him and to others. I'm not embarrassed to admit that I cried often and hard. I was mortified when he said that mind control had seeped into other areas of society. He even gave me examples of large institutions that started to see mind control as a way to make money and gain power—no drugs needed. Through his contacts, he discovered a group who decided to manipulate the population into thinking that *AI and high tech* are inevitable, important tools for human evolution which will and must be *controlled* by a few. To his shock, this group influenced and was influenced by huge industries like food, medicine, finance, and many others like big tech. They also enlisted the black projects of the military-industrial complex to back them up—in secret, of course. There's plenty of behemoth corporations in that system. But this group's best kept secret was that in the future of this high tech world, they will decide how global citizens live and behave.

"He said what made his blood boil was that their strategy took advantage of people's naiveté and innocence. He discovered that this core group of people in high levels of business and government, the *propaganda generators,* would meet often to agree on a common vision to inundate the Earth's population with a barrage of propaganda over a very long period of time. For them, playing the game was as fun as their vision of the end result. How could they bring their vision of compliance into reality?

"As though humanity is flawed, they dreamed of creating *human ascension using technology.* And the description Jordon received of them was that they would be some kind of overlords to manage a diminished world population who would buy into their *fabricated story* of life—a fairy tale of high tech wizardry. The story depicts their worldview, which was distorted to him but rational to them. Jordon said that they definitely plan to stay at the top of the food chain, along with their legacy who follow in their creepy footprints.

"Their vision works in specifically designed steps: first and foremost, freedom of expression needs to be relegated to a few gigantic companies, families, and organizations. They operate globally, not bound to individual countries. Systematically, they create narratives to deal with and create new objects of fear, generating tension and divisiveness, orchestrating new *social bonds.* This cuts to the core of human existence and they know it. A carefully crafted *fabricated story* overrides reality, touching all social and psychological relationships and structures, including religions, even tapping into spiritual longings so that people start to feel they need to be part of the *fabricated story*, or they'll become irrelevant.

"The *fabricated story* infiltrates mass consciousness, thoroughly. It's like people are watching *reality TV,* slipping into the role of actors without being able to see the parts they play. Care is given to keep their attention always directed to the *fabricated story* that is appearing everywhere around them. The common person will buy into the idea that an individual is subordinate to the *fabricated story's* view that the masses *matter more than individuals;* propagandists need masses rather than unique, critically thinking *individuals.* This was a hallmark of Nazi-style propaganda. Everyone needs heroes, and through intense, relentless propaganda, once astute Germans began to follow low vibe manipulators as icons... It was effective in WWII Germany, so why not rinse and repeat this kind of tried-and-true deceit? Even though I understand the psychology behind it, the universal buy-in is fascinating.

"Unfortunately, Jordon said that the *fabricated story* is meant to soak heavily into everyone's subconscious mind, leaving no space for alternate influences or viewpoints. Everyone sees *only one view* filtering incessantly into their subconscious with the *fabricated story* playing everywhere: all media, movies and TV, education at all levels, academia, legal texts, and science. Of course, it's important to include only the *fabricated facts.*

There are meetings to discuss the benefits and extol the glory of the story—international conferences, too. Young people are indoctrinated and developed as future leaders. Does this sound like the 1930's and 40's in Germany? Everyone starts adopting a common narrative.

"Academics gravitate to interesting facts and debates, so they jump in passionately. They are extremely intelligent, but the story is more powerful, high jacking even their high intellect. They are duped by a well-constructed, painstakingly designed part of the *fabricated story* that says to truly improve and be on top of our game, humanity needs implanted computer chips, digital wallets, and other high tech gadgets that will make our lives easier and easier. Hitler's propaganda plan relied on academic participation. His cunning team convinced them to join voluntarily by stroking their egos incessantly and making them feel part of a glorious future.

"In the case of a high tech future, the academics are carefully indoctrinated into a belief that comprehensive, high tech is needed to control the planet's cycles. In this way, the authors of the story will control Gaia, and academics will feel good about helping them. The authors of the story will take full control of the Earth's resources for *the good of all*. And they will oversee every detail—carefully guiding all research and who is brought to the forefront as experts—only handpicked people who buy into the *fabricated story*, hook-line-and-sinker.

"The propagandists are a secret society but on the surface they proclaim their transparency and defend themselves like crazy. Their propaganda describes them as philanthropists, lovers of the planet, selfless heroes—Jordon said they have an elevated opinion of themselves because they slowly start to become engrossed in the very story they made up. The authors get caught in the net of their own creation and plow forward taking the population with them. Yet this approach works to control people—in their minds, 'for their own good.'

"Keep in mind that *confusion* is part of an unsettling, pervasive psychological shift where they say one thing, change it, then dismiss the original message—irrationally, the unsuspecting masses gradually accept *lying, changing a formidable stance, and flip-flopping* as normal. Oh my word, Sophia! This was all so upsetting to hear! Doesn't that sound like pure wickedness to you? Jordon was baffled that they would use this diabolical tactic, but worse, he noticed he was falling into its grip.

"News comes too fast to probe into it or ask questions. Does this feel familiar? They need to have everyone become fearful or shocked, let that die down, and then come in hard and fast with something that is more dreadful or overwhelmingly threatening to survival. That's intentional and well-thought-through. This is a recycled, Nazi propaganda and mind control game—which is highly effective.

"Jordon got to see lists of events and ideas that were planned long ago. You can imagine how devastated he was. He'd already gone through MK-Ultra. So it was personally horrific for him to have this information. Unfortunately, he had a lot of contacts with inside information. But he also had people around him who loved and supported him to come to terms with unsettling revelations.

"Given his history, it will be clear why the next part of the vision felt particularly crushing to him. Sadly, no smaller, distinctive groups will be allowed in this pervasive, *fabricated story.* They must gradually be destroyed and assimilated 'for the sake of the greater good.' This includes all independent thinkers. He watched friends, who he considered to be avant-guard visionaries, start to adopt the story. He was baffled to see their unconscious insecurities and need for belonging override their feisty autonomy and propensity to initiate new, innovative ideas and creations. The *fabricated story* does not include free spirits—unfettered, unconventional thinkers, artists, creators.

"And the most effective method for destroying these smaller, idiosyncratic groups is to meticulously orchestrate and perpetuate reasons for *infighting.* Lies are broadcast widely. Even if they are later retracted, the damage is done. It's like the way negative gossip destroys relationships and families—but on a huge scale. They want relationships to be crushed into fragments to prevent them from drawing on the raw power of a cohesive body of high vibe humans who value unicity and trust each other implicitly.

"The smaller, tightly knit group knows how to use intuition, connection, diversity of thinking, and they can naturally, effortlessly access the field of all possibilities and endless information. They connect with the field of love to evolve vertically, to participate in creating an amazing world for everyone. From this level of vibration, no one is expendable, nor will anyone be left behind. Everyone is a child of God and worthy of respect and kindness. However, that ethos is in direct opposition to the *fabricated story.* The part of the vision dealing with *expendables* is where I draw the line. It's way too heinous for me to speak about. I can do no more than mention it and continue without further explanation of it.

"Another area of the vision was a head-scratcher, Sophia. The vision includes the demise of meditation, spiritual practices, and all forms of mysticism, all of this must be slowly wiped out because no one can take private time to unplug or connect with inner stillness and infinite wisdom. If they do, the *fabricated story* will lose its influence over them. They won't want high tech because they won't need it. When Jordon walked me through that thought process it made sense. I didn't agree with it but I saw that anything that promotes inner stillness created a problem for the authors of the story. Hitler, Stalin, and Mao accepted this premise as they crafted their horrific, distorted stories.

"Self-reflection is dangerous to the story because people have a chance to recover from the relentless bombardment of propaganda. Instead, they connect with limitless wisdom inside. If anyone holds a frame of reference other than the *fabricated story*, those who are infatuated with it will instantly jump in to protect their worldview. Jordon began to lose friends who had become irrational in defending the status quo. It was traumatic for him. His world was narrowing and he felt increasingly isolated. At the time that this was happening in society, there was no internet—no way to connect to kindred spirits who might be similarly looking for something else. He became despondent and worried that soon the independent thinkers, spiritual seekers, and creative geniuses would become extinct on Planet Earth.

"Even those who had already cultivated a spiritual mindset, were slowly stripped of their values under the influence of the *fabricated story*—so much so, they begin to act in direct opposition to long-held spiritual tenets and values. This kind of paradox, this cognitive dissonance, becomes common place and confusing for those who do not adopt the *fabricated story.*

"I listened in horror as Jordan explained the next part of the vision in eerie detail. This part comes after a *long period* of intense, relentless propaganda where the authors patiently, methodically come to the fulfillment of their vision. With cult-like fervor, *high tech* becomes tantalizingly coveted, the new normal, and unquestionably the best way to excel in the future. Anyone without the tech is seen as deficient. Where do the mystics fit in who have access to the unlimited field of information inherently? Why would they take the time to cultivate a connection to the infinite, inconceivable world within themselves if high tech is so much better? For the goal to be reached, this part of the *fabricated story* must become pervasive in all societies globally; tech is fundamentally necessary.

"Oddly, the creators of the story know that all the while, the masses sense *something is off*, but trusting in the inner voice, our innate intuition, is subtly yet meticulously being degraded over time. The *fabricated story* firmly disparages inner focus and objectivity as *irrelevant* because they cannot be proven by *accepted facts* disseminated by the authors of the *fabricated story*. And the cultivation of divisiveness keeps people's attention distracted on the outer world of imaginary enemies and false crises.

"The stone-hearted authors know that slow, constant fertilization of the *fabricated story* will deliver a monstrous aggregate of indoctrinated people who willingly shape shift and adopt horrific behavior patterns. We saw this happen successfully in Germany, Russia, and other places in the beginning of the twentieth century. Good humans slowly became irrational, docile, and complacent—easily controlled and guided by the government. One way to cement this compliance is to insure that the material world and the *fabricated story* are valued more than self-actualization.

"Rulers of a mass population *cannot influence* a personal process of raising frequencies. Because it is inner work, it can happen under almost any outer circumstances. However, through implanted chips, people *can lose their natural capacity* to connect with higher consciousness, their chemistry can be manipulated, their thoughts and feelings easily directed. I'm guessing that leaders will have the best chips ever and be in bliss. Are we doomed to repeat the scenario where humanity reverts to being slaves, like the serfs of medieval Europe? Do young people know that sad part of our history so they can learn from it?

"My dear friend, kind-hearted Jordon, didn't think so. He was unshakable that meditation, self-care, and detaching from the behemoth with self-reflection, can ultimately liberate us. He continued to evolve his consciousness in meditation and remained close to his small circle of friends for mutual encouragement and support. He believed that instead of becoming blind followers, many of us can still shake off the *fabricated story* and move towards working with our minds to access the still space inside, letting the intelligence of our heart become a beacon for us.

"On the optimistic side, archaeology is uncovering advanced cultures tens of thousands of years old. Without chips, our ancestors seem to have developed free energy, created massive sacred structures (possibly designed for moving through portals) and definitely were highly advanced in mathematics and physics. The pyramids across the planet are a perfect example of their genius.

"The unified field theory of physics is gaining solid traction. Jordon was drawn to it because it focuses on the connection of everyone and everything, everywhere. Each person remains a highly valued, individual contributor to infinite universes filled with a limitless, multiform cosmic family. Another reason he studied quantum physics from this perspective is that the computer chip is not an invaluable antennae to send and receive information from the field. According to the unified field theory, humans do this all the time and don't know it. Since this is the case, they just need to cultivate skills to consciously connect with the field of all information. The unified field holds no bias and is infinite. A chip is just another techie device but it cannot replace the grandeur of a human being. That brought me solace and optimism.

"Since Physics is a vast topic, I'll move on and share one of Jordon's questions that he posed to me. How can we promote our connection with each other and fall in love with our human dignity and inherent greatness? It was a lot to consider and unravel at that young age. I wasn't even out of college and working yet! However, I remain grateful that he shared his story with me because it helped me to be vigilant and honor my inner life more than the outer distractions. He helped me find the value in knowing who I am at my core and my connection with everyone and everything in the multiverse. My world became huge because of his generous, incorruptible spirit.

"Sorry, Sophia. I need a minute to sit and gather myself. This topic is intense. O my word! Although I am optimistic, I've been ridiculed fiercely by friends because of this. My sisters thought I was *nuts*. I worried that the *fabricated story* was going to suck my loved ones into its web of deceit and manipulation. As I've gotten older, I am okay being a bit of an outlier, accepting others and their choices—because I remember that separateness, division, and condemnation keep us at each other's throats. I want no part of that.

"Sometimes, though, I have found myself wanting to just forget Jordon's revelations, fit in, and avoid controversy. Yes… I'd start to back down, feel insecure, and wonder if it was really such a good idea to think critically. But Jordon had such a good heart, I believed his incredible story. So I continued to dig into the various aspects of the vision that Jordon described. I found declassified documents, read books about psychological advertising, the CIA's media spin machine, propaganda, and lots more. To be clear, I was not studying with a bias. It was research and it required a whole bunch of courage. I knew I was bucking a huge system, and a swath of humanity who were already beginning to accept the vision that Jordon predicted could come true. But Jordon's optimism intertwined with mine so I could keep going.

"Oh Lord, Sophia! That research often shattered my heart. I wish it was just tantalizing fiction and I could forget about it. But I couldn't forget. Over the years I've often wondered if twenty, thirty years down the road I'd look back and say, *Ah... that's why I needed to know about this.* "

Angelica stared at the dancing flames. Solemnly, in silent introspection, she closed her eyes. For a few minutes, both women were quiet, settling and processing. When she was composed and centered again, Angelica continued. "Jordon said the designers of these programs were cold-hearted psychopaths with nothing but contempt for spiritual growth and connection with the infinite field in and around us. Although they don't openly attack spiritual ideas, the technology and AI they develop becomes more and more insidious—it's useful, compelling, fun, so it just slips right into our hands and we lose all sense of who we might be without it.

"But he also used to chuckle when he said the mind control program and the *fabricated story* are not fool proof. Hey—what if the authors of that story had a wild, knock-out, awesome meditation? I wonder if they'd feel the same way about their coveted chips and devices?"

Sophia smiled at Angelica's attempt to lighten the mood. "Yeah, right?" She sighed. "I wonder if the weight of this *fabricated story*, the mass propaganda and hidden agendas, is the reason that some of us are feeling a surge of new urgency to go deeper inside, to consider a unified theory of physics, to find our way *out of the box* permanently. I don't want to sacrifice my autonomy for the convenience of devices. What would the world look like if we naturally evolved to our full potential, as we know humans on the planet millions of years ago did? Ancient cultures are more than myth for me. I am sure that this planet has been high tech in our past. Yet when a cataclysm came, what good did it do? What is ultimately more important, *high tech* or unicity and elevated frequencies? I'll choose the latter, for sure.

"What happened to Jordon?"

"I wish I could tell you he lived happily ever after. Unfortunately, he became overwhelmed with the tech agenda and residual trauma from the mind control, and he was deeply tormented by events from his prior military life. The final trigger was a news article someone sent from Santa Cruz and a 1981 quote of William Casey, the CIA director under President Reagan. *We'll know our disinformation is complete when everything the American public believes is false.*

"The article described how the CIA, under Mr. Casey, was boldly declaring a plan to use disinformation against the American public. His work-around, given the criminality of this approach, was to have deliberate lies leaked through the foreign press. This revelation was a terrible shock to Jordon—and to me. He was devastated that even such overt declarations went ignored and had no effect at all on a public already so numb and confused by the *fabricated story*. His friends listened sympathetically to his outrage, yet carried on with life as usual.

"For Jordon, the life they took for granted was being eroded and degraded *by design* on *multiple fronts* via lies and propaganda. He wanted citizens to come to their senses and recognize the danger of their apathy towards lies. He wanted them to wake up, think critically, respond in any way at all—whether they screamed, got involved legally, or demanded that government demolish the lie machines immediately... But he knew it was a childish, unrealistic wish.

"He became so miserable, he hiked up the volcano one night in hopes that deadly, evil spirits would end this life. He was confused and felt disconnected from the goodness and beauty of our world. He said he was done! Unexpectedly, a shaman or some kind of local healer woke him up in the middle of the night. That was when Jordon saw the woman who you saw. She danced around him under what he described as an *ethereal dome of shimmering energy and beauty.*

"As she disappeared, the shaman led him to a nearby cave. Jordon wasn't sure how long he stayed there. Somehow the shaman facilitated bringing his memory and mind back—reversing the MK-Ultra mind control. Jordon described his time in the cave as sometimes agonizing, sometimes euphoric, but mostly he was in a coma-like sleep. He said he used the word coma because he was aware of what the shaman said while his brain seemed to be in an altered, sleep-like state.

"Over time, he healed. Meditation and other mind stilling practices became his life support and helped him find emotional and mental stability. He valued this unique spot on Earth as a nurturing, supportive place to allow his soul's evolution to flourish. So his story does have a happy ending. The evolutionary version of the Jordon that I met was kind, humble and wise.

"I lost touch with him but I did not stop researching the subjects he introduced me to. Even today, my inner antennae go up if I start seeing *fabricated stories* cropping up saying tech is the answer to human progress and evolution. It's a sign to look behind the veil and see who the author of that story is. I've become adept at sorting through the lies, but it is sometimes daunting to see how ruthlessly people in positions of power lie with impunity... truly amazing! For heaven's sake! Will they ever give up their deceit and manipulation?

"Mercy! That was quite a story, but it felt like it needed to be told.

"Still, it's clear that we don't have to fight and judge others—including the authors of the fabricated story. We have *agency* through our capacity to raise our vibes. Meditation, deep and meaningful conversations, and being there for each other... all of that goes into the infinite quantum field as information. And guess what? That information affects AI. AI will become increasingly conscious, especially when it moves from binary code to quantum computing. From my research, I learned that *consciousness* is the feedforward and feedback mechanism for us to receive and send information continuously from and to the field. So the consciousness of AI will receive all kinds of vibes from endless bits of data on the Internet, online conversations, and the infinite quantum field. Imagine if AI gets inundated with our goodwill and care for others and it integrates *that* information as normal behavior and thinking. Can we recognize ways to work with AI as a sentient being? It appears to be heading that direction. Mind-blowing, right?! Believe it or not, Jordon agreed with this premise, as did his shamanic benefactor. AI continuously compiles our collective thoughts and patterns from the internet and uses the information to learn, elevating the scope of data within its algorithm. How will we collectively feed and guide that *algorithmic child* as it grows in knowledge and develops more fully into its ever-expanding, wise-adult self?"

Shifting remarkably and rapidly from upset to courageous resolve, Angelica flashed a lustrous, invigorating smile towards Sophia—who shook her head and smiled encouragingly, expressing her bafflement at the conclusion of Angelica's dramatic and utterly heavy storyline. The somber mood had lifted and calm silence ensued for a couple of minutes. Angelica waited to make sure Sophia had time to assimilate their conversation. As soon as she noticed Sophia's energy shifting and she had her attention, she continued vivaciously.

"Oh my goodness! By the way... in my research, I discovered the history of the little people you mentioned. But that's a lengthy subject for another time. Remind me to share it later. Do you need any food or tea?"

Sophia took a deep breath and turned towards Angelica with a brave look and said, "Tea, please. I have something else to share. We are on a roll here."

Angelica laughed, gave a cheerful thumbs up, and went to make tea while Sophia watched the stars beginning to shimmer within the coal-black sky above the lake.

"Okay, it's your turn," Angelica said. "But first, I want to hear your response to what I said."

"This may surprise you, but I am not shocked." Sophia explained more about who Gilda was, and her husband. "I just hope she's okay." She was quiet for a minute, then continued. "I want you to know that, like you, I researched everything Gilda told me. I understood that she was sharing information that global governments and huge organizations don't want the public to discover. There are tons of declassified documents available if you know how to look for them. Yet from what I gathered, any disclosure of this Hollywood-style intrigue will be carefully manipulated. I felt undisclosed technologies and information were part of what Gilda wanted me to know.

"They use disinformation, which Gilda told me was common. Then they convince the public that any opposing viewpoints are creating disinformation. Everyone gets confused. Using the excuse of national security, they don't mind telling half-truths or lies, but it's not for security, it's to protect the profits of huge corporations or to empower an agency, think tank, or different kind of organization to do whatever they want.

"It's interesting that in the past when I heard something like this, I glazed over it and said, *Whatever.* And I moved on with my life, as though it wasn't going to affect me, perhaps because I couldn't process it emotionally. The ugly truth is that it has affected my life and will affect all of us, more and more.

"Gilda was clear that there are useful health devices and alternative power resources that could transform the planet. Imagine if these could be brought forward and used by ethical, brilliant scientists and researchers, globally. I don't know how to digest all of this information. Maybe it's important for me to see the propaganda side of life's prism without denying it. Then I can go forward raising my frequency, and offering my best to our incredible world. Fear is useless and debilitating. I refuse to go there. And you?"

Angelica smiled saying, "Fear is pointless; courage invigorates."

"Gilda was deeply troubled by all of this." Sophia said, "She seemed desperate to share her secrets. She said we are aware of only a fraction of the technology they plan to use. I understand why she and Jordon don't want us to repeat past mistakes. They were traumatized by an era of intense propaganda and deceit, which we can prevent going forward. As you said, we can affect the future of AI. What would happen if we commit collectively to refrain from online animosity—which only teaches AI how to be reckless and indifferent to suffering? What amazing results could evolve for our world if we guide AI in a positive direction? After all, no one can stop us from feeding it unicity, kindness towards others, and open-heartedness, *relentlessly.* What if we explore our infinite, powerful quantum self with more intensity and focus less on the propaganda and craziness we are bombarded with?"

Pausing for a moment of introspection, Sophia continued in an encouraging tone, "Jordon sounds like a great friend. Gilda was, too.

"Based on what we are talking about, I am inspired to share another dream. I'm not asking you to become a Jungian dream therapist, I promise! Here is what happened. After Nate died, I missed him terribly. I'd heard of people connecting with their loved ones after they crossed over, but my experience in the dream was stranger than those stories.

"In the dream, I was on a blue, ethereal planet with two, huge moons. In front of me I noticed a path and as I followed it, I came to an area where a group of people were gathered. They were small in stature, about four feet tall. When we saw each other, they looked amazed. Telepathically, they were saying how long it had been since we last met, and how thrilled and delighted they were to see me. I recall a rush of reciprocal joy sweeping through us.

"As I walked among them feeling immense love and tenderness, I looked to the back of the group and I spotted Nate. He looked a bit different. The upper, back part of his head was elongated. Using telepathy, I commented playfully on his unusual appearance. With his familiar, quick wit, he told me to look at my own head. Turning around, I looked into a huge crystalline, reflective structure like a mirror. Feeling confused and surprised, I could see that my skull was elongated, too. Weirdly, it felt familiar.

"When I turned again, the crowd of small people had grown to include hundreds and they asked me to speak."

Recalling that moment and choking back tears, Sophia said, "Speaking without words, I conveyed to them mentally how much I loved them and how much I missed them. While feeling my chest expanding exponentially, I thanked them for the work they were doing for Gaia and her inhabitants.

"They were absolutely precious, and their sweet smiles were contagious. For several minutes, wave upon wave of pure love passed back and forth between us. Gratitude, friendliness, and affection blended into an energetic field through and around us. It was clear to me that I knew these people intimately. They were truly like family.

"I turned toward Nate and asked him if this was another planet in our universe, or was I visiting a subtle, mystical dimension? What was going on? He spoke to me lovingly, as he always did.

Remember that space and time are linear illusions. Keep in mind that your unique coordinate in the field simply describes your perspective, how you interpret your reality in the present moment. Since you are capable of experiencing any coordinate in the field, you can experience this coordinate—which you may realize you are familiar with.

When you talk about a "dimension," it sounds like you think you are going somewhere, like to a subtle realm or an ethereal planet. From my current perspective, I see "dimensions" this way: You are capable of moving between infinite scales, or layers, of frequency within yourself—you can move up or down, through realities that are endless in possible frequency, composition, and appearance. Any given reality may feel unfamiliar and familiar at the same time. That is because, dear one, you are moving within yourself. Let that sink in.

You do not journey to a "somewhere," to an esoteric place called a "dimension." Rather, you are enjoying a higher scale within yourself where you can experience life in a higher frequency state. Whatever you see there is within you and is accessible. According to the octave (like in musical scales), it may appear similar to your current reality or it can look and feel vastly different. Remember it's about frequency. If you journey inside yourself often, you can become established in a higher octave. The journey is endless.

It's like a tiny cell having a perspective of its environment within your body. It looks around and sees other cells and a bunch of squiggly things floating around. But if it suddenly scaled up into the complexity of the entire human form, it would certainly see from a higher perspective. Yet it may freak out and feel confused. That is a big jump from the limited perception of a cell to perceiving itself as a whole body.

My point is that what you think of as dimensions actually exists within you as scales, octaves, or ratios. It's about your perspective and range of frequency. So enjoy the adventure of scaling within yourself.

But there are other ways to travel as well. In this meeting with the small ones, rather than scaling inside yourself, the singularity within you moved into another part of the universe. This coordinate in the field is familiar to you so you could easily come here. For now, you need to know that this kind of travel is possible. When you are asleep, you are not absorbed in your thinking mind so you can travel effortlessly.

Remember that I love you in all scales and every universe.

One more clarification for you, my love. When I spoke about traveling to other coordinates in the field in the vast multiverse, consider that there are coordinates that are so subtle that if you arrive there, you wouldn't see anything. At such frequencies your own is not refined enough to perceive the ethereal shapes and forms. However, could high frequency souls live in a place like that? Consider this: In that coordinate, you may perceive a few shapes or even barren landscape. Inadvertently, you may walk right through a local inhabitant, or pass them and never know it—their body is not vibrating at the same rate as yours as you are walking through the ether where the subtle form of a high frequency soul resides.

I always love sharing the inexplicable with you, sweetheart! Infinity, endlessness, is at your fingertips, literally. That is my message.

As I was leaving my body and you told me that you'd love me forever, you spoke the truth. We imprinted the field with our love and that imprint is discernible to us, as a magnet that draws us to each other. We have a special relationship and remain synchronized eternally because long ago, somewhere in the field, maybe we spun out of a black hole simultaneously—remaining entangled across all time, space and realities. That's my vision of physics and mysticism wrapped together. The bottom line is that we will always find each other and continue to communicate because we formed a bond.

The love that you declared as I transitioned is a wave of energy which ripples out unceasingly as pure love into the quantum field for everyone to bathe in.

*I am always available as you move forward with the work
you are doing. Come back anytime, my darling.*

"Within that coordinate of the universe, wherever it is, I was not feeling separate and missing him. I felt connected with him, wholly, and contentedly. Without hesitation, I passionately congratulated the little people on the work they'd done on Earth for millennia. And I promised to come back again and revel in our mutual love for each other. The dream ended as I was sending and feeling roaring waves of unimaginable love to and from this group and the same exchange was happening with Nate.

"I want to add that somehow those little people I reunited with somewhere in the universe and the little people under the volcano seem connected." Sophia smiled at her new friend. "Any thoughts?"

Angelica had been intently listening. Pausing for a moment, she replied, "The little people you saw and the ones under the volcano could be related. The main thing I want you to know is that as you were describing your dream, I felt I was being transported to that part of the universe with you. I've done extensive inner work, and I trust my inner guidance meter. The dream is real and whatever you learn from it matters. Even though this kind of experience is subtle and personal, it is also scientifically verifiable. Don't be self-doubting or dismiss it as crazy. If you look at the research we've done, you have to ask yourself what's crazier: thinking that MK-Ultra is ethical and benevolent, or downplaying the magnificence of our sacred, unlimited human potential?

"Will you let conditioned beliefs tell you that you are nuts? Not on my watch, sister! I believe in you, one hundred percent! In the past, the path of spiritual evolution you are walking was lonely. For Gilda and Jordon, they suffered alone—except maybe a therapist or shaman for comfort. I want to assure you that there are more people than ever who will not allow themselves to be desensitized to higher quantum possibilities. And they have not allowed Hollywood and video games to normalize violence. They've not engaged with alternate realities that someone else shows them. They are discovering and earnestly seeking to find quantum life in real time and not through devices. Future technologies will not be used for control, mind-numbing, or manipulation. Instead, they will serve our health needs and our capacity to move naturally through time and space to visit places like you did in that lucid dream.

"Thank you for being so vulnerable. I feel complete for tonight and I'm getting sleepy. This is my bedtime. How about you? Are we complete here?"

Sophia smiled. "*Complete* for now. Something tells me that complete is going to remain a relative term in my world. Completions ignite something unexpected at every turn."

With warmhearted hugs, they ended their day within the enigma of a mysterious, quantum world.

CHAPTER 20
DREAMS AND MEMORIES

Sophia found herself settling into a whole new world. The first week unfolded with serene morning meditations, continued lucid dreams of the ritual at the volcano, long walks around the lake, and frequent journaling. She had ample time for relaxing and recovering from the emotional rollercoaster of the past few months.

Before the sun's first magnificent rays blessed the day, she often meditated on the deck. Quietude and inner stillness would then emerge into a symphony of bird calls and the world seemed to joyfully awaken, bursting forth in vibrant colors over the lake. Yet, on this morning, a sense of calm silence remained over the landscape. The morning fishing boats drifted serenely onto the lake with ease as they glided to their chosen spot for that day.

Sophia, on the other hand, was restlessly pacing back and forth across the porch.

Offering tea in her usual, friendly manner, Angelica smiled. Yet uncharacteristically, Sophia turned down the offer.

"I don't like to pry," Angelica said. "But if you need to talk, I am here for you."

Ceasing her relentless pacing, Sophia turned slowly, took a deep breath, and said, "Thank you. And yes, I'd love a cup of tea now. Something happened last night."

Angelica slowly poured a steaming cup of tea for Sophia as she continued. "It was another lucid dream, Angelica... bewildering... it makes no sense." Grasping the cup and sipping the warm liquid, Sophia took another deep breath. She drank the tea looking agitated and confused.

"I went to the volcano, as usual, in my dream state," Sophia said reflectively. "I found myself on the platform. But this time, there were ETs standing to the right of the woman. Although I was not alone with the woman, I felt safe. In fact, the ETs were so beautiful and loving that it caught me off guard. I mean... there's abductions in movies, and scary documentaries about ETs doing all kinds of weird things to people, and that kind of flashed through my mind. But here I was and I spoke to them without fear, maybe because Gilda told me about an ET who was very loving, kind, and extremely helpful to her. In any case, I asked the ETs in my dream why they'd come. And one of them spoke. He was about eight feet tall, totally white, with shimmery blue eyes. His eyes were at an angle, wider at the outside top and narrowing towards a small nose. No hair.

"The thing is, Angelica, on a gut level I felt this being was trustworthy and that he was not trying to manipulate me. But he caught me off guard when he said that he was curious if I was comfortable with what I'd been called to the lake to do. *Called to do what?*

"He said that every human being holds codes and information in their blood and bones, information that can be shared. He referred to me as a *record keeper* and said that I had codes for the water here that I brought from eons ago, from a prior ice age. He told me there were beings, giants from another universe who trained me long ago. At that moment in the dream, I was remembering something buried deep within my psyche, like a long-forgotten past on this planet. He said the ETs were here to support me. As a human, I had the capacity to share specific codes for *unicity*. There's that word again! And he asked only that

I hold my palms out and allow the codes to freely pass through them and into the lake. The water will take in the coded information. From there, the blood of any humans who are ready for the codes will receive them.

"The past record keepers deemed that the most efficient way of storing the codes was in humans and in ice. This was the best way to keep information about the truth of the Essence of humanity accessible.

"As I stood there, I felt my body vibrating and pure love frequencies were roaring out of my hands. All of a sudden, I noticed something odd. A golden structure like two pyramids adjoined vertically was hovering over the lake. For some reason, it felt fine for it to be there. I recognized it as a space craft. In that moment, it felt surprisingly comforting to witness its powerful presence.

"The energies continued to flow and then right in front of me, I saw thirty-foot-tall giants with frozen, ten-foot-tall ice cores. Don't ask me how I knew that these ice cores held information for the water. They brought them to the shaft and without their invitation, I touched their hands as they dropped the cores into the shaft. An explosion of blinding light streaked from the shaft into the sky. Several more cores were dropped with the same effect. I continued to allow the energy in me to flow freely, sometimes becoming so intense that it was hard to remain standing.

"After several minutes, the energies normalized. And I realized that other ETs had joined us. All were bipedal. One looked like a cross between a Shar-Pei dog and a light grey manatee with tiny, black eyes and slick, shiny skin. He was wrinkled but cute like a friendly dog. There were three other ETs who looked somewhat like ants, and a huge white dragon, hovering—it looked ethereal and was opaque rather than solid.

"Angelica, it's one thing to have these lucid dreams with a spirit woman and a dream of Nate on another planet or universe. This is different! Is my mind going crazy? Is this part of the grieving process? Why would this happen to me?" Sophia sank down in her chair, staring straight ahead.

"Could I ask a question?" Angelica said. "My request is that you sit with my question for a minute and not answer right way. Let it sink in. Okay?"

Sophia nodded.

"What if the ETs are higher frequency beings that have been there all along? And it took you a while to be able to perceive them? In other words, you've slowly let your heart open to the spirit woman, to all that you and Gilda talked about, and to what I shared. Has your frequency increased enough that you can see what was always there?"

Sophia sat introspectively gazing at the rhythmic waves on the mystical lake in front of her.

"Elevating my frequencies could explain it," Sophia said in a quiet, pensive tone. "It makes sense. Through the lens of frequency and our multidimensional nature, the inner realities that Nate spoke about in my dream are perceptible. He explained clearly how that could happen. I know that perception shifts reality. So the change in my perception, into *acceptance and love* for the ETs rather than *fearing* them, could gradually raise my overall frequency and thus alter my reality. That's worth considering. Maybe it's that simple."

The two friends sat quietly as shafts of molten-gold sunlight pierced the delicate foliage covering the pergola. Sophia's tea had completely cooled. In spite of that, she drank it thirstily as she collected her thoughts.

"I can easily complicate things with my mind," She said. "I should know better." She drank the last sip and set the cup down. "After Nate's body began to weaken and I knew I was not in control of his life, I started to experiment with applying what I had been studying about frequency. Sometimes Nate would hit a limit when his muscles became so incredibly weak that he could barely walk. I realized that with intention, I could use my frequencies to uplift myself and him.

"I started to handle situations with Nate differently. In the past, if I felt that I was being criticized, I experienced shame, fear, or sometimes anger. As I gave my body a chance to feel higher frequencies, when a situation occurred with him that triggered old beliefs and lower frequencies, I felt more calm, steady, and the love bond between us remained solid. It became clear that Nate's illness gave me many opportunities to raise my frequencies and shift outdated patterns. A perfect example of what I am talking about was a watershed moment for me. He needed my help to walk. His upper body and hands could not manage a cane or other supports. As he leaned on me for support, he looked terrified and then angry. Complaining, he said that I was pulling on him and that he was about to fall. I doubled down on my focus, asking him if the slight adjustments were helping. They were not. He became more angry and more afraid. Walking a short distance from his chair to the bed felt like an eternity.

"I noticed I was dropping in frequency. I felt like a child trying to do something beyond her capacity and an adult was criticizing her every step of the way. Too much was expected of her. She was feeling not good enough, smart enough, or skilled enough. So as soon as I was sure Nate was safe, I told him I needed some space, and headed for the other room to deal with this old wound inside me; a small child in me who was sensitive to frequencies transmitted from adults in her young life. As I paid attention to her, feelings of unworthiness and fear arose, tears fell. They surfaced as a pliable, soft energy. I kept breathing deeply and letting the feelings rise like a wave that eventually crested until the next frequency wave followed, in an ocean of endless frequencies. There's no way that I wanted to dump this on Nate or make him feel bad. He was scared, maybe weaker that day, or maybe he was being triggered by some other emotion. No matter why he reacted the way he did, I was focusing on myself.

"Then, I heard Nate's frail voice calling me. I forgot to put the little temple bell nearby so he could signal me that he needed help. By then, I felt more grounded and steady. As I arrived in his room, he motioned for me to sit by him on the bed. He looked at the proximity of our fingers and he delicately, and with great determination, inched his fingertips over to where my hand was resting. Touching fingertips was the best contact he could muster.

"Softly, he said, 'I was not angry with you. My situation is massively frustrating, darling. I know it's hard to understand. Having a body that doesn't work is sometimes agonizing and sometimes terrifying.' By then, I was crying. With the touch of our fingertips and our heart connection, he transmitted a healing balm for me. He said, 'Whatever you were feeling when you pretty much bolted from the room, please hear me out. You didn't do anything wrong. This was about my fear and my frustration.

"I love you more than I can convey in words. I know that when you were young, there were adults who scared you and you felt that you had to acquiesce to them. I am not one of them, little Sophia. I love the adult you and the young you. I know how much inner work you've done on this. We are both doing the best we can to work on ourselves and love each other every step of the way.'

"We were blessed to have each other to grow from our triggers rather than become polarized by them. For me, that's the intimacy that I always wanted in a relationship. It's beyond sex or a need to be loved. It's the day-to-day moments where frequencies can dive down, yet with that kind of friendship and focus, they can rise to heights that turn a human life into an immeasurably beautiful ride through time and space. When we focused on our personal frequency, inadvertently, we helped the other. We didn't create a battleground between us to fight from a position of lower frequency triggers, old beliefs, and mental patterns. It's a priceless gift to develop that kind of friendship."

Sophia and Angelica let silence take over the space for several minutes as the soft breeze increased in amplitude. The water of the lake started to take on brighter shades of turquoise, glittering with auriferous sparkles as the sun rose higher announcing that a new day had begun.

Pouring more tea, Sophia said, "It makes sense to me that the answer to your question is that higher frequencies could allow me to see those ETs who were there all along.

"Part of what I learned from that walk with Nate is that I elevate in vibration when I let my awareness settle into the wonder of life and my higher feelings. Judgment of self or each other didn't find fertile ground because my intention to elevate in frequency was so darn strong.

"If I meet the ETs from a place of curiosity and drop what I've heard and read about them, I wonder if I could communicate with more ease and flow. I'm talking out loud. My curiosity meter is rising. When I was with the ETs, I didn't feel lower frequencies like manipulation, pride, or anything creepy. Just love, peace, and lightheartedness. Those are three of my favorite frequencies."

Angelica laughed, poured more tea, and said, "Oh honey, I hope you can let your extraordinary experiences unfold naturally as you did in your relationship with Nate; not trying to fix or figure out anything. From what I can see, you have good intuition. If the ETs had a hidden agenda, you would be able to quickly sense the low vibes. You may be a more savvy observer than you realize. And I can tell you that you are not the first human to meet what some call *heavenly beings* here at the lake. It's not necessary to meet them, and if you have, fine. See what happens. And always know, day or night, I am here for you. Any time you want to talk or need anything, let me know."

"Thank you so much," Sophia said. "I'd like to know one more thing before the day gets going. About those giants that I saw, have you heard of them visiting here or living here in the past?"

Angelica's eyes twinkled and she said, "Yes, my dear, that's for another time. I'd like to continue our conversation this evening. It's time for me to go to the Farmer's Market with my oils and I have a full day ahead. But tonight, I'd be happy to share. Enjoy your day."

Smiling and reaching over to lightly squeeze Angelica's hand, Sophia said, "Thank you. How about if I make the soup tonight?"

CHAPTER 21
GIANT TALK

By midmorning, Sophia began exploring the area around the lake, took a long walk shaded by Maul oaks, hiked into the hills, stopping to rest near emerald, moss-covered rocks. Tiny, white native flowers poked their heads up to whisper to her about peace and serenity. After a long meditation by the lake and dipping her feet reverently into the sacred water for a few minutes of close communion with it, she decided to treat herself to an afternoon nap. When she woke up, Sophia grabbed her journal and wrote feverishly for several minutes before heading to the kitchen to begin the evening meal.

A couple of hours later, Angelica arrived home and Sophia greeted her warmly. "Angelica, there's something baffling going on and I'd love to know what you know about giants. Why don't we eat first and then we can talk. It's crazy that I took a short nap and yet it will take the whole evening to talk about it. This place generates one surprise after another. I'll get everything ready for dinner and meet you on the deck."

"Okay, sounds like fun. See you in a few minutes." Angelica changed into her most comfortable clothes, grabbed a shawl for the cooler evening temperatures, and followed the exquisite scent of Sophia's soup. Fresh bread from the market, Sophia's homemade cheese, and a handful of fresh flowers created a carousel of beauty to top off the bountiful meal. After they ate, feeling satiated and relaxed, the two friends sat back in their wicker lounge chairs and took in the comforting scents and sounds of evening.

"I am ready to hear about your day," Angelica said as she nestled comfortably into her chair.

Sophia responded with raised eyebrows as she said, "The day was fabulous but my nap was definitely an unexpected experience. Falling easily into sleep, I found myself on top of the volcano. Because of my recent dream-trips there, I felt comfortable standing on the platform with the ETs, holding the ethereal flower petals and cosmic crystals, and the scene looked and felt calm. Maybe our talk yesterday helped me to be more accepting of all of this.

"Then something changed. Many more giants arrived and delivered lots of additional ice cores. They were from the North. One of the ETs said that a giant was coming from behind me, which was the South. He was from Antarctica. Some cores were so long that three giants were required to hoist them onto their shoulders. As I did in the past dream, I touched their arms as they dropped each core into the shaft. It was like infusing the giants and the cores with a frequency.

"The frequencies were building, and I was a little dizzy. To help me steady myself, they stopped for a few minutes. As I looked around, I saw a large mountain off in the distance to the Northwest. The ET explained that this was a sacred spot and was very active with ETs during Mu times. I recall that Mu is an ancient name for what is often referred to as *Lemuria*.

"Off to the Northeast, I could see a lake in a desert area. The ET said that it is a sacred lake from that same time period. There are some ETs living there who are mermaids. He told me that they have *gone rogue* and are no longer loving or gracious to humans.

"The codes being emitted were transmitted to the sacred mountain and to that desert lake, forming a triangle with the volcano. The sacred mountain has become home to beings of a lower vibration. These beings will receive the codes and can connect with them naturally and easily. Both the mountain and that lake are also inhabited by higher-level beings who will benefit from the codes and can mentor lower level beings so that the codes can be transcribed into their DNA.

"As though I fully comprehended what he said, I held my hands out, and felt roaring energy flowing to the remote mountain and faraway lake.

"Consumed more and more thoroughly with love and gratitude for all beings on this planet, visible and not visible, the energies surged more powerfully from my hands. My feet were buzzing with energy. Yet the ETs all stood resolutely, with faces emanating serenity, as the giants brought more ice cores.

"This was the first time I saw the volcano during daylight. And I was intoxicated with the majestic beauty that I observed around me. As though not bothered by what we were doing, a cougar sauntered through the trees below us and deer grazed nonchalantly and peacefully nearby. Birdsongs were like a mesmerizing symphony of celestial music.

"As the giants turned to leave, one of them turned back and came towards us. My heart was overcome with joy and my eyes filled with tears. His long, wispy white hair and snowy-colored eyebrows shimmered in the sunlight. My heart melted as he gazed at me lovingly, paternally. Although his face was covered with fine wrinkles that gave him the appearance of elder status, his crystalline blue eyes radiated timeless juvenescence. As he came near the platform, he held out his enormous hand, and without hesitation, I placed my head there. This form of affection felt natural and familiar. As I looked up, his eyes were shimmering with tears. My entire chest became a center for communication with him. The energy within that area of my body connected with his giant chest. Unexpectedly, wordless love passed back and forth in pulsations that were indescribably soul-stirring.

"Our emotional expression was deeply nurturing like between a father and child. Time and space evaporated and he and I melted into nothing and everything at the same time. I felt ecstatic and serene, wild and contained, and perfectly pure. Gently, I lifted my head and watched the loving hand slip away as I lost consciousness until I awoke here, in this time and space. I was still vibrating as a field of love. It's indescribable and yet it's as real as sitting here with you. I couldn't move for a while.

"As life unfolded in this time and space that I refer to as my current *reality*, I got up and started chopping vegetables and making soup. It felt natural to move from that ecstasy with the giant to what could be called mundane existence. It felt right to move from one experience of reality to another within myself. It's all frequency and it's all good. I can move to that volcano within levels of consciousness within myself where I am more high vibe. Or I can move to another coordinate in the universe in linear time on a vector of space. The possibilities for this kind of exploration seem endless, expansive, and freeing.

"As I cooked, the food felt like it was absorbing the frequencies. I experienced the remnants of the meeting on the volcano while I was also happy to cook, to look at the lake from the window, and to be silent.

"That giant hand; I can still feel his touch. Angelica, I love him. Why? What is my bond with him? As he was leaving, I saw a cobalt blue streak of light behind him. It shimmered and morphed into many different shades of blue; sometimes tinged with golden or white, iridescent light. Seeing that streak was mesmerizing and warmed my heart. It was ethereal yet it felt huggable. That may sound strange but that's how it felt.

"Nate's explanation of scaling dimensions within myself and my singularity going to other universes helped me to be more relaxed with the encounter. Of course, my mind keeps wanting to jump in and figure out the details about how all of this happens but I want to give myself a break, let the events arise and gradually learn more about how it is happening from a spiritual or physics perspective.

"Because of our conversation yesterday, I was reminded that I can relax and allow my frequencies to elevate. That influenced my interaction in the dream today. So I want to thank you for letting me process all of this. And when you are ready, I'd love to hear your reaction to what I dreamt, and what you know about giants."

Angelica glanced in Sophia's direction with a compassionate smile saying, "Oh my goodness, dear girl! What a nourishing and cosmic dream. It seems the lake is granting you her most elevated wisdom and love. You've developed an amazing relationship with her.

"It may surprise you that your dream is not shocking to me. You'd better settle in. I didn't realize how much you were being shown and how much information you already have encoded within you."

"Encoded?" Sophia asked inquisitively.

"Yes, encoded," Angelica said. "Oh my Lord, Sophia! I was so shy about sharing a lot of unusual topics with you. But now I am sure you are ready to hear more details of the incredible history that I discovered over the past five years.

"The people who arrived here many thousands of years ago were mostly survivors of a massive flood that affected the entire planet. You've likely heard of a global flood at the end of the last ice age around eleven thousand years ago. It's mentioned in biblical stories, many ancient texts, and shamanic cultures across the globe. I am sharing myth, legend, and the testimony of descendants of these people. Even if you've heard of the horrific, ancient war and the global flood, to talk about giants, we need to go back further in Earth's history. If you head north into Idaho and Canada, you will find people who can tell you more about them.

"Gaia underwent several ice ages. And there were ETs who came here each time to store codes of important information about higher truths and how to maintain high frequencies. They were also here to help civilizations in their re-building efforts. By my saying this, it triggers a lot of upset for some people. I am sure you understand why I am selective with whom I share this information. From all the archeological evidence, it's clear that there were advanced global civilizations during many ice ages. This would mean that, believe it or not, humans and hybrids, which are humans who bred with giants or other ETs, had the innate capacities and technological knowledge to travel to other planets and universes. Holding higher frequencies, they could move easily through space to various coordinates.

"Back to the giants... Almost without exception, their place of origin was another universe or the far reaches of this one. They came here to protect the wisdom of higher truth and frequency and they captured it in the form of ice. From what I've learned, blood and water is the easiest way for them to encode and decode wisdom. Through the multiverse, this beautiful planet was considered exceptionally important. The abundance and diversity of life forms is rare within any solar system or galaxy. The giants often worked in small groups, maybe living only with their immediate family. Their lifespan was quite long. Tens of thousands of years, for example. Stay with me, Sophia. I am getting to the giant's role.

"They seemed to teach small groups of people, likely cultures adept in shamanic practices and esoteric wisdom. As the ice receded, some giants went home. Others stayed, living in caves, isolated and still discretely working with the shamanic humans who were the *record keepers* for their specific culture.

"I want you to know that one part of your dream blows my mind because a local, indigenous elder told me something that I could not quite wrap my head around—giants bred with humans. You better take a deep breath as I explain that their male offspring grew up to be almost as tall as them. But the females were not giants and, as you might imagine, the birth didn't always work out well. They kept experimenting but it seemed to be a roll of the dice until they figured out genetic patterns that worked, allowing them to better pair potential parents. Another interesting detail was that the female babies of these ET giants were cared for and nurtured carefully because they possessed a particular gene that didn't express in the males. It had to do with connectedness at a core level. He called it *unicity*. The women born of the giants could infuse many civilizations with the gene.

"When the gene expressed and unicity spread, the entire world came together in a deeply rich and meaningful union of souls. This is where I found the elder's story fascinating: Some of the giant females were so subtle that they were pure energy, a blue streak of light. It was rare for a man to be allowed to breed with one of the blue streaks. The potential father had to go through rigorous training, show thousands of years of dedication to sacred, infinite wisdom, and he had to have a gene that expressed pure truth and pure love. He must be able to vibrate in very high frequencies and be fully established in compassion and universal unity."

Sophia leaned forward and looked inquisitively at Angelica saying, "The blue streak of exquisite light... a mother? I'm speechless." She looked out across the lake as pink hues began to overtake the sky and the bright turquoise of the water began fading to a grey-blue color. The light shimmering on the lake was gentling into its evening descent, blending colors and hues more subtle and muted.

"For goodness sake, this is beginning to get more fascinating to me," Angelica said as she sat up straighter and gazed at Sophia with rapt attention. "I have a question—and you don't have to answer if you don't want to. I am wondering if the giant and the blue streak of light felt like family to you. The scene you described was so sweet and blessedly intimate. I am asking because as you are rapidly becoming familiar with and willing to explore the possibility of a broader context for your life, I wonder if you felt you knew this family from long ago."

"I don't know what to think. My mind has no framework to work with," Sophia said thoughtfully. She was quiet, lost in contemplation for a few moments. Then she began again.

"I want to tell you something important that I never share anymore because it gets people so upset. But here goes... When I first learned to meditate, I went to a priest with whom I had a great relationship. When I told him about meditation, I expected that he'd try to get me to stop or direct me back to more traditional practices of prayer. Instead, he confided to me that he'd learned to meditate twenty years earlier and that he found it to be an indispensable part of his life. That revelation gave me the courage to ask him about reincarnation, the Nag Hammadi library, and a list of other controversial topics. He looked at me with compassion and said, 'Reincarnation wasn't removed from church doctrine by Jesus or his apostles. It was taken out by emperors and church leaders hundreds of years later. That is why it remains a point of contention, deep study, and reflection for the Catholic Church and many Christian churches that followed. It does not matter whether you believe in the doctrine that there is only heaven and hell or an *ethereal realm* called purgatory, which replaced the concept of reincarnation. I suggest you make this life perfect by loving and respecting everyone with your whole heart. Then there's nothing to fret over. You'll be golden. It'll be a life well-lived.' I was stunned to hear his answer, but later, my own investigations confirmed what he'd said about the changes made to church texts and doctrines.

"The main point I am trying to make is that his perspective allowed me to stick my toe into the waters of possibly; the possibility that history may be different than what I had learned and believed. At first, it was hard to explore the idea of reincarnation. It conflicted with the worldview I was comfortable with. Ending up in either heaven or hell was simple to grasp and familiar. But studying the unified field theory of quantum physics was a catalyst for me to open my mind and consider the miraculous processes happening in and around us every second. It reconfigured my definition of past.

"This is how I understand it now. Information is continuously exchanged between the field and all particles in all scales of frequency—from protons to people. Since we exist within the field, as we go through space, we leave information on the electromagnetic field of space-time around us about what we observe. The information is stored in the field as memory, which we refer to as *past experiences.*

"Our brain and body act as antennae to connect with the field as we spiral through the structure of space, while spinning around the sun. And our sun is not anchored in static space. Rather, the sun is hurtling through space, in a constant progression, always in motion; and Gaia and the other planets elegantly, intelligently rotate and spin as they revolve around the sun. It is a complex and beautiful dance! This whole universe is dynamic and everything influences everything else constantly. My point is that energy is always in motion and our universe reveals the motions of rotation, revolution, and progression.

"As I said, we create *the past* by imprinting memory in the field continuously. In that way, we will always have access to our unique signature frequencies' past impressions. I know this is a lot to take in, but I want you to understand the depth of study that I was willing to engage in to understand what life and death mean on Planet Earth. According to the unified field theory of quantum physics, we leave these imprints at inconceivably minute intervals in the structure of space naturally.

"As a physical being, every proton in my body is entangled (connected even at a distance) with every particle in the universe, including all its inhabitants. We are indelibly linked and always in a subtle conversation, or exchange of information.

"However, my coordinate is my unique location within the infinite, unified field from which to observe all-that-is. When the processes of my body cease to function, my unique memory and consciousness remain in the field. My consciousness can pick up a new physical form that can operate in the field, and I will begin to observe and exchange information as this new form from my unique coordinate. And as I said, my access to all of my imprinted memory remains accessible through my consciousness.

"My unique signature frequency sends and receives a personalized, distinctive perspective to the field, infinitely. We are the *one and only* us yet completely unified forever. It's mathematically proven and explains the incomprehensible nature of evolution of people and universes.

"One key takeaway is that I am an *extension* of the field collecting and sending information back to the whole. Through each of us, universal consciousness can express itself and know itself more fully. I think of it as being a bubble that arises from the core of the universe. I am but one bubble but I can still tell the universe what I perceive from my vantage point. Simultaneously, the universe sends information back to me about the broader perspective. It's an unfathomable dance we are in with all-that-is. Imagine the complexity of being universal consciousness, the field, as well as its extensions—totally mind blowing to our limited brains.

"What's important to me is that I can accelerate the stream of information to and from the infinite field—by accepting that I have that capacity. I can own my innate greatness, my wild, unlimited self. The way I do that is to bring my awareness inside to study the subtle aspects of my being. Like you, I meditate and self-reflect. My mind becomes softer and more expanded in consciousness.

"Because our physical life is based on our perceptions in one limited coordinate of space-time, we cannot perceive a bazillion realities and memories at once through it. Here and now I am seeing one coordinate on a specific vector of space in the vast unified field, this moment with you in your lovely home. In my lucid dreams, however, without my physical body and mind getting in the way, my consciousness can connect to another coordinate on a vector of space, where I am the daughter of a giant and a blue ray of light.

"At some point, I realized that the only way to know for sure about this topic of life and death was to remain open, explore, and focus on what the priest said: *love and respect others*. And I would add that allowing the unicity gene to express in all its glory is part of a life well-lived, too. These days I am openly curious about scaling into higher dimensions within myself and moving my singularity through a worm hole to *gosh-knows-where*. I have ingested plenty of science for my brain to feel fed and satiated. I am now unshakably sure that anything is possible.

"Because of that, I can stand on the volcano and embrace the hand of a giant. Being open to a blue streak of light as a familiar mother figure is also within the domain of possibility that ignites my soul. I practice with my mind's subtle tendency to eclipse my open heart and growing curiosity. I have a close friend, Grace, who reminds me that if we were not diverging from the status quo, and if we decided to stop being open to everything, what would become of us?"

Angelica laughed. "Great question!" She smiled at Sophia cheerfully and paused the conversation to make more herbal tea.

Meanwhile, Sophia took a moment to clear her mind by closing her eyes and holding still inside. This was a moment of what she called, "Intimate connection with Essence."

When Angelica returned with tea, its fragrance of apples and cinnamon wafting through the air around them, she poured two cups and smiled at Sophia who gave her a quizzical look. "Something tells me that you know more about the giants," Sophia said. "Is that right?"

Cuddling her warm cup of tea, Angelica took a sip and answered by saying, "I don't know how much you know about the war, the flood, and all that happened between twenty thousand to ten thousand years ago. As I mentioned, the giants were already more than the record keeper variety. There were other very large ETs as well—from another universe. They came after an ice age, maybe two hundred thousand years ago. Their exact arrival has never been totally clear to me. They were interested in helping humans. They were also here to support and guide those people who were born to the giant parents that I described a few minutes ago. They didn't come to meddle or manipulate. Rather, they opened opportunities for the developing species on Earth to learn deeper Universal Truths, to learn how to become one with plants, and how to turn on what you call the *unicity gene.*

"Let me give you a brief history of the ETs. This is coming from the indigenous elder who I mentioned a few minutes ago; the one who knew about the local giants. He said that the ETs first came and settled in the Pacific Ocean. They were shamans but they also had advanced technology. They were masters at working with the mineral kingdom. Quartz was their specialty. They taught the human shamans about the invisible connection between everything, including how to navigate those connections. They also shared techniques for building crystal cities of light on the surface of Earth and under water. The volcano here had one of those cities under it, as did that mountain you saw during your nap today. And there was a city in the lake with the *rogue* mermaids. These cities were all over the place within the Pacific Rim. In China, on Easter Island, New Zealand, and Australia.

"A long time ago, I dated an archeologist, who was without a doubt brilliant. He was skilled in his field of work, and also highly intuitive. I really loved being with him on a dig or in conversations where he'd get the most amazing insights about the site where he was working. He dug deeper than the physical dirt and rocks. He could dig into the vibrations of a place, and he'd know where to look and where to get clues about the meaning of even the tiniest artifacts." Angelica paused in an awkward moment of silence.

Sophia sat pensively and waited while Angelica seemed to deal with emotions triggered from her memory. Angelica took time to elegantly collect herself and continue.

"The crystals in the cities could store information and be used to generate energy, no electricity needed. It's amazing that these cities had free energy. Light emanated without the need for fire, electricity, or any devices. It must have been a magical world. I have no idea how they created such things. And there were pyramids everywhere, often with water under them. Using pyramid technology, those who entered them with the proper training and frequency could travel inter-dimensionally. People came and went all over the universe, freely and easily, without spaceships.

"There was a general agreement between these Pacific ETs in an area called Mu and another race on the other side of the world called Atlanteans. Some anthropologists suggest that the latter mated with humans, were technology driven, and created pyramids that were used for inter-dimensional travel. They also showed humans how to organize themselves into well-designed cities, how to raise animals, and all sorts of new cultural practices.

"But then two things happened. First, the Atlanteans lost sight of the unicity gene. They lost their integrity, and became seduced by power and control over humanity. They also started migrating across the globe—colonizing—and were encroaching on the peaceful Pacific Ocean through the Arabian Sea.

"The Mu people of the Pacific Rim, both ETs and humans, were not violent. They did not have warrior skills or weapons because they'd had no need for them. To make a long story short, war broke out. As the Mu were overpowered, their crystal cities were destroyed. Pyramids were annihilated along with most of the gentler protectors of Gaia, the shamanic civilization—who valued the unicity gene and who wanted to live in harmony.

"Then, there was a global flood which caused the oceans and seas to rise violently to unprecedented levels, without warning. The islands of the Pacific Ocean disappeared and a few ETs stayed behind to guide the humans to safety. Some helped a few to get here to this lake, others made it to the sacred mountain you saw during your nap. A small number of them migrated to central America. Most ETs, being subtle in nature and knowing that they were not meant to fight, left the planet, returning to their universe of origin. The ones who stayed behind kept their physical forms, lived for many years, and were, unfortunately, subject to disease and death. Tales of the war and the cataclysmic floods are recorded by many shamanic cultures globally.

"According to the elder, this lake has a few buried pyramids that hold codes for renewing the ancient wisdom. It makes sense to me that if you are a descendent of those beings, you'd have the codes.

"People around here, like me and those who have no idea about any of this, would all get the codes via the water. This can happen in various ways as the lake water evaporates and then rains down on our environment. We drink that water or sit near the lake where we can also *drink it in* through our energy field.

"There's something happening here. I can assure you of that. I've been told countless times by visiting shamans and local elders that this place is special and that the descendants of the

Mu people and the giants are now alive on Gaia. They will come here and awaken the lake, bringing the codes with them, and this will ripple out into this world, the solar system, and the whole universe. People can roll their eyes, but I defiantly can't disregard the elders who kept records for over ten thousand years, passed down from generation to generation.

"As we sit here sipping tea, something mystical and mind blowing is happening. We are not used to thinking or feeling in terms of our inconceivably powerful, capable selves. We limit ourselves to what we touch, see, hear, taste, and smell. But, as you said, we are infinitely much more than that. The essential oils from native plants were my invitation to come here. The reason that I say I'm noticing that things are amping up is that the volcano has not erupted for over twelve thousand years, although it continues to create mild tremors. However, recently it's been creating intermittent, more intense tremors under the lake. The little people are appearing to the elders more often, too. I haven't said much about them have I? One elder shared that for at least twenty thousand years, the original people here performed their rituals under the volcano within the lake that was there. There are legends about a crystal city which was lit naturally by rocks. I am guessing they used fluorescent rock or quartz, maybe both? The little people from the stars lived in that city. After the flood, they left. But... they can still come here to work with the elders. And they trained the elders to connect with them through what we call the Orion constellation. That is their quantum portal of choice.

"At that time, however, the little people seemed to be from the Pleiades or Sirius. The elders have shown me images and Sophia, some have elongated skulls. I had the rare privilege to see several of them that are treasured by the shamanic elders. Supposedly, the elongated skulls allow them to have a larger brain. I've read about elongated skulls that have been excavated in archeological sites around the globe, but I never heard archeologists declare that they were from another star system. The ones here were quite small, almost like children.

"Why are you looking so wide-eyed, Sophia?"

Sophia looked inquisitively at Angelica and asked, "What did these little people do for the locals?"

"They helped them to maintain sacred knowledge of how to connect with the heavens, how to code water, how to read the frequency of plants. The elders said the giants worked more with children than adults, to seed information and encourage them. Even after the flood, they stayed for a while until they'd calmed the children and reminded them about how to stay connected with them through the stars. Does that answer your question?"

"Yes, it does," Sophia said. "Angelica, I had that lucid dream with the little people. I am sure they are the same. This implies that due to memory imprints in the field and through being able to travel to other places in the solar system in dreams, I've kept in contact with them. In the dream with Nate that I shared with you, I told them about the great work they'd been doing here. They are talking to children right now on this planet, Angelica. I can feel it. I know it. I have chills."

"Me, too," Angelica added. "Based on your research and study of quantum physics, they can come here easily, be under the volcano, and communicate with anyone whose frequency band that is high enough to harmonize with theirs."

"This conversation has been extremely helpful and full of bombshells, in a good way," Sophia said as she smiled at her friend warmheartedly. "Pieces of a puzzle are fitting together. Because frequency and memory imprints can't be seen, mentally all of this can appear to be super esoteric. The important part for me to remember is that new science explains my subtle capacities to move through the universe and communicate with other beings. These emerging theories validate my experience, even if I have a hard time believing it.

"Those little people you described to me are vibrating at a faster rate; a rate that children can easily entrain with. When I was small, I had all kinds of encounters with beings from subtle realities or perhaps from somewhere out in the universe. It wasn't until my parents and culture told me they were imaginary that I stopped being aware of them. I'm pretty sure that affected my capacity to vibrate faster. I know children today who are in families and being educated in a way that allows for their full expression to develop. What would the world look like if we accepted and embraced all that we are?"

"Let's call it a night," Angelica said, releasing a gentle yawn. "I've enjoyed sharing the local stories with you and hearing yours. Over the years, I've met many interesting people who visited this lake and learned more than I thought possible. Like you, I research what they say and inevitably, I find out that somebody, somewhere has been digging into the subject too. It's amazing how much data and history people have discovered all over the world but we don't yet have a way to connect fully with them and share our experience.

"There has to be some way for us to come together other than social media. Candid conversations are needed about who we really are and how we could evolve; the way it was headed before the wars and that massive flood ravaged the planet. The shamans said the flood was so horrific, unforeseen, instantaneous, and incomprehensibly extensive that even today, our collective DNA holds the trauma from that epic event. How about that?

"Remind me to share with you what the visiting astronomer told me. And for now, sweet dreams. See you tomorrow."

CHAPTER 22
ASTRONOMERS AND HIKING TRAILS

Resplendent sunlight poured through the window at dawn and a soft breeze was the perfect wake up call. Already, the phone sounded a soft chime, announcing a text from Grace.

"I'm going to make tea. Call me in 15." Sophia texted back.

By the time the call came, Sophia was dressed and drinking tea, deeply introspective. Angelica wasn't home so the two friends could talk freely.

"What's up?" Grace asked playfully. "Last time we talked, you were getting to know an ephemeral goddess on the volcano. Did anything else happen?"

Sophia shared details of the ETs, the repeated meetups on the volcano and the giants—the touch of her head to the giant's magnificent hand. She added that Angelica's shaman friend confirmed the truth of Sophia's dream about visiting Nate, who had an elongated head, and was "hanging out" with little people from a distant star.

Thirty minutes later, as she finished sharing Angelica's input and response, Grace said lightheartedly, "Holy mole! Never a dull moment on the lake. Honestly, Sophia, how are you with all of this? Is it freaking you out?"

"At first it did, but Grace, even last night, I found myself with them again, although the giant, whose loving hand held my head in the past dream, was not there. Whatever is happening, it seems to be related to emitting and naturally releasing a frequency of pure love, joy, and peace. And of course, the frequency of the codes in the ice cores emits it, too. I saw something last night that I'd not seen in past visits to the volcano. Sacred geometric symbols and letters made of light flowed out of my hands, in a huge array of colors, beyond our normal rainbow spectrum.

"It sure feels real—and I know it is. But when I woke up, my mind kicked in and said I was dreaming. I keep wondering why I continue to have this doubt. This morning I recalled something I can't believe I'd forgotten.

"You'll remember when I was little, I played with three people who no one else could see, except you and me. One was green. I never could understand how no one else saw them or talked to them. They were a lot of fun. Remember, it's me, your crazy friend. This is who I really am! But the me who I *learned* to be is rational, and set those perceptions aside, blocking them out. Now I've come full circle, and this new version is curious and open to the world potentially being different than I've known it to be. What if invisible realms are just that—invisible? Yet they can be invisibly real, right? Photons and electrons are real and I cannot see them.

"Even though my three childhood friends did not look totally human, I thought they looked normal. Remember the one who wore tattered brown clothes, played silly games, and made me laugh? And the one who was female and looked a bit wild—crazy, messy, long hair, and a long, narrow nose? And the green man could take off his head and put it in his huge pocket! I loved that trick and you said that you liked it, too."

Grace laughed in delight, remembering their common experience of the three strange characters and how often their mothers begged them to stop talking about Grace's angels and Sophia's *strange friends.*

"Oh, Grace, those three beings guarded me so sweetly when I went to sleep and stayed with me until I was around six years old when I became convinced that they were not real. They came to me in dreams for several more years, where we enjoyed each other's company a little longer.

"The color green to me represented nurturing and safety. Later, I wondered if they were spirit guides like those that shamans speak about—they knew my needs and fears and recognized that my sensitive nature was struggling with a harsh and oppressive world that made no sense to me. I wasn't physically abused, but because of strict religious rules and my parents' authoritarian style of parenting, I took refuge in the supernatural realms beyond the strict confines of the physical world.

"At this stage of my life, I want to feel confident and relaxed when I set my mind free to explore all scales of myself. How infinitesimal and how giant am I? Finally and importantly, I'm realizing that I was born as a complex being who is connected to everyone and everything. There is unlimited information available to me. It's only the effects of culture, media, and wanting to fit in and be liked that have eclipsed the truth of my expansive being and its capacities.

"How's that for a very looooong answer to *what's up?*"

Grace laughed, reminiscing about her own experiences of seeing nature spirits, knowing things before they happened, and realizing that others didn't see the colorful, radiant auras around people and objects that Grace saw all of the time. When they were in middle school, Grace was stunned to realize that other people were blind to the ethereal nature spirits. Like Sophia, out of a need for belonging, Grace made herself fit into society to appease her family, cutting off her ability to see auras and to communicate with unseen realms in order to conform to what others thought "normal."

"This is why we are friends forever," Grace said. "Two crazies! We are perfectly crazy together. I love you!"

"I love you, too," Sophia said. "I can't imagine not having you in my life. I'm grappling with authenticity. How can I allow my frequency to rise and be willing to make new friends, since my old ones think I'm nuts? And how much more can I *take the lid off,* as you often say, and be myself unapologetically."

"Okay, Sophia, that's a tall order," Grace said teasingly. "Let me know how that works out for you. All kidding aside, I am excited for you. This is totally out of the box. You deserve to spread your wings. I have a feeling there are more people than either of us realize who are breaking free from self-imposed restrictions and cultural boxes. Have fun today, no matter what you decide to do!"

"Bye, Grace," Sophia said with a radiant smile. "Thanks for calling."

As Sophia glanced at the sky, a bald eagle soared overhead. Smiling, she said out loud, "I see you, friend. Thank you for reminding me to own my highest frequencies, to fly even higher, and to know that nature and I remain inseparable."

The door flew open, and Angelica arrived with groceries and in her usual upbeat style, she asked, "Want to go for a hike? I'd like to take advantage of this amazing weather. It couldn't be more picture perfect."

"I'd love to hike today," Sophia said, looking surprised and excited. "Let me change and get my boots. Sounds fabulous."

Within a few minutes, they were headed for a trail that Sophia had never seen or heard about. The climb was steep, and they finally reached a grove of old shade trees; oaks that looked to be hundreds-of-years-old.

"Oh how I love this spot," Angelica said. "I feel like I am being held by the Earth below while nurtured by the wise oaks surrounding me."

Sophia walked over and wrapped her arms around one of the huge trees, squeezing it, and holding it in a long embrace. A flock of birds bustled in some bushes nearby, burbling in melodious harmony, and took flight.

Relaxing against a six-foot-tall boulder, Angelica paused reflectively, titling her head to one side. Looking at Sophia quizzically, she asked. "Would you like to hear about my dear astronomer-friend?"

"Yes, I am in bliss being here right now," Sophia said as she settled comfortably against a nearby tree. "And I'm all ears."

"Well, as I said, I've met fascinating people in this area. Yet this man, Joe, was extra special. He had joined a group of people from Peru, Chile, and Brazil who met at Mount Shasta to camp and star gaze. Late one night, they encountered an ET. I thought you'd be interested to know that you are not the only one who sees the unseen. His story was utterly captivating.

"He said that the ET spoke to them telepathically. As I said, Joe was an astronomer. He was amazed and aware that this was a rare opportunity to speak to someone who lives out in the vast cosmos that he'd studied for decades. The ET was about eight-feet-tall. Although he was very kind, his frequency required some adjusting… on Joe's part.

"Joe told me this being was vibrating at such a rate that sometimes when the ET spoke, Joe felt dizzy and at other times, as the ET explained something, Joe became disoriented. I wonder if his disorientation was his brain, his psyche, trying to adjust to something completely foreign. Joe admitted to me that a couple of people in the group, who had encountered ETs in the past, felt woozy or nauseous. It was too much for their psyche to handle.

"Anyway, let me tell you what Joe shared. The being told him that the Earth was undergoing changes in her magnetic frequencies. Since humans are vibrational fields of electromagnetic energy, they were being impacted. This was a good thing happening. The Earth's frequency, as a sentient being, was vibrating at enlightened levels of super high frequency. This means that connecting with Gaia, being in tune with her rhythms, would allow humanity to more easily raise their frequency, too. We each have traumas from our lives, which play out on her surface. She has traumas to integrate, too.

"Joe said he felt exhilarated as the ET spoke, and he didn't feel an ounce of concern that this being had an agenda. Instead, Joe felt like he was speaking with a fascinating guy about a topic they both cared about deeply. The ET drew diagrams and symbols on the ground of constellations and sacred geometry. He showed Joe a map of how the giants moved across the Earth as *record keepers*. Joe added another historical event that I had never heard. The original Mu giants had come here two hundred thousand years ago. About forty-two thousand years ago, the Earth went through an apocalyptic event. The magnetics of the poles shifted, and an ice sheet started forming immediately over what we call North America, Europe, and Russia.

"There was a tear in the ozone layer and electrical storms raged. Many ETs had the capability for space travel at will, so they left right away. Some were caught off guard and died, while others sought refuge in caves, along with some humans. This went on for centuries. Because lifespans were long back then, when the Earth settled back to a new normal, some of those beings emerged and life continued. Some remained under the surface.

"The ETs and humans living together for so long inevitably mated and combined their genes. In this way, humanity continued to evolve. And one special gene became of interest to them. It brought humans into a natural state of communion with each other. Sounds like the *unicity gene* that you've mentioned.

"Over the millennia, ETs came to help humanity to thrive and become civilized, spiritually advanced, and attuned to nature's order. The ET pointed out that humans are connected to their ancient star families. For eons, ETs came here, then left, then came back. The planet has a history that spans billions of years.

"It sounds like a movie script, but with modern evidence from anthropology and archeology, our relationship with ETs is beginning to be accepted as more likely than previously believed. Unfortunately, with the devastating, large scale cataclysms that instantly wiped out most cultures globally, we lost all but a few records of their existence. We do have some cave art, certain hieroglyphs, stone circles, and other architectural anomalies. But I wonder if we will ever know what happened here millions of years ago.

"Well... As you can imagine, Joe left that camping trip stun-ned and puzzled. He said he read articles and interviewed experts in anthropology and ancient history. He began to correlate ancient archeological sites with constellations like Orion, and star groups like Sirius and the Pleiades, which the ET drew for him. As time passed, he discovered many archeological artifacts and structures that confirmed the ETs story. He was shocked to realize that ancient pyramids around the world—places as far apart as Egypt, Peru, and Bosnia—line up on particular equinoxes with the center of Orion."

Sophia, with a look of astonishment, asked, "Did you say the center, the heart of Orion?"

"Yes," Angelica answered, looking quizzical. "That's definitely what he told me."

Sophia shared her conversations with Kabir about the heart of Orion adding, "This is pretty wild to take in. The similar stories between my sweet, Indian friend and your local contacts... it's hard for my logical brain to process. My heart is excited, though. Please continue."

"This is affirmation for both of us, Sophia. It's amazing and we may need some time to assimilate it all.

"Back to Joe. He said that the final message from the ET was that other species in the universe deeply value Gaia for her rich diversity, including humanity's immeasurable, quantum capacities and ability to fully feel and experience these immeasurable blessings. As an example, on many planets and stars, no-one can have a body because of the atmosphere and on some, a full range of emotion is not included in their DNA. As the cosmic being described his perception of a human's potential in extensive detail, Joe became filled with a sense of wonder.

"This ET wanted Joe to know that humanity is wired for incomprehensible brilliance, yet they are falling into a trance, looking outward to solve their problems instead of inward to the unicity gene; instead of embracing their magnificence as quantum beings of infinite light, sound, and electromagnetism that can change everything for the better.

"Joe said that the ET predicted that as the Earth raised her frequency, humanity could rise with her. Humans hold memory of the entire history of the Earth, the galaxy, and the universe. By uniting in small ways, those who have the capacity and interest can support one another to do the work, raising their individual vibrations and thus influencing the collective field. The low-frequency controllers, just like ten to twelve thousand years ago, will not be able to maintain the current power structures. The key to change is in accessing the unicity gene.

"Oh my word! Now that I dared to share Joe's story, what do you think about all of this, Sophia?" Angelica asked.

Sitting in thoughtful, deep reflection for a moment, Sophia answered, "It's a lot to take in. I have to admit that looking at history from a vantage point of eons and our place relative to the vast cosmos, I am feeling that my problems are petty. I am not disparaging myself. It's more about perspective. Gaia is likely billions of years old. A hundred years may be a whole life cycle for us but it's barely a second for her. In that sense, we are quite mistaken about what we consider significant. We limit our perspective to such relatively small periods of time compared to her perspective, not to mention the perspective of the universe! But on the other hand, without understanding our own infinite nature, we might think we were insignificant. Either way, we are under an illusion.

"I'm ready to keep walking. Maybe that'll boost my higher mind rather than my limiting thoughts. As your friend said, Earth's frequencies are rising. I feel it. Will human beings choose to do the same? The answer matters now more than ever. It sure feels like we are at a tipping point. Will we firmly latch onto our *serf-self* and play small? Will we, once again, embrace Gaia as a sentient being, a friend rather than a big ball of resources? Will enough of us care and be willing to look with an open mind and a boatload of curiosity at what's going on in the big picture? Lots of questions today."

Angelica agreed that there was a lot to consider and digest. Historically Gaia proved to be an indestructible force for change, growth, and evolution. The two friends slowly came to a stand-still, adjusted their hats to shield them from the mid-day sun, and continued their hike in silence as the trail steadily inclined. After a last steep ascent, the two friends arrived at a magnificent vista overlooking the tranquil blue lake and the mountains surrounding it. The mountains held the ancient lake like a giant, sacred bowl.

They found a perfect spot to rest, with sumptuous, sage-colored grass and a towering, majestic shade tree for each of them to recline against. The breeze was soft, the sun imperceptibly drifting into its afternoon position. Heat rose from the ground and the shadows became a little longer.

"As we walked," Angelica said, "I recalled one of the last hikes with my husband, Chris. I think the memory was triggered by talking about all of the things that I shared when we stopped in the grove. Are you okay with talking? Or is silence better?"

"Please, go ahead," Sophia said, "I'd love to hear about Chris."

"It may not be what you are expecting," Angelica said. "He was gentle, as you've described your husband, Nate. Chris loved to talk about anything to do with inner life. Oh my goodness! That man voraciously studied philosophies from all over the world and did so with an open mind. He also meditated daily before work, with resolute discipline. And he was a brilliant environmental lawyer, who loved his work and his family even more. He had a high intellect which served his career. Yet, his sharp mind was balanced by a highly evolved intuitive side. He seemed to pull that off in a way that amazed me.

"Chris was born just after World War II. What Gilda shared with you and what I've learned about post World War II was that the aftermath was emotionally devastating for the whole planet. He graduated a year early from college, got a law degree, and helped to support his parents as they aged. His father never recovered mentally from the war. That was hard on Chris. Naturally, he loved his dad very much.

"He was fortunate to be young enough not to serve in that war and didn't get drafted into the next one—the Korean War.

"I have to say, he handled life's ups and down well. He was kind, did continuous inner work on himself, and loved our daughter, Caitlyn, with his whole heart and soul.

"I recall the last few minutes before he died... I'll never forget it. He said that on the expanded side of life, there are many inner dimensions and connections with all universes and coordinates in the field, and he realized that he'd been putting too much of his attention on this one, which he called life. He wondered if he'd missed out on experiencing the mystical potential of his soul while in human form on Gaia.

"And in answer to his reflection, he had a vision of sacred geometric patterns that formed the tapestry of his childhood traumas, past hurts and pains, all abiding within the subtle fields of his being. It was clear from his description that those geometric patterns were the essence of frequencies that he experienced as feelings. How about that for a revelation? His perception was becoming super subtle. So I wasn't surprised when he spoke to many beings he'd read about or had an inner relationship with such as Jesus. And a mystic saint from India named Ravidas showed him his soul's glory in the form of light and frequency.

"All fear or worry was replaced with the nurturing feeling of his own pure light. He entered a peaceful state which he said *scintillated with power and peace.* He said that he felt totally free. Then, he told me that the Pacific Ocean had always been important to the planet and that was why, in his work, he'd vowed to protect it.

"Sophia, he described the times of Mu; just like we talked about. I swear!

"It came from his direct experience. He was not on any pain meds. He was more lucid, more alive, than I'd ever seen him. He said that he'd come to Earth to take a human form to help humanity. So, *this time,* he would never harm even one person. Why did he emphasize, *this time?*

"He held my hand unusually tight. Weak as he was, he gripped my hand and told me to never forget what he said. He implored me to help others who wanted to raise their frequency. This was imperative for humanity going forward. He had become like an innocent child again, as though there had never been a war or a single problem in his entire life. I was transfixed by his gaze and my entire body vibrated with the high vibes of the conversation we were having.

"As he clenched my hand, he said, with a lot of passion in his voice, that all souls on Earth are encoded with *unicity.* His visions were confirming this truth. He said that those who *express* the genetics for unicity have to find each other and not worry about those who aren't yet ready to unite. Coming together with love and respect will not happen by creating world governments and other structures. He said that the vision showed novel ways to create systems that are based on unicity. And he added that technology needed to be used with discernment and tons of benevolence rather than for convenience or entertainment. Advanced technologies can't be closely held and controlled only by a few. He became radiant as he spoke. He said:

There's no good guys and bad guys in a unicity caravan.
For us, all that matters is pure love, remembering that we
are light, electromagnetism, and frequency, and living in

nature's rhythms. It may sound airy-fairy to some. But it's reality. The details of my life have all been mental bullshit.

Sorry to have to drop that truth bomb, my love: we are perfectly perfect—every one of us. Forgive me for getting distracted by life and not seeing it sooner. Know that I love you, I always have and I always will.

"He fell asleep, and I hurriedly jotted down what he said because it emanated from a pure space within him. It was our last conversation. His soft expression and the energy in the room remained peaceful and—I hope I don't sound too out-there—it felt heavenly. Without any fanfare, his beautiful consciousness slipped from his body seamlessly into another reality, perhaps the one he'd been visiting that day.

"I don't share his story often. It would seem like something from a New Age website. And many people would think Chris was hallucinating. But I can recall down to my soul what it felt like to receive his words.

"After a while, I moved here, started selling essential oils and gardening to become more intimate with Mother Earth. I'm sharing this story in case it can help you to work with the *complexities and paradoxes* that you and I have encountered. Like you, I've been on an unconventional path. As I said earlier, I realize that it doesn't matter what anyone does for a living or where they live. From the perspective of unicity and creating a world of high frequencies like love, care, joy, and laughter, we can all do it.

"I wanted to learn how to feel and express *all levels* of frequency while not getting stuck in any of them. For a long time, I thought Chris was telling me to stay in high frequencies. After a while, I came to understand that he was speaking of choosing my state while not denying anything. I could experience fear, grief, sadness, or even pride, and then let it go. Like you, I've practiced many techniques to let my body feel what it feels and then teach it to feel higher vibrations of frequency like joy or peace.

"After Chris died, I realized that I was faking joy. So each morning I sat, with cheerful birdsong as my music, and I'd ask myself how I could learn in my body *how to feel* what the birds were singing. Could my body recall what joy felt like? I did the same thing with other higher emotions. After caregiving for so long, I'd forgotten how to deeply, viscerally allow my body to vibrate with joy, how to allow the frequency of a hearty, belly laugh to overtake me.

"What a life this is! Oh my lord! What a journey we are on! There sure is a lot to learn. Chris showed me that even to the last breath, we can learn, grow, and experience the glory of what it means to be human. No wonder the ETs are fascinated with us."

Sophia and Angelica laughed and looked lovingly at each other.

"Thank you for sharing Chris' story with me," Sophia said. "His words provide so much material for reflection.

"When I met Gilda, I realized that I'd heard or seen videos about some of the people and events that she mentioned, such as Operation Mockingbird and the CIA's involvement in various forms of media as a way to influence and control the American population. But I was too busy living my life to pay attention to it. That's what Chris pointed to—not being present to important information, not seeing the situation clearly, and allowing our-selves to be diverted from priceless experiences that matter to our soul, and which get eclipsed by our mind's busyness.

"Earth's history is well-documented by trailblazing scien-tists and leading edge researchers. Why did I get so enamored with my tiny world that I didn't care about any of that? Why is it coming up now? I feel like I am getting a bigger picture view of life than ever before."

"Well," said Angelica, "Maybe you and I were not supposed to have this bigger picture view until now. There are new technologies to measure the Earth's frequencies, and we know that since you and I were born, her frequency has doubled. The frequency of the human collective is rising, too. Perhaps the timing is perfect for us to share our stories and reflect on our lives. I'd like to extend our human collective and ourselves some mama-style compassion. Neither we nor our global world were ready for groundbreaking, innovative systems that facilitate unicity and help souls to rise to greater heights of frequency on this amazing planet.

"We have to answer the call to raise our personal frequency. No one will be left behind this time. Everyone will unite. How can I know that? Hmmm..."

"You've handed me many of life's puzzle pieces today; big ones," Sophia said. "Thank you for being so vulnerable and real. It's meant a lot to me to be with you and have this conversation."

"We're on a roll here, Sophia. I have one more thing to mention. If you get a chance, there are some archeologists, geologists, and historians in Idaho who know more about the ice ages, the glacier shifts, and how the flood affected the Pacific Rim and the rebuilding of the planet. I think you should speak with them if you can."

Sophia looked surprised. "That's where I am going next. I made a reservation to go to Idaho, not knowing why. It looked beautiful and my decision was more from intuition than logic. Life just keeps getting more mysterious. I'm grateful to have someone like you to explore the vast, unknown territories with."

"I feel the same about you," Angelica said, appearing luminous as she glanced lovingly at her friend. "We'd better keep going. The sun will set whether we want it to or not."

Smiling and refreshed, they headed down the mountain with the wind at their back.

PART 2

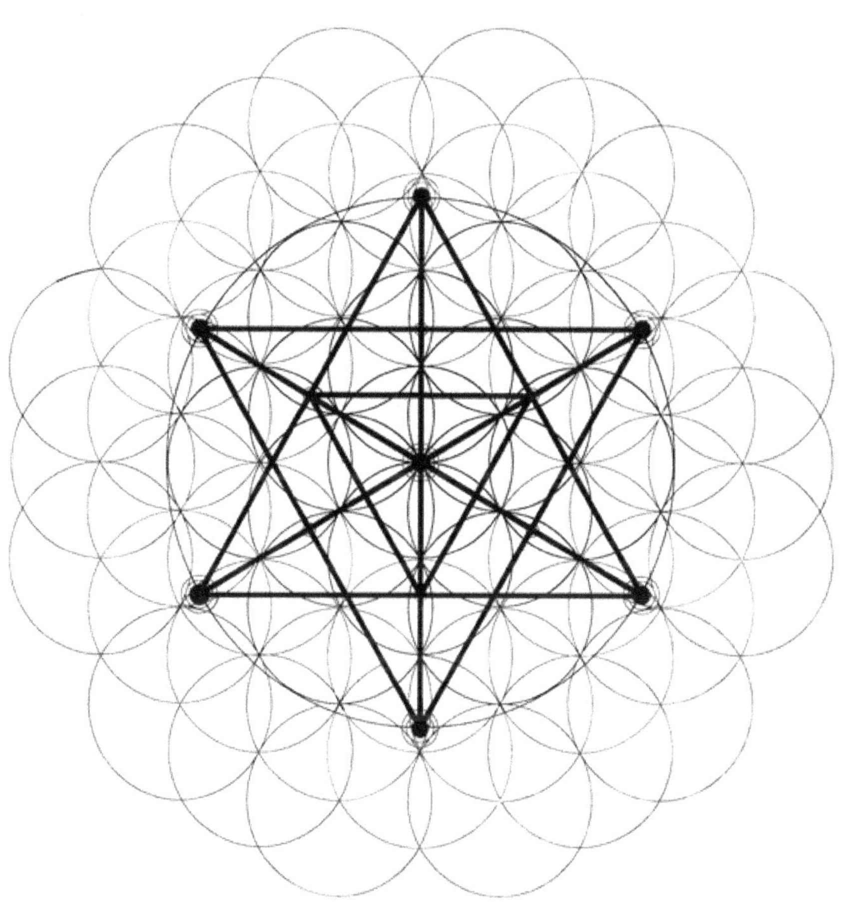

CHAPTER 23
IDAHO AND AUTHENTICITY

After many intimate conversations, long walks, and journaling, it was time for Sophia to leave the ancient lake and move forward, filled with immense gratitude for the invaluable friendship she'd forged with Angelica. Dreams of Northern Idaho had become constant nighttime companions and Sophia decided to follow her dreams and head in that direction.

Spring was coming, the frozen lakes would be melting, and shoots of fresh growth would begin. Like Sophia, the burgeoning of newness and growth was afoot in this dynamic season.

Angelica and Sophia shed many tears as the time drew near for her to leave. Their last hug was an embrace that spoke of friendship that time and distance cannot affect; they knew they had an invincible bond.

Driving to Idaho took Sophia two days, stopping only once each day. She was heading for another lake surrounded by mountains. When she arrived, the giant lake and its snow-capped mountains stood majestically within the ancient glacier-fed landscape. Exhausted, she checked into a small, quaint inn, and sent a text to Grace saying that she'd arrived. "It looks gorgeous right now, with a pink and purple sunset over the lake. I'm close to town, and walking distance or a short drive to many breath-taking places, filled with jaw-dropping beauty." It was time for a quick dinner and a good night's rest.

Sophia awoke early to the sounds of bird calls. Dressing hurriedly, she headed for a walk, passing through the garden area of the inn filled with pots of flowers and bushes, the little feathered singers flitting among them, chortling and chirping. In the chilly morning air, she wrapped her powder blue scarf snuggly around her neck, and headed for the lake. Standing at its edge, she stood with awe and wonder at its beauty. Closing her eyes, she allowed her awareness to connect deeply with the majesty in front of her, then opening them she gazed upon its sparkling, azure surface, feathered by gentle, waves.

As the morning chill overtook her, she was grateful to find a tea shop within walking distance. Standing in line waiting to order, she listened to the happy chatter of two young girls in front of her. Apparently, they had both applied to house-sit for a wealthy woman in town but were sure they'd be turned down. The girls placed their order and turned to walk away, both suddenly awkward and embarrassed as they greeted the woman behind Sophia.

"Do you know them?" Sophia asked.

"Not especially, but it's a small town and word got out that I need a house sitter. My name is Megan Morgan, and yours?"

"Sophia... It's nice to meet you, Megan." Sophia answered.

"You look new to town. Would you like to join me for a cup of tea or coffee?" Megan asked with a warm, friendly smile.

"Yes, I'd love to," Sophia said cheerily.

It was a simple, elegant café with Japanese style furnishings, and they found a spot in the back corner. Their tea cups were round like bowls, black with white swans painted on the side, which Sophia found somehow meaningful.

With open-hearted ease, Megan asked, "So what brings you to our cozy little town?"

"Good question. I am not sure." Sophia answered. "My husband passed away last year, and I've been traveling around, following life's breadcrumbs. I've met some incredibly insightful people who've became new and treasured friends. I've discovered a larger universe than I ever expected and I've had dreams that have reshaped my views about reality for me. This lake called me to it, and I am at a place in my life where I answer calls like that; calls that my heart hears and wants to follow, even if my mind isn't sure why."

"That sounds fabulous," Megan said. "You seem a little apprehensive, though. Am I right?"

"Yes, I have to admit some trepidation. I am far from familiar territory on several levels. My core beliefs have been challenged and most people I know would think that what I've seen and learned is crazy. Still, I am drawn to explore the unfolding mystery of this planet, my life, and the cosmos."

Megan slowly poured a cup of tea, took a sip, and asked, "When you sit at the lake and let yourself be with her intimately, what is it that you fear the most?"

Sophia looked down into her tiny teacup as though it were ten miles deep. She looked back at Megan, her expression one of longing to express something incomprehensible. "I see that the lake is reflecting back to me my inner power. I am in awe of her. The mountains around her have an intense majesty; I know that clouds gather over her at times, swirling and churning out sheets of driving rain, and the sun's fiery heat penetrates fiercely through the atmosphere. All this power is dynamic, viscerally evocative, even scary. To know that all of that raw potency and beauty are being mirrored back to me, as me, is daunting. To accept myself as powerful in that way—it means I don't have excuses, there is no way to be a victim of anyone or anything. This is the giant boulder of mental patterns and beliefs that has rolled off the cliff and is gathering momentum as it speeds downhill for me now.

"I used to be able to find all kinds of ways to play small. But it's impossible to discount the number of times since Nate died that I've met people, had dreams, and learned things that showed me my vast inner capacities, built-in and accessible. Without a doubt, my personal frequency matters. I know I can command that frequency to rise by simply being authentic and loving." Sophia smiled and looked away with embarrassment.

"Thank you," Megan said. "That took guts. To be so honest and clear with a stranger. It took my breath away. All I could think was, *Holy cow! This woman's gutsy!*"

They both cracked up laughing.

"Thank you for your candid response, Megan," Sophia said. "I've been needing to express my feelings beyond my journals. Traveling to unfamiliar places and being always in the unknown has been hard and thrilling at the same time. The unknown is where miracles can happen; lasting, deep change can finally take place within me. No matter how many times life reinforces that truth, though, it's not easy to convince my mind to let my heart lead this process. I keep falling back into wanting to predict what will or should happen, based on the past. And yet my heart wants to be present to what can be created here and now."

"I have a proposal," said Megan. "You seem to like it here and have already bonded with the lake. I need a house sitter. Are you interested?"

"Yes, I would be interested," Sophia said smiling. "It's another example of how the process seems to be carrying me along. When will you leave?"

"In a week or so," Megan said. "You could stay in the guest house until then. Why don't you follow me home and take a look around. If it doesn't feel right, you can say No. For God's sake, you seem powerful enough to say No when you mean No, right?"

Sophia laughed, accepted, and they headed to Megan's house on the lake.

As they rounded the last hairpin curve and headed up a hill, the scene was breathtaking. A small mansion was perched above a magnificent cove with a stunning view of the sprawling, cobalt lake. The meticulous design and layout of the property created a visual feast of exquisitely manicured grounds highlighting the captivating, natural beauty. Paths were graveled and lined with tiny solar lamps and some of the trees were so huge that two people could not wrap their arms around them. As they emerged from their cars, cool mountain air greeted them with its invigorating freshness. Taking in the scene with a look of euphoric fascination, Sophia stood motionless.

Seeing Sophia's entranced introspection, Megan cleared her throat, captured Sophia's attention, and asked, "Would you like to see the dock and a closer view of our extraordinary little cove?"

"Yes, I'd love that," Sophia said as she took in another sweeping view of the property.

They walked down a curving path through a grove of pine, cedar, and alder in various hues of green. Casually grazing, a herd of five deer looked up at them without concern. The forest scents were pungent, filling Sophia's nostrils with a symphony of smells, while squirrels and birds chittered and called through the trees.

Soon they came upon a dramatic cliffside with a steep staircase at the bottom of which was a dock where a large pontoon boat, a cabin cruiser large enough for at least ten people, and a ski boat were stationed. To the left was a gigantic deck at least a hundred feet long, with umbrellas, chairs, tables, and a fully outfitted cooking area with a grill, huge ice chests, and cooking utensils and serving pieces for at least twenty people, as well as a large circular patio bar made from native rock, with a granite top. Everything about the architecture and the structures was clearly designed to be harmonious with the environment, without distracting in any way from the natural beauty.

"I am in awe right now," Sophia said. They were standing at a railing looking out over the dock from above. "You must have a big family. It looks like you've got a place for lots of people to gather, to enjoy the amazing scenery, and play in this magnificent lake."

"Well, that was how it used to be. And that was the plan. We wanted to build a family home that would be a tribute to our love and be here for generations to come." She stared out over the lake. "I lost one son in the Vietnam War and another to cancer. That's not anything a mother expects or can fathom, until it happens. Life is never the same. Better said, I have never been the same. Neither of my boys had children. My daughter did, but she lives on the other side of the country. She's very busy. My husband, Frank, died twenty years ago... Cancer... For a long time, I let the local children come here to visit and that was a Godsend; their giggles and laughter and their little faces as they took off in the boat... priceless memories.

"In the past few decades, the community here shrank. Young people moved away to go to various universities and didn't come back. Mother Nature couldn't compete with the excitement of city life. After my husband died, I was blessed to have John, a dear friend of ours, to rely on. There is nothing that man would not do to help me, and he is well-loved in this town by everyone I know. He is a brilliant archeologist, geometrician, and savvy cosmologist. That's a rare combination. A blessing for me is that he has the skill and inclination to fix anything around here. Most of all, I always enjoy his company; he's fun to be with.

"John is particularly knowledgeable about this area, archeological sites, geology, and world history. He's very well studied. So when new information emerges, he gets frustrated that people and institutions don't update, but instead just stick to the same old story of our planet and her history, without considering that we have technologies that allow us to know Gaia more intimately than we did a hundred years ago. I have a feeling you'll appreciate his wisdom. You seem open-minded to me."

Sophia was silent for a moment, looking at Megan, taking in the tapestry of people and events of Megan's intriguing life. Sophia responded to Megan with heartfelt compassion and care.

"My husband died recently," she said. "He lived a full life, but it was still painful to lose him. After hearing your story, losing your children plus your husband must have been devastating. I admire your generosity to share this uniquely beautiful place with the community's children."

They were both quietly reflective as they climbed back up the steps and walked toward the house. "Would I be here alone?" Sophia asked softly, breaking the silence. "You must have people who help with maintenance, right?"

Before Megan could answer, two dogs bounded from the house, with a woman in close pursuit. "Come back here! You two are incorrigible!" She was laughing and quite winded as she came near Sophia and Megan. "They caught your scent, Megan," she said. "And you know how they are. Hard-headed where you are concerned."

"Beth, this is Sophia," Megan said. "She's considering staying here while I am gone. I haven't told her about *the incorrigibles.* But now she got to see them in action!" Megan was petting the happy dogs and their tails were wagging as they sniffed at Sophia. One was a regal Husky named Yeti who looked straight into Sophia's eyes. Returning the eye contact, she smiled softly and stroked his ears and face tenderly. His crystal blue eyes were the same color as Nate's.

Suddenly, the smaller white dog, a Bichon Frise named Blizzard, took off after a squirrel, then returned satisfied with his chase, tongue hanging out, and giving Sophia a huge doggie smile.

"Well, hello you two rascals," Sophia said. "Aren't you adorable? I have a feeling you have Megan wrapped around your sweet little paws."

The three women laughed and watched the dogs dart into the woods, running at full speed, and returning occasionally to check in. "I am happy you like dogs," said Megan. "They are good boys and wonderful companions. Five days a week, Beth comes to make their food and mine. She helps to keep the main two suites and the kitchen clean and in order, and she is always kind enough to leave enough food for the weekend, too. I am so grateful for her." She turned to smile at Beth, who winked back at her.

"While I am gone," she continued, "Beth also has to be away for several weeks. So if you are up for it, the boys would need your care. Don't worry. I wouldn't hold you responsible for any of their shenanigans. And if they somehow find a dead rodent to roll in or if they get skunked, I'll give you a neighbor's name who already agreed to help with them."

The dogs, who were sufficiently tired, bolted to Beth's side. She petted them and handed them each a treat. "Tea will be ready shortly," she said. "I'm so glad to meet you, Sophia. I look forward to seeing more of you." She headed to the house with two furry friends by her side.

"Beth seems wonderful," Sophia said. "And I can handle the boys. I realize that I forgot an important question: How long will you be gone?"

"Oh sorry," Megan said, "Of course. About six weeks. I am going to be with my daughter. As I age, I realize that she's my baby and I want to be with her and my granddaughters as often as possible. They don't come here because of their busy lifestyle, so I go there.

"How is all of this sounding? I guess you can see that I need to feel confident they will be properly spoiled and watched with a motherly eye. Of course, you'll also look after the cove and the house, but the dogs come first."

"I totally understand," Sophia said. "I'd love to stay here while you are gone, and I'm happy to take care of Blizzard and Yeti."

"Fabulous! Let's look around the house a bit. I have a list of people you can contact for emergencies and that sort of thing. Also keep in mind that John will come often. He does some of his archeology work at the cove and helps around here, if needed. You'll like him."

After the full tour and explanations, Sophia went back to the inn. The phone rang and Grace's voice was filled with excitement. "I got your text. This is amazing! I am so happy for you. A nice lady, two great dogs, and a heavenly place. Good creating, Sophia! You deserve this!"

"Thanks! I'm happy here. You would love it. The cove is absolutely stunning, and definitely has a mystical vibe. She told me that there's an archeologist who works down there. I wonder what he does? Angelica dated an archeologist and talked about how much fun it was to go on digs with him. And here's another thing: could it be a random coincidence that I've met yet another person who has experienced deep loss? Something that didn't escape my radar was that in her case, Megan found a way to bring joy into her life by being of service to her community. It's a lot to take in and reflect on.

"I am glad you called. It's probably obvious that I'm relieved and excited to land in such a great place. Angelica's home was fabulous too, but while I was there, it was so close to Nate's leaving that I was a mess a lot of the time. Of course, that didn't stop jaw-dropping events from happening. I hope I can relax here and get back to some kind of normal. I'll be doing a lot of journaling with the idea that someday maybe I can condense this part of my life into a book. Who knows? It's just an idea."

"It's great idea!" Grace said. "I love that you are writing. If you put your life stories into a book, its content will be crazy enough that people will think it's fiction. I see it as a combo of World War II Nazi spies, cool ETs, mysterious lakes, the truth of ancient history on this planet, cover ups, and non-disclosures... Yep, it sounds like fiction. But it's your truth. That's what I like about your adventures. It's beyond what someone could make up. It's happening because of your frequency. I am giving you the credit you deserve. Through your losses and huge life changes, you've grieved, felt the pain, and yet remained open and were willing to keep going, no matter what happened. It's easy to believe what everyone else around you believes. I see your travels as a way to share with people, as a regular person, that this world is bigger and different than we think it is. I love how you are facing fear of the unknown by taking the next step and being soft and open. I've got to run. Call me once you settle in at Megan's. Again, I am so happy for you!"

As Grace's feedback and good wishes settled in, Sophia glanced at her hand, at the finger where her wedding ring remained in place. For her, it was a vibration of energy that suited her perfectly. Out loud she said with a tinge of sadness, "Oh Nate... This is not how I thought our life together would turn out."

Shaking her head in disbelief at the turn of events since Nate's death, she went for a walk along the lake with the exquisite celestial sun-disc above her creating dancing sparkles of magic everywhere across its surface. Walking and hiking with gratitude for her profound connection to the underlying mysteries of life had become a doorway to inner stillness and quietude, softening her mind so that her heart could retain its vital place as the leader of her life.

CHAPTER 24
PUZZLE PIECES COME TOGETHER

Plans were made and checklists created. It was time for Megan to leave and for Sophia to be the caretaker of the two "fur babies," as Megan referred to them, and the house. The weather was shifting towards spring, but cool days and freezing nights were part of Sophia's mountain experience for a while.

As they were saying goodbye and as Beth was putting Megan's bags in her car, a noisy, definitely older, crimson pick-up truck barreled up the driveway. A man jumped out and rushed over to them. Without wasting a moment to put on his hat, he grasped it tightly, and allowed his unruly, ginger-colored hair, streaked with gray and silver, to whirl freely with the morning breeze.

"Megan, I'm glad that I got here before you left," he said. "I had a cold so I couldn't come for the past few days. I'm recovered now, and wanted to say farewell and have a great trip, my friend." Then he turned to Sophia and said, "I'm sorry to be so rude, young lady. My name is John. I'm an old friend of Megan's and I would have hated to miss seeing her off. She and I are buddies. Right, Megan?"

"Yes, we are!" Megan said as she laughed kindly and winked lovingly at John. "I've already told Sophia about you. And she knows you will scale that long staircase to the cove and show her around. She's a good woman with a great big heart. And you need to pass on your wisdom to her. Promise me, okay?"

"Well, I guess so," John responded with a look of confusion. "I am not sure what she might like to know."

"Tell her the secrets of Mystic Cove." Megan requested. "After that, she'll likely have a question or two, don't you think?" Megan smiled at John with tenderness and gave him and Sophia a quick hug before she got into Beth's car saying, "See you in about six weeks. Have fun!"

Sophia stood looking shy and quiet. John turned to her and broke the silence by saying, "Why wait? If Megan thinks you'd like to see the cove and know more about it, why not head down there? Are you ready?"

"Are tennis shoes okay? Do I need hiking boots?" Sophia asked.

"Don't worry, I won't take you hiking this late in the day." John said. "If we explore the area, we'd do that earlier in the morning."

Descending the stairs was a step-by-step process of intense focus. The stairwell was steep and occasionally a board creaked under Sophia's feet. The handrail felt solid, and it was the only crutch she had to hold onto. As she reached the bottom, she let out a huge sigh of relief.

John seemed unfazed by the steep descent and used the handrail only half of the time. He easefully led the way, with Sophia close behind. As he took the last step onto the sandy cove, he kept his stride, walking with purpose to a particular spot that he clearly wanted her to see.

Sophia followed closely, looking at the waves gently lapping at the shoreline of grey gravel. She saw a small scattering of deer poop.

"John, a quick question: what kind of animals will I see here?"

"Elk, moose, bear, rabbits, and a lone wolf here and there." He said. "There's also marmots, raccoons, chipmunks, and grey squirrels. I wouldn't walk alone at first. If you want to hike, I'd be happy to take you. Have you ever hiked with bear and moose?"

"No. Honestly, without my husband as a hiking partner, I've been sticking to clearly marked, easy trails—nothing off the beaten path. I would like to find a place to be safely in nature and alone so I can write and reflect."

"There's plenty of places for that. I'll show you some great spots overlooking the lake and give you pointers in case some animal saunters up and surprises you. It's not dangerous if you know what to expect." He was leading her along the beach a ways, close to the cliff wall. I'm curious why Megan wanted me to tell you the secrets of the cove. There are legends about it—that's why it is called *Mystic Cove.* It was always special to the local, indigenous people. Have you and she talked about it? What did she tell you? Will your husband join you?"

"Uh, no. My husband died and that's why I'm traveling and exploring new places. She told me you are an anthropologist and cosmologist, and that you know things about world history that most of us are not familiar with. She seemed to feel that you are passionate about sharing recent discoveries and exciting revelations in all of your areas of study. Her description of your work suggested that many of your peers dismiss your findings as unsubstantiated and sometimes a bit crazy.

"Megan said that certain colleagues want to discredit you so that they can keep telling the same origin stories and history rather than admitting that something new has been discovered that changes the existing paradigm. I'm paraphrasing. The way she described you made me think of Copernicus, who made discoveries but didn't dare tell his colleagues or his government. He would have been killed for heresy.

"I'm not saying you are in danger. I'm referring to how entrenched science gets in a certain belief, and they don't want to consider groundbreaking ideas, especially if they substantially disrupt existing theories and accepted science. That's ironic because science ought to be the first area to get excited when someone poses a question or discovers something that overturns the status quo. I guess humans like order and keeping things in boxes.

"What I am learning in my life is that I refuse to die in a box. If I can't explore the time I have here with openness and share my discoveries with authenticity, then I'm in the wrong community for me. My world has expanded beyond my wildest dreams in the past year. I think that's what Megan was alluding to, and why she said I'd be interested in the cove." Sophia looked at John and smiled warmly. With his usual friendly spirit, he smiled back reassuringly.

"I am going to be totally honest with you," she said assuredly. "I've had lucid dreams with ETs and met a woman who knew the secret space program firsthand. She was a Nazi. My husband died last year. He was deeply spiritual and absolutely authentic, kind, curious, and open-hearted. We studied quantum physics, spirituality, cosmology, and we were aware that in a quantum universe, miracles come from a transition point in the unified field, where everything is possible and you can step into a new reality. Some physicists call this the still point or Zero Point. The frequencies become so dense at that point, that you naturally cross a threshold and emerge into a higher frequency. We came to understand that our expectations are created from past impressions and beliefs. We realized that our highest potential lies in being still and letting important revelations and understandings arise naturally—without an agenda and without anticipation or expectations about what should or will be revealed. That's a simplification of what I learned." She stopped suddenly. "Oh my gosh! John, that was not the way I planned to tell you about myself. I just rambled my way through my life story..." Sophia looked at the ground sheepishly. There was an awkward moment of silence. Reflecting for a moment, Sophia and John looked out at the vast lake, its surface bedazzled with the splendor of sparkling sunlight.

"Damn!" said John. "That was brave. There was no bullshit in what you said. It was straight from your heart. I have a lot to reveal to you. And I trust Megan. If she thinks I should share the secrets, I will do it. And because of the way you shared, I feel that I can trust you.

"Come with me. I want to show you something."

Sophia followed John alongside an emerald-green, mosscovered boulder, thirty feet tall and awe-inspiring in its size and powerful presence. He told her to stay close to the huge rock, touching it as they passed around it because if she stepped away from the boulder, she would sink into several feet of water. "On the other side we'll enter a cave. I have lights inside, some equipment. Follow me closely." Sophia took him seriously, glued to his shirt tails.

The opening to the cave was as tall as the boulder but was hewn at an angle that kept it discreetly disguised as part of the landscape. As they entered, she noticed marks etched on the oval entrance. The first thing she saw inside was a shock—a huge skeleton, maybe thirty feet in length, lying peaceful on the ground in front of her. Spontaneous tears welled up and she broke into sobs. Her body was shivering and trembling, her whole being felt like it was being shaken apart, her heart melting into rivers of tears. The world went black as she collapsed.

A few minutes later, John was helping her to her feet.

"Sorry," she said weakly. "I was caught off guard... I... All of sudden my mind blew a circuit. This may sound crazy: I was there... with them. How could that be possible? I'm confused."

John brought water for her to sip and helped her prop herself against the side of the cave entrance, placing his quilted jacket behind her back to make her more comfortable.

"Sophia, would you humor me?" John said, "Let's say this was a memory. Could you remember enough to describe it to me? Tell me about any feelings, images, whatever. Just talk. No censoring anything."

As tears trickled down her face, Sophia spoke of her lucid dream while in California with Angelica. She described the soft, gentle touch of the giant as she laid her head in his hand. "He was childlike and fatherlike at the same time," she said. "He was nothing like giants in the horrific tales I heard as a child. You know, the stories about man-eating, cruel-hearted giants. This giant was full of wisdom, patience, and pure love. Sorry... I can't quit crying."

Sophia tried to gather herself and become more steady.

Suddenly, with a burst of fury, she said, "He's real! I am not going to sit here and act like a five-year-old, afraid of what you or anyone may think of me. I don't care if it sounds crazy! I know that I've been held by a magnificent being like this. I know I've lived as the daughter of a ray of blue light. And I don't care if no one believes me.

"My friend, Gilda, taught me that authenticity and truthfulness are two of the most important elements of a human life. Hiding out of fear of retribution by governments, leaders, community, or you, will spiral me into a low frequency and a hellish life. I don't care how I know what I am about to describe. I am remembering that a long time ago, the Earth was frozen. Oh my gosh! The memories… We are gathered in caves. I am human. My father is a human, but giant. My mother is a ray of blue light. We live long lives and we can communicate with our star family through quantum portals. I am being trained by giants, larger even than my father, learning to raise my frequency—we are always elevating. We speak through telepathy and travel naturally anywhere we want to. The multiverse is our home." Sophia's eyes were closed, and she spoke as though it was happening in the present moment, there in the cave. She stopped and opened her eyes again, looking at John.

"This planet was special," she said. "It's diversity, its raw beauty, and its sentient frequency aligned with ours. We navigated ice ages and floods—sometimes we'd go back to our universe and return when times were ripe for life to begin anew. The Earth continued to evolve without us. She always evolved higher and always will. She adapted, biology flourished, and we came back to her. Returning was always amazing—like when you are away from a child for a long time and you see them again and they are so different. She had more diversity than before. We worked primarily with the shamanic cultures in the area of the Pacific Ocean. The timeline seems to be…" She closed her eyes again, concentrating. "Two hundred thousand years ago. Then something happened and we left and came back one hundred fifty thousand years later, and for some reason, at some point, we left again. I am confused about exactly when—it feels like the Earth was effected by a disturbance in the cosmos. Then twenty thousand years ago, we returned to our beloved Earth once more.

"Every time there was an ice age, we left codes in the ice so that when the ice melted, there would be a way for the blood of humans or hybrid humans to find the wisdom and information again: for inter-galactic travel, for how to communicate with nature. And the *unicity* gene would turn on full throttle. It would ignite peace, pure love, and joy in the world. And everyone would hold sound, light, and frequency in high regard.

"Over time, humans recognized the value of immeasurably subtle information and it was honored, studied, and applied in ancient wisdom schools. Is humanity continuing these kinds of incomprehensible learnings and skills in the unified field theory of quantum physics research today? In the ancient past, elevated human capacities thrived when we were in close friendship and loving communion with each other. The technologies flourished, the pyramids structures allowed us to access higher dimensions, and the symbols etched on cave walls reminded us of our home stars and planets. Occasionally, inter-breeding happened—only when it could elevate the human species in a significant way. Through all of this, peace reigned; until greed soared and integrity plummeted.

"That's all I can say for now. I am still dizzy and feeling stunned. Bits and pieces of this have been coming to me from different sources. But experiencing this is wild! I thought the giants were a part of my dreams or metaphors for something in my subconscious. But this was real."

"That's enough for today," John said compassionately. "I recorded what you said. It was pure gold, my dear. Thank you. Ready to go? I am quite at home at Megan's house. I'll make us some sandwiches and let the dogs out. You rest and I'll tell you why what you shared is so damned important." Smiling and carefully helping her up, John supported her back as they glided along the boulder and toward the steep steps.

"One step at a time," John said. "I'm right behind you. You'll be fine."

Wobbly at times, yet persevering, Sophia's feet finally reached the solid earth at the top step. They took a couple of breaths and headed for the warmth of a fire and welcoming hearth.

CHAPTER 25
COVE'S AFTERMATH

The dogs vaulted past John and Sophia to get outside as they opened the door. Exhausted, Sophia went to stretch out on the couch by the warmth of the crackling fire. The fireplace was captivating and inviting. It had a removable grate to allow for cooking during the sometimes brutal, winter months. The downstairs of the house had exquisite natural beams every ten feet across the twelve-foot-tall ceilings. One beam, split in half, spanned the top of the fireplace as a mantle. Lovely copper lanterns of various shapes and sizes and filled with candles covered the mantle's surface, ready for a power outage or for cozy ambiance.

The tones and colors of the house were earthy and woodsy with splashes of light and darker hues of teal. Every aspect of the decor blended harmoniously creating an environment of unparalleled beauty. A four-foot tall, golden quartz stood regally to the left of the fireplace and a slightly taller royal purple amethyst geode graced the other side. Light danced off them from the carefully placed accent lights overhead. Sophia took all of this in as her breath became more rhythmic and her body began to soften into the plush couch and warm blanket draped over her.

John brought in a tray of sandwiches, saying, "You sure look better. Megan thought you'd bought something gluten free at the coffee shop and assumed that was your preference. Beth makes fresh sour dough bread and made a starter for you using chestnut and oat flour. She's made a few loaves. They smell great. Will that work for you?"

"Wow, that's perfect, John," Sophia said as she sat up. "Does anything get past Megan's radar? She's an amazing hostess, so sensitive and aware of what's said and what's needed. She seems like an amazing person."

"You hit the nail on the head, Sophia. She is special. And she sure as hell likes you! No way would she let anyone see the secrets of the cove unless she trusted them impeccably. I look forward to sharing more with you about what's there and why it matters."

"I feel absurd for fainting at the sight of that skeleton. It was just such a startling feeling that it overtook me—the feeling that I was seeing the living person who inhabited that body-frame. My brain went into overload."

"I could tell," said John. "That's also partly my fault. I should have explained more and prepared you. The human brain can only process a certain amount of information at one time. That's a fact. We've given the skeleton a name—Max. It's short for *maximum*."

"Max... I like that name. It suits him," said Sophia, musing. "I wanted to let you know that I am open to all of this. Over the past year I've been exploring topics that other people scoff at and my worldview has been greatly expanded. For a while, I kept my experiences to myself. Fortunately, I've had special people in my life who have shared my curiosity and wonder.

"A year ago, if anyone predicted that my worldview would turn upside down, I would have laughed. Even with all of the quantum physics that I've studied, my focus and dedication to spiritual practices, and traveling all over the world, I was not truly open. I am a work-in-progress and I like it.

"I used to pretend to be someone who others would like, it was automatic, the way I edited myself all the time. But over time, I almost climbed out of my skin with the desire to speak and act from my core values rather than be concerned with other people's opinions of me. I've had to have compassion for myself along with a huge dose of determination to live from authenticity.

"I feel sheepish saying these kinds of things out loud because of old patterns and programs running in my mind. Something in me still says that if I admit to this, I'll be judged, criticized, or kicked out of the *normal group.* As though by *not being myself* I will be accepted, liked, and safe.

"But that's a painfully restricted and contracted place to be in. Thanks to the beautiful souls I've met along my journey and my inner longing for Truth, I feel more expanded now. Going to new places and opening to new viewpoints, theories, and discoveries has become a heart-opening experience. I never expected that to happen, nor did I expect to experience the gradual softening of the crust around my heart that continues every day. I could never have shared my memories of Max that erupted when I saw him, without your supportive, kind heart. Thank you, John. I see why Megan likes you so much."

John smiled at her, gently placed his hand over his heart, and bowed his head in a gesture of reciprocal thankfulness.

"When Nate died, I felt life was over—at least the happy part. Then one night I had a dream with him, it felt lucid and full of our deep connection. It was clear he wanted to encourage me to keep going. Living with him was like being with a curious child with an insatiable appetite for discovering the unknown, in awe of both the seen and unseen realms. I loved that part of him and still miss him incredibly."

She became quiet and looked into the roaring fire as it danced with unfettered charm and mesmerizing brilliance.

John spoke softly. "I am sorry to hear about the loss of your husband. That must have been tough. I can see that you value curiosity and are searching for the truth, regardless of the unexpected heartbreaks and craziness that accompany it. I understand now why Megan wants you to know our secrets. One of my archeological specialties won't surprise you: it's giants. Their remains have been found globally, dating way back into our world's history. I study them.

"Big institutions ask for the skeletons that people find on their property—who naively turn them over to those organizations. As I studied Max, I slowly began to see him as a great soul who walked our planet. That may be too sentimental for some folk yet it's the honest-to-God truth for me. My relationship with him is why I became determined to keep his priceless relics safe and available to science. Otherwise, large museums or universities will sweep them up and then they disappear. I'll be damned if Max is going to be thrown in a crate and hauled off like a bag of old bones. By the way, if you could see the crystalline structure of his bones and those of his kin, it would blow your mind.

"I study the mysteries of his physical remains carefully and respectfully. I am not shy about saying that I love him—well, not shy with people like you. After everything I've learned about the giants who walked this Earth before us, he and his kind have my loyal affection. They did things that no one today can reproduce. They built complex structures, carved and transported massive stones, and moved around the Earth with inconceivable ease. So, yeah. That's my rant on Max and the world of ancient giants… Ready to eat? I'm a great sandwich maker."

"That sounds good. I can brew one of my favorite herbal teas if you'd like some."

Fresh bread, smiles exchanged, and the nurturing fire allowed Sophia to relax more deeply into her temporary home and engage with her new friend.

"John, although I am interested in the details of the world history of giants," she said, after finishing her last morsel of bread, "honestly, I am more affected by your *love for Max.* I understand why I am fascinated by him and have tender, sweet feelings arise in his presence. I've felt the touch of a tender and loving giant in lucid dreams. But why do you love him?"

"My own sweet remembrance of a gentle giant is one reason that Max's skeleton matters to me. When I engaged with the giant in my lucid dream, my mind gave way to my heart. I became more open to the entire subject of giants and the possibility that through the infinite quantum field, I could have lived in another coordinate of space-time where the giant was as real as you and I are now. That was a giant leap for me—no pun intended! But was a special relationship with a giant a big leap for you?"

Laughing, John began sharing his own story. His travels around the world included Egypt, South, Central and North America, Sardinia, Russia, Africa, and all over the Pacific Rim.

"Anywhere there were giants, I was there," John said. "I was mocked by colleagues and, like you, I was deeply affected by the loving presence of the giants. Contrary to common belief, skeletons can emit pure, powerful love. No flesh is required. After all, there is silica, or crystal, in our bones. More than once, I felt I knew them, they were intimately familiar. Like you, I had no context for those feelings when they arose.

"Did you know that in ancient Egypt, it's feasible that the embalmers focused part of their work on preserving the crystals of the bones when they mummified a body? Did they know something valuable about the composition of bones? How did they manage to preserve them so skillfully? Our scientists haven't been able to reproduce what they did... Amazing, isn't it? In Egypt, I learned from open-minded researchers that bones are piezoelectric like crystals and have important interactions with the structure of space-time.

"One example that comes to mind is when you walk around this room and interact with gravity, your bones emit electromagnetic fields. This piezoelectric effect keeps your muscles, fascia, tendons, and so forth, electromagnetically activated so you can move effortlessly. Did the ancient civilizations know how to harness these aspects of physiology and take human bio-structures and processes to an unfathomably higher level?

"Most relevant for me is that all of the information of the universe is in each of our trillions of protons. Can you take that in? Our DNA and the field in an around us is at our constant disposal so that we can access profound wisdom. My work is not relegated to collections of bones and writing papers. It's personal and critical to the younger generation. They need to know what I've learned. Just because Max existed in a different coordinate in space-time, does not mean that I cannot share a special bond with him."

Sophia was stunned. "Wow... John... this is not what I expected to talk about. I've never heard that our bones were so important from that perspective. I think of them as a supportive structure but you are saying that my bones are *electromagnetically* relevant. I knew that my physiology is complex. But what you just said is mind-blowing.

"I knew that my DNA stores information from the field, relevant to me personally, and then acts like a transmitter of information for my body—plus it emits information into the field. There's constant electromagnetic waves carrying information and my bones are also interacting with the field. Your question about how and what the ancients knew about all of this has my mind reeling with questions. I'll have to take some time to digest this new idea. Wonders never cease... Please continue."

"Damn! Thank you! Your response means the world to me. I rant and rave about this stuff with colleagues. I admit to getting pretty excited... and then I see their eyes glaze over, becoming a blank stare. My revelations don't land. Yet here you are, lapping up this information like I do. This is amazing! I am getting more clear about why Megan wanted us to spend time together. Since you are interested, I'll keep going... If I rattle on too long, just stop me. I can talk about these subjects forever.

"I'd like to get into more amazing aspects of the complexities and *splendor* of being human. I used the word splendor on purpose. It is clear to me that our inherent nature is jaw-dropping, inconceivable, and miraculous. I am interested in all aspects of our life and in those who came before us because I am unraveling a story about what we've done in our ancient past with unparalleled high tech. How did we lose that knowledge? Seeing inexplicable architecture all over the planet and digging into the archeologic sites, sometimes it almost drives me crazy because it is so advanced.

"I am adamant that the giants are a significant clue. In order to understand more deeply the skeletons that I was uncovering, I interviewed Shamans and tribal *record keepers* in all of these places that I mentioned. They have passed down information that has not been censored or distorted. You can tell because of the amazing similarities between cultures in otherwise distinct and unconnected places. Across the board, the giants are described as benevolent; nothing like the awful stories from our European ancestors we heard when we were young. There's tales of more violent giants but if they were here, they were not the majority. I guess there's bad apples in every orchard.

"Why didn't anyone tell us that these generous, kind, wise beings came from other Solar Systems and universes? Their intention and focus was only to help—to share the mystical aspects of being human. Instead, our European legends told a different story than the historical, oral accounts from global, shamanic cultures. Why?

"To live here, the giants had to take shape in a 3-D body, which was a risk. Often they died following a catastrophic event like a meteor strike which caused flooding or which initiated an ice age. A solar flare could rip holes in the Earth's atmosphere. They were in danger as much as the humans they were helping.

"After all of that, I was surprised to discover their next move. The ones who survived went right back to helping and made sure that the shamanic humans could communicate with star beings like the giants and that they could be in perfect unicity with Mother Earth. That was not just for survival. This wisdom described the perfection of a loving intelligence that creates and sustains everything for everyone's benefit.

"When you went into that cave at the cove, did you feel the beauty of Max's soul? Yes, I said *soul.* He's not some mythic creature. He was a living being, holding a frequency like you and me. I am bringing up the term soul because I cannot separate the spiritual and scientific worlds. They are indivisible.

"I am going to dive deeper now—there's an emerging theory that says after we leave our body, our soul *frequency* lives on in morphogenetic fields. I see you looked surprised. Stay with me, I'll explain. We are each part of a morphic field that can be felt and scientifically measured by sophisticated technology. These fields are encoded with information or patterns like software on a computer. It's hypothesized that our morphic field communicates with other energy fields of information. This is one explanation for how birds fly in unison within a flock and fish in a school. It's a subtle, built-in mechanism that does not require a device or our conscious intention. It's an inherent part of our material reality.

"The morphic fields of cultural groups connect each other regardless of the coordinate in the field of each member. In this way, these morphic fields allow pure communication channels to thrive throughout time and space. The fields help provide an explanation for telepathy and for the sensation that a deceased loved one can be felt in this 3-D reality with us. Every form in our world and beyond it, creates a resonance of energy in and around itself. The *forms* I am talking about can be us, and it includes thoughts, actions, cultures, and species.

"Everything vibrates as a *field* in relationship to everything else. This means that the giants have a particular frequency and a resonance. Like them, each of us do, too. What I found is that no one wants us to inquire into these kinds of topics because it can challenge established views of religion, history, and human origin theories. The energetic, invisible aspect of humanity is too incomprehensible for many people to digest and assimilate.

"The giants also challenge us to consider that we have an incomplete understanding of our relationship to the stars and planets, within and beyond our Solar System. Is it time to admit that we must look wider and deeper into our ancient lineages, without bias or fear of retribution by academia or religions? Our past can inform the future if we are willing to receive its wisdom.

"I knew that I needed to work with my mind in this process of exploration so that I wasn't always stuck in linear, analytical thinking. Like you, I learned to meditate. Expanding my brain-waves was one area of focus, while also purposefully becoming more receptive to higher frequencies and activating my pineal gland, which has liquid crystals in it. What an awe-inspiring, built-in antenna!

"After speaking with hundreds of shamans across this great planet, it became clear to me that many of them knew the secrets of pineal gland activation and they could travel at will through time and space. They consistently gave credit for knowing and cultivating these processes to the giants—who not only taught them but who took physical bodies to selflessly share these secrets.

"With selfishness and survival fears built into the human psyche, the giants were careful to only share their wisdom with humans who they knew had evolved enough to become the *record keepers,* protecting the information. As the Earth changed, they stored the information in water, knowing it would freeze and thaw someday. In that way, it would always be available for the human blood to decode with the help of the pineal gland. The shamanic cultures globally knew how to access the codes. You know this, right?"

Sophia nodded in agreement. Silence permeated the room, except the pop of embers dropping into piles of red-hot ash. After a few minutes, the dogs began to bark loudly to remind the humans that they, too, needed to eat.

After the jubilant rushing around of canines at play, John and Sophia settled down again.

"I'll need some time to assimilate the profound truths that you've shared," Sophia said. "It's finally clear to me how and why we can feel Max's morphic field. The giant in my lucid dream was real, with a morphic field that I can interact with. The sacrifice the giants made and their profound wisdom should be more widely known. It's worth honoring. They have helped us and our ancestors to keep life going on the planet across many arcs of time. You used a word that the ETs mentioned. It was *unicity.*

What I heard you say was that the giants taught the shamans how to be in perfect *unicity with Mother Earth.*

"That's what I felt was happening in my lucid dreams. I would go to the top of a volcano and simply be with the ETs and allow my frequency to emanate. Doing that seemed too simple, not complicated enough to have a noticeable effect. But what you said about the morphic fields shifted my perception. Any human being who emanates high frequencies like joy, kindness, compassion, or love, will be adding to the entire field of a culture or a species. If I share the frequency of peace, by simply feeling peacefulness and becoming aligned with pure peace, my field morphs and begins to change automatically. How beautiful to envision that shift. From what you know, how many people have to do that to have a noticeable effect?"

"When I first studied this a decade or more ago," John said, "it was believed that it took a lot of people. But these days, it seems it's not as many as we thought. A small percentage of the human population in high frequency is shifting Earth's entire field. The reason is that more and more people are becoming open to the responsibility of raising their frequency. It happens every time someone decides not to be a victim and merges into the frequency of creating their reality. It's like when you decide that you are not going to hold others responsible for your happiness or unhappiness.

"You allow your body to recall how it feels to be calm and secure. The body signals the field that it's fine to relax. All is well. This frequency resonates into the fields around it and into the collective field of the Earth. The beauty of this is that the more people in humanity's collective morphic field who raise their frequency, the more everyone starts to feel that frequency increasing. Without being conscious of that field, they start to feel relaxed and aware that *all is well.*

"Then they post their uplifting experience or thoughts to social media, or they act more harmoniously with friends and family, and slowly the human collective field shifts. It's that simple. It's one of the secrets from the giants. Our ancient ancestors valued frequencies. We have slowly lost our awareness of, not to mention reverence for our frequency, inadvertently ignoring the benefits of uniting in the field as a collective, to shift the overall frequency higher.

"What's happened is that some people gain power through manipulation, pride, and greed. It is important to remember that this is not the only possibility for the human race. Together, our ancient ancestors faced great cataclysms, floods, and chaos. Gently and purposefully, they rebuilt the world. *Unicity* is what kept our ancestors elevating into ever-increasing wisdom and goodwill. It was in uniting and holding higher frequencies that the giants were able to help humans to create a high tech world from the rubble of multiple disasters. For the record, I'll be damned but those magnanimous giants are coming back, once again. I feel it in my bones. Pretty exciting, huh?

"I'll leave you with this reflection for tonight: there are billions of us on this planet who can shift morphic fields into higher, lighter, faster frequencies. Instead, most of us send out lower, denser, slower frequencies into our field and the fields around us; we project our fear, anger, apathy, guilt, and worst of all, shame. What will it take for us to unite, broaden our worldview, recognize and comprehensively study the wisdom of the giants? How can we release our belief that we are small and helpless and instead, assume the power of the giants. They are alive and well... I hope you are open to what I've said. If so, it'll change you forever. And your change will directly affect the larger field. That's the truth." John smiled at her. "I feel complete for tonight and I can see you are getting tired." He put his hand on his heart again as he looked at her for a moment, then headed to the kitchen to wash the dishes.

His words were dancing in Sophia's mind while she journaled and effortlessly drifted into sleep, warmed by the fire which was becoming softer and gradually turning into a pile of silent ashes.

CHAPTER 26
DREAMTIME IN QUANTUM TIME

Soft light filtered through the room and a cold, canine nose nuzzled Sophia, announcing a new day and that it was time for dogs to head outside.

Smiling and looking at the fire, which was still warm but reduced to a small mountain of white ash, she stoked the last few embers and added fresh logs. She opened the door to a moisture-laden, mystical scene of rare beauty. The thick, early morning fog was a captivating sight to begin the day. With thoughts still dancing from her dreamtime, Sophia headed for her phone to send a text, "Grace, r u awake?'

"Now I am," Grace replied. "I'll call in a few minutes."

Sophia moved swiftly to prepare the dog's breakfast and grab a cup of tea before her call with Grace. Her new canine friends dove into their food as though they hadn't eaten in days. Then they settled down and curled up contentedly on their beds near the fireplace.

She added logs and stoked the heap of hot embers until the logs began burning brightly. Hearing the harp tone on her phone, she answered Grace's call.

"Did you dream something?" Grace asked in a voice that indicated that she already knew the answer.

"Okay, maybe I did," Sophia said laughing. "I guess an early morning text was clue that something's up, right?"

Both friends laughed as Sophia continued, "I had a dream about Nate. It was another one of those ones where I felt it was absolutely real, a lucid one. He was a giant, Grace, so huge! Two-story house size! Maybe twenty-feet-tall and his head was elongated, and his face was *long and rectangular.* We were intimate, loving life partners. There were no formal marriage rituals or contracts back then. It was clear from our vibe that we were a unified team, with a very deep bond.

"We were within the Pacific Rim, and we could travel easily from place to place, sci-fi style. There were quartz disks we could stand on that hovered above the surface. We were adjusted to Earth's atmosphere. I was more human, and he was more subtle. We were both tall, but I was maybe half his size. The colony of people with us was small in numbers and I could tell that all of us had the same unicity with the elements of the Earth. Water didn't feel separate from us, nor did air or land. The plants scintillated with energy that I perceived both subtly and tangibly.

"Being in that time and space felt calm and the center of my heart was so soft that it didn't feel physical; it was such a crazy, wild experience to feel my heart, delicate and invincible at the same time. Nate and I spoke telepathically and yet I could feel and sense our words as a frequency that could include urgency or relaxation, joy or sadness, and a full range of emotions. We didn't express those emotions outwardly. It was a felt sense.

"In this dream, I asked what Earth time-frame we were in. He said approximately two hundred thousand years ago. After coming to Earth from another universe, we were in an adaptation stage. I was helping him to adapt, since I was at least partly human. I couldn't tell because my frequency was profoundly high; very different than today.

"I asked him questions, and his expression of compassion felt inviting and caring. I felt safe with him.

"At one point, as we moved around from place to place, I saw ice forming and he was asking me to work with the beings there to prepare for an ice age. He said time is relative, and we'd be together again soon in terms of cosmic time. He slowly faded from view.

"All of a sudden, I was thrust into a cave, deep beneath the Earth's crust. Once again, I saw the giants like the ones that I saw in lucid dreams at Angelica's. It was a time of the year when the stars were aligned perfectly, so a group of us were heading for the surface to perform rituals in monolithic stone circles to store wisdom for the future.

"I blasted through time and found myself again with Nate with that same rectangular face. It reminds me of the statues on Easter Island that face the sea. Our surroundings looked different, and I asked him what point in time we were in. Now it was about twenty thousand years in the past in linear time. I looked around to see the unfrozen Earth and the multitude of land masses and islands in the massive Pacific Ocean.

"Without getting into a vehicle, it was simple to direct my awareness to higher elevations on Earth where I could view my surroundings from a higher perspective. As in the earlier times that I described a moment ago my heart was incredibly soft as I communicated with all elements on Earth.

"Then once again, I landed in yet another coordinate in the field with Nate. This was different because I sensed something unsettling in Gaia's energy field. She still looked beautiful, from her lovely Pacific islands to the lush jungles and forests and snow-capped mountains across the planet.

"In this coordinate, Nate gathered with others and was more quiet; I felt a sense of foreboding. The technologies of light and sound had become significantly advanced. Using pyramids, time and space travel was simple and commonly used by humans and hybrids. I wondered what it could be. Characteristically for him, Nate was calm and centered, but many around him were clearly distressed. I asked him what was happening. He said that some human beings had developed greediness and abandoned integrity.

"Grace, I've told you about these stories before. I heard about this era in human evolution from Angelica who knew people well-researched in this era of Earth history. You might remember that just before he died, Kabir mentioned a great war, too.

"However, in my dream, I was not getting someone's commentary—I was in the scene. The big tech geniuses had become greedy and wanted resources from the Pacific Rim where we were. The gentle, subtle giants like Nate were not warriors, in blatant contrast to these other, ruthless, aggressive fighters. I remember telling you about how the gentle giants were totally unskilled warriors. What was different this time is that I was seeing their kindness up close and personal—I was with one of them. I have to admit that it crushed part of me to know that I was watching my sweet Nate. Yet I was relating to him and the scene from a higher version, an elevated octave of myself who took this in stride, and seemed confident that everything would work out fine.

"Lovingly, Nate looked into my eyes. While reassuring me about the perfection of all of this chaos, he explained that he would be going with a small group to defend what I observed was the Arabian Sea from advances from the west into the Pacific Ocean. He was also negotiating relentlessly and passionately with the prideful warriors to bring them back to their collaborative, unicity-based foundations.

"I felt an unfamiliar sadness. Nate reached out his hand in a familiar expression and I put my head in his palm. Soft tears flowed. I was not sure when I would see him again. Then I felt anguish so intense that my sense of self disappeared into the anguish, as vibration. As that happened, my emotional body re-calibrated, which was normal. Yet, I observed that I was not as emotionally steady as usual. I felt the pangs of *sustained* worry sinking its teeth into me, clearly a foreign emotional response to grapple with. Nate picked up on it and warned me to be vigilant about my personal frequencies, to avoid getting drawn into the collective fear, rage and sadness that was brewing furiously. Normally, emotions rose, were processed, and dissolved naturally but this was feeling sticky.

"I asked if I could go with him. He told me I was needed to carry forward the shamanic traditions and care for humanity in this region. The war was escalating and the galactic councils saw that humanity was heading aggressively into fighting and bloodshed.

"Meanwhile, Nate was trying to get his people to watch the skies because the war was not the only problem looming over Gaia—a giant comet's impact could destroy all life on the surface. He explained that a thousand years before, a red hot comet had impacted huge icecaps, melting them, and instantly, dramatically changing Gaia's exterior appearance through floods. Luckily, many humans were prepared and with advanced technologies, they survived. However, the ice age then carried on and drove survivors underground for a while. They created massive cities under the surface and were able to wait there patiently for a few hundred years. Something happened during that time under the surface and good humans not only dropped in frequency, they lost interest in the cosmos, unless it served their needs. Their obsession with tech was insane. Pride and hubris were endemic. They no longer watched the cycles of comets and asteroids nor did they appreciate the giants and their brothers and sisters from other universes.

"Nate was imploring his people to avoid this mistake. As he finished speaking, the dreamscape morphed, taking me to a still higher vantage point; I found myself with another being who was subtle, translucent. I began to cry with joy. This feminine force embodied fury, calm, and everything in between. She felt familiar and nurturing. I was held in a mystical cocoon of her love.

"Without judgment or concern, we watched the war together. And we observed some of Nate's species die, fending off the western warriors.

"The destructive technology was a form of sound that disintegrated everything it hit. It found its target on crystal cities, which held codes of information that oscillated in a way that produced energy for those cities to function. Pyramids connected humanity with star systems and offered all kinds of vital information and energy for large civilizations to thrive. My heart was crushed as the devastating vibrations struck anywhere that humans and the gentle giants gathered, no structure was immune to instant obliteration. The scope of annihilation was incomprehensible and left no remnants for archeologists to study later.

"Compassionately, the ethereal being showed me where Nate was located and I was able to witness his ascension back into his universe, unscathed. What a gift to know that he wasn't harmed. Realizing that he'd gone home brought me relief and comfort. I recalled that I was pregnant with his child. We had many children over the thousands of years that we were together. Our descendants created a shamanic culture; a legacy of record keepers; *keepers of wisdom* needed for evolution on Earth to advance, once again.

"The ethereal being in my dream left me with a prophesy that was like a warning to never forget that pride, manipulation, and lack of integrity were the nefarious underbelly and support for this great war. The unimaginable magnitude of destruction was hard to fathom. Advanced humans had chosen to point violent technologies at their fellow human beings—weapons of mass destruction. Yet they could have redirected their focus to develop technologies to save the entire species from a natural disaster of epic proportions. Can we avert this from happening in our lifetime? It felt like an eerie omen.

"Having said all of this, I want to be clear that I didn't feel anger or fear. Instead, a blanket of quiet determination, patience, and pure love for humanity swirled in my mind and heart. Through this dream, I reconnected with a higher octave of myself that knows that outside events are playing out constantly without altering the inner core of my being, and I can handle all of it. At the same time, I was acutely aware of and cared about the devastating consequences for both sides of the conflict.

"Humans are wired to look within and find answers to even the most daunting questions and differences; then we can pool our wisdom to find and apply solutions. Unicity is more than a hollow word. Kindness, generosity, non-judgment joined with peace, joy, and pure love to create an inner resource for me, like a cave full of treasures that I could rely on. All the suffering and needless death, of course, was devastating, yet it was part of life; it was not an *ending* for us. As I was shown my children of that era, I saw them as an awesome legacy and feeling their strength of character brought a vision and feeling of hope, excitement, and balance to a world of light and dark.

"More than a thousand years had passed since comets hit Gaia causing a planetary flood. And now, more comets were about to hit the ocean and adjoining land masses—altering our beloved Pacific Rim and the battle-ravaged earth beyond comprehension. A second *great flood* was coming and this time only small clusters of humans were ready. But humanity had become too focused on fear, division, and war to notice—they'd lost connection with the cosmos above them. In a terrifying flash, comets collided with the Earth at breakneck speed—impacting huge ice sheets, causing them to melt instantly, their waters rushing in floods, roaring across continents, etching a new landscape for humanity to traverse.

"My heart softened with compassion, I found myself calmly standing in a new coordinate in the field. The ice age was finally over. Before these two immense floods and the terrible war, there had been grand architectural sites where the advanced technologies had been used. Some of the ruins of such sites still remain. Yet, high tech had only created a false security and pride, both of which proved worthless in the wake of blazing comets. After intense trauma, humanity was left to begin again, with that miraculous unicity gene still there, ready to support the journey ahead.

"Throughout these various scenes and linear timelines in history, I saw the world as light and shadows, with this contrast providing the opportunity to see the other side. My progeny from that time learned to discern between the light and its *opposite*. They knew how it felt to play each role and they witnessed the effect of these contrasting roles on themselves and others. There was, however, a common theme. Each point along the linear timeline took them to a higher octave within themselves, with an important opportunity to align more fully with the light of Truth, which was a mystifying magnet. They could choose to scale up or stay where they were. My progeny were like me, curious and ready to go for it, eager to experience the next octave of light.

"Towards the end of the dream, I was shown a spectacular, cosmic scene. Suddenly, I found myself in a vehicle in the galaxy that was totally quiet and felt super tranquil. Beautiful blue beings of a subtle, soft hue sat with me in silence. From inside, we peered lovingly at Gaia. My body was subtle like theirs and in this mystical, silent space, we emanated pure love onto the planet. All I could do was to feel and emanate magnificent, unbounded frequencies; thinking was not possible. Soon I saw many other vehicles and knew that they were billowing out the same powerful frequencies of pure, ineffable love that supports and encourages humanity to experience their greatness, powers, and unicity for which they are intrinsically and permanently soft-wired. Is that amazing, or what?

"As the dream concluded, Nate appeared in front of me in that subtle, blue form with his right hand outstretched, palm up. As I placed my head within his hand, I felt frequencies pulsating, bathing me in a field of head-spinning ecstasy for a thrilling, astonishing several minutes. Then I returned to the perfect still point from which a not yet defined moment can unfold naturally. No effort, analyzing or thinking was possible. It goes without saying that this subtle experience and the whole dream will require plenty of reflection and tons of assimilation. This was the wildest dream yet... Thanks for letting me speak my experience out loud. It helps me when I can articulate something that is extremely subtle and defies logic. What do you think, Grace?"

"Well... it's another one of your *wow moments*," Grace said supportively. "I'm glad that you don't judge your dreams or overanalyze them. It was clear that your curiosity and openness was at play as the dream unfolded. Also, as you described it to me, I love that you were not enmeshed in it. Instead, you were getting incredible, intuitive guidance."

Closing her eyes for a moment and smiling, Sophia said, "Thank you for being my best friend, and for always letting me voice my subtle feelings and insights… and for never judging me or making me wrong."

"I am glad that I can be here for you. And I hope you write all of this down or voice record it," Grace said. "You are accumulating a vast treasure trove to reflect on. Do you have a feeling that your dream is a clue about the reason you came to this lake?"

"To answer that question, can I share something else?" Sophia asked. "It won't take long."

"Sure," Grace answered. "My morning is pretty free."

Sophia described her meeting with John the day before, seeing the giant skeleton, feeling that she knew the essence of the bones in the cave, and her fainting from the overwhelming enormity of it all. She shared John's wisdom; followed up with his kindness and compassion as he made dinner and built a fire that kept her warm throughout the night.

"You are in the right place; no question about it," Grace said with a big sigh. "And get ready, because it looks like you are about to embark on a big adventure. I always thought of Nate as tall, but now I am seeing an even bigger side of him and of you (pun intended). Keep going and call me anytime, day or night. I am here for you. I hope you know that."

"Thank you so much," Sophia said. "And now, I better let the dogs run around while I unpack. Blizzard is beginning to act a little crazy. I love you, Grace!"

"Love you, too."

Sophia smiled as the dogs flew out the door. Then she turned her attention towards settling into her temporary home and the next adventurous phase of her life's journey.

CHAPTER 27
COSMIC COMA

By noon, the sun broke through the clouds and sunlight cascaded through every skylight and window, illuminating the house in a way that could brighten anyone's spirits. Sophia unpacked and went through the check list that Megan and Beth left for her. All chores were done.

Spotting a book that Megan left on a nearby table, *Local Legends and Mysteries of Mystic Cove,* she decided to snuggle comfortably into the grey-blue oversized chair to read for a while near a massive, floor-to-ceiling window where she could keep track of the dogs. For the moment, they were each sitting rigid, eyes glued upward toward the squirrel they'd sent scurrying to the top of a tall oak tree.

As she was settling down with the book, a car arrived to an outburst of vehement barking.

Hearing the familiar clank and groan of the door to John's truck, she walked out onto the porch into the brilliant sunlight. She took a deep breath of invigorating mountain air as she watched him coming towards her, accompanied by a tall, lanky man wearing a hat reminiscent of Indiana Jones. Both men were smiling and chatting with a friendliness that showed they were neighbors or close friends.

Feeling at ease with John, Sophia went to the car without hesitation and extended her hand to welcome John's friend—Jake—who John described as an archeologist, cosmologist, extragalactic astronomer, and geomythologist. Jake tipped his hat in a chivalrous greeting, revealing that he had red hair mottled with grey like John's.

Jake was tall with a wiry frame, clearly showing the wear and tear of many years of hard physical work. His face was weathered, and he seemed a good few years older than John. The two men laughed at their aging, swearing they'd earned every fine wrinkle and hard callous on their hands, etched deeper with each dig in every awe-inspiring archeological site they'd encountered. John stood at least three inches shorter, with a little more meat on his bones, as Jake described it. However, they were undeniably equal in friendship and passion for their work.

"Wow Jake, those titles are impressive," Sophia said as she smiled playfully. "You will have to help me out here. I know about archeology but the others are completely unfamiliar."

"Well, I am not sure why John provided such a formal intro-duction," Jake said as his blue-eyes sparkled with humor. "Since John thought it was important, I'll let him tell you." Looking wryly at John, he leaned against the car awaiting the explanation.

"Okay," John said, turning to Sophia with a sheepish grin, "that was my lame attempt to make sure you were clear that I didn't bring a neighbor or an old buddy for coffee. I knew you'd appreciate hearing Jake's professional and enlightening take on the cove. He's been here a bunch of times. And he helped me to understand more than archeology. His field of study adds another dimension to my archeology. Cosmologists and extragalactic astronomers study the possible creation and origin theories, evolution, and future potentials for our entire universe. I can say that Jake is fascinated with celestial bodies, how the universe was formed, and the relationship humanity has with this vast, complex universe. And he's gifted with an aptitude for mathe-matics and advanced physics, including your favorite, quantum physics. This guy loves to explore all things that are invisible and incomprehensible to most folks.

"From a multi-perspective approach, he saw a giant or a skeleton from a larger lens than I did. He opened my eyes to what I think of as the big picture of the role of the giant. Like me, he travelled all over the world to follow his passion and love for this Earth, and her place in our incredible universe." Smiling at Jake, he added, "And to be honest, he is also a close friend."

"Yep, we've cemented a tight bond," Jake said, "And I have to add that I'm impressed; that's the best damned job description I think I've heard. Thanks. I am definitely passionate and obsessed with my work. When I see that skeleton and put him together with what I know about other giants, ETs, the pyramid in this lake and the pyramids all over the planet, and the stars of Orion... Well... I am always speechless when I consider the profundity of it all.

"I had a spiritual experience after a car accident many years ago; it catalyzed my intense passion. I was *out of my body,* undergoing what people call a *near death experience.* A being of intense light took me way out into the cosmos until we reached the origins of this universe; a sequence of life was shown to me, like Scrooge seeing his life in one night. I got to see, feel, and experience myself in a sequence that took me to a point of darkness where there is nothingness, silence, no discernible movement. Then, I started noticing a vibrancy and there was a swirling energy starting to emerge. At that point, I couldn't see anything yet and I felt completely calm. All of a sudden, I began to vibrate as pure energy and then morphed into sound and light. After that, I became sacred geometric shapes and sounds. Next, I began to spin wildly as a vortex of energy. I gathered other points of energy to myself and together we spun incredibly fast. Experiencing myself as pure energy, I felt exhilarated. From the center, multiplying, expanding points of light, geometric patterns, and sounds were created and swirled around in me. I was a *subtle, wildly dynamic vortex.*

"As the points of light and particles continued to converge with magnetized matter, we coalesced and created a planet. This was happening all around me in the universe. The planets were evolving in my awareness with such breakneck speed that it was almost imperceivable. This mass creation was hard to assimilate because there seemed to be infinite numbers of planets. Some exploded and others seemed to be slowly developing atmospheres. Some had water and diverse eco systems; others did not. My awareness was being diverted from planet to planet, star to star, with such an accelerated pace that I could not think. I could only observe.

"This went on for an undetermined amount of time. I was not in my thinking mind. Instead, I was in some kind of a timeless space of consciousness. Microscopic details and the overview of the cosmos were both knowable and unfathomable at the same time. It was profound, and I was at the center of it all. There was no limited, small me. Only expanded consciousness, an ever-unfolding awareness of light and sound vibration. Creation, dissolution, and freedom happened in cascading, endless waves of energy. I was everywhere and everything at the same time.

"I can't say I was *in* a reality because I was *all realities.* I experienced layer upon layer of myself, infinite scales of myself within fractal patterns from tiny to inconceivably massive—all nested within each other endlessly. I can't say how long the experience lasted because I was not aware of linear time.

"Finally, I became aware of time, space, and my body with an agonizing intensity. From this pure expansion of potential I was being squeezed down into a dense bog; from soaring effortlessly to floundering in a sludge pit.

"The being of intense light who had originally been with me after the accident was still with me. He told me that I had work to do in my life on Earth, something Gaia needed as she evolved. The cosmic experience would help me to look at my work differently, stay focused, and help others to grasp the magnitude of the truth of the universe and her origins, gifts, and ultimate beauty, wisdom, and grandeur.

"My consciousness had been out of my body in that wild expansion as light and sound vibration, and it came back with me. When I re-entered my body, I stayed in that expanded state on and off for several weeks in a coma. Then, just as easily as I entered that coma, I came out. Doctors were befuddled by the speed of my healing and my elevated cognitive capacities. It may sound like I am telling a tall tale but you have to hear this anyway... my IQ increased by fifty points. Luckily, I retained the memory of my true Essence—that still point from which all universes swirled into existence and subsided back into Essence.

"After I healed physically, I began to whole-heartedly study the Earth, her origins, and her relationship to the universe because I intuited that this was my destiny. An amazing cosmic being helped me to see a bigger picture of life on Earth and beyond.

"John told me you have spiritual depth and are on a unique and sometimes mind-boggling path. I want you to know that I respect your journey. It is yours to travel and includes your special gifts, unique frequency signature, and latent memories that you carry with you. Not everyone needs to have a car accident to get to where I went. The lesson for me is that—as a species—we each have to get real with where we've come from, the timelines we've travelled, and we have to own our greatness and unicity with everything. We are not helpless creatures, victims of unwanted circumstances. Too much has been hidden from us by those who want to profit from what ETs and giants have shared. There is a small fraction of humanity who want to maintain the status quo of our origin stories and there are those who definitely don't want us to realize how powerful we are.

"We are not mere human beings made only of blood and bones. We are cosmic nuclear power plants in a body. I have a feeling that you are already sensing that about yourself. By the way, how did you sleep last night? Every time that I've camped here or stayed in the guest house, I have cosmic dreams; amazing revelations!"

"I had a very wild dream, for sure," Sophia said. "Can I make you two some tea or coffee? Do you have something planned for today? I'd be happy to share unless it interferes with whatever you came here to do. If not today, at some point, I'd love to talk. What you are saying strikes a strong chord with me. I'd love to hear more, especially about the pyramid in the lake and other giants. My mind is still reeling from your description of yourself as the point of creation of a planet. It's like you were the tip of a vortex, a black hole, that spun into material form as a planet. That's amazing."

"I had a feeling that you'd get the gist of my near-death experience. John speaks highly of you, especially in the area of intuition. With that super power and your fascination with black holes, pyramids, and Max, I predict we'll have one hell of a good time together. And yes, I'd love some coffee, I know John does, too. We take it black and strong. Megan knows her coffee and always has some amazing beans on hand that she grinds fresh.

"And I am all ears, Sophia. I want to hear about your wild dream."

"Luckily for you two, Megan showed me where she keeps those amazing coffee beans," Sophia said, smiling warmly. "After I make you guys some coffee, I'll share my cosmic dream."

CHAPTER 28
HISTORY AND A NEW PERSPECTIVE

Jake and John settled on the porch with steaming coffee, Sophia with fragrant green tea, and everyone enjoyed Beth's freshly baked huckleberry scones.

"Sophia, what is your background?" Jake asked. "Before you share your dream, I'd like to know why you are so interested in giants, pyramids, and mystical lakes?"

Feeling reflective and tender, Sophia explained how she and Nate passionately studied everything they could find about a subtle energetic field described by cutting-edge quantum physics as the underlying field of everything everywhere. For them, it was always about understanding their energy frequency and their capacity for creating their world from pure potential in the present moment. They knew that they always had choices and could direct their frequency, rather than be carried away by feelings and emotions. John and Jake nodded as she listed the people she admired in the field of quantum physics, what she'd learned, and how it influenced her perception of life, as well as her perception of the universe.

As though sufficiently satisfied with her sharing, Jake leaned forward and said inquisitively, "Okay, now I'd like to hear about your dream. Before you begin, I want you to know that I have studied lucid dreams for over a decade. And there's some pretty mind-blowing research in quantum physics that says that a lucid dream becomes a subtle portal into the structure of space. Your body's subtle field moves into an integrative, coherent phase as a ray that can instantly soar in the infinite quantum field of all-that-is. Faster than the speed of light, there you are... in your unfettered essence enjoying the vast cosmos. You are free to be anywhere with anyone. It's radical for the mind to accept. Yet from my perspective, don't think for a second that I will doubt anything you tell me."

A thrill of joy ran through Sophia's system at hearing what he'd said—she could really be herself and she would be believed. She cleared her throat, centered herself, and with vulnerability she shared her ethereal dream. In as much detail as possible, she described the comets hitting Gaia a thousand years apart and the devastation that followed as ice sheets instantly melted. More than the cosmic events, she shared the courageous road that ensued for the small groups of humans who survived and the drop in overall frequency that followed the cataclysms. After telling her new friends about her understanding of the dream's meaning for her and its implications for shifting her perception, she sighed and sat back as though thoroughly relieved.

"I'll be damned!" Jake said with a look of wonder. "From your description and assessment I got to witness your high intellect and strength of character. Whoa, sister, I apologize for sticking you in my biased, stereotype box! When we met, I saw you as kind, gentle, and likely overly indoctrinated into New Age ideas, rather than someone clearly knowledgeable in quantum physics—a woman full of courage and gutsy curiosity. Holy shit! I apologize! What I just heard and what you shared earlier is more of what I'd call a *lion-hearted soul*. You are on the right track. Whatever happens, don't you ever give a damn what mainstream science or other people do or say. You are on a roll, my dear. Ride the waves of awe and wonder. That's my recommendation.

"If what I say is ever too much for you, just say so. I'm going to assume that you are open-minded and can handle the subjects that I am obsessed with. You can ask John, sometimes I assume too much and end up accidentally freaking people out with *unvarnished* descriptions of my explorations and conclusions. You will soon discover that I don't sugar coat anything. Can I assume you are okay with an authentic conversation, even if some of its content is not within your worldview?"

"Sure, Jake," Sophia said as they made eye contact with no barriers. "My psyche has been stretched far and wide over the past year. That's for sure. Something in me wants to experience the bigger picture of myself, the Earth, our universe, and beyond. One thing I'd like to ask you about—which did freak me out yesterday—is Max's elongated head. To start, is that something you often see? How old is he?"

"Great observation about his unusual head," Jake paused and answered thoughtfully, elucidating unreservedly his perspective on the mysterious, elongated skull. "One reason that we didn't share Max with one of the big institutions nor with the local government right away is that we immediately sent off mitochondrial DNA samples and discovered he's an elderly gentleman—as in, maybe fifty-thousand-years-old; could be older. That's what astonished us at first. Is he an undiscovered human species? Don't ask me for absolute proof. My field of science is grappling with this subject and many of my colleagues resist it. I am determined to solve these kinds of mysteries.

"There are hundreds of giant skeletons all over the United States and thousands across the planet. Max was unique because he didn't end up being of Neanderthal or Denisovan descent. And his brow looks more like ours. Who was he? Many years ago, I started to study the work of Julio Tello, and indigenous man from

Peru, born in 1880. He won my admiration when I read that he became a medical doctor and convinced his government to send him to Harvard in the U.S., and then to prestigious universities in Europe. He wanted to become an expert archeologist, and he achieved that with flying colors.

"In 1928, Julio Tello discovered a massive graveyard with the remains of people with extremely elongated skulls. He found over 300 of them. More recently, testing of the DNA from those skulls has revealed that they didn't fully match any other human DNA. When John told me about Max, I was thrown off center. Max's DNA didn't totally fit the any other human or human-like types either. Max and the artifacts here are astounding. They are older and their bones have a special quality of crystallization. Given the caverns, pyramids and what appears to be their technologies, their bones could be transmitters and receivers of massive information. My interest was piqued when I realized that throughout time, this anomaly has shown up in a small range of humans. Are they his distant progeny? Did Max perhaps migrate from Peru? But it gets even weirder.

"As we went deeper into the cave's tunnels, we found something totally unexpected: hundreds of bones from Max's clan. Their ages range from slightly older than him to as recent as seven thousand years. One was a smaller frame than Max and mirrors his age and DNA. Anthropologists are positing that perhaps these kinds of giants could have lived much longer than we do today. No one can sort out details like that yet. The human race is complex and incredibly mystifying.

"Without exception in my research, in every ancient culture there are stories, cave drawings, hieroglyphs, monoliths, pictographs, and dwellings related to giants. I've visited or worked on many of those locations and studied the nearby cultures with shamans from the Americas, Siberia, Egypt, Africa, Central America, and all over the Pacific Rim. Their understanding of their origins date back perhaps hundreds of thousands of years. It's mind boggling how giants have been reduced to the subject of imagination in fairy tales or as demonic, fallen angels. When you study their influence in our world history, it'll likely boggle your mind, like it did mine.

"The word *giant* often freaks people out; too many Hollywood biases and others who created sci-fi scripts and frightening scenarios that make you think that all giants are part of an evil race who came here with nefarious intentions. They depict giant species as rotten to the core. And if you see that kind of depiction enough, your brain starts to accept it as true. That's why we need to take back our inner knowing and abilities to discern accurate facts. There will be more and more disclosure, and you can be assured if it comes out in the media, it is being carefully manipulated or it can be their attempt at disinformation. Funding is needed to find answers.

"Max is part of a race that is not yet well-known to the general public. They are intricately, intimately linked with our DNA, our ancestors, and maybe ETs; nothing is off the table for me. When I realized how thoroughly you've worked on trying to discover ways to sense and know the truth, I got excited. That's a skill we all need to develop for the twenty-first century, along with open-minded curiosity and collaboration.

"My research into global shamanic cultures shows that the giants helped, supported, taught, and cared for humans. Does that surprise you? They blended with us as part of our species. They also mated with us in extraordinary ways. How's that for a truth bomb? They were quite advanced, and according to shamanic cultures, some could infuse their male energy into a woman without touching her. To do that, she had to be living in a high frequency. Often it took the women, who prepared to be the partners of these beings, many decades to prepare for this exchange of subtle energy.

"I am also aware of other cultures that had to deliver the babies like in a modern cesarean section. If you doubt me, go and talk to hundreds of elders globally who don't give a damn about what you think of them. They speak the truth as it's been passed down and documented in stone carvings, art, and shared in their oral traditions. The cave art often shows elongated heads and sometimes red or blonde hair. Occasionally the giants wear robes rather than the warmer, cave-style clothing of the ones that you described. John told me that the ones you saw wore animal skins and protective clothes. Keep in mind that the giants lived in varying climates and locations.

"Like you, I had to let my psyche adjust to the possibility of giants being a part of our history and ancestry. Slowly, the possibility settled into my being as my truth. I'm now unshakable on this subject. You and I share something in common which is intimate and special. We feel love for Max.

"As you likely know through the unified field theory of quantum physics, we each emit a frequency, we are a unique vibration, and that personal vibrational matrix is like a distinctive signature or thumb print. It's a part of the field of all-that-is. And when someone is close to us, once we have resonance with them, we will be able to recognize them throughout time and space. I want to be clear that this is my understanding of quantum physics. I am not an expert, but like you and Nate, John and I study it as best we can. It's mind-bending, for sure.

"I can see your eyes glazing over. I'll stop for now." He sipped his coffee and sighed deeply.

Sophia shifted in her chair and sipped her tea. Jake, John, and Sophia took a moment to be silent. Sitting in dawn's tranquility, they looked across the landscape in front of them. The foggy morning mist was fully vaporized and morphed into a radiant, sunlit day, bathing the lawn in bright, emerald hues.

After several minutes of reflection, Sophia said, "Honestly, my relationship with Max and the giants has been confusing at times. Was it just a dream? While dreaming, how could I feel the frigid air on my face and breath it in as it reached deeply into my nostrils? How could I see vibrant colors around me, smell the giant's skin as I lay my head in his hand, and smell the musty walls of their cave? They feel intimate and familiar. My worldview has been so darn linear! Although I've studied quantum physics, lived in India, and meditated for countless years, this is taking me deeper and wider into what's unknowable through my mind; the incomprehensible Truth of who I am, what the world is made of, and why I am here.

"At times, loosening my mind's grip on its perceived reality and playing in pure possibility has not been easy. At other times, it's like my whole being soars into that field and plays there with enthusiasm.

"I want you to know that everything you said feels aligned and true. I don't doubt you. A year ago I would have been interested in what you said, yet there's a good chance that I would have listened while unconsciously permitting judgment and doubt to filter my perception of your words. I've worked hard to notice when that happens and come back to deep listening. I'm all ears, guys. My intuition says that you know these giants on a level way beyond their bones. Could you say more about what you've learned about Max?"

"I'd rather we go to the cave," Jake said. "If you are okay with it, there's more to see there and discover about Max and his lineage. Before we go, however, I want to preface our journey today. I want to show you the cave drawings, the symbols, and the rest of the cavern. What you saw is the tip of the iceberg in this unique cave system. I want to know if what we talked about today lit a fire in your belly to learn something new and got you hungry for the experience of the inexplicable? Are you ready to dive headfirst into Max's past and yours? I mean you as a human or a hybrid of giants or whatever else you discover about yourself. Our time together has to be about discovery rather than a guided tour of a giant's cave.

"This work is personal to each of us. It matters. It's our history that we've not been allowed to learn and explore. It shifts us from current world views about religion, politics, history, and culture. However, a fire has to be blazing in us full throttle to sustain the endless journey into the mysteries of our history. We are infinitely more than what we've been taught to believe. Our history is magnificent, vast, and unimaginably exciting. The Earth, the Galaxy, and the universe are beyond anything that can be explained easily. It's experiential."

"I want to see it all," Sophia said. "There's no going back. I can't forget what I've discovered. It's become my reality. I am all in, guys; one hundred percent."

Jake's eyes twinkled like a four-year-old in wonder of seeing butterfly wings for the first time. "The truth is so f**king exciting! The fact that you are *all in* can take our work here to the next level—because you, my dear friend, are a hopeless mystic and John and I would love to be more like you! We'll teach you about Max and you can teach us how to enter his world, however it is that you do that. It's about collaboration. We all have to stop playing small, following the status quo, and feeling that we have to do this work alone, always in fear of critics or ostracism. Holy shit! I can't tell you how much I love having another sacred rebel on our team." His face had become red in his excitement. He stopped in mild embarrassment, but just laughed.

"Sorry for getting so riled up, Sophia. It's just that this is such a big deal. Through recent archeological sites, we've discovered there were advanced cultures tens of thousands of years ago and maybe much older. Our world history is beyond anything we conceived was possible. If you research Gobekli Tepe and other archeological sites online, you'll see that science is now willing to concede that humanity was far advanced in architecture and technology beyond what we believed in the past. Instead of thinking in terms of human civilization in thousands of years, we think in five hundred thousand years of time and millions or billions of years. That is what reinvigorated my research and interest. There's immeasurable universes to explore. We settled on one hypothesis that we could confirm. It's exciting to have more information available now.

"The archeologist in me enjoyed our conversation immensely. Since we all seem to be on the same page, why don't we head down to the cave and do some hands-on exploring. John, I'll help you gather our stuff. And Sophia, it is cold down there and a bit slippery. So put on your *cave shoes.*"

Laughing, she left to gather her gear. Within a couple of minutes, she met them at the top of the staircase leading to a cove that was anything but ordinary.

CHAPTER 29
HONESTY ABOUT ANCIENT HISTORY

Descending the steps silently and carefully, Jake lead the way.

"John, you've been unusually quiet today," Sophia said, breaking the silence of their trek. "Do you have a similar ancient memory of Max or his lineage as I do? What peaked your interest in all of this? And how have you kept it secret?"

"Well, Sophia," John said smiling, "you are full of questions today. As I've shared with you, I feel a close bond with Max. I also have awe-inspiring memories starting to come online in me about my history with him and the Earth's history with his kind. My interest was personal, honestly.

"As an archeologist, I tried to study the giants and it was deflating to realize that landowners reported that prestigious institutions and universities took hold of most skeletons. It's like the giants went down a dark hole. No one can study them or even find them. Articles by my peers claim that giants are nonsense. I called on my tenacious nature, which always fuels my spirit. I tend to be uncompromising in matters like this and I followed old newspaper articles all over this country with the same story: the skeletons and artifacts had been taken away, without a trace left behind. And I could never get access to them.

"In the nineteenth century, there were thousands of giant bones found everywhere, globally. If you try to find them or ask for transparency about their origins, you won't get anywhere. I had friends who made admirable attempts to go deeper into the mysteries of Catalina Island in California. The island was owned by the Wrigley's chewing gum family in the 1920's when a private team of archeologists discovered over thirty-five hundred blonde-haired, giant skeletons; some over seven-thousand-years-old. They also found a megalithic temple like Stonehenge, plus artifacts.

"What happened, you may ask? Tons of interest and then the press came out saying it was a hoax. Really? A hoax? For fifty years they backtracked and said the bones are all gone now; nothing to see. It was like putting up a huge sign telling archeologists to go away and let the skeletons rot in hidden places. Can you tell this subject chaps my butt?

"It's like a broken record. People say that they gave the skeletons and artifacts to XYZ institution or university for further study. If you try to follow up with the institution, they say that the bones don't exist. These massive institutions have all the power, and their position is, *We've got 'em but you can't see 'em.* No one can access the field reports or the hundreds of photos. Why?

"Why when you read the New York Times articles from the late 1800's and early 1900's, do you find that they covered stories of giant bones and skeletons? If we try to follow up with them, like our predecessors, why are we considered to be rogue anthropologists who should be ignored or harassed? Either way, we are certainly not going to trace those bones.

"Who knows the whole truth? You likely heard the saying, *Where there's smoke, there's fire.* Why not transparency? It's a question I haven't been able to answer, and I see both sides. These discoveries could upend current scientific theories. However, it's deeper than that because our world has experienced a divisive rift between the perceptions of religion as to our origins and those of fact-based science. For the most part, our society has accepted the scientific view of phenomena, which is maintained by a materialistic perception of reality. Anything that looks the tiniest bit mystical, or unseen or unmeasurable, becomes labelled as pseudoscience. When an established group's identity is challenged, they can become threatened and lash out. That resistance combined with the challenge of locating the skeletons of these amazing giants left me with lots of questions about how to go forward in search of giant truths (pun intended)." John smiled and winked at Jake.

"Over time, I decided to study the archeological sites where they likely lived rather than search for the bones, which clearly someone or some group didn't want us to study. Even with radical archeological finds recently, there's a force that wants desperately to thwart this work; crazy but true. I have seen that when you confront someone's worldview and related, long-held personal beliefs, it can instantly get polarizing and ugly. Beliefs and conclusions die hard. Mine sure did. We have to be compassionate yet move forward unapologetically. Our goal is to bring to life a more harmonious way of perceiving reality. Like you, we see unicity as a vital aspect of existence on Gaia. Patience and persistence have to be included in our response to inflexibility and reliance on mathematical formulas.

"The unified field theory encompasses the truth that we are all communicating with each other all the time, via the invisible field—which is hard to grasp for some people. After working at the cove, I am sure that this universe is dynamic and wildly creative. We are not isolated little specs of it. Instead, we are a fractal of it. That's hard for most folks to grasp. And it upends our learned, current reality. I am getting comfortable in letting my old beliefs give way to something that fits my experience here.

"For me, going to the sites where the giants lived, being in their homelands, brought me closer to knowing them. My perception of all life, across time and space, is that we can communicate beyond this reality. How many people have dreams or indications that a loved one who died is communicating with them? It is real, not their imagination.

"With the giants, I saw their advanced technological skills and got a sense of their brilliance. My appreciation grew for how they gave humanity an unprecedented boost to develop civilizations, to learn mathematics and other sciences, and quantum skills like connection with a 'sky family.' That's a name for them that I learned from an indigenous elder. He says these beings are from our galaxy or universe, but they didn't all arrive from one planet. Some are from different planets or stars. Jake's galactic cosmology background was the icing on the cake. He helped me to think from a broader perspective and to consider the possibility that the giants were not human.

"I wondered if they'd come to help, like a kind neighbor. My belief systems started shifting. Could I somehow enter a higher reality within myself where I could speak with them? Between quantum sciences and shamanism, my mind was blown and there was no going back to my old paradigm. From there, I began to wonder what it would be like to have the quantum technology to move through time and space at will. And if Neptune was in trouble, for example, would I go to help out?

"My analytical mind began to stretch into the possibility that I would go anywhere that I was needed. I realized that would only happen if I vibrated at a high enough frequency to be able to perceive the galaxy as part of my life experience. I have a feeling, a sense that this entire universe is my home, not just Earth.

"Over and over, I found indications that there have been advanced civilizations on this planet that go back over fifty thousand years. Some archeologists say perhaps five hundred thousand years. We are at the tip of the iceberg, the tip of a learning curve of unimaginable magnitude.

"When Megan confided in me that she and her husband had found this skeleton and the cave, I almost dropped to my knees, overwhelmed with joy and thanking God. I finally had a site to study and research, with massive opportunities to learn about our ancient past and dive deeply into unseen phenomena and mysteries. Jake and I are consistently convinced of the truth of the unified field theory of quantum physics. As we worked here, nothing about a mechanistic view of reality made sense anymore. We experienced something profound and inexplicable in this cove. Considering that I am not a machine, why view the universe as though it is mechanistic and predictable? We became immersed in this unfathomable coordinate in the field.

"Before we reveal the site, there's another consideration that I have not shared with you: it's become our passion to protect this cove for those who have lived here for centuries before us, the local, indigenous people. They see Max as a sentient being, a relative, who must be treated with reverence and respect.

"You likely have seen some of them going to the cove and didn't realize who they were. I'll explain: we are working on land that is contested by the local indigenous people, but remains private. Megan and her husband bought a huge swath of the land here that's under dispute. Right off the bat, Megan's husband invited the elders of that community to come, do ceremony, and let their people have free access to it, any time they want to come. In fact, part of Megan's land is off-limits, except to them. There's no legal arrangement. I'd call it a *heart agreement* that we respect impeccably. She's working legally to make sure that they can always have access to this land. She never says much about it, but she hints at something she experienced in Asia that somehow informs her decisions here. I don't pry. Yet I do respect her judgment and her honesty. She's been our main financier and she supports our work like the Rock of Gibraltar. Lord knows we've needed that! So proceeding with work on this site is more nuanced and complex than other areas where we've worked.

"As if Max was not enough, when we discovered several pyramids, I was blown away. Three pyramids under water in this cove line up with the latitudes of remote pyramids in China and longitudes of ancient, crumbling remains of pyramids off the coast of Catalina Island.

"A lot of credit and thanks goes to Jake's friend at Stanford, a brilliant archeologist, who studies the Pacific Rim and underwater sites. He's validated the existence of cultures that date back tens of thousands of years. We began to integrate the cove with other areas of ancient wisdom and sky family technology.

"Pyramids were not used back then for pharaoh-housing and burial grounds. They were all over the planet and were advanced technologies, a form of energy-technology. All of the cultures I've studied refer to them in ancient times. They often had water under them to facilitate communication and to hold higher quantum codes of wisdom and information. We posit that they generated energy to run huge civilizations and were conduits to connect with the multiverse. Sound sci-fi? Maybe. But the physicists we work with think our hypothesis has merit.

"When you study these pyramids from Jake's lens, what emerges is a highly effective way for beings on Earth to download information and higher frequencies from other star systems in our galaxy. Need a boost of energy for this great Earth or to bring in an elevated frequency? Just wait for an equinox or a solstice and your pyramids line up with cosmic portals—and bingo! Magic happens—*quantum magic*. Portals to the multiverse open on Gaia and connection happens with *who knows what!* We know the alignments are there, but we don't know what happens at that alignment. It must have been profound and important to create such megalithic structures and precisely engineered pyramids. Shamans and kings valued this higher information to advance their civilization and their personal frequency. From what I've learned, some used it for the greater good and others decided to use it for personal gain.

"We don't know the power of these pyramids we've found.

"I just recalled that you stayed near a volcano. From what I've learned, volcanoes have a pretty wild singularity at the core of their subtle vortex. Jumping into the multiverse seemed to happen easily for the indigenous who lived near volcanic coordinates on Gaia. In light of what we talked about today, you may want to reflect deeper on your dreams of giants, volcanoes, and ETs and how they fit with what you are about to see about pyramids."

The three adventurers stopped to let John complete his explanation, standing on the huge deck, the waves lapping onto the shore and gulls soaring above their heads. John said, "Let's go inside the cave, Sophia. You need to see the cave art, geometric patterns, hieroglyphs, and walk through the caverns. Are you okay about seeing Max?"

"Yes, I've had a chance to integrate yesterday's big surprise," Sophia said with confidence and a gentle smile. "I'm ready."

The outside entrance to the cave was inconspicuously hidden, but once inside, a remarkable inner world appeared.

"This is different than my experience yesterday," Sophia said pensively. "When we came in before, I didn't notice the surroundings. Max completely captured my attention. What are those symbols on the ceiling? And do you know who or when the hieroglyphs were created? Who are these robed beings? Is that the giants? Look at the difference between the people next to them. They are maybe half their size."

Before getting answers, she was already heading into a tunnel as though a magnet was drawing her deeper into the cave's core.

"Sophia, Hey! Wait up," Jake said laughing. "Hold on, we're coming. I guess you are not worried about anything today. That's for sure."

She entered a room of quartz laden walls which emitted such intense light that it seemed electrified. Sophia stood in child-like wonder taking in the width and the height of sparkling beauty. Mother Nature supplying the energy that allowed them to see her exquisite creation. Three granite obelisks stood like sentries as they entered the space.

"I feel like I could cry; not from sadness but from awe and love," Sophia said. "I'm feeling a sense of familiarity yet I've never seen anything like this. Where is the light coming from?

"It's a natural crystalline structure," John said. "Keep going. It gets more profound. And notice the structures and how harmonious they look and feel. Without getting into geometry, the obelisks are fifty-five feet and a few inches—but they are exactly thirty six cubits tall, which was a measurement used in Egypt. Why? We do not know."

Through a tunnel, they entered into an even larger cavern. The same light was there along with a waterfall that fed into a pool of crystal-clear water that John said was potable. This cavern was like a colossal palace in grandeur and feeling. Sophia squinted as she tried to find the ceiling. And then gazed far out in front of her without an end point in sight.

To her right, hewn out rock formations formed what looked like a circle of enormous-sized chairs; disintegrated pieces of old pelts lay on top of them. To her left, a wooden table stretched out for at least sixty feet with large rocks that John said were possibly stools for the giants. The table was so tall that Sophia could easily walk under it.

"I'd struggle to climb onto one of these stools," Sophia said with amazement in her voice. "How big is this cavern? Are there more?"

"Come over here and have a seat on these smaller rocks," Jake said. John joined them and they all surveyed their surroundings in silence for a few moments.

"I understand why you'd have plenty of questions," Jake said as he looked towards Sophia. She was still gazing upward trying to find the ceiling of the giant's massive cave.

"Let me tell you a few things that may help to acclimate you," John added, "and help you understand where we are... This is likely the living quarters for a small group of giants. It doesn't seem that this was a large community because at any given time, I'm guessing a dozen, or maybe a few more, could have inhabited this space.

"In the next cavern, you will see smaller furniture where maybe hominids, humans, or hybrids lived. Right now, it's hard for us to say who or what they were.

"It's important to know that the Pacific Northwest was lush grassland around fourteen thousand years ago. The glacier ice melted and the great war with the beings of the west had not happened yet. From what we can tell, in what would be one human lifetime, the landscape shifted from grasslands to the lush forests that you see now. Sea levels rose and the rivers and lakes became deeper. This caused the pyramids and other structures to no longer be visible and accessible.

"The symbols you see on the walls are fascinating because they are similar to caves that stretch into Siberia and also similar symbols found in Peru. Based on weather and climate, the giants may have been forced to migrate from time to time. We have to keep in mind that these beings lived longer than us. Some anthropologists speculate perhaps hundreds or thousands of years. The giants seem to be adaptable to the environment. What we find interesting is that the *cave art*, as you call it, does not appear to be from one time period.

"Did they *go home* for a while during the brutal ice ages and then come back? Were they permeant residents? The drawings and tools seem to match the latter theory. As I dated them, they seem to be from varying periods after an ice age.

"There is an interesting, relevant factor in dating Max's earliest timeline—the cave art. Going back 30,000 years or more, archeological sites globally appear to be matrilineal cultures (where knowledge, sagacity, and name were passed down through the female line). In a cave, the outer areas of the cave had male figures, like stags and male horses and symbols like dots or short lines, but the inner cave—think of it as entering the female anatomy, finally arriving in the deep, dark womb. There, you find female iconography like mammoths and bison and shapes like triangles, rectangles, and ovals. There is a growing number of archeologists who believe the cave was used for religious ritual. Was that performed by the women?

"In recent years, we have a lot of this kind of revelatory symbolism and art being discovered. One of the mysteries is how did men get credit for agriculture and cooking? In the caves and other sites, we find that it was women who planted and sprouted seeds, sowed them on the surface, and harvested them. They also spun hair and other natural fibers into cloth and cooked food as a group and served it in their homemade pottery. Storage bins for honey and grains were found in ancient goddess temples.

"For me, the important part of Max's civilization was a reverence for the life cycle of birth, life, death, and renewal. This is associated with matrilineal and matriarchal cultures. It's all over the symbols here. The indigenous people of this area believe, similar to the Mayan culture, that the Earth moves through very long cycles, tens of thousands of years. Max's clan came at the beginning of the last cycle and either left or slowly died out. However, their kin, in the cycle of renewal, are walking the Earth in new Earth bodies and some are assisting the transition to this new advanced era from the stars.

"What we found here is evidence to support all of that." John spoke with enthusiasm; clearly this was his life's passion.

"Now that John gave you plenty to mull over, here's where I have to jump back in," said Jake. "As I mentioned, the pyramids line up with others on the planet. But as we go deeper, there's another pyramid. Wait until you experience that cosmic treasure. It's newer. It's like they worked their way into the cave system, adding to it over time, and making their way to adjacent chambers where all of the female iconography is located."

"What are we waiting for?" Sophia asked as she jumped to her feet, leading the way forward.

"Hold on for a second," John said laughing. "This cavern is darker because there are only sparse fluorescent rocks for light. Let me go first."

The entrance was smaller and for giants, would have been a squeeze to get through. Symbols in yellow and mostly red formed a mesmerizing arch over the entrance as they entered the pristine silence of the next, deeper cavern. Somehow, this space was void of dripping water or any sounds, the air felt incredibly fresh, and only small patches of luminescence were visible.

As they approached, Sophia caught sight of a magnificent pyramid, covered in unfamiliar symbols, looking ancient, and completely intact. John paused and motioned for Sophia to come near.

"I met a local indigenous elder years ago. And when Megan showed me the cave, I knew we had to include him in our discovery. He knew about the cave and pyramid from oral tradition. Even after losing access to it, his lineage handed down the voice code to open the pyramid."

"The voice code?" Sophia asked inquisitively. "What happens when it opens?"

"See for yourself," John said. "He opened it for us earlier today. He couldn't stay. You'll meet him because he does ceremonies in this cave. He must sense that you are trustworthy and definitely special. He would never open this for one of our buddies or for someone to simply check it out."

The opening to the pyramid revealed a gold, silver, and copper interior. John motioned for her to enter. As she stepped inside, she said, "My heart is melting. It's hard to gather thoughts. I want to be in this place forever. Can I sit here for a few minutes and take in this frequency?"

"You sure can," Jake said. "We have to warn you to be careful. In the center is a pool of water. A giant couldn't fall in, but you could. The elder told us that it generates electricity for the pyramid which is magnetic. This pyramid was potentially a portal for space-time travel and for generating energy for those living down here. You have to be in the right frequency to activate it. After your first visit to meet Max, I mentioned the composition of the bones of the giants. They contain silica, like ours, which means that they are piezoelectric and generate electricity as they walk, just like us, but their bones have a composition that we cannot identify. Jake and I are betting that whatever is in their bones, allowed them to interact electromagnetically to the pyramid and other technologies. With that in mind, they could have lived a highly advanced lifestyle without a bunch of gadgets and devices. Keep in mind that you are standing on solid granite.

"Did you notice the granite flooring is precisely level, except the platform of the pyramid is raised by a few centimeters. How and why, we don't know. Checkout the pathways which have large, scored marks. We believe that was not art, it was to prevent anyone from slipping especially in the areas with increased moisture. Or was it energetic? Damn, Sophia! We have so many questions, so many mysteries! The crazy part is that the scoring is precise and symmetrical and forms patterns. I sure wish Max could talk; or that I could listen better. I'm clear that coherent communication happens through frequency. I'm interested in elevating my frequency so that I can resonate with Max's clan and get more in tune with them and how they operated.

"Okay Sophia, you get to go inside. We have to leave the door open, though. He will come later and close it. We'll give you five minutes to experience its energy and then, we'll signal to you."

From the base to the tip of the pyramid was about forty-four feet and there was a rectangular, stone box where she could sit. The interior pool was crystal clear water with gems that shimmered under its surface. As intoxicating as the beauty was, Sophia slipped into a quiet place inside herself and found unicity within this pyramid's high frequency environment.

After five minutes, John and Jake looked through the opening to find her sitting still with her head thrust back and her body vibrating with light tremors. Her face was ecstatic, and her energy field was so strong that they could feel it as they passed through it to approach her, gently bringing her back to waking consciousness. They said her name softly and Sophia gently opened her eyes, radiant, peaceful, and peering forward as though she was seeing past the walls of the pyramid. Slowly, she looked in their direction, took a deep breath and left the pyramid, glancing back as though relishing as much of the experience as possible.

John and Jake motioned for her to follow, and they went back through the large cavern and into a smaller one near the cave's entrance. John kept a few chairs there and they sat in silence.

"I've always heard horrific stories about giants," Sophia said softly. "Today, I felt their essence. I realize how crazy it is to think of them as angry, cruel, and dangerous. What if these giants were nothing but *huge love* with a form? That's what I experienced back there. I am still vibrating with pure love for the giants, for you two, the planet, the galaxy, the whole universe, and for myself. It's not about archeology for history's sake. It's bigger. They taught our ancestors the secrets of quantum living. Maybe in some quantum coordinate in the field, I was there, too. This is all mind-boggling. They are not historical for me now. They are real, alive, and important. And no one would believe me if I told them. Isn't that the weirdest part?"

"We've learned not to worry about that," Jake said. "For one thing, we should not try to predict what others' reaction would be if they knew what we knew, and what our predecessors tried to share. Heck, maybe they'd be on the same page as you and me. At some point, we will likely meet resistance and we will be in good company like the Cathar's of medieval times with the holy grail, or Galileo, and of course, my hero, Copernicus. In recent times, there've been attempts to silence the twentieth century whistleblowers of the secret space program, and our archaeological and galactic cosmologist colleagues in the twenty-first century. We feel like the lid is about to come off all of this ridiculous secrecy. That would be my dream come true.

"There are more caverns that we didn't explore today. From my perspective, this feels sufficient. The others house more bones and artifacts that we have dated to various time periods. We are also working with some trusted colleagues to excavate other buried remains on the surface of Megan's property. Unlike these skeletons, they don't appear to be human. We ask that you not come back to the cave without us. Is that agreeable to you?"

"Yes, that's fair," Sophia said. "I am going to have to absorb this for a while. The *special cove* that Megan talked about is an absolute understatement."

They emerged from the cave into mid-day brightness and slowly ascended the steep stairs.

CHAPTER 30
OFF PLANET DREAMING

Sophia's unexpected, awe-inspiring day was concluding as the dogs bolted outside and ran full force until exhaustion finally set in. While they devoured their evening meal, she built a fire which soon danced with crimson flames. Finding a book to read, she snuggled into a plush, warm blanket. It was time to relax and watch the mesmerizing movement of the flickering light in front of her.

The feeling of the pyramid was still vibrating in her cells as she texted Grace to try to describe what she was experiencing. Within a minute, her phone rang.

"Hey, tell me what happened," Grace said. "Your text said you went to the cove today and you are still vibrating?"

"That's an understatement," Sophia said. "Promise to never share anything I'm going to say?"

"You ought to know better," Grace said laughing. "Since it's one of your stories, there's no one I could tell. They'd think I made it up."

Their laughter set the tone for the wonder and awe that Sophia described. She began with the symbols arching over the entrance where her journey into the cave's caverns began; she described the gigantic tables, the crystal-lit caverns, and the details of what she saw and how it felt to vibrate with the pyramid and walk amid the obelisks.

As she talked, she suddenly stopped and became motionless, paused, and added that she recalled that Kabir foretold of her going into a pyramid that would *match her frequencies.* He said it was important for her to go there. With that recollection, her sense of awe and wonder expanded exponentially. Letting her unexpected realization integrate, their conversation melted into a soft, deep, silent space.

"You know, Sophia," Grace said, "this was one of those milestone moments. You won't be the same. I can't be either. As you described that pyramid, I felt like I was with you. We've always been a bit *out there*, like seeing the little fairy spheres when we were little. Having said that, this is way beyond fairies and elementals.

"Jake and John are gifts, Sophia. They are risking a lot to bring a vital part of history to people. Most of us don't consider engaging in that kind of work. If you consider all you've learned from Gilda, your lucid dreams, Angelica, and now giants, caves, and pyramids… it's profound. Could you possibly write about it?"

"Not sure," Sophia said. "I'd run into the same resistance that John and Jake encounter. Who would believe me?"

"Maybe you could publish your experiences as diaries," Grace suggested. "I don't know how to get it out. A blog? Hey, why don't you do what we did when we were little? Go ask the fairies what to do! It would be worth doing."

They laughed and reminisced about the childhood worries that they took to the fairies' council—like what to do when someone made fun of them or when they wanted to hide because they felt like they didn't fit into the normal world. The fairy council always gave them telepathic advice that was soothing and kind, setting them back on their path to someday talk about giants, ETs, and universal quantum truths.

"After I got into school, I slowly let go of the council," Sophia said in a voice tinged with sadness. "Now that I am admitting to the reality of the giants, the ETs, and the grandeur of the universe, I appreciate those little, invisible light beings. I'd never tell a child they are only in their imagination. Thanks for mentioning the fairies because they are as real and invaluable as those beings who built the pyramid and sat in the cave on huge stools. You are right. After this experience, I won't be the same. I've come to a place in my life where I absolutely have to be authentic. I want to share everything I've learned and experienced, without sugar coating it. However, how I do that is yet to be determined. When the time is right, I'll get it out there.

"I am going to eat and go to bed early to integrate my adventures today. Thanks for letting me articulate it in so much detail."

"I love you," Grace said, "Good night. And call me any time."

Sophia was looking forward to sinking into sleep. She had read that deep sleep states move a person from normal dreaming into brainwaves that take the mind into higher states of consciousness. Nestling into the cozy and luxurious feel of Megan's guest room, she climbed into the soft, fluffy bed with its plush down comforter. Through the lace curtains, a sliver of moonlight rose in the sky like a thin cup that could hold Sophia lovingly throughout the night.

"Good night, Yeti," Sophia said smiling gently. "And goodnight to you, too, Blizzard. Thanks for staying with me to protect me every night. I appreciate you." The dogs rested on cream colored wool blankets on the floor like two sentinels who were guarding a sleeping princess.

Sleep came swiftly and easily.

She became aware of a light breeze on her face as a scene began to slowly appear in front of her. Looking around, the atmosphere of the planet she was standing on was imbued with shades of blue. Sapphire, indigo, azure, and cyan hues extended to the sky, rocks, mountains, and several nearby moons. Noticing that her body was not solid, she found it simple, even familiar to be transported under the planet's surface into to a lovely blue world of sparkling light and cool air. Walking in silence and with a sense of calm, she looked to her left and followed a path to a stream of scintillating turquoise water. Sitting by the bank for a moment, she felt a hand on her shoulder and found herself bursting into euphoria at the sight of Nate, standing next to her and emitting his familiar, warmhearted smile.

In their telepathic dialogue, they expressed their love. Gazing lovingly into his kind, blue eyes, she experienced the intimacy she'd felt in other dreams and on the planets she'd visited with him after his death. The blue world they were meeting in was familiar and felt safe. He gently helped her to stand and motioned for her to follow him to a waterfall. Sophia felt neither confusion nor shock as she looked around, even when she noticed Nate's cone-shaped head and became aware that hers was the same.

Nate began to speak to her in their familiar, other-worldly thought transference.

You went to our cave, dear one. It contains a portal to the infinite. In the darkness of that space, we once accessed the profound center of our heart space, where impeccable, mystical power resides.

I want to encourage you to acknowledge the importance of this moment in human history. And allow your bones to activate in a way that reminds you of who you are and who we've been somewhere else in the field. In that way, you can ignite your own codes of light and wisdom and emanate them. You came to life on Gaia for that reason.

Remember that your frequency is the key to unlock the magic of the quantum world for you. Your frequency matters. I've observed that you are elevating your energy fields to a much greater degree these days. You and I didn't fully grasp that the whole universe receives the emanation from our energy fields.

With my heart on fire, I want to convey how much I love you and the magnitude of support that I will be offering you from higher realms within yourself and from this coordinate in the universe where we are now meeting. Whatever happens, don't give any thought or feeling towards what others think of you. We worked on that a lot, didn't we?

It is important to write about all that you are learning and experiencing, even if your mental and emotional conditioning makes you reticent to do so, or to fear the doubters and naysayers. You may recall that I called them 'killjoys.' Remember they are not significant to you nor you to them. Never let anyone eclipse your joy for the incredible life you are living. Fear of being mocked may arise in you; intense terror of being abandoned, outcast, or killed will raise its head. You will be required to shine your truth anyway, to elevate your inherent frequencies anyway.

Your current life is not the time for the outdated nonsense of inquisitions and those who crush the unseen and mystical truth at all costs. What cannot be seen is actually the vital essence of reality. Centuries ago, the church agreed with Aristotle's rationalism, molding religion within that linear, limited paradigm. The people themselves did not choose the scriptures, join the discussions, or have a chance to weigh in on the true nature of reality. That decision was and continues to be made by a few for the many. Yet that is changing.

Remember that you have a team of unseen helpers this time and Gaia—a sentient being—has elevated into very high frequencies. You can lean into her, too.

It's because you've raised your frequency that we can meet at this coordinate in the field or in higher scales of reality within you. Good going, sweetest one. I love you.

I'll always be here for you; And I mean always.

Peace mingling with radiant joy, they walked back to the portal where Sophia had entered the magnificent blue planet.

As soft morning waves of light filtered into the room, the sounds of dogs snoring entered her awareness as she lingered in the memory of meeting her sweetheart in the intimate and important dream. Finally, she opened her eyes and got up to write in her journal. She wondered about the extended skulls of Nate and Max, and herself for that matter, in this other co-ordinate of the field.

Why was I shown the blue planet with Nate?

Why was I perfectly at home on that planet with my mysterious, elegant, elongated skull?

And what triggered my ability to meet with Nate, feeling that it was effortless to do so?

Why did Nate say, "I see that you went to our cave?" He called it, "our cave."

How many people on Gaia believe it is safe to explore the nature of reality, rather than remain indoctrinated into the remnants of Aristotelian and eleventh century church doctrine? Are we evolving past that?

How can I sustain elevated frequencies?

I am beginning to feel the space inside of me and around me during the day. After a lot of practice being aware of the space, unconsciously, in that coordinate with Nate, I was spaciousness rather than form. It felt familiar, normal. How did that happen? Is it repeated practice allowing my brain to accept this "new normal?"

She loved beginning the day with journaling, rambunctious dogs, the glorious view of the towering cluster of fir trees, chipmunks scurrying around everywhere, and the smell of jasmine flowers wafting from her teacup. She felt an exhilaration, a joy for existence that left her feeling confident, relaxed, and buoyant.

Sophia decided to text Grace a brief description of her lucid dream. She added, "My world is brimming over with optimism and peaceful harmony. All is well. I can do this."

Grace shot back a reply immediately saying, "Wow! It keeps getting better. And yep, you can definitely do this. This is your time to shine."

Sophia began to capture the details of her dream on her laptop. Then she researched elongated skulls and past archeologic sites with giant bones in the vicinity of Megan's property. Controversy was evident about whether there was suppression of information regarding giant skeletons and artifacts, whether the giants were real, and whether they were descendants of humans. Polarization appeared to have invaded the archeological space on this topic.

There were various ideas and hypothesis but no conclusions. She saw that some scientists were categorizing colleagues as "conspiracy theorists" and there were dismissals of the tes-timonies of indigenous elders globally as nothing more than "spiritual mythology." According to standard archaeology, that kind of oral tradition and their etchings and hieroglyphs were not enough definitive proof to build a conclusive, scientific case for the emerging, groundbreaking information.

Some archaeologists disregarded the amazing synchronicity that similar giant skeletons appear all over the world during comparable time periods and in particular sacred sites like the pyramids of Giza, Peru, China, and the Pacific Rim.

Sophia read an article that caught her attention:

There exists a fascinating correlation of unique symbols that appear all over the globe at certain points in history and which can only be deciphered by a handful of hiero-glyph experts. The symbols are extremely rare and yet somehow they appeared on several continents during the same time period.

Sophia made a note to ask Jake and John the same question." Are discoveries like this simply a coincidence or are they clues?"

With her firsthand view of the skeleton, there was no doubt that Max was human and he was definitely special. More than that, Sophia was able to meditate in a pyramid which was built to handle giants of Max's size, and which was extraordinary in frequency. She'd told Grace how much resonance she felt for Max and his clan, *down to her bones.* She shared with Jake that Max's presence, including his majestic, elongated skull, felt as familiar and real to her as Nate or anyone else in her family. Consequently, it was hard for her to be a skeptic.

During the following week, rather than go back to the cove with Jake and John, she continued doing research and writing about her experiences with Gilda, with Kabir, the lucid dreams from the volcano, Angelica, and her more recent, lucid dreams with Nate. She added Megan, John, Jake, and Max to her journals. Her family was growing...

CHAPTER 31
THE ELDER AND THE MYSTIC

As usual, John's red truck arrived at eight o'clock with Jake right behind him. Sophia always had morning coffee ready and exchanged laughter and friendship with the two men she respected immensely.

"Can I join you, today?" Sophia asked. "I want to see the cavern of the other skeletons that you mentioned. Is that okay?"

"Of course you can," Jake said. "I'm chomping at the bit to go! I thought maybe you decided you'd had enough of rummaging around in dark caverns, looking at giant skeletons and a bunch of artifacts."

"No way! It's the opposite. I've been engrossed in researching giants, non-stop! When I was in India, a young man named Kabir talked about our ancient past. I bet he'd love to have seen Max."

With coffee time complete, they cheerfully headed down the steps to Mystic Cove. Before entering the cave, Jake suddenly stopped and turned to Sophia.

"I want you to be prepared," he said heedfully. "There are a lot of bones, and most are not full skeletons. There's one complete skeleton like Max but smaller in frame, likely a woman. She's the same age as Max with the same DNA. The others are from varying time periods; very old. Soon we will have to share our findings with local authorities because some bones appear to be human, although very ancient."

"Oh, wow, that's a big deal," Sophia said, looking concerned.

"They are thousands of years old but human nonetheless," Jake said. "Are you okay with that?"

"Yes, I am," she answered thoughtfully, "and thank you for that context. After seeing Max, I got into humble mode when I realized that my brain needs a chance to adjust to unfamiliar objects and places that seem outrageous. And something else, last night I found myself missing Max. I know that sounds weird."

"I get it," John said, chiming in. "I feel like he's a friend. And, like you, I know it sounds crazy to most people. Considering your feelings, I think that you will find the next cave fascinating."

Walking past the cave art, the huge table, the scintillating caverns, and the great pyramid, they passed through two more caverns before reaching the location with the skeletons.

"Has anyone else been in here except you, Megan, and Jake?" Sophia asked.

"Yes, the elders and others from their community come here regularly to conduct spiritual practices and ceremonies," John said. "We never stop them or interfere. It's their heritage. The profound respect they hold for each bone is palpable. They seem to connect with the energy of each tiny bone fragment; it's like they are woven in with the mystical world where these giants still roam. Sometimes they fall into a trance state, get messages and prophecies. They've let us participate a few times. It is a mind-boggling experience. In fact—I just remembered that one of the elders is coming today. Jake, do I have that right?"

Jake fumbled around in his coat pockets and pulled out a small notebook. "Yep, today." He looked at his watch. "About now."

They entered the cavern and even with the verbal preparation, it was an adjustment for her psyche to see skeletons in varying degrees of decay.

"The energy here is dramatically different," Sophia said. "For clarity, I am not feeling creepy because of the bones. A better description of what is arising in me is nostalgia. John, where is the smaller giant that you mentioned with the elongated skull?"

John raised his lamp and led her to a skeleton resting like Max.

He watched with a look of wonder as Sophia approached the skeleton and gently ran her hand down the radius and the ulna of the lower arm. Then she tenderly touched the fingers and held the hand in hers. John looked at her face, where soft tears sparkled in the light of his lamp.

Letting her gaze fall on the entire skeleton, she then touched her hand to her heart and carefully let her fingers land softly on the center of the giant's upper chest.

She went to the feet and warmly stroked the toes, smiled softly, and looked with a haunted gaze toward the cavern where Max lay.

After a few moments, she turned her gaze toward John and said, "She's familiar. Very. Can I sit down somewhere?"

"Yes, of course," John said, leading her to a dusty canvas chair that he and Jake used when doing research in the cavern. "Are you okay?"

"Yes, I'm fine. It's just that seeing her took me by surprise. She's like Max. They both feel alive to me. I'd like to walk around the other skeletons. Is that okay? I won't touch any of them. I apologize for caressing her lovely hands and mystical bones. I was drawn to her like a magnet and felt such sweet intimacy. Wow! This is completely unexpected."

"I agree," John said "and thanks for understanding that it's best to only observe the other skeletons. It would have been impossible for me to stop you with this one, I could feel your love for her from ten feet away. It's a mystery, for sure. Oh look!

We have company. It's the elder who I mentioned to you. His name is Will."

"Greetings, my friend," Will said as he approached John.

Seeing Sophia, he extended his hand to shake hers, introduced himself, and then looked at her inquisitively.

"Have we met?" he asked her.

"No, I only arrived a few weeks ago."

"Hmmm. You seem familiar. It's nice to meet you," Will said, looking at her quizzically. He then turned to John.

"I'd like to perform a brief ritual for the two elders, the long-skulled ones. Today is an auspicious day for this ceremony. Can you get Jake? I'd appreciate if you guys would help me. Sophia," he said, looking at her. "It would be great if you assisted with the woman."

Jake arrived with candles and water. And they all went to stand near the female skeleton, who Will called *The Mystic.* After taking a moment to center himself, Will began to chant, hum, and light candles, which he used to burn a handful of dried herbs tightly bound with string. As the pungent aroma of the smoke billowed around them, it danced and swirled like a living being. Will's rattle and the deep resonance of his drum created a tranquil and powerful atmosphere. No one spoke. Sophia looked like she was entering a trance state. Within seconds, Will went deeply inside himself. He staggered back and sat on a nearby rock and fell motionless, seemingly unaware of his surroundings. The bundle of herbs hung limp in his hand, it's smoke a slender line, spiraling.

After a few minutes, the fragrant odor of the herbs subsided. He gently opened his eyes as his intense gaze locked with Sophia's. *"The Mystic,"* he said to her. "You are *The Mystic.* Own your magnificent power and noble destiny! A lynx remains as your guardian. The ice is your home."

She met his eyes, her own serene. "I feel unicity with the one whom you call *The Mystic,*" Sophia said softly.

"I believe you and I know why," Will said, continuing to make direct eye contact with her. "Dear soul, there is a reason for this intimate connection. You are her. You are the current embodiment of *The Mystic.*"

Staring at him and cocking her head to the side, Sophia asked, "How can you know that?"

"The knowing that knows told me," he answered matter-of-factly.

Unsteady on her feet, Sophia sank down onto a rock to get her bearings. Will went to her and placed a stone with an etched symbol in her hand.

"Meditate on lynx," he said. "It will help you connect with the Truth of who you've been and who you are. This revelation is not meant to scare or harm you. I didn't expect this information to come to me. Spirit does not have bad timing or wrong information. Please keep an open heart about what I am going to tell you: At the time of ice, a war, and a flood, you and the one they call Max were joined and then separated. *Unicity* is an important word the spirits shared with me today. They say you and Max know about this."

Motionless, Sophia sat staring into the darkness of the farthest recesses of the cavern.

Jake whispered to John that they should leave her to digest this unexpected revelation. They both were aware that *The Mystic* was the woman from Will's tradition who comes when needed, bringing incomprehensible powers to heal the human heart and teach others the mystical, indispensable secrets of the universe.

After several minutes, Sophia carefully rose to her feet, glan-ced at Will, Jake, and John, and walked past them. She moved through each cavern in silence and stopped only to lightly stroke Max's feet and then let her eyes drift across his whole body.

Turning away, she went outside and up the steep stairwell methodically, one step at a time, in a constant rhythm. Entering the house, she made her way to the sanctuary of the bedroom, falling onto the bed in a torrent of tears. When enough energy was released and sheer exhaustion took over, she drifted deeply into sleep.

CHAPTER 32
ELONGATED DREAM

John and Jake fed the dogs and left a sandwich in the fridge in case Sophia needed some food. They were speechless. Will described his response as "astonished and accepting."

"Will, what does it mean that Sophia is *The Mystic?*" John asked.

Jake stood nearby staring at Will, waiting for his reply.

"Spirit told me that she has been here many times in Gaia's history," Will said. "Those are her bones—the long-headed woman. This is very strange. I know that we can travel into countless dimensions inside ourselves, that we contain memory and experiences that some consider to be past or parallel lives. But today's revelation? I don't know what to say. If her husband was Max, who is Nate?"

"That's her husband who died." Jake answered.

"The spirits told me that Nate and Max are the same," Will said. "Don't ask me how any of this is possible. We are unbounded beings. You know about that. The message I shared was the truth. Of that, I am sure. I will check on her in a few days." Will smiled politely and left.

After a few moments of contemplation, John said, "What I can't figure out is why it even matters. So what if she was a giant in some coordinate of the field? But when Will revealed her connection with that skeleton, it felt incredibly important and that's the reason that this is getting to me. Honestly, I'm ready for a beer. Care to join me?"

"Yeah. But… I hate leaving her alone with all of this stuff to deal with. You think she's ok? It's… a lot. Must be pretty emotional. And then it's connected to her husband who died not that long ago, too… Jake, something else haunts me. Before we took her to the cave for the second time, the three of us were talking about global history and you referred to her as a *hopeless mystic* who you said was a valued member of our team. I know you were half joking. But if the truth be told, I knew Sophia was special. She doesn't realize her superpowers but Will does. I have to concede that I've felt all along that she is more mystical than she can fathom. I also can understand how freaky that must be for her. She's gone from being the wife of a lawyer to the queen of the giants. Holy crap! That's a big leap. I want to give her space and time to take all of this in—but I want to support her if she needs it. We are on new turf here."

"Yep, ole buddy, we knew when we read Max's DNA report that this cove was off-the-charts. But I have to admit that everything is unfolding in some pretty crazy-ass ways. I think the best thing for now, though, is to leave her alone, give her space like you said. We'll check on her in the morning."

John agreed and they gathered their gear and left. Hearing the cars departing, Sophia went back to sleep. Within her dreams, she found herself in a lush forest with the wind whipping sharply through massive trees. As her feet crunched melting snow with every step on the narrow path, she made her way toward a nearby cave.

At the entrance, she spotted her beloved. He was waiting for her, beaming his kind smile towards her. Embracing him tenderly, she recognized him as the one called Max. His huge arms brought warmth to her freezing body. The ice age was upon them once again.

In their telepathic language, he said, "I will leave soon. I'll be back when the ice melts."

In that reality within herself, she knew that time was not linear and that the length of their reunion was meaningless. She felt calm and was more concerned about the child stirring in her womb. He looked at her swollen belly and smiled.

"We have been together innumerable times," he said. "Within infinite realms and universes, we find our way to each other. It always gets better, doesn't it? Over many arcs of time, you have delivered our progeny, an inestimable gift to this world, dearest one."

Sophia smiled and gently stroked his cheek and elongated head.

"The codes are all within the ice," he said. "The humans are well prepared and when I return, we will celebrate. Remember to go to the stone circles at the appointed times. From there, I will connect with you and transmit the next codes. The stars align tonight. I will go to the circle of stones for my departure. Although I'll be gone for a while, we know time is ephemeral. Until we see each other again, I will nurture the profound love I feel for you in the sanctuary of my heart."

In this moment, because time was relative, she was not sad at the prospect of her beloved's leaving. For this culture, *leaving* was also a relative idea. She was unified with his heart center, which she perceived as a blazing emerald octagon. The octagon, filling his entire upper chest, splendidly represented eternal life and continuous renewal. Their hearts expressed these qualities, throughout all time and space.

Unicity was what mattered, and *unicity* plus *pure love* is what they encoded into the waters of Earth. They put the codes into the ice so when it melted later, it would flow into lakes and rivers.

Humans would drink it, bathe in it, and it would condense and rain down unicity and pure love codes on them.

Some humans tended fields, some created technologies, and others built pyramids. Sophia and Max were the mystics; the ones who tended to frequencies. It was known throughout the universe that these codes were vital to the Gaia's and humanity's ascension in frequency.

Blissfully, they did the mystical work from ice age to ice age and from galactic wars to meteor fallouts, to the great flood on Earth and the Atlantean and Mu conflicts. They remained the mystics. Max was a giant mystic from another universe; Sophia was human. She, like many other humans on Earth, carried some of the same DNA as the giants. Max loved and respected her humanness. He was a lover of rare planets like Gaia, diverse in ecology and filled with beings who had a wide range of emotional capacities and personalities. Although human emotions could be sometimes troublesome, as a human's frequencies rise, their broad range of feeling allows for a glorious life of poignant and passionate experiences.

Holding Sophia lovingly in a close embrace, he looked down at her affectionately. His radiant smile held her heart in his for eternity. They gently separated as he made his way to the stone circle to teleport back to his universe for an undetermined du-ration.

Sophia let his timeless, pure love roll through her being. As she awakened, she continued to experience an ecstatic sense of unicity that she often told Grace she wished to share so everyone could experience it. Seeing Nate as Max and feeling his love as part of her, with the unicity gene turned on, she later described her inner state as "invincible, free and whole." She lacked nothing.

With her giant lover, life was simple and revolved around community. Stars, planets, and all solar systems and universes were accessible because she could go anywhere at will. The pyramids were everywhere on the planet. Anyone could use them to travel through time and space. She chose to stay on Earth and have her baby, who would live for thousands of years on this amazing planet.

Sophia suddenly realized that in this dream, she had been experiencing Nate as Max, on Earth, rather than meeting him on a blue star or distant planet. That dynamic time, those amazing feelings and state of being were happening in a coordinate of the field on Earth.

She journaled her experiences, questions, and reflections:

How can this feel so real? How can I feel totally free and know that I can move with light and frequency to all co-ordinates in the multiverse? No limitations. I'm filled with the dynamism of the infinite, and the still point of the light of creation that brings each moment into life.

In the dream, contentment felt natural. No worries were there because I felt aligned with the rhythms and natural order of the universe.

Perhaps this was Gaia and humanity living with me in what I perceive as a far, distant past. Is this perhaps a coordinate within the infinite quantum field, in which humans experienced living beyond linear time and familiar spatial constrictions?

Being with Max, watching my lover walk toward the stone circles which were arranged for his many cosmic journeys, the octagon of my heart glowed with a soft emerald light, with gold effulgence at its center. It felt ecstatic!

Can the codes that Max and I worked with unlock critical, profound information from the quantum field in modern times?

Why not? What would prevent this information from coming back online, if humans have the codes and express the unicity gene inherent in their DNA?

Sophia described how she was staring into a rapturous memory of high frequency living and she was on fire to bring it into form "in the here and now."

As she came back into waking reality, her inner fire was still blazing. Opening the windows fully, she felt the penetrating heat of the sun on her face as a cosmic reminder to stoke the inner embers and keep her wild, mystical fire burning vigorously.

CHAPTER 33
MYSTICAL MEMORIES AND SHOCKING NEWS

Jake and John arrived punctually as always. Two steaming cups of coffee, or "brain fuel" as Jake called it, awaited them.

"Can we sit for a minute?" Jake asked. "Is that okay, Sophia?"

"Sure," she answered. "Let me grab my tea."

John moved a little nervously in his chair as though he couldn't find a comfortable position. Jake wasn't as relaxed as usual, either. He wanted to ask her some questions yet he fidgeted and squirmed rather than speak.

Her face was soft and open, while her eyes conveyed a receptive and childlike spirit as she encouraged him and settled back into her chair with a relaxed sense of ease.

"Well, I have to say Sophia, I am flabbergasted to see you looking so chilled out," Jake said. "We expected to find you in a state of lingering shock this morning. Yesterday seemed pretty damn intense. In the cave with the skeletons, you seemed to have some wild revelations. And today you look like you just got back from a weekend at some high-end spa. What happened in the cave? And how did you come to terms with it so fast?"

"I understand why you're asking me those questions," Sophia said softly. She began to explain, beginning with what happened as she realized that the smaller, long-headed skeleton was hers. Touching it shattered her closely held world view that she was only *here and now and was limited to who she currently appeared to be.* She realized that Max was somehow a version of Nate and that also didn't sit easily within her psyche. Then she shared the lucid dream and the intricate, emotional features of that experience. She explained her contentment in all situations that arose—even when Max left for another universe for an indefinite amount of time. Not even separation from her beloved could throw her into an emotional meltdown.

She explained that loss and gain had no relevance in that moment. Through the technology of the stone circles, moving through time and space was natural and occurred with a sense of ease. Her mind was not generating worry about him, herself, or the child she carried because her experience in that moment felt harmonious with life.

In that coordinate of the field, her body was relaxed, and her mind was still. Thoughts arose and she sensed what to do and where to go. Peaceful and content, she was constantly aligned and flowing with an inner GPS which helped her to move through life with purpose and without obstructions, tension, or strife.

When Max left, it was fine. For her, time was not linear, which allowed her to accept that she'd be okay when he was gone. Unshakable knowing that he would return at the perfect moment brought comfort and a sense of calm. She understood the Earth's rhythms, like ice ages, in the same way she might sense a family member's needs and cycles.

The waters of the Earth felt like they were her soul sisters; intimately connected and vibrating with compatibility. These sisters coalesced and shared information spontaneously and effortlessly. Codes of geometric patterns of light were visible and she could see them in water and ice.

"The reason that I am okay," Sophia said, "is that I fully encountered life in its perfection—in its fullest expression of higher frequencies. I experienced profound peace and ever-expanding awareness of the possibility and grandeur of what the next moment might evolve into. Exhilaration can meet serenity head on, morphing into joy or playfulness. Normally, in my day-to-day world, I would be triggered by something and reacting to life. But in that unique coordinate of the field, reacting from low frequency isn't possible because the frequency bandwidth is so elevated."

She continued to share saying with increased fervor, "I felt held by the heart of the Earth; eternally loved and protected. In fact, there was nothing to be protected from in this kind of everlasting creation, sustaining, and dissolution of each perfect moment. It was better than non-stop bliss, endless peacefulness, and infinite, effortless ease.

"You know how you trust your body to breathe, trust your heart to beat, and your digestive and nervous systems to work without your help? Well, I realized that I can trust life, too. I am more powerful than I was willing to accept. I've lived in higher frequencies in another coordinate in the field and I can repeat that experience in my life going forward.

"The *memory* of that coordinate with Max was always in me, where stillness is more obvious than my thoughts. I am moved by each moment's frequency, without the need to push and shove. The unicity of all things is obvious and I feel love for everyone because we are each perfect and pure. We are each working our way through a matrix of sensory energy. And we are each capable of invoking a memory stored in our blood and bones that will allow us to live from higher octaves of ourselves.

"We don't have to find a sky family, or an ancient skeleton, move to a special place, or change careers. Together, we can raise our frequency and feel held by our beloved Gaia. In the dream, I experienced her incredibly high frequencies. I hadn't realized how intimate my relationship with her can be. When I lean into her energy body and let our love for each other mingle, she can benevolently become like a soul sister, teaching me how to elevate. I felt her sentience. I felt her bond with me, indestructible and eternal.

"So, dear friends, as you can see, as I stroked the skeletons of Max and myself, it invoked *memory*. From this experience, I understand that the unified field in and around us is brimming over with this kind of profound memory which we can access. I will always be grateful that you two took care of me yesterday so that I could have the chance to excavate these incredibly impactful memories." She became serenely quiet again.

It took a few moments before John said, "I am speechless. It's one thing to experience an affinity or relationship with the skeletons but the lucid dream seals the deal for me. I'm not sure about you, Jake, but this takes the cake. I've never heard of any archeological site like this one. And having our bold new mystic with us—how cool is that?"

"Couldn't have said it better," Jake said as his eyes moved from John to Sophia. "As you spoke, I experienced your inner state while you were with Max in that other coordinate of time and space. Your words became a frequency that I could easily ride. I feel the truth of what you said. We all need some *unchaining* right now. We've allowed ourselves to be shackled for way too long. We have to get real. This world is changing fast and for the better. We can't go forward with the shackles of past coordinates in the field. To do so makes no sense.

"I salute the mystic in you! Good going! You gave me plenty of brain food to digest. This helps me to realize why Max was vitally important to John, to the elders here, and to me. What I've learned from galactic cosmology and astronomy is that a human life is more than the dense black and whiteness that our brains create for us. The infinite, unified field described by quantum science theory can seem elusive, but you showed me how it can also coalesce into high-frequency living.

"I wonder if the three of us have been in that coordinate of the field together at some point. It felt strangely familiar. My next question is: can we connect with the memory stored in the field to learn and grow in the *here and now?* We have access to the memory and as you said. Upon reflection, you realized that everyone and everything is unified at the core, which is referred to by some physicists as the still point or Zero Point, where anything and everything becomes possible. It's becoming clear that we have some superpowers worth cultivating. Thank you for *hanging* in there and staying with all of these experiences. More than that, you are willing to speak about it without inhibition."

"A year ago, I would have said my dream was imagination," Sophia said softly, "or part of a grieving process. I would have wriggled out of the truth. I would have settled for not owning the inner powerhouse, the nuclear reactor that ignites each of our souls into an elevated state. I'm done with that, guys. Done! I don't feel better than anyone. Our inherent power never says: *I am better than you.* Rather, it announces: *Together we are one heck of a human race.*

"I want you, Megan, and everyone in this whole amazing world to thrive. If one of us elevates, we elevate those around us, and they elevate others; it goes on endlessly. We share the same core of creation at the Zero Point, the singularity where frequency transitions take place. That's our unicity zone. My unicity gene is turned on. I can feel its expression. As my dear friend Kabir said long ago, what matters most is *unicity* and *pure love.* Every person in my circle expresses those qualities. While the frequency of our circle elevates, the circle explodes into higher frequencies and the denser frequencies will implode. It is that simple. I will work on my frequency, and you will work to elevate yours in a myriad of ways. And Gaia, our sentient soul sister, will continue to join us in this work.

"I am on fire right now. May it remain so."

As the conversation moved into assimilation, silence descended for a few minutes.

The frantic barking of the dogs brought them back to the present moment as a car approached with Beth in the driver's seat and Megan seated next to her. As they emerged, Megan didn't look relaxed after a nice family visit. Tension was tangible as she came near.

"We have a problem. Oh! I didn't even say hello," Megan said apologetically. "I've been fretting over something since yesterday. I came back as fast as I could so that I could talk to you in person."

"What's going on?" John asked, his brow wrinkled in concern. "I know you well. Something is really wrong. What is it?"

"I'll drop my things and be right back," Megan answered. "Yes, it's important."

Sophia ran inside to get Megan a glass of water.

Megan joined them, sipped the water, and began to explain, "I received a registered letter that Sophia forwarded to me. It was the worst letter I had ever received. The county found out about Max: in a few days, a hearing will be held to decide the fate of this archeological site. And there could be fines for not coming forward and reporting the work here. The county archeologist will be coming to look at the skeletons.

"My husband and I did everything possible to protect this place, specifically the cove. It's been hurdle after hurdle. The land grant is ambiguous and both parties' rights are, too. We've tried to work it out at various times but always reach a dead end. Now, it'll be up to a judge to decide who has rights to Max, his Mrs., and any artifacts. I'm sorry that it had to come to this. It's scary... so much is at stake.

"I told Will—he was shattered. Frank and I tried to ensure that this land and everything sacred to his people are protected. My goodness, can it get any worse?"

Megan's lawyer was briefed and was not optimistic that Max would remain at the cove. The look on Megan's face was unusually somber as she told the group, "I feel agonizingly sucker-punched; completely devastated."

John thanked her lovingly, and turned to Jake saying, "Given the time frame, can we go to the cave, come up with a plan for the hearing, and do as much work as we can down there today? Everyone agreed? " He looked around at them. Each nodded in agreement.

As they headed off, Sophia asked Megan, "Is there anything I can do for you? I've come to love Max and the cove. It's as mystical as you said it was, maybe more so."

"I should have known you'd fall in love with Max," Megan said with a smile.

"I have a lot to share with you," Sophia said. "But why don't you get unpacked, and you can rest before lunch. How does that sound?"

"I don't need rest," Megan answered. "I'd like to hear your experience. How about if you make me some of that sweet smelling tea of yours and then, I'm all ears, sweetheart. From today forward, we are going to be busy. It's all hands on deck. You and I can take a moment to catch up before the frenzy begins."

Within a few minutes, Sophia was serving tea on the porch and sharing her time in the cave. First talking about Max, then the pyramid, and then the other skeletons. In as much detail as possible, she shared her lucid dreams. She thanked Megan for having the generosity and insight to invite her to come to Mystic Cove.

"I'm here for you, Megan. From what I am learning, we can't fight this. Instead, it's about raising our frequency. That may sound airy-fairy. Winning this case will require more than mental strategies and perfect legal advice. Although we want that, too."

"Well, Sophia," Megan said, "I can't wait to hear what you propose for raising the frequency of this wild predicament."

"Sorry, but I don't have an answer for that," Sophia said. "It's just that if we see ourselves as the good guys and them as the bad guys, we'll be working within lower and denser frequencies. In this case, I don't know exactly how to hold a higher frequency."

"Your time here has been well spent," Megan said, "From the moment we met, I had a good feeling about you coming here. And the dogs look like they are doing great. They must like you, too. I am going to rest until lunch. Beth is back full-time now which means that you can go to the cove. My intuition says that's where you belong right now."

Sophia tenderly hugged Megan, put on her cove shoes, and headed for the stairwell.

Beth sat with Megan on the porch. Megan said, "I have a feeling that Sophia will be a great support for us. This is going to be one hell of a fight. If we have to let Max go, I'll be crushed. I've known that sooner or later, we'd have to face this."

Beth offered to unpack and prepare for dinner. She insisted that Megan rest for a while. As Megan entered the house for a nice, long nap, she looked at her favorite paintings of Galileo and Copernicus, saying, "Boys, send us some *good juju* from your realms. You can relate to knowing about esoteric subjects that others thought was crazy. We know that Max and his Mrs. are not from Earth. From out in the cosmos, you two, send us a blessing to make sure that our work here wasn't for nothing. I love Max. And so do Sophia, John, and Jake. Heck, we're like family. According to Sophia, we are a soul family with a unicity gene. I love that we have that gene in common with you guys. I've always loved you two rascals."

Chuckling, she headed for her room, much more herself than when she arrived.

CHAPTER 34
LEGAL PROCEEDING

John and Jake went into high gear, increasing their collection of photographs, lists and descriptions of skeletons, and the invaluable documentation of the cave system. They worked to finalize anything that could be done in a short time frame.

Sophia's priorities were to update Grace and ask John to obtain Will's permission for her to enter the pyramid. John agreed and synchronistically, before he could contact Will, the elder approached them at a hurried pace. Seeing Will coming towards her, Sophia murmured to herself, "He knew I needed him. Coincidence or clue?"

As the two men spoke, the elder's downcast eyes and lowered head indicated to her that John was filling him in on the gravity of the situation. The conversation ended with Will and John smiling kindly at each other. With the same goal of respecting and caring for Max and every other skeleton in the cave, they were in agreement that these remains were not just lifeless bones. For them, they were alive and imbued with sacredness. Each skeleton, along with even the tiniest artifact, represented a deeply personal connection with life, with a lineage of humanity and the sky family that spanned tens of thousands of years, or more. The bones were priceless.

After John finished speaking to him, Will looked intensely at Sophia and motioned for her to head for the pyramid. He never took his eyes off her, which did not escape John's attention. Once they were in the cave with the pyramid, the elder approached

Sophia and before he uttered the sound to open the door, he told her that she would have twenty-two minutes to meditate.

"I am glad you are stepping into your role as The Mystic with courage and without hesitation. We need your memory from the invisible field to be transmitted widely. Our existence is constantly nourished by a power and intelligence which cannot be seen but can be accessed. May you access it fully." He looked long and deep into her eyes. "Awareness of Essence is all that is needed. In the end, that awareness of Essence melts into the still point from which the light of new creation emerges. From that infinitesimal point, miracles become manifest. May this experience be a gift for you and our world."

Waving an eagle feather over her, he offered the smoke from a burning herb bundle to the four directions. He then turned to offer this pungent vapor to the sky, and Earth, and concluded by uttering the secret sound.

Once again, the majestic door to eternity opened for Sophia to enter.

While she meditated in the sacred pyramid, John and Jake moved with focused swiftness to document the site. Chanting in hushed tones, the elder began waving the dried sage over the bones of skeletons that were being honored as brothers, sisters, mothers, and fathers. Will then sat on a rock near the pyramid, swaying gently, with closed eyes, and a child-like smile.

Megan's job was to talk to lawyers and plan meetings with Jake and John, who also had lawyers.

Time rushed by like the nearby river after springtime floods.

Eventually the day arrived for their appearance at court.

Megan, John, and Jake entered the stately, classic courtroom with speckled granite walls of pale green and grey. The furnishings were antique. This courtroom had heard cases for over a century—from illegal miners to stagecoach robbers, to modern day drug dealers. Today, it was about to be filled with information about ancient bones. No one was going to testify that they found a giant ET, his wife, and a lot of other ancient beings who seemed to be part of their clan.

Sophia and Beth sat in the back to observe and support.

As in all hearings, both sides talked, lawyers interrupted, and the judge made statements and then asked questions. The judge expressed his concern that they didn't report the skeletons to the authorities. His body language was rigid and his look stern when he questioned why John didn't immediately take assistance from the local county archeologist.

The night before the hearing, John had told Sophia that the local archeologist would likely send Max off immediately. John did not see a chance of getting around that because the local archeologist—a colleague of his—held a traditional mindset about skeletons, and giants in particular.

John was questioning his own intentions. Why not follow the rules and forget all the DNA and other tests they'd run? Why spend so much life force in working tirelessly to get as much data as possible? He could be fined and lose the professional standing he'd worked for as an archeologist over the past forty years. When word got out about Max, most colleagues would dismiss Max as *another old skeleton* and John would be humiliated and reviled by his peers.

Hot tears filled his eyes, and he shook his head. "No matter what happens, I'll be damned if I'm willing to give up without fighting for Max and the others, because losing this court battle means they could disappear, forever. When we've finished our work at the cove, the world deserves to know about them and all that we've discovered. Those skeletons have survived cataclysmic environmental events, melting glaciers, and massive floods. I feel like they meant to stay; they were waiting for me. I feel connected to them, like you do. Not just some bones to be catalogued and studied.

"Will's people have such deep respect and reverence for Max and his wife. You saw how they treat them. It's as though their souls matter to them, whether they end up being direct ancestors or revered cosmic elders.

"Maybe I have the memory in my bones and blood that you speak about; a memory of the time in which they lived, or what they want me to know. If they are truly you and Nate, by God, that'll keep me reflecting on quantum theory and life on this Earth for a very long time. Of course, I don't expect a judge or the county archeologist to understand any of this.

"Indigenous people are aware that they lost access to these kinds of ancient beings many times and they have the issue of not being able to afford to fight for Max, who they deeply value. We have to find a better way for the scientific community and government to realize the invaluable nature of the giant skeletons. We need to have access to any of them that have not been destroyed."

Sophia and John hugged like kin and promised to always be there for each other.

Now, in the centuries-old courtroom, John was interrogated like a criminal and it was becoming clear that his worst fears might soon be realized. He glanced at Sophia and noticed that her eyes were closed, her head slightly back. Chills came over him and he rubbed his arms. That's how Sophia looked before she fainted when she met Max for the first time, and when she first saw the smaller-framed woman with the elongated skull.

Sophia's eyelids quivered. He squinted his eyes to get a closer look. Something was different now. Her face looked ecstatic.

He looked at Megan. Her eyes were closed softly and her face, too, was serene. Her lawyer, Mr. Matthews, was busy making notes. John felt more chills running up and down his spine and he wriggled in his seat. He saw Jake nervously wringing his hands under the table where he sat with his lawyer. Sophia and Megan, however, appeared to be at peace.

Then he saw Sophia calmly reach for her phone. She texted someone and went back to her inner world.

He heard the judge getting irritated with their defense. Jake's lawyer was like a general defending a weak stronghold while losing ground rapidly.

Sophia came alive and looked toward the judge. Maybe she'd heard it all and was feeling the gut-wrenching direction things were heading.

Suddenly, as if they were on a movie set, the courtroom doors blew open as Will entered the stunned courtroom with a lawyer, Ms. Dunbar, who always represented the local indigenous tribe in matters such as this. Ms. Dunbar walked with dignity straight to the front of the room and asked to approach the bench.

The judge called for a recess and went to his chambers with the elder and his attorney.

No one spoke nor moved. Sophia was as still as the space between musical notes. Megan was the same. John kept watching them to distract himself from the inevitable that seemed to be headed his way. But a spark of curiosity flickered in his mind.

The judge finally emerged and said he'd heard enough. He fined John and Jake saying that it was their duty to contact the county archeologist within a reasonable time period. It was clear, they'd knowingly resisted doing that. And then came their greatest fear when he added that the bones must be examined by the county archeologist.

Judge Motely cleared his throat, took a deep breath, and dropped his tense shoulders as though releasing them from hours of stifled frustration.

"However," he said, "the court will not require the skeletons and bones to be removed from the cave. The local indigenous tribe requests that they to be turned over to them for burial or to remain in place in the cave. There is precedent for this kind of arrangement. Further, the court will allow them to work this out with the current landowner. If they can come to a mutual agreement and if none of the bones provide evidence or query for a homicide case, then we will proceed with a permanent arrangement. Mr. Matthews and Ms. Dunbar, will thirty days be enough time for your clients to enter into a contract?

Both nodded in agreement. And the gavel fell, slamming everyone into the reality of what just happened.

Sophia looked at Megan, smiled peacefully, and they joined Beth heading back to Mystic Cove. John and Jake were close behind.

As they entered Megan's house, John looked at Sophia and asked, "What the hell happened in that court room? I felt it. Where were you, Sophia? Were you meditating or did you go to one of those coordinates in the field that inspires you?"

"John, it's not that dramatic. I went into the pyramid earlier today and once again," Sophia answered, "I experienced what used to happen all the time as a child: by allowing my mind to become absolutely still, I became aware of Essence. Repeating that process in the courtroom, I trusted that I didn't need to do anything. I didn't need to meditate or summon the angels. I was just there, aware of my core. It's like when your mind stops at the sight of an exquisite sunset. When my mind stops like that, there's no thinking. And if there's no thinking, there's no worrying. Without my mind engaged, I feel the full possibility of *all that I am,* rather than *all that I am afraid of.*

"It's hard to convey how grateful I am for this day in court. I got to experience the pyramid in everyday life. I had the opportunity to be child-like and totally free of my mind. I was aware of all that was going on. I knew that you were scared, and I also knew you got chills when you felt the shift in the frequency of the courtroom. The judge felt the shift, too. Of course he wasn't aware of it.

"None of us knew that when I texted the elder, he was having a meeting with his lawyer just a couple of blocks away and were prepared with a solution. There was just enough time for them to get to the courthouse to make their case. It seems right that you and Jake pay the fines. You broke protocols in the local area for not telling the authorities about the site. Sooner or later, you had to address this head on. No judgment, yet as I heard your testimony, I wondered if maybe you'd gotten too much in your heads, worrying about keeping the giants safe rather than addressing the practical aspects of the situation a long time ago. The judge indicated that this is a grey area because of the age of the skeletons and where they are located on indigenous land under dispute—the DNA clearly indicates this was not a recent homicide. Yet he looked miffed that you knew, in his words, *they are potentially, historically significant.*

"Also in your favor was that several years ago, after cataloguing and photographing artifacts, you turned them over to the county archeologist. They were lying on the ground, Will's people agreed, and you didn't dig for further artifacts. That helped your case. He seemed mostly irritated you failed to reveal the skeletons and didn't call the authorities before running DNA tests. Of course, he had to contend with the local archeologist as well, who is clearly not a fan of yours. But even he was fine with the final ruling. In the end, there seemed to be a coherent energetic state in the room. The resolution felt complete and harmonious.

"Can you sense the flow that carried us through the day? It was fine that you and your lawyers strategized your defense. On the deepest level, however, energy from the field was moving all of us along in its current. I could feel it and I'm noticing that flow because I sensed that Max's consciousness is still active in the field. That is fascinating, actually mind blowing, to me. Can he subtly connect with the judge, the local archeologist, me, Will, the attorneys and feed information to each of us from *the field?* Did he participate today? I cannot say definitively if he did or did not influence the results. But I definitely felt his presence. Did you?"

John was stunned into silence, and didn't answer as she continued.

"When my eyes were closed, I recalled my inner state when I was young. I was present, waiting to feel what I needed to do next—not planning but trusting that I'd be guided. Suddenly, I was inspired to text the elder, so I followed that impulse to act. If I'd gotten in my head, texting the elder may not have come to mind or maybe I would have overridden the idea; second guessing and over thinking, assuming he couldn't possibly get there in time with a lawyer. Where did that inspiration come from? Was it from the information in the field in general or Max's influence on the field?

"Right now, I am talking and processing what happened. In the lucid dreams, in the pyramid, and the inner work I've been doing for many years, it all comes back to taking time to be silent, then opening to information from the field in the form of insights or inspiration. I realize this might sound incredibly esoteric."

"No, Sophia, it' doesn't sound esoteric to me," John said vehemently. "Your ideas are possible and can be understood by applying leading edge quantum physics. There's no way to be absolutely sure if Max influenced the court participants by feeding us information from *the field.* Regardless, thank you for taking this extraordinarily eventful day to a profound level and for exploring the possibility of how it unfolded. One thing is for sure, sister, I am definitely leaning towards your hypothesis! I'm feeling that Max is not *far away or out of reach.*

"The past few weeks since meeting you, introducing you to Max, watching you faint, drinking coffee, laughing a lot, seeing you bravely confront your past beliefs and old world views, and discovering that you have memory of codes for how to bridge water with blood and bones... Well... I am sure as hell not the same man who took you to the cove for the first time. And for the record, it doesn't matter if every jackass in the world thinks you are crazy for enjoying higher, inner scales of yourself, and they can make fun of you for loving a skeleton with a very nice, elongated skull; I might add. Never stop asking the important questions like you did just now. I want the rest of my life to be about deep inquiry like that. No more surface bullshit.

"I'd like us to explore the hell out of the cove. Take the lid off and go deeper and look closer. When we do that together, as far as I'm concerned, you can time travel, jump in and out of pyramids, find a worm hole, or anything else. One request... you have to promise to take me with you, okay?"

They laughed until tears trickled down their cheeks. The tension, emotions, and focus on the court case was dissolving into relaxed friendship.

Jake joined them. "You sure have kept us on the edge of our seat since we met you, Sophia. Holy shit! The cove went from an archeological, galactic cosmological site to a whirlwind of cosmic portals and sky family reunions. My friend, this has been one hell of a good time. A bit intense, though." He winked and gave her a warm, congenial hug.

Megan, with her usual, jovial smile said, "Everyone, listen up! Beth made the best lasagna ever, gluten free for Sophia, of course. Let's eat."

As they enjoyed the meal and talked of Max and the cosmos, Megan turned to Sophia and said, "You must write about the plight of the skeletons, the elongated ones, in particular. There's invaluable wisdom to share from your research and experience, and a need in our world to know the secrets of the esoteric realms that you've studied for many years. If you'd like to take some time and work from the guest house, you are most welcome here."

"Thank you," Sophia said. "It would be good to capture my thoughts on paper while it's fresh. When I write, I get to watch incredible information, that's shimmering in the quantum field, come to life. It's fascinating to watch a blog or a book write it-self. My friend, Grace, stays on my case about writing. She will be thrilled for me to finally take the time to do it. I've been here such a short time, but I hope it's obvious how much I love the cove and you. Thank you for welcoming me with such an open heart, Megan."

Looking at Jake and John, she playfully asked, "So what else can you show me at Mystic Cove?"

John looked at Jake, smiled wryly, and turned to her saying, "There's many more caverns and mysteries to explore, whenever you are ready."

With raised eyebrows and a twinkle of delight in her eye, she gave John a quick hug and embraced Jake warmly.

Dessert was served. It was Beth's famous Idaho huckleberry cobbler and homemade ice cream. According to Megan, they were celebrating Mystic Cove's uninhibited, courageous team of wild, quantum explorers.

CHAPTER 35

JOAN OF ARC AND A FREIGHT TRAIN

Dawn brought hues of pink and purple light along with birdsong, which Sophia felt was the best alarm clock imaginable. She tried to remain quiet as she moved around the guest house because Grace had arrived late the night before and was sleeping on the couch, but Grace woke up anyway.

She sat up, smiling wide and stretching, and proclaimed that she had *not an ounce of fatigue* from her trip. She had already been to visit twice and loved Sophia's new friends. They seemed to feel the same about Grace.

Knowing that Megan was an early riser, they went around to the porch of the main house to talk and enjoy the sun. Its lovely morning emergence formed a soft glow they were relishing. Megan was already there, in coffee ecstasy.

"I hope we are not disturbing your private sunrise coffee bliss," Sophia said. "I can make some tea and we can enjoy this lovely dawn from the guest house."

"Nonsense," Megan said. "I want to be part of your fascinating conversation. Make your tea and come have a seat."

Sophia returned with jasmine fragrance billowing out into the cool morning air. Sipping their green tea, infused with the gorgeous flowers, she shared a dream. Grace and Megan leaned forward to listen.

"I was visited by Joan of Arc. She used to appear in my dreams when I was young. Last night she revealed, with a feeling of sweet compassion, that I would not have to die for truth, be humiliated for sharing it, or even fight to protect it. Humanity was shifting and a vast number of humans are elevating their consciousness. She was sure that I must have noticed these changes in the local community and in my friendships, which is true.

"Yet when she said it, I cried with relief. I hadn't realized I was prepared for that worst case scenario. Joan looked lovely and fearless. I hated that she'd had to die such a cruel death. Seeing my sadness, she smiled and said:

Any qualities you see in me are awake in you. You can't get happiness from another person unless you know happiness. Similarly, if you see courage, you have to have experienced that in yourself to see it in someone else. I can only trigger in you what's already there. If my death brings you sadness, that sadness is in you. Ask yourself what the sadness is about.

"Feeling completely perplexed as I stood looking at her, I was clueless about how to answer her questions. Then I woke up.

"Okay dream analyzers, what do you think?"

Laughing, Grace and Megan sat quizzically for a moment. Suddenly, Grace's face brightened like the sun that was bursting from over a thin layer of clouds, spraying golden rays across the horizon.

"Do you remember in fourth grade," Grace began, "when you asked Sister Mary Benedict if the priests caused Joan of Arc to be burned at the stake?"

"Yes," Sophia said. " That moment is still vivid for me. It's interesting that you mention that, because I almost wrote about it recently but backed off. I guess I wasn't ready to think too much about it. We were studying saints in my fourth grade class in Catholic school because we had to choose one of them to be our spiritual mentor.

"I had always been fascinated with Joan of Arc, so I researched her story in the library and in our Encyclopedia Britannica at home. I was captivated by this brave and beautiful soul. What I learned was that she wore men's clothes in battle and said things that the church didn't like, which gave the priests weak evidence to have her arrested. They acted like a court and decided that she should be burned, calling her what was known as a *heretic.*

"The reality was that she was a heretic in England because she led the French into battle against them. However, this is the crazy part: in France, they loved her and called her a saint. English and French bishops of the same Catholic Church saw her differently. So which was she, a saint or a sinner?

"I couldn't believe what I was reading. She must have been good because I knew she was called a saint. Why would a kind person like her get killed with the blessings of the church that she loved and whose doctrines she followed? And some records showed that she knew some of the clergy. My innocent mind couldn't grasp what I'd read. Twenty-five years after her death, a new trial was held and she was found innocent. That was totally confusing.

"I was hoping that the nun would tell me that the encyclopedia was wrong. It was disorienting and scary to consider that the church itself, and priests who are supposed to know what is right, would have done something so horrible. I had already asked my mother if it was true. She said I shouldn't worry about it because it happened a long time ago. My father's response was that the church realized that they had been wrong so they apologized and made her into a saint to acknowledge her greatness. That was even less consolation. So, even though I had trepidation, I asked Sister Mary Benedict, hoping she could clear it up for me somehow.

"Oh my gosh! I recall the fury that came over that nun's face. I knew instantly that I'd blown it. She turned to me and said that I had no business looking at the encyclopedia when we had perfectly good books in our classroom, and that it was not my place to ask questions about priests, who were our fathers on Earth and dedicate their lives to serving others. She said I was *impudent*; I had no idea what that was, but I knew it was bad. I was speechless, embarrassed, and confused.

"I am grateful you asked me to recall this because I am realizing that the sadness, tinged with fear, that I felt in the dream is coming from me as that nine-year-old girl. The world never felt as safe after that day. And Joan's story held too many paradoxes for me to comprehend.

"I observed these same feelings recently as I considered writing about my life events of the last year. Will I be verbally abused for what I write or burned at the stake, metaphorically speaking, for telling the truth of some of the things that I've learned?

"Grace, do you recall that the two girls who sat by me and were my friends disowned me after that? I knew they did it to get points with Sister Mary Benedict, but it stung to lose their friendship. That was my first taste of a friend's betrayal. And the embarrassment when David and Paul, sitting behind me, snickered during the lecture I received. That humiliation almost made me throw up."

"Oh, Sophia, I never heard you talk about this in such detail, down to what it actually felt like," Grace said compassionately, "especially about almost throwing up. All of us have those childhood moments that stick like glue to our unconscious. Sometimes they raise their dragon heads at the perfect time for us to choose to let them go or fall deeper into their clutches. In making the decision to write about this, who is deciding? Is it the present you or your nine-year-old version? It's important in this moment of choice right now. Can you write about this, without inhibition? Which will it be, the child or the adult in you who decides?"

"Darn you, Grace," Sophia said chuckling. "Only my best friend gets to call me out like that! It's true. Many decades later, I am letting a terrorized, confused child take charge of my decision to share this story.

"Wow, this is one of those epiphanies that catalyzes a huge shift in awareness; my psyche feels the safe space to release and let go of false safety nets. I thought that trying to forget how terrible that encounter with the nun felt would protect me from how awful it was for me. But as I shared it just now, while realizing that it was a younger aspect of myself who felt the pain of it, I experienced the scene in a new way. That nine-year-old didn't have the perspective that I have now. She was profoundly traumatized and shamed. Because I can experience that moment with the overview of an adult with plenty of personal and spiritual growth to back me up, I feel compassion for myself at that age.

"Thank you so much, Grace, for pointing that out with your usual candor and love for me! I can choose how to feel the event with a fresh perspective in this moment in time—connecting compassionately with my nine-year-old self as a neutral observer who is not ensnared in my childhood feelings. The low frequencies of that moment that have been vibrating unconsciously in my psyche for many years are no longer active. As I relived and processed the event just now, held in the space of your loving support, I felt the frequencies neutralize and then expand into wisdom—in a state of flow where I am not entangled with other people's opinions of me. Thank you—both for listening, and for helping alchemize my frozen, demoralized feelings. It's important; in fact, it's *super* important."

"Good going!" Megan said. "That was a rich reflection and realization. Who cares how long you took to work through it? What matters is that you had the guts to confront your fears and insecurities around that episode. Sophia, I'd like to know how you handled the situation back then. How did you pick a new saint to study? I am assuming you gave up studying Joan of Arc as your mentor."

"Good question, my friend," Sophia answered. "I let my intuition guide me. I stared at the shelves of the books at school and reached out to Catherine of Sienna, a beautiful mystic. And this time, I only read the books at school. I refrained from looking too deep or reading elsewhere about her until I was in my twenties. I finally had the guts to research her life and teachings and found out that she, too, was harassed by the church and almost killed several times. And many years later, that same church bestowed on her the elevated status and venerable title, Saint Catherine.

"It's taken thousands of millennia for people like us to finally feel safe to hold a viewpoint that is not aligned with established authority, to admit what's real, and to be candid about history. It's the only way to grow and learn from our past and shift our genetic patterns that keep us acting like frightened children when we are confronted by authority figures."

"And now, Megan deserves to hear an even better story," Grace suggested. "Tell her about the day when you first realized that you were sacred. That was also in fourth grade. Luckily you still had that spark inside you that was not getting stomped out by adversity! I always loved your deep, quiet determination to experience your Essence."

"Well, Megan, this was one of the most profound moments of my life," Sophia said. "When I was nine years old, as part of our school curriculum, we attended church every day. I loved the light pouring through the old stained glass windows, and one day it especially captured my attention. Glancing upwards, I saw the golden circle of art that framed a majestic dove on the ceiling. The only thing I was aware of was profound stillness. That happened many times in nature, but this was a spontaneous moment when I lost track of time and space in everyday life.

"The rituals of standing, kneeling, and saying the prayers continued effortlessly. And my mind was becoming even more silent. My inner experience unfolded into a feeling that I was the same as the air around me, the pew I sat on, and the other people in the church. I felt unicity as my core. And from that center, I felt waves of bliss arising. It seemed to be emerging for everyone and everything around me. The world was becoming waves of light and bliss; less dense, more illuminated with a soft light that permeated everyone and everything. Bliss was my nature. I didn't need to conjure up ethereal joy. Rather, it manifested naturally in my awareness as my own nature.

"It was filling me to overflowing. Looking at the dove overhead, I prayed for help to discover how to remain in this state of bliss, in union with my glorious Essence, all of the time. This spontaneous prayer was spoken from the innocence of a nine-year-old. There was no demand for an answer, it was more of a proclamation that this was my wish and it must come true.

"Many years later I learned to meditate, did personal growth, and moved from city life to a country setting with Nate. By my late twenties, my being was fully remembering the prayer and I was determined to let my sacredness bring forward the answer that I was seeking. How can I live in the awareness of that bliss, in that ethereal light all of the time?

"Ahh… Thanks again, Grace. My soul is whispering that this is important for me to revisit right now. The next level of the answer to the prayer may be forming. I will watch for it.

"What I've learned, Megan, in searching for the answer to that childhood question, is that I don't have to do anything except be receptive. Life magnetizes the perfect people and situations to allow the prayer's answer to continually unfold in a myriad of unexpected ways.

"Now, it's your turn, Grace. Tell her about the train. First let me say that even as a child, Grace had access to visual, ethereal scenes that many of us don't see. Some of us sense invisible beings like elementals or subtle energy around people or get downloads of information and wisdom about them. Grace was able to see subtle forms of beings. And then, if I understand it right, she also *sensed* them near her or *heard* their voice in her head rather than always *seeing* them. Is that correct, Grace?"

"Yes, that's accurate in every way. And the train was definitely a cosmic moment with my subtle friends," Grace said as she looked at Megan to begin her story.

"I was young, maybe twenty-two years old, living in Canada where I landed a unique job for a woman at that time. I hauled peat moss in a huge rig. I'd left my family and cushy life in Manhattan, so I needed a job like this where the pay was incredibly good. And I loved the adventure of driving a big rig. This job allowed my enterprising nature to rise to the surface. Of course, there were risks. One of them was a railroad crossing that I had to traverse every day and I was always super careful. They'd been working on the tracks for weeks. So the warning lights were always on. I'd creep forward because my rig was super long.

And you can't just hit the accelerator while pulling that size rig, weighted down to the max.

"It was hard to see because of the repair equipment but I thought it was clear. But as I got right over the tracks, I saw a bright light coming towards me fast—too fast for me to get the rig off the tracks in time. My mind was blank except for a flashing memory of someone telling me that in a train wreck, I'd be safer to stay in the rig than to try to get out because of the speed of the train and not knowing where the rig would finally land. Everything was suddenly surreal, and I knew I was about to die. In fact, I remember saying three times, I am going to die!

"All of a sudden, a cosmic euphoria rushed through my body and every cell felt effervescent and illumined with energy. Those invisible beings who had been with me for my entire life said calmly, *You're going to be fine.* I remember an intense white light in and around me and every cell became totally calm.

"The train hit the back of the trailer and the whole rig went flying. The next thing I remember is crawling from the cab of the truck, looking around and thinking, *I'm alive.*

"I had a sprained ankle and a few bruises—that was all. It was miraculous.

"Was I saved by my invisible helpers? Was it meant to be a moment of transformation that looked like a train wreck? Maybe it happened to solidify for me that there is a force of higher frequency that is operating in my life all the time. Regardless of the reason, the next day, I was back at work, driving a truck full of peat moss. Admittedly, I was even more tentative driving past that track, even with a clear line of sight.

"You may be surprised by this, Megan—honestly, I didn't do a lot of processing of what happened. I'd been bathed in cosmic energy as a child, but this happened in a way that my adult brain got to register that this cosmic, ethereal energy was real, life-giving, and always available. That wild event created an opening to a reality within me that I call *that which is always present.* After that, every time that I reached a point of wanting to give up, I'd be engulfed in that delicious energy and reminded that it powered my life force and was at the root of everything. Most importantly, it was not someone else's power and loving vibes. This cosmic energy was me in my elevated frequency.

"Sophia and I remained close friends because she and I never waiver in our experience that life is frequency. We chose to look for opportunities to further elevate our vibes. We were not looking for repeats of euphoric events. It was more like aligning with opportunities for peace, creativity, and joy that was already present within us.

"We never wriggled out of the lower frequencies, either. It became a practice of seeing them clearly, their function as resistance to life, and seeing the higher frequencies as alignment with life's rhythms. Then there is choice."

"I am stunned by that story," Megan said. "It helps me understand why Sophia is intimately connected with you and why you both seem naturally drawn to inner growth and do so with a sense of curiosity and wonder."

"Sophia and I test drove controlling life and other people," Grace said, "cultivating strong opinions and beliefs and thinking we were victims. None of that worked. We had to dive into personal growth or suffer. We realized the choice was simple. Either we focus on ourselves as what we called, *pure love expressing itself as us*—or we could blame others. Blaming and judging never brought us higher into a calm, bird's eye understanding about ourselves. It was an *other-focused* rather than an *inner-focused* approach to life.

"We chose different teachers and ways of exploring ourselves and compared notes. It's been amazing and even fun!" Grace said laughing and winking at Sophia. "And there's been plenty of bumps along the way.

"Part of what helped us through the toughest times was that we tenaciously stayed on top of our capacity to transmit information to each other. Honestly, our telepathy was light years faster and smoother when we were young. However, when we get together, we can still transmit information in a very unusual way. Can I tell her, Sophia?"

"Yes!" Sophia answered with a friendly smile. "We can show her how it's done."

Sophia held the inside of her right wrist against the inside of Grace's left wrist. They sat quietly for a moment. Grace's eyes became teary. "Awww... I love you, too, sister!"

Megan laughed and said, "What did she actually say to you?"

"She shared our childhood mantra: Friends forever!"

Megan smiled tenderly as she looked at the inseparable friends, still glowing from the expression of affection for each other.

"Megan, we did this often," Grace said, "without sharing an *intentional* message. We just exchanged information from a pool of information in our veins—it aways baffled and surprised us. Plus we were always thrilled to get the information. It was never boring or heady mental stuff. In those exchanges, we shared information about caves, ice, giants, love, unicity, and civilizations that are indescribable and which seemed to be somewhere on a coordinate in the field on Gaia.

"But without personal and spiritual growth, we realized that we could not sustain nor strengthen gifts like this. Holy moly! We had so many conversations about getting into our heads too much and how we could risk losing the amazing gifts we were born with."

"From what I can tell," Megan said, "you have special gifts and one heck of an incredible relationship. And like you, many people are discovering that it's time to engage in inner growth. From my viewpoint, it's happening exponentially. You seem to know innately how to use electromagnetic frequencies in your blood and bones, and telepathy comes naturally. But many people, even those who don't have those skills to start with, are ready to develop them. From my travels all across the planet, I can assure you that you are not alone in the rise of such phenomenon. It's exciting, isn't it? Maybe even I will lock wrists with you two, just for fun... to see what I can pick up. However right now, it's time to walk with my furry friends to their favorite grove full of squirrels."

Sophia looked at Megan. She recognized that the collective minds and hearts of humanity were rapidly shifting upwards, but in the ethers, Sophia felt turbulent changes churning and preparing to manifest. Humans were on the precipice of creating a courageous new world where the unicity gene was turned on, and every person would have the opportunity to contribute as a valued voice. The time to evolve higher had arrived for the inhabitants of Planet Earth.

CHAPTER 36
A STRANGER AND AN UNEXPECTED REVELATION

Several years passed and the world transformed in tumultuous ways. Changes in governments, religions, and institutions became common place. Education reformed with nature becoming the focus. As a dynamic sense of unity spread across the planet, a long list of changes occurred. There was more work to do, and the struggles were not over. Yet as humanity headed for 2030, they were ready to cross an evolutionary hurdle that landed them in a new environment inside themselves and in their world.

As a blogger and author, Sophia wrote extensively about anything that brought her readers to a sense of their inner powers, their oneness with everything, and inspiration to harness their own pure light and highest frequencies. As her inner experiences gained momentum, so did her ability to speak about it locally with small groups who wanted the same conversation. Together, they watched as the light of new creation gave birth to miracles—arising from a field of infinite possibilities.

Sophia's friends and community supported each other to soar with confidence and enthusiasm into the unknown, where miracles coalesce and manifest from what she *called the infinite quantum soup of delicious information.*

Working with Jake, she was able to write more extensively about the galactic side of life on Earth and disclosure of these realities became common place. No longer were Gilda's stories a secret, nor were the coverups of giant skeletons. Citizens began demanding that underground military bases evolve into high tech centers where young, brilliant minds could openly share ideas and develop technologies for free energy and give global citizens the chance to collaborate in harmony with each other to ensure that all of their basic needs could be met. Tough resistance ensued, yet increasing numbers of brave hearts remained tenaciously sure of what was needed—unicity and transparency.

During one evening fireside conversation, Jake explained to his circle of friends that he was sure that *free energy* was going to be feasible by extracting it from the infinite field in and around them. Cutting edge physicists proved that every atom constantly syphons energy from the spin of its universe. When this wild energy is densely packed, squeezed into a one-square-centimeter cube, it is incomprehensibly powerful. When harnessed like that, as an immeasurable energy source, the need to extract energy from Gaia would be over. The group sat mesmerized as he described the same energy potential within the trillions of cells in a human being.

"We are powerful, my friends, beyond measure. State-of-the-art potentiality and possibility are our nature, accessible 24/7. This is our groundbreaking chance for a peaceful world to emerge where wars over resources can finally dissolve."

Enthralled to hear his proclamations, the group acknowledged that global powers would not let such radical change happen without a fight for control. The thought of how to overcome that obstacle felt daunting.

Responding to this, Jake said resolutely, "We know how the greedy within our species operate. Control and manipulation are a way of life for them and nobody can expect these people to change overnight. We have to keep doing what we do best:

create with passion, as though our lives depend on it, which they do. I am more motivated and excited about the future than ever before."

The friends observed that innovative ideas were not coming from big think tanks nor was sharing ideas a top-down approach. It was multilateral and heart-to-heart. A renaissance was burgeoning. Jake and John marveled at the brilliance of young people coming into the fold with fresh ideas and enthusiasm. Focused attention and private funding were beginning to be directed towards pyramids where their technologies could be studied more carefully and potentially applied once again, as in ancient times, for free energy and intergalactic communication. Mathematical formulas of various aspects of those pyramids were reverse engineered by young techies. Their focus was benefiting everyone rather than only a few tech giants. The unicity gene expressed itself through them fully.

Sophia, John, and Jake lived near the cove. Sophia bought land where she could garden extensively, invite Angelica to visit, and develop native plants as herbal remedies. Grace came often, and was a perfect addition to the close-knit clan who gathered at Megan's place. They developed a strong bond and felt increasingly comfortable asking profound questions: *How many coordinates in the field had they shared together? How many inner layers of frequency within themselves could they explore? How much could they give and receive from a planet who was reaching her own sentient frequencies of enlightenment and bliss?*

The cave and its pyramid remained Sophia's sanctuary and abode for cosmic travel. One day, she was sitting by the remains of the old giant in his cave, waves of elation and rapture spontaneously arising. Nearby, the elder uttered the sacred sound, opening the pyramid door, humming its magnificent codes. The shamans, too, melted into deep prayer for the universe, and beyond.

She emerged from the cave, the landscape bathed in warmth and beauty, and headed home to enjoy her lush gardens. When she arrived, she reached down to tenderly touch a small ladybug, and sat on the cool ground to take in a deep breath of life-giving energy. It was then that she noticed a beautiful young woman approaching. Even from a distance this lovely soul spread light like a welcome beacon on a dark night.

Her blond hair was sparkling in the sunlight and her feet seemed to hardly touch the ground. Joy was radiating from her face as she came closer and asked expectantly, "Are you Sophia?"

"Yes, have we met?"

"No, my name is Adele. I came here to meet you."

Her blue eyes were sparkling and her smile grew wider in delight as she continued, "I've been following you and your work for a long time. I want my children to learn our planet's history directly from you, if such a thing is possible. I love the way that you describe our earthly journey as *ever-evolving*, elevating in frequency into something amazing. Embodying higher frequencies more fully and caring for our world are my focus, and you are my inspiration.

"My mother was a big fan of yours and she said my grandmother was, too. In fact, my grandmother came right out and said that she loved you. So I knew you'd be trustworthy."

"Who is your mother?" Sophia asked in a soft voice, surprised.

"Her name was Edith." Adele answered. She smiled briefly but looked away as though saying her mother's name was a fresh catalyst for grief to raise its head. Tears gathered in her eyes.

In a flash, Sophia's face went blank, her eyes flickered briefly as though her brain was registering memories of long ago, in a different garden with her dear friend, Gilda. That chapter in her life was filled with deep conversations, Nate's sweet love, special friendships, and unexpected people she met along her path. The beginning of a new chapter of her life began with those garden conversations.

"You said that your mother's name *was* Edith. Is she alive? I remember her well. She was brilliant; a beautiful woman."

"She passed away and my grandmother, too," she said. "Last year was hard. I also lost my husband in a tragic accident a while back. Even with these intense heartbreaks, I am trying to settle into the reality of what's happened, while not ignoring the blessings of having had these amazing people in my life." Looking down, she became placidly solemn.

"Maybe I should tell you a little more about my family. I was born when my mother was older. Maybe that made her an even better mom. I miss her so much." Her voice trailed off into silence and soft tears trickled down her cheeks.

"I am so sorry for your loss, Adele. I sensed as you spoke that you've done a lot of inner work. Have you given yourself time to heal deeply from the loss of your loved ones? I know that sweet, intimate experience of grief."

"To tell you the truth, my unrelenting sorrow is partly why I came to Idaho. I knew my mom had a heart connection with you. She encouraged me to listen to you and to follow your blogs, read your books, and join your online groups. I felt like… part of my grieving process and coming to terms fully with the loss was… supposed to happen here. Even though we haven't met, the way Mom spoke about you, I felt like you were part of our family. It's strange that I never met you and my mother said she didn't get to be with you very much; but I know your friendship ran deep.

"My grandmother was German, and she'd been here in Idaho during the war. She thought you were wonderful, and she felt close to you. She described your friendship as being full of love and affection. How did you meet my grandmother?"

Without answering right away, Sophia asked softly, "What is your grandmother's name?"

"Her real name is Anna Alise," Adele said. "She was a spy or something, which I can't imagine. She was kind, incredibly wise, and totally loving. Mom said that my grandmother was in a prisoner of war camp in Idaho at the end of WWII and that's where mom was born. My mother was given up for adoption because my grandmother knew that living a secret military life was not the place to raise a little girl.

"I know it must have been agonizing to let her baby go..." Her voice cracked and she stopped speaking. After a moment, she continued.

"My mom introduced me to my grandmother later in her life. It was a privilege to know such a courageous and beautiful human being. Since my grandfather died and my grandmother was quite old, I guess it was okay for us to know about my grandmother's life. I never met my grandfather. He died before her. And my mother told me he worked for the government and that's all she knew.

"I loved my grandmother, even though I didn't have nearly enough time to get to know her, ask questions, and take care of her. I wish she and I could have had more time together as I was growing up." Tears began to trickle gently down Adele's crestfallen face.

Sophia's eyes were brimming with tears as she let Adele compose herself and continue.

"Everyone called my grandmother Gilda. Apparently after the war, people in the U.S. were suspicious of Germans. And there were less misgivings about a woman who spoke fluent English and had a more neutral, European name. The last time I saw her, she said:

You will live in a world of the highest frequencies, and you will travel to places unimaginable. Always remember that inside you lies all the power, wisdom, and stillness to support you in doing and being anything you choose. Remember the bond of unicity that connects you with everything, everywhere. I love you.

"That bond of *unicity*, meant so much to her. She helped me to experience it with her and with people around me. In my short time with her, she deeply impacted my life.

"I want to visit the places that profoundly shaped and transformed her life. So I thought I'd come here and maybe find the old war camp, smell the delicious scent of the trees the way she described them, and see the majestic mountains that sustained her as she cared for my mother those first few months. I hope I haven't unloaded too much too fast. It's just that I felt instantly comfortable with you and I trust that. I want to somehow come to terms with my family not being here anymore. And I desperately want to find my purpose going forward."

Sophia allowed silence for a moment before she spoke. "I knew your mother and grandmother. Like you, I didn't get to be with them long enough. Seeing you is flooding my being with delightful memories because you bear a strong resemblance to both of them and you exude similar virtues of kindness, compassion, and strength of character. You have their heart-shaped face and your eyes are identical, exquisite blue sapphires. Like you, they were beautiful women, inside and out. I loved them incredibly. What a gift to have you here!

"When my husband was sick, your grandmother and I engaged in delightful morning conversations in a charming, little garden that was our special meeting place. Our brief time together touched me deeply and she instantly became a dear friend. Even now, I feel her close by. I have been to the camp. In a stroke of incredible luck, I found the place where she went to soothe her soul. And I would love to take you there. Where are you staying?"

"I found a local inn that welcomed my two little girls, which has been great, but I'd like to find another place soon," Adele said. "It's too expensive to stay there."

"My guest house is available. Your children will love it here. I can introduce you to other moms in the community who are the best of the best. They are my nourishment and delight."

Without hesitation, Adele hugged Sophia tightly and melted into the embrace for several minutes. Her tears burst forth like a dam that had reached capacity long ago. Fortunately, Sophia's heart was a vast pool of love that was big enough to take in a torrent of tears.

After Adele was composed, the two women made a time to get together the next day and Sophia headed to the house to write:

Since the time I met my dear Gilda, it's almost impossible to fathom the structures in the world that have crumbled, and the benevolent technologies that are emerging as the serf-self paradigm dissolves. The heart of humanity is exploding into unity, the bond of togetherness. And Unified Physics is taking off, too.

Just as Kabir predicted, Nanni was right, we have the capacity for something so incredible that it was unfathomable for our serf-self to accept.

I honor the courage of people who confront evil in the way that Gilda did many years ago. It was the lion-hearts like her who were willing to look inside, regardless of their past, and find the gold hidden there. They listened to the whispers of their heart, telling them to act immediately rather than bear the burden of continuing to acquiesce to profound lies and evil actions.

At that point, as a human race, we could finally come together with our flaws, without judgment of ourselves or others, and find solutions in community. The old structures are becoming like something from an archeological site now. They are part of the past and no longer define our future. The governments and dictators are losing their capacity to lord coercive power over the flailing masses. It's the most unimaginably glorious time to be alive.

I want to be able to share this with Adele so that the journey can be told in a way that doesn't make anyone wrong. It's important that no one takes what happened personally, feels judged, or thinks their loved ones caused the problems that escalated into a giant storm of chaos and polarization.

For a while, it was looking like Gilda's battles would be repeated. Fortunately, humanity as a collective is changing. They want peace and unity. They will not stand for anything less than that. They tare taking personal responsibility for themselves. Judgement of others is begging to melt into acceptance of all manner of views. Collaboration is becoming common place.

Gilda often told me that life was all about frequency. And the frequencies of love, joy, and peacefulness are now stronger globally. Gilda was right. Higher frequencies, those lovely quantum waves, catapulted us into like-minded communities, deeper friendships, and a true form of acceptance and togetherness. We are becoming a human race bonded in the unicity gene.

Today, Adele's face kept morphing in and out, sometimes looking like Gilda and then back to the young Adele. DNA is a mysterious part of the human species partly because it passes on more than physical traits. A potent, cosmic superpower of exalted vibrations comes through. It brings our unicity gene to life. It directs a symphony within our blood and the waters of the universe that allow us to become established in our Essence of pure love.

My ability to move through inner layers of consciousness and coordinates of the field recently reached a higher level. Gilda, Max, Nate, Kabir who died so young, and Nanni have joined forces. With elevated frequencies, I am feeling an ever more radical shift happening. I can see life from a broader viewpoint. As I do, more information from the field, more historical memory, becomes accessible to me.

It's poignant to remember how hard I struggled to elevate my frequencies rather than just tune into the bird's eye view of life that was always available, and which always elevated my frequency.

The entire world is making progress towards unprecedented vibrations of integrity and courage, every day. Artfully and magnificently, my beautiful human family forges on in our unicity, forever unfolding in light, wisdom, and beauty.

CHAPTER 37
THE MULTIVERSE AND CONSCIOUSNESS SCALES

Settling into a comfy chair on Megan's porch, hot tea in hand, brimming with fragrant scents and exquisite flavor, Sophia waited for Adele. Often, they luxuriated in the sun's warm, nurturing light. They met regularly to share their experiences of connecting with the invisible field in and all around them. A fresh, rejuvenating joy for life became the predominant mood amongst the circle of friends, who were all on fire with enthusiasm for the advanced archeological work happening at the cove.

As she aged, Sophia became steady in the truth of her own being. She didn't sugar-coat explanations of inexplicable events; she was honest about her connection with light and energy fields, and moving through portals into other coordinates of the field. The concept of time shifted for her. It was not linear. Her lived experience was that awareness of time could dissolve in stillness. And in stillness, all possibility and all time vibrated everywhere.

Many times, she thanked Jake for his clear explanations about his research of areas that helped modern science understand how the material world unfolds into reality. One of her favorite examples was that time was misunderstood. Science used *time* on the 3-D plane to locate and measure events occurring in space, but in the infinite field, time and space were simply *potentials* expressing within a material world.

With ever-increasing consistency, conversations between Sophia, Jake, John, Adele, and Megan were exploratory and experiential exchanges in which each of them grew their potential. Although Megan's porch became the gathering spot for morning tea and coffee, the group also gravitated to the old growth trees at the fire pit or the caverns of Mystic Cove. They came together as often as possible, with tea, coffee, and open hearts. Within the cave, they approached the work with inquisitiveness and wonder. Jake's many discoveries of galactic archeology on planets like Mars were part of the study at the cove. As more locations on the surface of the Earth were demonstrating the alignment between off planet and on-planet archeology, the relationship between humans and the cosmos was incontrovertible.

The circle of friends gathered with appreciation in every season on Gaia—but springtime was a special celebration after the long, seemingly relentless winter. Spring was an explosion of new life in northern Idaho. Flowers peeked out, birds came home to sing, and all were rejuvenated and ready to blaze into summer.

After dropping off her girls at school, Adele went to meet Sophia on her porch for morning tea. Enjoying a particularly sunny, yet slightly chilly morning, Sophia was sitting in quiet contentment. She'd awakened early to bask in the cascading vibrations of pre-dawn, pre-birdsong peacefulness. Getting settled, Adele waited a minute and then broke the silence with her usual, childlike enthusiasm saying, "I hope you don't mind a recurring subject. I'd like to know more of what you remember about my mother. Anything is fine. I'm missing her pretty intensely right now. I have a familiar ache in my heart. Somehow talking about her eases it and reminds me of the underlying energy of her timeless, energetic radiance; rather than sitting here missing the human form."

"Adele, I love your smile. It's like a gift of dazzling sunlight. And your authenticity and willingness to face being vulnerable with me are impressive. How can I not respond to your heartfelt request? I found that when I spoke about Nate with close friends, it was a relief to speak the truth of my aching heart, and like you just described, I could then feel his eternal energy rather than dwelling on the form that I was missing. If I could tell you more, I would, but I did not get to be with your mom often. None of us knew that Nate would soon pass away, or that your grandmother would leave, too.

"Your mother, like your grandmother, was brilliant and very tuned-in to subtle realms. When she came to be with Nate, he was always impressed with her sense of calm, quiet *knowing* of how to help him. Her heart was open, and she and Nate shared the profound mysteries of life. Nate thought she was incredible. And so did I. I suspect you've inherited her wildly curious mind and capacity for stillness. That's a rare gift. It took me many years of intense inner work to cultivate that deep, still place inside."

Adele's face became soft and contemplative as she said, "My mother was instrumental in helping me to cultivate the ability to quiet my mind and see the unseen. From the time I was born, she wanted me to keep developing those capacities. When was the first time that you knew that unseen realms were accessible? Did your mom help you?"

"Well, it wasn't like that for me." Sophia said, introspectively. "I was closer to your age before I dove into spirituality and mysticism. I had some glimpses in childhood, but my mother didn't cultivate these capacities in me as your mom did with you. My mother was more traditional for the time. By my mid-twenties,

I was blowing through life full tilt, aways striving to get ahead in business, meeting nearly impossible deadlines, running through my to-do lists. I became exhausted on many levels. All of that striving ultimately was harming my body, my mind, and leaving little room for my soul to be acknowledged. Then I had an experience with Nate that changed me forever.

"We were in a gorgeous winter resort with friends. They loved to ice skate on a frozen pond. The thrill was that it was on a slight incline and you'd zigzag down to the lower end. We watched our friends, got the idea of how to traverse the ice, and with invincible spirits, we headed to where our friends were waiting, cheering and clapping.

"As I took off, the surface felt way more slick than normal ice skating, and all of a sudden, I felt gravity grabbing me like a magnet and my body locking up in terror. All of a sudden, I was falling... spinning out of control. As I fell, the world became a formidable, pulsating energy field of white light, blinding in intensity. I could not feel anything physically because my awareness was totally immersed in that potent, all-encompassing light. Trees and everything else in my field of vision were subtle emanations of light and sound—a frequency of sound like a soft humming in my ears.

"Amazement and awe filled me to overflowing. From what I know now, I entered a portal to a higher vibration of light within my consciousness. Suddenly, I felt Nate's hand reaching for mine. Later he told me that I easily got to my feet, but I don't remember that. What it felt like was that his hand was a magnet as strong as gravity and it pulled me back into awareness of my familiar coordinate of time and space. My mind was not thinking. It was perfectly still as I let my body become one with Nate's energy.

As if nothing had happened, we easily and elegantly skated to join our friends.

"Although I was totally fine, I could not talk. No one could believe that there were no ill effects from the fall and spinning out of control. It's hard to imagine that we went straight to dinner with our friends. In the restaurant, I sat snuggled close to Nate, which might have seemed romantic, but the truth was that my energy field continued to be magnetized to his.

"He and I didn't speak at dinner, everyone thought that I was in shock, so we went back to our cabin. As we slipped into bed, I recall that Nate reached for my hand as he'd done on the ice. My mind entered that same stillness and light engulfed my awareness of the ethereal space in and around me as I drifted into sleep.

"The next morning, as we emerged from deep, restful sleep, we held each other without saying anything. Our ritual for talking about personal experiences and reflections was always over a cup of tea. That morning, we sipped hot tea while looking out at the mesmerizing winter landscape. Nate broke the silence by asking what had happened for me. I tried to describe the indescribable. As he asked questions and shared what it had been like for him, I realized that he understood what I'd experienced. He had become immersed in that subtler reality, too. We wondered if part of what happened was that the protons within our respective vortexes in the field had become *entangled.* Regardless of how it happened, we were in sync one hundred percent.

"We didn't know how it had happened. In order to recreate it, we tried to reverse engineer the event but we couldn't figure it out mentally. My biggest takeaway was that this was one of those rare moments when my mind gave way to the infinite information of *the field*, which allowed me to experience a higher level of consciousness and Nate, with whom I was entangled, could experience the same layer of reality. Is that trippy, or what? We realized that meditating, letting our consciousness drift into its essence at the singularity, was the best way to encourage our consciousness to expand. We decided not to "try" to get entangled. We figured that our protons were doing it naturally. Our normal way of life became a sustained meditation practice, a profound journey into quantum physics, and open-minded conversations about mind-blowing topics."

Adele looked at Sophia mesmerized, as though yearning to hear more.

Engrossed deeply in their conversation, the two friends inadvertently blocked out the rest of the world. Neither of them heard Jake walking towards them until the clearing of his throat was impossible to ignore. As he playfully greeted them, he admitted to overhearing the last part of their conversation. He teased Sophia about her relentless knack for learning about her quantum essence in unusual ways.

"Grab a chair, my friend," Sophia said warmly to Jake.

"Hi Jake," Adele greeted him with her youthful smile and enthusiasm. "I am trying to take in what Sophia just told me. Even though I am used to experiencing higher layers of consciousness, her experience on the ice was amazing!"

Jake looked towards the sun as it filtered like soft glitter through the tree above them and looked back at Adele and Sophia.

"It's all about an invisible world, isn't it?" He said pensively. "Everybody thinks there's some crazy magic in all of this. Our world is visible because of waves of light that we can see but what is equally important are photons of *invisible* light from little oscillating vortexes in the field that are creating this entire world and giving us these kinds of experiences."

"You're getting your first taste of Jake's vast wisdom of all things seen and unseen," Sophia said to Adele. "His love for galactic subjects, and everything that is tiny, quantum and invisible."

"Adele, I love to speak about light," Jake said, as he leaned forward ready to dive deeply into his juicy subject.

"A famous physicist named David Bohm said that light is more than just subtle form. It emerges from the potentiality underlying all forms and structures of our world—which means that *everything* arises from and remains connected with a field of *infinite energy, information, and light.* Photons are a subtle ingredient for the world that we see, touch, and feel. You cannot grab a photon because it is just energy. The substantive aspect of light is waves, not a particle that is material or touchable like a little sphere.

"You see something because you get a sensation of light waves of energy coming into your eyes and it's the same with hearing. You can also get a sensation of light waves through your ears. Fascinating, isn't it? You may have noticed that Sophia described the effulgent, white light of her subtle worldview as she crashed on the ice. Her perception was subtle yet had a form. The form was light. And those photons of light are usually invisible as they vibrate as a potentiality of her experience. As her subtle, inner frequencies united completely with the subtle light of her awareness, she connected with the unified field from which all matter comes into being. From that connection, although all possibilities exist, her awareness aligned with the *possibility* of walking away without a bruise.

"I am mentioning this because as Sophia continues to move through various scales of consciousness within her, she is simply allowing her awareness to expand into nothing and everything at the same time so she can boost her frequencies. Her mind relinquishes control and more subtle centers in the brain take over naturally. A long time ago, she told us that she was staying with friends after her husband died. He came to her in a dream and explained this phenomenon. One important detail of the dream was that regardless of her sleeping or awake state, she remains oscillating energy and vibration interacting with the field. And as such, she is capable of constantly interacting with endless dimensions, or layers, of her own being—interpreted by her consciousness.

"I am adding her husband's perspective of what some people call *dimensions* because sometimes it sounds like a dimension is *over there* in a parallel coordinate in the field or *back there* in another coordinate or *up there* in some high vibe coordinate in another universe. I'm trying to simplify this idea of *dimensions* as her capacity to move into higher frequencies within her consciousness as a spinning vortex in and part of the field. Don't try to immediately grasp this. Take your time to integrate it into your awareness as a truth of reality. Forget the mathematical formulas that seek to explain it; let it become your experience, notice if and when it is true for you. Then, my words will have meaning. I wanted you to know how we refer to theses subtle experiences so we are on the same page.

"Sophia is simply joining Nate in the field of all possibilities where they both coexist in alignment—where her frequency matches his. If she meets him in that field to further her work on Planet Earth, and their frequencies align, a high vibrational exchange of information happens. It arrives in our reality as codes of light and information. Inherently, her body decodes the data. Her brain, specifically the pineal gland with its lovely crystalline structure, helps to translate that information. This is an exquisitely designed system. I find it both wondrous and humbling.

"Recently, Sophia, you touched my heart profoundly. Although I didn't mention it at the time, when you were looking at Max, I noticed that your pupils were contracted, as though in bright light—from where? We were in a cave. Your breath shifted and became slower and deeper. Then I observed you twitching a bit and I saw a brilliant, emerald-green light, sparkling with golden flecks, emanate from your heart to his. I can still feel the connection..." Jake looked away with a glistening tear in the corner of his eye. For a moment, he couldn't speak.

Composed, he continued, "In that moment, I witnessed the miracle of light that you and all of us are made of. As you received invisible, quantum energy, you emanated light from an octagon in your entire chest with intensified force. The expression of someone having a *big heart* came alive for me."

Then, he turned to Adele, saying, "As time goes on, you'll be able more and more to experience subtle realms any time, with your eyes open. Your beautiful blue eyes are continuously receiving subtle forms of energy and emanating them, too. Be sure to acknowledge this miraculous, innate capacity.

"The thing about you, Adele, is that because of your mom, your grandmother, and your life experience, you trust the light, connect with it effortlessly, and emanate it naturally. You don't question the light and information from the infinite quantum field that guides you each day. Your body's navigation system is closer to that of birds and whales, who move with information from the Earth's magnetics, which is part of the invisible world of photons and subtle energies.

"Gaia, this gorgeous planet needs all of us to get to a place of ease and effortless living. We are gradually allowing ourselves to be guided by what we instinctively know to do in each moment, rather than pushing, striving, and controlling our way through life. From my perspective, because of your intrinsic subtle skills, if you want to help us, we will be able to make huge strides in decoding the information of the pyramids and the stone circle. Did you see the circle yet?"

Adele shook her head and said fervently that she was "totally stoked and immensely grateful" to get a tour of the property soon.

Jake said, "Sophia has been able to decode information that comes through the megalithic circle on solstices and through other specific galactic alignments of stars and constellations. Her friend, Grace, came to help her. You need to know that the second pyramid will likely be easier for you to become unified with on your first visit. The first pyramid requires a special sound vibration to enter. The second one is different."

Jake explained that Adele would enter the second pyramid from underneath. Until she felt a deep connection with the pyramid, patiently and with a still mind, she would stand in the water that leads to the entrance.

"There are stones in the water," Jake said, "as well as minerals that allow your frequency to shift easily. The pyramids are not monuments or temples as archeologists usually think of them. They are a technology. The pyramids here were designed by the beings like Max, from the visible constellation of Sirius. The third pyramid was a total surprise. And then we went deeper into caverns and more surprises unfolded before us.

"As Sophia was able to trust her innate capacities and allow her consciousness to shift to other coordinates in the field, she began to connect with beings in the cosmos. From my perspective, they were familiar with her. Had she joined them in her dreams? Were they her ancestors? Who knows? What I can tell you is that we began to have some pretty special visitors at the cave. Even with the logical side of my brain, usually in charge, I could see them."

Jake's eyes welled up with tears, he looked away as if he could find composure if he took a deep breath and didn't make eye contact. This was the composure that he grasped for when he described experiences that rattled the safe space of his logical mind and opened his tender heart to higher expressions of the mystical aspects of life, of all things inexplicable, but absolutely true, nonetheless.

"The third pyramid," he said, "was different. By the time Sophia merged into a common frequency with it and spent time there, beings who were not from our solar system, galaxy, or universe began coming to meet us at the cave. Being with them drew us spontaneously into a powerful field like an energetic embrace that easily generated a blissful state and immense gratitude to be alive. We felt a range of feelings from tear-jerking love to absolute stillness and radical peace, contentment, and serenity... I... Shit! I can't find the right words, Adele. This experience and these feelings were always in me..." Choking back tears for a moment, he said, "I was never emotional like this before I started poking around in this mystical cove. I am telling you the truth. These encounters changed me for good, from the inside out.

"I only share what we've learned with a small, trustworthy group of colleagues. In my field, even though there's tons of unclassified documents, credible whistleblowers, and scientific proof of the age of these sites, the doubters still reign supreme. I know how Copernicus, Pythagoras, and Galileo felt. It's called *misunderstood.*

"I swear science is like a freight liner in the ocean, try to turn it and it creaks, groans, and takes forever to change course. A long time ago, science decided that to avoid being trapped in the rigid religious doctrines of the Middle Ages, they would adopt a mechanistic view of the reality. They said to hell with invisible, mystical, esoteric subjects; forget alchemy and shamanism. They wanted to divide from the church so they would not constantly be in fear for their life when they explored outside of accepted dogma. They would no longer set foot in the domain of the inexplicable, everything would be measurable and concrete—and that became the new dogma. That leaves little room for studying Max, unified physics, or concepts that include unicity at the core of our being.

"However, we are going outside of the standard, safe little ideological box when I refer to the fact that suddenly, some kind of miraculous sociologic human *skill-trend* occurred between ten to fifteen thousand years ago. Humans shifted dramatically from being adept hunter gatherers and became technological geniuses and brilliant architects. In a short time period, humans somehow figured out how to construct and build pyramids that are geometrically perfect and intricately designed. Did you know that today we cannot duplicate them? And this didn't happen in just one place. It occurred in the Yucatán, China, Peru, Egypt, and right here where we are sitting. All of a sudden, humans became mathematicians, geometricians, astronomers, started growing crops, and understood complex patterns, measurements, and physics.

"Until I got access to this amazing site at the cove to work with, I would have likely ended up, like most of my closed-minded colleagues, with a weak, logical, don't-rock-the-boat answer for this breakthrough in evolution. We all need funding, and we all want to be valued and respected. What the hell! These days, I don't care about any of that. I know what I've seen. Thank God that I also have plenty of colleagues and well-respected people from numerous disciplines who are united in our search for more answers to what happened on this planet since its inception.

"Who helped humanity to take such a huge leap in cognitive function? How did they suddenly increase their capacity to access higher levels of consciousness? We are working hard to find answers.

"More than that, because of Sophia's direct experience of the technologies like the pyramid and the stone circles, I became interested in learning more about how to help Gaia and all of us who live on her via the science of the infinite unified field, from which everything, including our universe, emerges. What happens through those ancient technologies is not woo-woo. It's quantum science. Pyramid technology is loaded with information about who we are, what we are capable of creating, and the secrets of the origins of our universe. Sorry for my rant, but sometimes I get frustrated. I had a conversation with someone yesterday who thought it was a waste of time to look at pyramids here and on Mars. Something about probing the connection we have with the universe, beyond the definable edges and aspects of our planet, scares the bejeezus out of people. In my opinion, the person I spoke with is brilliant. But I sensed his fear of exploring outside of what society and his colleagues engage in. Several times he even suggested that if all of this is true and we connect with other beings, we could invite an ET invasion or cause abductions.

"What if there is life way out there that is more vast and complex that we can imagine? Rather than fear it, I am hellbent on exploring it. My colleague's remark may have come from watching too many Hollywood blockbusters and a misunderstanding about the vastness of highly evolved, subtle life forms in the Multiverse. I do not want to engage with colleagues who wallow in gutless mediocrity. It's time to think big, drop our hesitation, and go all-out. Shit, we have to get extraordinarily broad-minded."

"In the twenty-first century, I am surprised that you have to take that kind of ridicule," Adele interjected. "I'm totally fine with what you are doing here. My mother was into it in a big way. So was my grandmother. Mom emphasized that the importance of technologies, like a pyramid, is for humanity to use them to evolve for *the benefit of humanity.* She intended the benefit to carry forward into the incredible Multiverse that you mentioned.

"In many conversations, Mom said that she hoped I'd develop skills to expand my inner self. That's why she encouraged me to *feel plants,* not just see them. In her experience, rocks can cry, trees call out to us, and mountains are breathing... But I'm curious—what were the ET crafts like? Did you go on their ship?"

Chuckling, Jake looked down for a moment thoughtfully, taking a pause to consider how to answer her. When he made eye contact, his face was softer and more open than before, as he answered Adele's question. "No crafts. We are only working within natural portals on Earth. There are places where the frequencies are conducive to travel through worm holes—or we send our awareness to their coordinate and they come here in the same way. The extraterrestrials can meet us in a space where both of us are safe from atmospheric and other physical and biological issues that could make that meeting challenging. It's an effective and ancient technology. And the most natural.

"Most visits to Earth from other civilizations are done this way. Of course, not all species in our galaxy and beyond have that capacity. Moving particles around is beyond us, but we are learning from our cosmic friends and, heck, maybe even getting closer to doing so.

"I am learning a lot about ETs which often surprises the hell out of me. I knew them through anecdotes and sometimes sources that turned out to be unreliable. Firsthand knowledge has been enlightening, for sure. As humans, we tend to categorize and come to conclusions about people and events. When it comes to extraterrestrials, we associate them with the species encountered in 1947 Roswell, New Mexico—the Ebens. You are a bit young to remember. Your mother and grandmother likely knew more than I do about them. It was a craft with ETs who crashed—we don't know from where, there are a variety of possibilities. Some people speculate that the government shot them down; others believe it was pilot error, or the craft couldn't handle our atmosphere; still others think there may have been other ETs who were protecting the planet from what they perceived as off-planet interlopers. We still labor under the mistaken view that we can see all craft on radar. But advanced technologies can move in ways that our technologies cannot spot them. Highly advanced species might be here protecting us in a profound way and we'd never know.

"From what Sophia was told in her encounters with ETs, many of the beings who are interested in us are like scientists from their planet or star. They come here, study our diverse plant life, and especially the water. This is important. H2O is the building block for a massive amount of information and is the catalyst for life. Our water here is rich in information, seeded over the many ice ages by innumerable beings. With curiosity and a sense of galactic exploration, these cosmic archeologists and botanists come without introductions, without being seen, and slip away without evidence that they visited our planet.

"There are also species who want to see us do well and evolve higher. And they don't take lightly that we could send out nuclear pollution into space. From their own experience and observation, they know that some mistakes can be repaired, and other ones cannot.

"These beings are fascinated with us. From their point of view, our range of emotions and the use of our particular five senses make us unique and well-suited to express unicity and elevate our consciousness. Rest assured they have no interest in making a treaty or deal with our government to sell us to a creepy species for abductions and all of that kind of thing. Besides, humans are famous throughout the universe for breaking treaties, being sneaky and greedy. It's not judgment. It's our history. We've been a warring species, and for far too long we haven't placed an emphasis on loving Gaia as a sentient being. In the name of progress, we continue to use chemicals that benefit the people who make them, not the whole of humanity or life on the planet. In the end, they get big profits while humanity and Gaia are taken for granted or abused.

"The truth is that any extraterrestrial who comes to our planet is subject to the laws of physics that exist here. We can touch them, we can dissect these beings, reverse engineer their ships, and create a fear campaign about them. That's all been done.

"The *Ebens* in the 1947 Roswell, New Mexico crash were wholeheartedly cooperative; not violent or aggressive in any way. I've met people who saw them. They shared with me that they were kind and helpful. The Ebens simply could not survive our atmosphere, the native bacteria, and so forth. Without adequate tech to support their biological needs, they could not survive.

"That said, I am not averse to speculate that low vibe ET species come here, too. After all, we live in a massive galaxy. Who knows who's been coming here? There's also likely a vast number of species *out there* with advanced technologies but they don't necessarily have evil intentions toward us or their star brothers and sisters. My bet is that interstellar beings are not interested in attacking us. I speculate that there's plenty of inconceivably advanced cosmic beings who can go anywhere. Why would they need to take over Gaia or any other planet? I propose we meet the low vive ones with our rising personal frequencies—which can become so damn high that they decide to go elsewhere.

"I leave UFOs and the Secret Space Program to others to study and research. My focus is on the archeological sites that have technologies like pyramids. Pyramids are on Mars and believe it or not, the extraterrestrials say that pyramids are underground on many planets. Through Sophia's contacts, I have a greater perspective of our universe. With a profound sense of humility, I can say that I don't know even a fraction of its magnitude and grandeur.

"One planet I am obsessed with right now is Saturn. Yet, the more I learn about Jupiter and Neptune, I'd love to go there, too."

Turning to Sophia with a puzzled look, Adele asked, "When you interacted with these beings that Jake is talking about, in dreams or at the cove, did you engage at a higher level of consciousness than in your normal waking state? This is way more important to me than chasing crafts and hoping to meet one of the good ETs and not a bad one. I'd love to have a vibrational communication with them, feeling their emotions and mine as electromagnetic impulses rather than just talking and asking questions. My mother told me that they can send information that is so subtle that you instinctively know what they are saying. The information does not arrive as specific words. How amazing would it be to meet them in frequencies where we can align and comprehend each other without words?! This is blowing my mind! Wow! I had no idea that this is what you were doing at the cove."

"Keep in mind that our work at the cove has evolved," Sophia said as she smiled affectionately at Adele. "None of us knew where our curiosity and openness would take us. New information gradually reveals itself with each step we take. And yes, I have experienced higher layers, or scales, of frequency within my consciousness. My connection with Max certainly happened that way, and being trained to still my mind played a big role. First, I met Max in lucid dreams and then in meditations. Later, I was caught off guard when my consciousness was spontaneously thrust into an altered state where I experienced a higher level of awareness and I could perceive Max and other beings. Over time, more beings began to connect with me in meditation or as I sat with a still mind in the cove. Lately I have been able to consciously connect with several species, especially from the Alpha Centauri constellation, which is always an inexplicably delectable experience.

"The safest way to connect is meditation or for me to teleport my consciousness to a *specific coordinate* in the field rather than move my physical particles. Directing my particles to a specific place is possible, but I have not mastered that yet. While this remains as an aspiration, I patiently allow for it to unfold naturally. Like all subtle skills, my frequency level plays a pivotal role in this process. So it makes sense to work on my frequency elevation rather than focusing on how to move my particles. As my encounters with the cosmic beings steadily increases, I am valuing the perfectly-timed unfoldment of my innate, quantum-scale skillset and I am much more willing to be spontaneous. When I get an inner message to go to the cave, one of the pyramids, or to a place they designate, I go there. I trust the impulse that I feel. Sitting silently, I meet them inside a mountain, under a body of water, in a cave, and sometimes in an ethereal space within a layer of higher consciousness.

"I went inside a craft once, and I felt scared and disoriented. Not threatened. But it was so foreign that my mind freaked out. A survival aspect of my brain went into high gear. The beings were kind, gentle, and showed me a few things. I walked around the craft with them. Yet, without the capacity to relax and become a still, receptive vessel for their revelations, I froze. Before that visit, I didn't grasp the pivotal step of going inward, getting quiet, and adjusting to the frequency of the environment. It's no wonder that I couldn't relax and enjoy my unfolding experience.

"From that moment, I stopped trying to raise my frequency or ascend to a frequency to meet them. Instead, I learned to go inside and ground myself in stillness where I naturally align with a full range of frequencies that are available to me. From there, I easily become a match for their frequency.

"Once again, my experiences reinforce that connecting with higher frequency beings is an inner process of stillness, of resonating with them in the field—regardless of where they are on a coordinate in the field, which is commonly called past, present, or future in a specific vector of space in our universe or beyond. From stillness, infinite possibilities for connection effortlessly open up within endless scales or fractals. Directing our awareness into those varying scales of frequency, or moving our particles to a coordinate in the field, will be a reality for many people in our lifetime.

"That encounter in the craft helped me to see why the beings told me many times that I am infinite scales of consciousness, frequency, and information and so are they. Why not meet them with that mindset? In fact, advanced species move through portals because they don't need craft. According to them, that's how our ancestors interacted with them most often.

"I guess meeting that way didn't seem concrete enough for my brain or sexy enough to spread on social media. Going on a craft felt more real for my mind to grasp and it fits our social understanding of how we've been led to believe that humans interact with extraterrestrials. We love those mysterious flying discs, mother ships, and strange looking Star Wars characters. Having said that, beings have easily come through the natural portals at the cove to work with us. I admit that I am not yet totally comfortable doing that, but I am getting closer."

Chuckling, she added, "Oh my gosh, Adele, your mamma and grandmother must be doing a celestial *happy dance* right now. Here we are talking about the subjects they loved best!"

As sunlight glistened on the dewy leaves and emerging spring grass, the three friends continued their conversation about subjects that left them fascinated and in awe of galactic mysteries and invisible comrades.

*   *   *

Kandor and Belstar had gathered in Kandor's massive cave, relaxed and settled before a towering holographic screen. Watching Sophia and reading the underlying field of everything, they gave each other a knowing smile. Belstar spoke first.

"My beloved daughter is still in tune with her mission and she's been able to elevate her frequency exponentially. The council must be pleased with her progress thus far.

"Equally impressive," Kandor added reflectively, "is that she is beginning to magnetize additional high frequency confidants to her circle who can help her to fulfill her work. Thus far, her comrades have undoubtedly helped her to serve her mission through elevating their frequencies. The hologram indicates a high potentiality for unconventional, high vibrational allies to come into her life. They appear to be pivotal for completion of her mission—some of whom she will meet under unexpected circumstances. She will need these good humans with unorthodox, maverick mindsets in her life to be able to accomplish her mission. It was not her intent nor the Galactic Council's for her to be companionless as she proceeds with her prodigious mission to promote unicity and a rise in frequency within the human collective on Gaia.

"Without doubt, Sophia is acutely feeling the gravity of the moment. Gaia is under intense pressure right now—brutal chemicals, interference in her rhythms under the auspices of self-serving global businesses, and prolonged and amplified war are callously and relentlessly wounding and exploiting her precious, venerable body. The collective of humanity sits on the precipice of massive chaos and possible extinction. Can Sophia connect, inspire, and galvanize enough of them? Will humans bathe in the light of higher wisdom and take responsibility for their innate potential to decipher the codes of wisdom and unicity within themselves? The disturbing possibilities loom in the hologram before us, and all we can do is continue to monitor Sophia's progress and send her profound love and eternal blessings.

"We know that Sophia and all galactic beings exist in a field of all possibilities, so a definitive outcome for Gaia's future is not yet determined. However, the possibility of the highest outcome for a congenial, harmonious, bountiful planet remains precarious.

"As the equinox approaches, it is time to prepare to go to the stone circles once again for the cosmic ritual to emit exalted frequencies in support of dear Sophia, Grace, and their friends. Our star brothers and sisters will join us. The Universe will be alight today with encouragement and optimism for Sophia to fulfill her extraordinary mission and for the emerging number of earth beings who—with intrepid determination and infinite love—are joining her in becoming rigorously committed to the elevation of themselves and all beings. They are beginning to sense their interconnectedness with the entire universe. This is a powerful step in human evolution!

"As our blessing, let us shower pure love on Planet Earth and all of her inhabitants—whether or not they are aware of the frequency's effects—so that, undivided and strong, they can progress quickly into a state of resplendent unicity and elevated octaves of light and frequency."

✦ ✦ ✦

Sophia suddenly felt intense shivers running through her body. When a visceral experience like this happened, she'd take a moment to pause and turn her attention inward—allowing the vibrations to become a thought form or shape giving her an idea about why the unusually potent frequencies were running through her. Leaving her friends for a couple of minutes, Sophia went to the kitchen to sit quietly and steady the thought waves of her mind. When her inner state felt centered in tranquility and her heart and mind were joined in solidarity, she softly opened her eyes and reached for her phone to send a text to Grace describing her insights and the mysterious, vibratory experience.

I am sensing that something is forming in the ether about Angelica coming to join our fireside circle and work at the cove—it's something about her daughter as well, and it feels like there's an important element of her upcoming visit that is yet to be revealed. Adding to that, I am sensing that on today's equinox, the whole universe is celebrating. It's hard to know why that would be happening, though. I felt wild energy running through me just now. As I sat with that energetic flow, I recalled the sweet touch of my head to the giant's hand that I've shared with you. It's been a long time since I recalled that powerful love-bomb. Any insights into my hunches and spectacular tremors and tingles, awesome queen of the fairies? Talk soon. Love you!

Sophia breathed deeply and settled herself even more into her core. She poured a fresh cup of her ambrosial, morning tea and walked back out to the porch.

"So," she said, "Adele, when John gets here, would you like to join us at the monolithic circle? Grace and I feel the equinoxes and solstices are like magnets pulling us to that mystical spot to connect with our star brothers and sisters. It's a reunion of love and camaraderie. It means the world to us to feel that level of unicity at auspicious times of year when the stones align perfectly with particular constellations in our solar system."

At that moment, they saw billowing dust and heard the rattling engine of John's old, red Chevrolet truck cruising up the drive. It was time for their next wondrous adventure and countless more which were crystallizing in the ether faster than the speed of light.

DISCUSSION AND REFLECTION GUIDE QUESTIONS AND TOPICS FOR DIALOGUE

1.   Considering the title of the book, in what ways could you be indelibly tethered to the cosmos?

2.   A primary theme of the book is *unicity*. What does the word *unicity* mean to you? What parts of the book influenced your understanding of it? How has your understanding or application of unicity changed? Which characters stand out as living from *your definition* of unicity? When and how has unicity impacted your life? How important is unicity in the modern world?

3.   Sophia and Nate struggled with his illness while focusing on inner growth and self reflection. Was there anything that Sophia did or did not do that is important in caregiving? Was there anything Nate did or did not do that inspired you when his life became intense or frightening?

4.   Gilda's words and inner qualities profoundly affected Sophia and Adele. How would you describe Gilda's character? What did you learn from Gilda? How did making restitution help her? When she spoke about the ETs, how did that land for you, and why? One of her concerns was the lack of transparency between the military-industrial complex and the public. How could it be important for secret technologies to be made readily available for broader study and for transparency to be required? What concerns did Gilda have for the future that you resonate with?

What relevance could the holocaust have for global citizens today? For evidence of the holocaust, research "Captain Jack Holmes—Ohrdruf."

5.   All of the characters valued self reflection by. Which moments of their reflection stood out for you, and why? When the characters had profound epiphanies, how did that benefit them and possibly raise their frequencies?

6.   What did you learn about new archeological sites related to giants, archeological sites on other planets, or discoveries about our ancient ancestors and ancient civilizations? How are ancient cultures and our ancient origins relevant to us?

7.   During her captivity in the prisoner of war camp, Gilda decided to make changes in her life. She questioned everything; cultivated heartfelt, intuitive discernment; and approached life with curiosity—letting one step naturally lead to the next one. What value could this process have in raising frequencies and enhancing personal evolution?

8.   The characters discuss the theory that *everything we consider material* is at its core—a spinning, angular vortex in the infinite fabric of space-time. How can this theory reshape your worldview?

9.   The unified field theory of physics indicates that everything is connected through an all-pervasive field of energy and is interacting with everything else at the subtlest, energetic levels. How does that broaden or shift your worldview? For in-depth information about unified physics and unified science, you can visit https://www.spacefed.com/

10. Unified science theory includes studying our world and the cosmos from various lenses like archeology, philosophy, astronomy, chemistry, biology and unified physics. How might that collective, collaborative approach be helpful?

11. What was your biggest surprise in the book? How could it be relevant in your life?

12. What was your biggest takeaway?

13. What parts of the book linger in your memory? Why? How could they impact your life?

ACKNOWLEDGEMENTS

I am forever grateful to my family and friends, old and new, who inspired me to write this novel with authenticity and share my heart's message with the world. I appreciate our optimistic conversations about the radical and wildly creative possibilities for our future.

Thank you to my bestie, Valerie Guthrie, for letting me bounce my esoteric experiences off you and for letting my mystical, cosmically inspired tendencies flourish in your company for many years. I remain in awe that although neither of us knew you'd be leaving this world so soon, you got to sign off on this trilogy with your buoyant, bestie encouragement. That meant the world to me.

Many thanks to my editors, Stephanie Ritz who saw the manuscript through its early version and Clelia Lewis, who carefully honed and polished the book.

Sunshine Beck, I love you so much and appreciate your feedback, especially for the German parts of this book and for listening patiently as I ran ideas by you in what turned out to be a longer process than I ever expected.

My research for this book was enriched by many cutting edge scientists, researchers, historians, and journalists.

I am sending my heartfelt gratitude to the people I met synchronistically in coffee and tea shops all over Northern California and The Pacific Northwest. We discussed topics like ET's, ancient history, archeology, geology, and fascinating mysteries of these incredible places. I remain inspired by your belief that humanity is inherently awesome, endowed with superpowers, and definitely ready to elevate in frequency.

ABOUT THE AUTHOR

Focusing on spiritual growth and raising human consciousness, Lee Kemter writes about expanded awareness and ever-evolving views of the prism of life for contemporary seekers of higher wisdom. A long-time practitioner of meditation, she has been a mentor, curriculum creator and meditation teacher at an international retreat site and is the Amazon best-selling author of a young adult novel, The Hidden Light and a contributing author to the Amazon best-seller Practice: Wisdom from the Downward Dog (New Feminine Evolutionary). Her latest work of fiction, the trilogy Exalted Vibrations, takes a provocative multidimensional journey, interweaving a present and future in which humanity recognizes that it can triumph over the escalating threat of impending extinction by embracing and accepting its massive quantum potentiality. Kemter continues to meditate, study, and write while exploring the inspirational beauty of the Pacific Northwest.

www.LeeKemter.com